Novelists and in 2015 he won the Eccles British Library
Writer in Residence Award. He lives in London and
teaches creative writing at Royal Holloway, University of
London. *A Weekend in New York* was longlisted for the
JQ Wingate Prize.

Further praise for *A Weekend in New York*:

'Intimate, funny and agile . . . Masterfully done.' *Daily
Mail*

'What's most striking about the novel is Markovits's
[Anne] Tyler-like ability to be both completely unsparing
about, and warmly accepting of, the sheer weirdness of
family life.' James Walton, *Daily Telegraph*

'Elegant, absorbing . . . What a fine ear Markovits has for
the way people talk. His dialogue put me in mind of David
Mamet's remark that modern US drama is mainly about
people not talking to each other . . . Each exchange is a
prolonged, expert rally, with the book as the ball, bearing
the imprint of each family member in turn.' Xan Brooks,
Guardia

'Markovits is excellent on gradations of failure. He also has the patience and precision to capture the elusive minutiae of our inner lives and interpersonal relationships.' Claire Lowdon, *Sunday Times*

'Sophisticated and engrossing . . . full of authentically captured emotion and wonderfully acute observation . . . the imprint of Saul Bellow is evident [yet] Markovits's voice feels wholly his own . . . This is a subtle, ruminative novel of family life, generational conflict and compromise [and] marks a novelist coming into his own.' Jude Cook, *Literary Review*

'A good writer makes the reading easy and Markovits makes for a smooth, immersive ride . . . Markovits has a lively eye for the small, ingrained moments of everyday life, and this gives his writing its authenticity.' Alasdair McKillop, *Herald*

'The characters' cool and sometimes startling insights into their own behaviour are [a] pleasure.' *New York Times*

---

by the same author

The Syme Papers
Either Side of Winter
Playing Days
Imposture
A Quiet Adjustment
Childish Loves
You Don't Have to Live Like This

BENJAMIN MARKOVITS

A WEEKEND IN NEW YORK

ff

FABER & FABER

To Inga and Dick

First published in 2018
by Faber & Faber Limited
Bloomsbury House
74–77 Great Russell Street
London WC1B 3DA
This paperback edition published in 2019

Typeset by Faber & Faber Limited
Printed in the UK by CPI Group (UK) Ltd, Croydon, CRO 4YY

AUTHOR'S NOTE:
In 2015 I held the Eccles British Library Writer's Award. The prize allowed me
to focus on researching and writing this book and I am grateful to the Centre
for its support and the staff at the British Library for their assistance during the
period of the award.

A CIP record for this book
is available from the British Library

ISBN 978–0–571–33806–1

10 9 8 7 6 5 4 3 2

"All happy families are alike . . ."
Anna Karenina

Whenever Paul qualified for the US Open, his parents, his big brother, his two sisters, their various kids, traveled to New York to watch him play. "It's like Christmas," his mother used to say. "Our family reunion." She was German, from Flensburg originally, right on the Danish border, though she had lived and taught in the US for the past forty years. All of the Essinger children called their parents by their first names, Liesel and Bill.

The first week of the tournament ran through the end of August; the second encroached on September. Most of the Essingers had academic jobs and couldn't afford to miss the start of term, but Paul rarely made it into the second week. When he was twenty, playing as an amateur, he reached the third round and afterward dropped out of Stanford to turn pro—he wanted to concentrate on tennis. The next year he lost in the quarterfinals; his ranking hovered briefly in the twenties. But that was as high as it got, and he spent most of his career snaking and laddering between the fifties and the low one hundreds, depending on injuries.

His mother, who had no real interest in sports, was basically puzzled by her son's athletic success—it seemed just another part of what it meant to have American kids, kids who were somehow foreign to you. His father was both inordinately proud of and at the same time bitterly disappointed by Paul's career. Bill had spent his own childhood hitting, dribbling, catching, striking, putting balls—around the park, the court, the diamond, the fairway, the green—but it had never occurred to him that one of his children might have an international ranking. And yet what that ranking meant is that half the time you saw him play in the big tournaments you watched him lose.

"I'll probably retire after this one," Paul had told his father on the phone. "I was lucky to get through the qualifiers."

"See how you feel," Bill said. "That's not what you need to be thinking about right now."

"There are very limited possible outcomes to what happens next week. They don't depend much on what I say to you."

It was always a burden, getting tickets, finding places for his family to stay. His girlfriend Dana bore most of the brunt. It didn't help that they weren't married, which she thought made the Essingers look down on her, especially after their son was born. A worry that Paul always responded to in the same way: don't be crazy. But it fed Dana's other anxieties, about her career, or lack of one, about her past. Another thing that didn't help: the apartment she found for them belonged to her ex-husband.

Paul had asked her to pick up his parents from the airport, but they were landing at five, which meant if she brought Cal along, well, it was feeding time at the zoo—you can't expect a two-year-old to sit in traffic. Inez, their nanny, took Friday afternoons off, so Dana and Cal could "hang out" together, which sometimes meant pushing him to that play-

ground in the park near 86th Street and sometimes showing
him off to friends, in coffee shops or their apartments. Dana
looked forward to these afternoons all week, even if, two
years into motherhood, she was still a little nervous around
Cal. Secretly she would have liked to get rid of Inez, though
she liked Inez, too—she was so . . . not just patient, but full
of energy. Dana could be one or the other. *What am I supposed to do all day* was a thought she had on a lot of days.
But she didn't get rid of Inez, because . . . oh, who knows.
Because Paul could afford to keep her. Because she suspected Inez was better at looking after Cal than she was—better
for Cal, that is.

"Can't they get a cab?" she asked Paul.

"Bill won't pay for a cab."

"So you pay."

"He won't let me pay. You know that."

She was lying in bed in running shorts and a T-shirt,
which is how she slept in the summer. Their seventh-
floor window looked out onto the central courtyard of
the apartment complex. Paul liked to sleep with the air-
conditioning on, a throwback to his Texas childhood, but
she always opened the window anyway—and could hear
the New York sounds coming in. Traffic noises, tires on
the wet streets (the night was still sticky after an afternoon
shower). Even the distant consoling laugh track of a neighbor's television. One of the doormen called out something
in a happy voice, probably to a guy delivering food.

Paul, with the pillows stuffed behind him, messed
around on his laptop; his face looked greenish in the back-
lighting. Usually about a week before a tournament he

started to turn inward. He would read when they were in the room together or stare at his computer or play with their son instead of talking to her. She sometimes thought he preferred Cal's company—not just loved him more, which was understandable, but preferred his company. Maybe *she* did, too. But that was only because Cal gave you some kind of response.

"So why don't you pick them up?" she asked.

"Marcello's thing. They're having a memorial for him before the Open starts. What he meant to American tennis, at some midtown hotel." When Dana didn't say anything, he said, "It's not like I'll be having fun. You know what these things are like. It's basically a publicity exercise. The USTA is making a film about him. But I really liked the guy, he meant something to me. Sometimes you have to show your face. I can pick up some takeout on the way home."

"It's you they want to see," she said.

"They'll see me when I get home."

"Fine."

He gave her the look he gave when he was refraining from saying something that maybe struck him as petty or mean. "All right, I'll pick them up."

"It's just that I don't know what to do about Cal."

"Leave him with Inez."

"Friday is her afternoon off. And she's flying to Tempe to see her mother."

"What, now?"

"She's having her pacemaker replaced."

"On the weekend?"

"On Monday morning. Inez wants to spend the weekend together beforehand, in case something goes wrong. I mean, it's a routine operation. This is just a kind of superstition. But I'm not someone who will get in the way of one of my, I don't know, employees . . ."

"I just don't want my dad making Liesel get the train to Jamaica, and then the Long Island Rail Road and then another train at rush hour, with all their stuff."

"So they should get a cab."

"He won't. It doesn't matter. It's not your fault. I'll pick them up."

"Of course I'll do it," she said.

She switched off her bedside lamp, and the imperfect darkness of the city evening came into focus in the window. She lay on her side and looked out across the airspace of the courtyard; maybe a third of the windows showed a light, in funny patterns like SAT answer sheets. The way she had said "employees" upset her slightly—this is the world she grew up in, where people talked conscientiously about their staff. She heard her mother's voice, discussing their cleaner; as a kid it drove Dana nuts. And she knew what Paul thought. You hire people to do a job, you pay them to do it, end of story. There's nothing to be embarrassed about. But he didn't have to spend time with Inez. You have to be friends with these people, or pretend to be friends at least, and that makes it awkward when you pay them or make decisions about what they can or can't do.

"It's not just picking them up," she said. "Do they have to stay in Michael's apartment? I'd rather pay for a hotel."

"What's wrong with his apartment? He won't even be there."

"You know, Paul."

She turned over to look at his face, in the green glow. His hair was cut short, what he called his jock haircut, to hide a receding hairline. But he didn't much care, and when he wasn't playing, he let it grow long in tufts around his ears. The skin under his eyes seemed vaguely sun-damaged, not freckled but slightly abraded. He spent a lot of time in the sun. But he still looked like a sensitive boy, the kid who speaks only after raising his hand. It took her six months, when they started dating, to realize that his shyness was just a form of self-control. He didn't have to be shy.

"Michael's got a great apartment. Let's all move into his apartment."

"You're kidding, right?" she said. "Don't you think it's weird? Please. Turn that thing off. I want to sleep."

"They don't care."

"You think that's true, Paul, but it's really not. You think your family is above all that, but they're not. Your father has opinions about these things. Your mother has opinions. They don't mention them to you, but they let me know about it, believe me."

"Come on, Dana," he said, and shut his computer, and put it on the floor by their bed, and turned around again and tried to pull her toward him. She was almost as tall as he was; her legs were just as long. "What are you feeling so anxious about? I'm the guy who has to go out there and lose."

"That's what I don't like. That's what you don't realize. It's harder on the rest of us."

"I'm sure it must be," he said.

FRIDAY

The rain continued fitfully overnight, then all day long the city steamed and gathered heat. Dana got caught up in the general weekend exodus — people trying to get out early. Fallen branches and leaves had collected on the hard shoulder of the Parkway; the waters of Meadow Lake looked almost sealike. To keep Cal happy on the car ride to JFK, she had given him a box of graham crackers. This was his dinner. He worked his way through them slowly and methodically, but not very carefully. There were wet crumbs everywhere by the time they reached the airport: on his fingers, on his pants, on the seat, and on the floor. She tried to reach around and clean up what she could from the driver's seat, but it was no use. Her hands were sticky; the traffic kept pushing her along; she had to circle. When she saw Bill, she felt a little surge of anxiety and shame.

Not that Paul's father would care much about the state of her car. He stood by a pair of suitcases, looking vaguely homeless, in his sports jacket and dirty chinos, in his running shoes. He also looked exactly like what he was: an econ professor. In the humid afternoon, the mustache of his beard curled over his lips. He stared right at her, and then past her, at the car behind her, and the car behind that one. She pulled over to the curb and even when she rolled down her window and shouted "Bill!" he glanced at her for a moment with the baffled, almost angry air of a bumped-into stranger.

Then he turned around and called out, "Liesel, Liesel, she's here." Liesel appeared through the glass doors, wheeling another suitcase, looking friendly and flustered. Bill said, "Let's go, come on. I don't expect she's allowed to hang around."

"Even inside the air-conditioning isn't working properly," Liesel said. She had short gray hair, a round, handsome, very brown face; she wore a striped shirt and jeans and a juniper-red hippy kind of bead necklace, which Dana had found and Paul had given her for Christmas. "Hello, Dana. This is very sweet of you."

"You must get used to this in Texas," Dana said.

"You never get used to it."

Bill, bending his back and not his knees, lifted their suitcases into the trunk of the car—a Saab 900 turbo—then climbed into the backseat next to Cal. "Hey, Cal," he said to the boy, in his 1950s dance-show host voice. "What's doing?"

Liesel dropped her handbag on the floor of the passenger's seat. She sat down heavily and swung her legs in, one at a time. A year before she had had a knee replaced; now the other knee probably needed surgery, too, but they were putting it off. When she was in, she gave Dana a smile of relief. "It's cool in here." Her eyes were a little shiny with tears from the salt in her sweat. Dana, who loved her, almost felt her own tears rising.

Bill said, "Does Paul really fit in this car?"

"Well, he sits in front."

"Even so."

For some reason, the presence of strangers upset Cal, and he began to cry as they turned onto the Expressway. Bill tried to comfort him, he offered him a graham cracker, he took off his watch and gave it to the boy, but Cal struck it out of his hands. Bill picked the watch up from the floor and started to clean up some of the mess—not just the cracker crumbs, but other wrappers, empty juice boxes, raisins, old Cheerios, and receipts. He had found an empty plastic bag and was putting them in it.

"Oh, just leave that. I'm sorry," Dana said. So he did care.

"It's fine. Why not make myself useful?"

Cal continued to cry, a steady, not very hopeful kind of crying, very sure of itself— as steady as rain on a gray afternoon.

Bill even tried to clean up some of the debris from Cal's shirt and between his pants and on the car seat. "Okay, buddy. It's okay. I think he wants Mommy."

"He's hungry," Liesel said. "I've got some chocolate."

"He doesn't like chocolate."

"Every kid likes chocolate."

"Cal doesn't."

"Well, he can play with the wrapper."

Liesel reached in her bag and found a piece and gave it to Cal, who went quiet; Dana felt very slightly annoyed.

The traffic coming in had gotten noticeably heavier since she set out. There were cars backed up both ways, trucks inching along, people honking. Exhaust fumes hardly rose in the thick heat. Even the city skyline, which she could see in the distance, looked vague, worried by midges. Yesterday's storms hadn't cleared the air, there were more storms predicted over the weekend.

Bill said, "Is Paul out hitting balls?"

"They're having a memorial service for Marcello. That's why he couldn't come. He says he'll pick up some food for us on the way home."

"He shouldn't do that. I'll go and get something." Bill was suddenly in a good mood. "I could go with him."

"I always liked Marcello," Liesel said. "All of these people exaggerate everything, but he didn't exaggerate so much."

"You have a lot of luggage."

"Bill brought his work along."

"I don't know how long we're staying," he said. "If Paul makes it to the second week, we'll cancel class. Who knows how many of these things he has left. I don't want to sit around all day doing nothing. So I brought my work. I'm assuming there's a space to work in this apartment."

"There's space."

Liesel said, "It's very generous of Michael to let us use it. I don't know what he likes. We brought him some Texas honey. It can sit on the kitchen counter, it won't go bad. And if he doesn't like it, he can throw it away."

"Really, he doesn't mind at all. He's hardly there. He's one of these people with houses everywhere. When he comes to New York he mostly stays on Long Island. Anyway, he's not in New York now, he's in Sacramento. For some reason. He probably feels guilty toward me, I don't know. He's always been very generous to me. That wasn't the problem. He doesn't mind."

They were coming up to the Triborough Bridge, the lanes spread out, and Bill began to take out his wallet, which was in his pants—he had to squirm a little to extract it.

"Let me pay the toll," he said.

"Please. I don't even think about it. We have E-ZPass."

"How much is it? Five dollars? I'll leave it on the seat."

She had joined one of the lines and could turn around to look. "Please, it will just get lost." But he stuffed a bill into the backseat pocket. Cal had fallen asleep, which meant he'd be a nightmare later on. Paul would probably want to keep him up anyway. It was okay. She could let it go.

"Look at this city," Bill said.

His father had grown up on the Lower East Side, then moved upstate after law school and marriage. But he sometimes brought his boys into the city, to catch a ball game, or see family; once or twice he took them along on business. And still New York stood in Bill's mind for the larger, louder, brighter realism of childhood.

It was like entering a forest—your sense of scale began to adjust itself. All those warehouses, parking lots, billboards, and lanes of traffic. Some of the billboards worked like TVs, the images shifted electronically, you couldn't take your eyes off them. They told you the weather, the time; people's faces were blown out of all proportion. Not just movie stars, but local news anchors. He saw an advertisement for the History Channel. What was it like to look up at yourself on one of those things? What did it do to you? Earlier in his career Paul used to advertise for a brand of tennis ball. Sometimes they (he and Liesel, sitting at home in Austin) even saw their son on TV. It removed him slightly from them, from their sphere; it seemed to have an effect on Paul, too. It took something away.

Dana followed the signs to the FDR. She tacked into the far lane and waited in traffic at the 96th Street exit. Kids were playing basketball behind a tall chain-link fence. Bill said: "I got the feeling from one of our phone conversations that he's not in a very optimistic frame of mind."

Cal's sleeping had somehow changed the atmosphere in the car—it was grown-up time. One of the things Dana both liked and resented about the Essingers is that they talked everything through. Her own mother had a very different sense of conversational etiquette. "I don't know if he's optimistic or not. He never says anything about these things to me."

This was more of a confession than she meant to make; she realized as much after the words came out. Not just a confession, but maybe even a slight betrayal—of Paul. Of what he was like with her. Eventually she said, "I'm sorry our apartment isn't big enough for everybody. Do you want me to take you to Mike's first or should we go home?"

"I don't care where," Liesel said, "so long as I can use a bathroom."

"You can use the bathroom at ours."

They crossed through the Park, between the dirty high stone walls, under the bridges, following the cabs, but still you could feel the green density around you, like a kind of subconscious for the city, the core of nature that you're stuck with; emerging again on the West Side was like coming out of a dream. More buildings, more people, more traffic. Even the cross streets had cafés on them, pet boutiques and dry cleaners. Liesel felt her heartbeat accelerate slightly, a kind of happy anxiety. She had lived for forty years in America but coming to New York was like arriving again for the first time. Her undergraduate years were spent in Berlin. She was an elegant young provincial woman, men took her to the theater, they invited her to concerts, and a part of her life was still lived out in her imagination in big cities, without kids.

They found a parking spot five blocks from the apartment (the service entrance made it slightly nearer), and Bill sat in the car while the women went up. Liesel took her handbag, and since Cal was asleep, Dana carried him. "Just give me a minute," Bill said. "You can leave the key. It will take me a minute to get everything together." There was something very faintly conscious about the way Cal adjusted himself in Dana's arms, pushed up, shifted his head against her neck, so that she could feel the heat of his skin against hers. Somehow his eyes were closed for both of them, there was no one else.

They walked through an arch into the courtyard, and a woman sweating in her running gear said, "You've got a sleeper. Poor Cal."

She was stretching out her calves, leaning against a wall.

"Oh, hey Mandy," Dana said. "This is Liesel." And then, with a little laugh, "my sort-of mother-in-law. Amanda Frankel."

"Excuse the state of me." Amanda stopped stretching and pushed back her hair. "The things we do."

"I never did," Liesel said, smiling. Afterward, in the elevator lobby, she went on: "I'm always amazed how everybody knows everybody else's kids' names."

"Her daughter is the same age as Cal. He calls her *that girl*."

Liesel didn't always listen well—she followed her own trains of thought—but these often intersected with the conversation anyway. "It's nice that he has friends in the building. Kids the same age. It doesn't really matter who."

"He has friends." They were in the elevator, among the mirrors, watching the light shift from floor to floor. "There are kids he doesn't like. He likes Poppy."

It was funny for Dana to find herself subtly taking Amanda's side. Because they had a complicated relationship—she was one of those mothers you compare yourself against.

The front door of the apartment was very heavy. It was an old building, and Dana had to twist her body and use Cal's weight to help her lean and push it open. She got her foot in the door and held it for Liesel, who went in and struggled to find the light switch in the hallway.

Dana said, "I'm giving up on his bath" and walked through with the boy in her arms. She took him to his bedroom and laid him in his crib, clothed and dirty. There was a chair beside it, an awful hospital-style rocking chair for nursing mothers, very comfortable, and she sat down for a minute, even though Cal was clearly deeply asleep. One of her favorite things about having a baby was that it allowed you to opt out of grown-up time occasionally. The presence of her in-laws always put pressure on her. It was a kind of atmospheric intimacy; she got used to it after a while and almost missed it when they left.

Liesel was sitting on the sofa in the living room, with a glass of water, when Dana came out. The big window was behind her, which showed the rooftops of lower, cheaper buildings, untidily asphalted, sprouting shiny steel vents and grids and pipework, water towers, and boxes of electrical significance. Sometimes you could see a deckchair left out, somebody sunbathing, or a few potted plants and trees. Beneath them, at the bottom of a kind of canyon, the river of Broadway flowed.

She said, "It's so nice to be here. He must have been very tired."

"I didn't think he would stay down, but so far so good."

Liesel set her water on the glass coffee table. The sofas were comfortable but not particularly to her taste — Italian, bright green; the soft rug on the floor was oatmeal-colored. Everything looked simple and expensive. Instead of paintings on the walls, there were large framed photographs in black and white, including photographs of Cal and Paul and Dana. She had probably spent the afternoon cleaning up, preparing for their arrival. Unless they paid for someone to clean up. You couldn't keep a place this neat with a two-year-old boy; maybe all the plastic was in his room. Suddenly for some reason she felt sorry for Dana, but also a little ashamed of her own strong opinions.

"I didn't mean to be rude about your friend. My kids tell me I'm always so critical. Really, I'm just embarrassed. When they were small, all the mothers knew their names, and said nice things, and I could never reciprocate."

"I like Amanda,' Dana said. "But she annoys me, too. Maybe I'm just competitive. She's one of those women who works hard to please her husband. Like, he pays the bills so she has to look good. That's why she goes jogging."

"I hope you don't work very hard to please Paul."

"Well, sometimes I work out with her, too. But not for Paul."

There was a silence, not awkward or comfortable, and after a while Liesel said, "I should help Bill, but it's nice sitting down."

"I can go."

"You've done enough, I'm just being lazy." She leaned over across her knees and picked up the glass and drank some more water. "I brought you something from Austin. It's very small and you don't have to wear it if you don't like it."

"I'm sure I'll like it."

"Don't be sure," Liesel said. "It's in my handbag. I'll get it in a minute."

For a minute Bill sat in the car, not moving. It was too hazy out for much sunshine or shade, but there was a faint breeze and the trees on 91st Street stirred in a hundred different ways. He always liked the summery effect of trees on the concrete jungle. Liesel wanted to move to New York. She wanted to retire and spend at least a part of her year in a big city. It made sense for him, too, he grew up two hours' outside, but for some reason he was resisting. Even though he liked New York, his childhood was happy, the associations were good, the presence of Jews, in the streets, in the shops, gave him pleasure; but it all felt like a long time ago and he didn't want to confront his nostalgia on a daily basis. Plus, there was the space issue—he was used to having a certain amount of real estate to walk around in.

When Paul bought the apartment, shortly after Dana got pregnant, Bill was surprised. It seemed an odd move for a guy pursuing a career in professional tennis, a guy who traveled a lot and needed good weather to train, who was about to have a baby. But Bill didn't say anything at the time, except to Liesel and the other kids. *Dana wants to live in the city* was the reason he heard. She used to be a model, she was taking classes in photography at the New School, and she had enough connections in the business to get work as a personal assistant, if that's what she ended up wanting to do. None of these reasons appealed to Bill. He was suspicious of his son for marrying an unusually good-looking woman; he was suspicious of photography, both as an art form and as a road to a meaningful career; and he didn't much like the kind of people Paul seemed to be associating with, fashion-types, celebrity hangers-on, everybody young and good-looking, the kind of people who live to be seen at certain parties. Well, who knows why anyone lives the way he does or she does.

But when Paul bought the apartment it's also true that a part of him was pleased. He took pleasure in his children's homes in the same way that some grandparents take pleasure in their grandkids. The apartment was large and light, an old building, with attractive features like solid brass faucets and mosaic-tiled floors in the bathrooms.

The address was good, halfway between Central Park and Riverside and around the corner from a subway stop. For a son of his to have made it to this extent in the city from which his grandfather and great-uncles had moved out two generations before . . . I guess that's one kind of progress, from the Lower East to the Upper West.

It surprised him, frankly, that Paul could afford to live like this, unless Dana had brought over a substantial amount of money from her first marriage—something else he wasn't terrifically pleased about, by the way, not that he judged her for it or held it personally against her. But there's a cost involved in attaching yourself to unstable lives. Instability is catching; and the fact was, Paul and Dana weren't married, in spite of the kid, and for whatever private reasons. His career earnings couldn't much exceed a couple million dollars, unless Bill had miscalculated the value of sponsorship deals. Even that kind of money doesn't allow you to live an anxiety-free existence in New York.

But maybe, again, Paul had other business incentives for being in the city. His tennis career was on the last lap. He was still a nice player to watch, with a deft, clever serve, soft hands at the net and a tricky slice backhand. He covered the court well, but his forehand was kind of a placeholder, a lot of topspin but not much penetration. So he didn't trust his approach shot; he stayed back. The guys you came up against these days were like basketball players, they were like football players, not in the normal run of human beings. Paul lifted weights, he was six foot one, but he couldn't generate the kind of power from the

baseline you had to at least be able to respond to at the
top level of the game. And somewhere along the way he
seemed to have accepted this fact, which is what upset Bill
and partly explained the move to New York. That's the
problem with failure. At some point it requires an acceptance of failure; you have to make internal adjustments.
Okay, so Paul was making them. As a mid-level American tennis star, good-looking and presentable, with two
years at Stanford to his credit, and a handsome girlfriend
who had connections in the media, Paul could try to make
the transition from player to former player gracefully and
maybe even lucratively.

Bill was aware that he had a limited sense of how people made money in this field, and that his other kids, if he
tried to explain his thought processes to them, his con-
cerns for Paul, would tease him for being delusional, a
Jewish mother, a worrier.

So he worried, so what. Then again, if Liesel got her
way, they could live around the corner from Paul. He
noticed a couple of real estate signs in the apartment
windows, Corcoran and Douglas Elliman, beside the air-
conditioning units or sitting on top of them. Tall windows,
with high ceilings behind them. Nice apartments, though
Bill probably preferred the East Side. Smaller scale. Liesel
wanted a balcony or a garden. There were two suitcases in
the trunk, both with wheels, and another duffel or carry-
on, which was known for inscrutable reasons in the family
as the shoe-bag. He also had his briefcase. If he could sling
the shoe-bag over one shoulder, he could rest his briefcase
on one of the suitcases and wheel them both along. But

this required a certain amount of careful arrangement; he began lugging all the bags into the street. He locked the door and told himself that he had locked it, and put the keys in the front pocket of his jacket.

The last time they visited Paul, he took them out to a Chinese/Cuban restaurant in the neighborhood, which was inexpensive and really very good. Bill thought, I'd happily eat there again, or walk with Paul to pick up the takeout, or go myself for that matter, if Paul wants to talk to his mother.

In the elevator lobby, he came across a woman returning from her run. In her thirties, quite pretty. Her face was sweaty and red, full of pumping blood; you could see the faint dark hairs over her lip. She wore black Lycra running shorts and a tank top, which pressed against her figure suggestively. She helped him by wheeling one of the suitcases into the elevator.

"What floor, madam?" he said, in his bellhop voice. She told him and he pushed the button. "Good run?"

"On Friday nights, my husband comes home a little early so he can put the kid to bed. So I get half an hour. And this is what I do. Who knows why."

She dabbed a hand against her forehead to keep the sweat out of her eyes.

"What's he do?"

"He's a lawyer. At Cravath."

"I know Cravath. I once did a little consulting work for them. I'm surprised they let him out early."

"It doesn't always happen. But they're only young once, right? It's good for them to have a little time together, just the two of them. Without Mommy shouting at everybody."

"Yes, ma'am."

She got out first, making the tired-but-happy face, taking a breath, and for two floors he thought, it amazes me, though I shouldn't be amazed, that there is still such a thing as a cultural connection. When he rang the bell at Paul's apartment, Dana let him in and helped him with the bags, which they left in the hallway next to Liesel's purse. Liesel was still sitting on the sofa. The kettle boiled, you could hear it in the kitchen, and Bill said, "It amazes me, when really I shouldn't be amazed, that there is still such a thing as a cultural connection. I ran into a woman in the elevator, obviously Jewish, very attractive, and for five floors we have a pleasant and even intimate conversation. That wouldn't happen in Austin. There might be friendliness, on both sides, or politeness, but you wouldn't get this kind of . . . easy . . ."

Dana said, "Excuse me," and then called out from the kitchen, "Liesel, milk, sugar?"

"Nothing. Just black. Thank you. I'm sorry, I'm just sitting here."

"That's fine. You probably ran into Amanda. She talks to everybody."

Bill was standing in the doorway between the two rooms. "Well, my kids would shout at me for saying this, but I wonder if what's really going on is something Jewish. This is why a thirty-year-old woman talks like that to an old man. It wouldn't happen in Texas."

"Oh, she flirts with everybody."

"No, it wasn't flirting."

Dana came in with Liesel's tea and put it on the coffee table. "It's hot," she said. "I'll tell her you thought she was thirty. She'll like that. I see her all the time. Her daughter is probably Cal's best friend."

"Before I forget," Bill said, "let me give you your keys."

Liesel stood up at last. "I'm going to get you that present." She walked on painful knees into the dark hallway, where the suitcases stood. Even in her jeans, in her long-sleeved shirt (like a painter's smock), in her comfortable shoes, she had the air of a famous woman. Her short bright-gray hair, her brown neck, her berry-red necklace. Dana was conscious of being alone in the living room with Bill.

He looked in the pockets of his chinos, front and back, and began muttering to himself, "Oh for God's sake." But he found the keys at last in his sports jacket and dropped them in her hand. "Listen," he said. "I'm only going to say this once. Let me pay for a hotel."

She stared at him for a moment. "It's fine, don't worry about it. You can stay at Michael's."

"I'm not talking about us. I mean for Paul. He needs to sleep right the next few days. I don't know what your arrangement is, but it can't be easy for either of you, having a baby."

"Cal is sleeping through. It's fine."

Then Liesel came back holding a bracelet. "It's Mexican silver," she said. A plain arrangement of links, slightly tarnished, but with a depth of color, a faint dark undertone from the copper content. Not the sort of thing Dana bought for herself, but she liked Liesel's taste, she admired it. Her own mother had very severe standards: certain labels, certain cuts, certain colors. The Essinger aesthetic cost less money; they picked up things in flea markets and put together odd combinations. Dana had a good eye; she was sympathetic to other people's sense of style and not always confident in her own.

"It's lovely. Thank you," she said and put the bracelet on her narrow wrist.

"This is why I give you presents. You were well brought up. You say please and thank you like you mean it. And everything looks good on you."

"It's true, I like it."

"Well, I saw it and thought, that's pretty. I wanted to buy it, but my kids have too much of everything, so I thought of you."

"I said to Dana," Bill broke in, "if Paul wants to sleep at a hotel for the next few days, we'd be happy to pay."

"Why should he sleep at a hotel?" Liesel said. "He can sleep here."

"I don't care where he sleeps, but he needs to sleep, he needs to be rested on Monday. They say it's the night before the night before that counts."

"If Cal wakes up," Dana said, "there's a spare room. Don't worry. Paul doesn't sleep well in hotels."

"Do you do that? Does he use the spare room?"

Dana looked at Bill; she wasn't quite sure what was being asked. "Sometimes. But Bill, please, sit down. Let me get you a drink. Paul bought you some caffeine-free Diet Coke. One of those really big bottles. If you don't drink it, we'll never get through it."

"I can get it," Bill said, but he sat down instead on the

green sofa. "Oh brother. The trip is always longer than you think. It didn't used to wear me out so much. Did Paul tell you when the rest of the kids were coming in? Are there plans?"

"Paul never gives me any of the travel information. I always have to ask everybody. Jean is coming in late tonight—she's going straight to Michael's, the doorman can let her in if you're asleep. Susie is still undecided. She may take the train down Sunday with the kids, if she can face it; otherwise she'll come on Monday by herself. Nathan has found his own accommodation. I don't know what. Anyway, they're all driving in tomorrow morning. He *says*, in time for brunch. Anything else? I think that's all. Let me get you a drink."

While Dana was in the kitchen, Liesel said to Bill, "You shouldn't have said that about the hotel. It's none of our business."

"She doesn't care. It was a straightforward practical suggestion."

"Well, you shouldn't have said it."

They were still sitting in the half-dark, the sun had recently set, but then the lights seemed to come on, there was a flash of summer lightning, totally silent, and afterward a shower of rain. It spread itself against the window, which was open a foot—along the sill, a row of houseplants pattered in a flurry of drops. You could feel in your breath the sudden fall in temperature.

"I hope Paul's not walking home in this."

Liesel said, "We should close the window," and got up to close it.

Dana came in and switched on the overhead light. "You don't have to do that."

"If you don't mind my saying, they could probably use some water." But she regretted this comment and added, "If you give me a jug I can do it myself."

Always with her kids Liesel felt a little hemmed in, by the ways of giving offense. Her younger daughter, Jean, was constantly telling her off, but when Liesel got tired and hot, things came out that she didn't mean or didn't mean in the way they were taken. Her children were very sensitive. Their partners, too. Anyway, what does it matter if you let your plants dry out? You have a small child, you're tired, you lead busy lives. Although it's true she couldn't quite guess how Dana spent her days. Not with Inez around. And a cleaner, probably, who did no more than an adequate job. There were leaves on the dusty sill; one of the succulents had a foam of mold growing along the branches. But this is none of her business and Bill shouldn't have said anything about a hotel.

She went with Dana into the kitchen to find a jug, and Dana, stretching her long arm, lifted a glass pitcher from a shelf.

"How's Inez?" Liesel asked.

"She's fine, she's okay." Dana started filling it at the sink. "She's gone home for the weekend to see her mother."

"Where's home?"

"Arizona. You know, Inez is really a very impressive person. She's started taking accounting classes at CUNY. At night, after she leaves us, she heads downtown. The campus is somewhere around City Hall. Getting back to her apartment takes her like an hour and a half—she lives in Hunts Point."

After turning off the faucet, she stopped for a second, listening.

"What?" Liesel said.

"I think that's Cal."

"I'm sure he's fine. Leave him. Or do what you want."

Dana didn't move, her head was bent, in the listening position, and she thought, oh, I don't know, I just want to see him, she'll think I'm fussing, and said, "I'll just go check. He didn't have his normal bedtime routine."

"I can't hear anything," Liesel said. She carried the heavy jug into the living room and spent a few minutes watering the plants, picking off the dead leaves and arranging them in a pile on the sill.

She didn't mean to tell Dana what to do, but sometimes Liesel couldn't help herself. Dana was one of those women with . . . one of those mothers with . . . too much time to think about everything. She needs a job. Part of what upset Liesel (she felt at that moment surprisingly upset) was the impression she had received of some unhappiness, or not even unhappiness, maybe loneliness or detachment, from Dana. Paul was in some ways her least revealing child, the least likely to confide in her. And he can't be an easy man to be married to. But Dana also—partly it was a question of social class. Liesel had been trying for years to break through her good manners. But you don't have to do it right now, at the end of a long day and the beginning of a long visit. When you're tired everything seems to matter, when really it doesn't.

This is something else Jean often told her. Jean was her most consoling child. Even if she was also living the farthest away, in London, and in her own life slightly adrift. For a while it seemed she wouldn't be able to make it. Because of the expense, apart from anything else—late August flights cost twice what they do in September. And she was becoming rather proud of her financial independence, such as it was. Bill offered to pay, of course, but Jean didn't want to take their money. This is stupid, Liesel said to Bill. If we want to spend our money this way, let us spend it; but then Jean decided to come anyway. They were all coming. All of her children. I don't care when she gets in, Liesel thought, I'll stay up.

Bill dug out a pack of cards from the shoe-bag and took them to the guest bathroom. He always played solitaire on the pot. Then Paul walked in, carrying in his arms two large rain-spotted paper bags of food.

"Hey guys," he said, putting them down on the dining table. "Good flight?" Liesel turned around happily to look at him. He came and hugged her, with an arm and half his side, and said, "Is that the buddy?"

"What?"

"Is Cal still up?"

Paul wore a black suit and a very clean white shirt and a black tie. In clothes like that you couldn't see the strength in his arms, but she felt it when he hugged her. He had hands like wrenches . . . he could open any jar. It always gave her pleasure—my strong young man. Of course, he wasn't so young anymore; in his suit and tie he looked like a perfectly respectable grown-up, somebody who made a lot of money and had expenses to meet and responsibilities to live up to.

"I can't hear anything after a flight," she said. "My ears."

"Where's Bill?"

"In the bathroom."

"Let me just give Cal a quick kiss." But he came back a minute later with his son in his arms. Cal had his sleep sack on, he wriggled his legs, he looked wide awake. "Hey buddy, what's up kid," Paul said, with his mouth in his son's warm hair. "Have you said hello to your grandmother?"

Dana had started bringing plates and cutlery into the room. "Of course he has. We met them from the airport, right?"

"Hey buddy, you want to get out of this thing? Let's show them what you can do." He sat down on the sofa to unzip the sleep sack and let his son loose between his legs. "All right, go. Go, go." Cal ran toward the coffee table and Paul watched him run, then caught him at the last minute, reaching his arms out and plucking him easily into the air. "I can't remember," he said to Liesel. "He must have been walking at Christmas."

"Yes, he was walking."

"But kind of like the guy from *Men in Black*."

Bill came out of the bathroom with wet hands. He wiped them on his pants. "Hey, son," he said. "What's in the bags?"

"I picked up some chicken and rice from Flor De Mayo on the way home."

"Is that that place you took us to?"

"How was Marcello's memorial?" Liesel asked.

"Yes. Is that acceptable to you?"

"Sure," Bill said.

"Fine," Paul said. "Let's talk while we eat, the food's hot. What are you doing?"

Dana had picked up Cal's sleep sack, which was on the floor, and was trying to take her son out of his arms.

"Taking him to bed."

"He can sit on my lap and eat a little chicken and rice."

She gave him a look. "Okay, but I've had him all day. If it's daddy time, it's daddy time."

So Paul said, in one of his father's voices, "It's daddy time!" and carried his son to the table.

He always looked forward eagerly to seeing his parents, and yet whenever they came, he felt a slight buffering against them, a reluctance to speak or reveal himself. It was easier talking on the phone, that was the relationship you were used to, the phone relationship. Which meant that seeing his parents again always brought with it a moment of disappointment. You could fudge the disappointment and pretend it was caused by something else. By the fact that whenever he saw them again, he noticed their age and couldn't help checking for new symptoms of it. His mother limped to the table on her bum knee. His father rocked back and forth on his haunches to stand up. He made noises like sighs. He said, "Here we go." But none of this is what really upset Paul, and he played with Cal on his lap, gave him forkfuls of food (some of which ended up on the floor) to hide behind his son, so he didn't have to look at them.

Liesel wanted to know about Marcello. "How was it?" she said again.

"Fine. I don't know. It was a public . . . event. There were a lot of people there. People like photographers. And then the other people being photographed." He took a bite of food and swallowed—you could see the muscles working in his throat. "I guess I was being photographed, too. Not that anyone cared much. But I said to Dana, sometimes you have to show your face. So that's what I did. I'm sorry I didn't pick you up."

"Doesn't matter, son," Bill said.

And Liesel said, "I remember when he first came to our house. I think it was the only time he came. He was so short and fat, I thought, what do you know about tennis? He said he could tell that this was a house of Europeans, that Europeans lived in it, something like that. He said, your son is very good, he will maybe make a career. I liked him, but I don't think I took him seriously."

"He said we should move to Florida."

"I don't remember that."

"He said if I wanted to have a career I needed to play more, I probably needed to go to one of these academies."

"I don't remember that."

"Yes, that's right," Bill said.

"Did you want to go?"

"I don't remember there was much of a discussion about it."

"That's not true," Bill said. "Your mother and I talked about it."

Liesel put down her fork. "I don't remember any of this."

"I mean with me. It doesn't matter, I would have hated it anyway."

"And Marcello was wrong," Liesel said. "About the career, I mean."

"Well, I don't know."

"Do you know this Borisov guy?" Bill asked.

"Who's that?" Liesel said. "I don't understand anything."

"My first-round match. He's young. He's Bulgarian. We played twice before, both three-setters. I won the first. He beat me five months ago at Indian Wells."

"Big serve?"

"Not particularly. Bigger than mine."

"Baseliner?"

"More or less. A good all-rounder. He's solid. He covers the court. Two-hand backhand. Doesn't come to net much because he's happy trading shots. One of these diet and fitness freaks. He's probably favored against me, but it's not a bad first-round matchup, all things considered. Either way, I mean. For either of us."

"That's no way to talk."

"Well, at my stage, one of the few things I've got going for me is that I have a pretty realistic sense of what my prospects are."

"I don't think that's true," Bill said, and Paul laughed, because it could have meant anything.

After dinner, Paul insisted on walking his parents to Michael's place.

"We'll get a cab," Liesel said.

Bill was putting on his jacket. "We won't get a cab but I'm perfectly happy walking."

"Don't be stupid. It's fine. We'll walk together."

That left Dana with the clearing up. Cal was still awake, and jazzed with sleeplessness. By the end of the meal he had started flicking food, and when Paul took his spoon away, he screamed to be let go, and ended up under the table quietly pushing the pieces of chicken and rice around the wooden floor. So Dana had to deal with him, too.

"Just get him to bed and I'll clear up when I get home."

"It's fine," Dana said. "Just go."

"Look at me like you mean it. Look at me like you mean it."

"Don't tell me how to look. I'll look how I want to look."

"I don't think that's how you want to look."

"Oh screw you."

"I'm kidding, Jesus. If you want to clear the table, clear the table, but don't be pissed at me, because I'm perfectly willing to do it when I get back."

"That's not what I'm pissed at you about."

"So what are you pissed at me about? So what are you pissed at me about?"

"Let's not do this in front of your parents."

"They don't care."

"Of course they care. I'm not pissed at you. I just want to get Cal to bed."

"Just put him in front of the TV and I'll do that when I get home, too."

"He's tired, he's two years old, it's ten o'clock at night. He needs to get to bed."

"So put him to bed."

"Fine."

"So I'll put him to bed."

"Fine."

"Come on, Cal," Paul said. "It's beddy-byes." And he pulled his son from under the table and lifted him in his arms. Cal started kicking and screaming. He had his mother's high shoulders and small round face, which looked very pretty on a boy and handsome on her. But not so good now, with his childish features incredibly mobile and expressive—like some kind of grief athlete, pushing himself to the limit. He seemed suddenly very long and skinny. Paul was much too strong for him and pressed him against his lap on the couch and forced the sleep sack over his legs. He wrestled the kid's arms through the armholes and began zipping up the zipper—it was a surprisingly violent demonstration of calm superior strength. All the while Dana said, "Let me do it, it's fine, I'll do it, just give him to me," until the zipper stuck and Paul abruptly quit. Cal almost threw himself onto the floor. Dana caught him and held him, with his long body against her chest and his head on her shoulder. He stopped crying, but his breathing had so much momentum behind it that they could hear him taking in air.

Paul said, containing himself but holding back something gentler than anger, "I just want to walk my parents home. Is that unreasonable?"

"No. Walk them home. I got this. It's fine." And then, to Liesel and Bill, "It's good to see you. I'm sorry. I'll see you in the morning. Everybody's tired." She carried Cal down the corridor to his room, with his hands around her neck. Paul could see that his eyes were already closed.

"*Mensch, du,*" Liesel said to Paul. "*Wir können alleine nach Hause.*"

Sometimes she still spoke German to her kids, when she felt tender or worried or angry, when the old simple relation kicked in again. We can make it home alone. *Du bist einfach müde*, she said. *Ihr seid beide müde. Du sollst ihr helfen.* You're tired, too. You're both tired. You should help her.

"She's fine. I want to walk with you."

The rain had stopped and the air had cleared when they stepped into the courtyard. Bill, who could be meddlesome in some ways, but not in others, said nothing. He wasn't in the business of giving advice to his kids, especially about their parenting. A fountain splashed in the middle, surrounded by dripping dark-green plants; rainwater ran noisily along the curb, too, into the gutters. There was a kind of circular drive around the fountain, where the residents could park and drop things off and turn around. Someone sat waiting in a black Mercedes SUV with the motor running and the wipers going. Waiting for what? Or just getting out of the house? People in the city lived in such close quarters. But then a girl ran ahead of Bill and Paul and Liesel, with a backpack swinging one way and then another across her back, and climbed in. Pigtails, maybe she was ten years old. One of these divorce arrangements, a weekend pickup? Who knows. Bill couldn't see if the driver was a woman or man.

It was cool, almost cold, but still faintly humid, which suggested the heat would come back. Mosquito weather.

At least in the meantime you could breathe again. Car headlights spread their reflections on 86th Street. Paul carried the shoe-bag and dragged one of the suitcases along the ground. He was still in suit and tie.

"A weird thing happens at these kinds of events," he said. "Not that I've been to many before. There's a pecking order, there's always a pecking order, but it seems particularly odd in the context. So a few people made speeches, some of Marcello's players. I mean an actual pecking order, you could go down the ATP rankings. Sampras said something, Courier said something. Guys who won slams. As if there were a natural correlation—these are the guys who knew him best and meant the most to him. Which they probably did."

"Did you say anything?" Bill said.

"I don't know. Not really. I gave a quote, whatever that means. To this woman from *The Times* I'm half friendly with. When she was an intern there she used to—I tried to be nice to her. We're talking about levels of intimacy defined by whether or not you can remember someone's name."

"What did you tell her?"

They were walking down Amsterdam, past the bars and newsstands, against all that traffic flowing relentlessly the other way, in little pulses, from light to light. They crossed over at 83rd and got dripped on by the awning of the Hi-Life Bar & Grill. A few people still sitting outside, drinking cocktails, had started to feel the cold—one of the women had draped her boyfriend's leather jacket across her shoulders.

Eighty-third Street itself was darker and quieter; there was no traffic. They passed a gym, a car rental outlet, and the tall steps of an apartment building. There was a school across the street and then the night sky came down into the space opened up by a playground. It was too cloudy for stars.

"Nothing I want to repeat," Paul said.

"But I thought you liked him."

"I did. I really liked him. But you can't say that you like somebody in this context, it doesn't mean anything. Even if it's true. Even if you think it's one of the nicest things you can say about somebody, *I really liked the guy.* And the fact is, the whole thing, you look around you, you're in this big shiny midtown hotel, and all these people are there, dressed up, and you recognize half of them because they're more famous than you. And everybody is about as sad and genuinely moved as it's humanly possible to be, given the setup. And the whole time I'm thinking, this is what it means to have an effect on the world. All these photographers, TV cameras, journalists, and celebrities. You know, it was impressive and moving, but at the same time you want people breaking down and making a scene, so that they have to be carried out, just to show everybody what's really going on here. Because Marcello's dead. And then his sister got up to say something. They had a mic rigged up on a little stage where I guess the jazz band plays over Sunday brunch, and that's what they had to do. They had to carry her off. She said, I don't know what she said, I couldn't hear her, but she started crying and then her daughter came up and did this funny thing. She had a little pink jacket in her hand and she covered her mom's face with it, like her mom was some kind of criminal making her way through the court reporters, and led her off the stage. Which wasn't easy, there were three or four steps. I don't know what happened after that. But I thought, thank God for that."

Liesel said, "You can't force a two-year-old boy to do something he doesn't want to do."

"What are you talking about?"

"You can't force someone to go to sleep."

"Oh you can force them to do plenty of things. You're bigger than they are. You know better. It's all force." He walked on a little and said, "Half of it's force."

"It's not fair on Dana to leave him like that."

"He was fine. He was basically asleep. In my experience, you get to a point in the evening where they're so tired you have to pick a fight just to push them over the edge."

"This is why Dana wanted to put him to bed two hours ago."

And Paul turned toward his mother and said, sweetly and almost amused, "Are you trying to pick a fight with me?" and Liesel thought, it's true, he can be very patient.

"Oh, I'm tired, too. I'm sorry. I worry about Dana."

Paul said, "She's fine."

Michael's apartment was on the fifth floor of a Gothic pale-stoned building two hundred feet shy of Central Park. The doorman, Eduardo, who knew Paul by name, gave them the key and helped Bill with his bags to the elevator, which opened up straight into the apartment itself. Then Paul spent a certain amount of time turning on lights. The living room was full of comfortable, expensive furniture, side tables with vases and busts, plants in brass pots and several Tiffany lamps, but the ceilings were high, there were French windows, and even with their bags left by the elevator door, it didn't feel crowded. There was a marble fireplace with a spider plant growing out of the grate, and a kind of Roman frieze above the mantelpiece: loosely clothed women and boys dancing.

Bill sat down heavily on one of the sofas. "So where does he watch TV?" he said. He took off his shoes. "Jesus, I'm tired. Who is this guy?"

"You don't have to stay," Liesel said. "We'll figure everything out."

"There's a TV in the study, in one of the cabinets." For some reason, Paul wanted to talk about Michael, maybe for Dana's sake, but he waited for another prompt and then went on anyway. "He runs a hedge fund; I think his grandfather was lieutenant governor of Virginia. They're like American aristocrats, but Michael's also one of these people who thinks that making a lot of money qualifies you as an intellectual."

"How well do you know him?"

"I don't know, I know him. I basically like him. He was honorable to Dana over the divorce. Everybody's still friends. He makes an effort with me. That kind of thing."

"How do you meet someone like this?" Liesel had for some reason taken indignantly against the apartment. She looked for the kitchen, which was tiny, really just a staging area for caterers, and came back with a glass of water.

"Who can cook in a kitchen like that."

"I don't think he cooks much. He orders in. He throws parties."

"Everything here is for show—he doesn't care about the rest. It's not a home, it's a public space."

"Stop it," Bill said. And then, to his son: "You should go back. Get some sleep."

"Don't say anything to Dana," Paul told his mother. "She'll see it as a reflection on her."

"It reflects that she was lucky to get out. Did she live here, too, when they were married? No wonder she left."

Paul said, "She didn't really leave. It wasn't like that." He went into one of the bedrooms, and then another. There were several doors leading off the living room; he found the study and the television and turned it on and off. "I left the remote on the couch," he told his father. "It's pretty straightforward. It doesn't matter where you sleep. The beds are all made up."

"I'll stay up for Jean," Liesel said.

"I'm sure she can figure it out." He stood there for a moment looking at them both. Liesel had collapsed into an armchair. Bill was lying on the sofa, with his feet in their socks rubbing against each other and pointing upward. "You okay, Dad?"

"Terrific."

"Is there anything you want to do in New York?"

"See you play."

"I mean like visiting Aunt Rose."

"Maybe I'll do that, too."

"You can see her on Sunday."

"Or next week. It doesn't matter."

"If you stick around."

"That's right. Don't worry about it."

His mother, with her gray hair and her brown face, slightly pink from tiredness, her large eyes, looked vulnerable without her glasses on. His father was in one of his slightly heavier phases, you could see it in his untucked shirt. Paul thought or felt something like, you've got to carry this body around year after year, without a break.

"Let me know if there's anything I can do for you."

Bill said, "You can get some sleep."

On the walk home, under the dripping sidewalk trees, seven or eight blocks, ten or twelve minutes, Paul felt childish, faintly contracted, as if the edge of his self had retreated a little behind his eyes but was looking out. The doorman was smoking under the arched entrance of his apartment building, and Paul tried to say one of those things you say in passing, funny or funny enough, but couldn't think of anything so just nodded his head. In the elevator he caught sight of his reflection. What do *you* want? he said, half joking, almost angrily, out loud. Dana had gone to bed, but his heart beat very slightly faster to see the light still on in their bedroom—she lay among newspapers.

"How was Cal?" he said.

"Fine. Tired."

"What have you been doing?"

"I called my mother."

He changed and went to the bathroom and brushed his teeth, making more faces in the mirror. The mug they put

their toothbrushes in was always too full, and his razor fell
out when he put the brush back in. He caught it cleanly
in his left hand; lately, this kind of thing had been happening again and again. Physically, at least, he seemed sharp,
he seemed in tune with something. A few days before a
tournament he tended to become sensitive to omens. Well,
okay, maybe the signs were good. Then he climbed in
next to Dana under the duvet. The papers rustled; she put
down the section she was reading.

"How did that go?" he said.

Something had shifted. She didn't seem mad at him, or
she had gotten over it, whatever that meant.

"She's reading your mother's book."

"Is she? Does she like it?"

"I think she does. She wanted to talk to me about it. She
says it's very personal."

"Well, it's a memoir."

"That's what I told her. It's funny, my mother would
never want to write about herself, but she's been telling
everyone she knows, my daughter's mother-in-law has
written this book. She even said to me, am I allowed to call
her that? She thinks you guys must all be obsessed with it,
and I told her, I don't even think you've read it."

"I've read it."

"You have not read it."

"I know the stories anyway. She told them to us when
we were kids."

"You should read it. It's very—"

"Okay," he said, which is what he usually said when
he wanted to close off a conversation. Dana looked at

him. Lately their mood changes had not kept pace with each other, but for once she decided not to worry about it. Talking to her mother had cheered her up—she was an upbeat, narrow-minded, but also intelligent woman. One didn't complain, there was nothing wrong with conventional views. It was useful sometimes for Dana to remember, the Essingers were a funny family.

"Do you know," she said, "for a second tonight, I thought your dad was propositioning me." Paul stared at her, and she went on, "He looked me right in the eyes, and said,"—but here she began to laugh helplessly, she was trying to do his voice—"*Listen, I'm only going to say this once. Let me pay for a hotel.*"

"What was he talking about?"

She could hardly get the words out. "He wanted you to—"

"Just say it."

"—sleep at a hotel. So you—could get some sleep."

"But I don't want to sleep at a hotel," he said at last.

"Well . . ."

"Don't make me sleep at a hotel," he said, pulling her toward him. They lay like that for a minute with the lights on, until Dana could breathe again and wipe the tears from her face.

SATURDAY

Michael's apartment had a wide though impractical balcony running off the living room, through French doors. There were slender-limbed trees outside. From the sofa, you could just see their green tips, silently restless in the morning breeze. If you opened the doors (the key was sticky in the lock) and stepped onto the balcony and leaned over the balustrade you could almost touch them. From that position, you might also be able to make out Central Park itself, over the arch of leaves—more green trees rising on a hill.

Liesel leaned and looked. Bill had gone out to get milk and a newspaper; Jean was still asleep. This is the kind of thing Liesel wanted from living in New York: the ordinary business of life, the way it involves you in the city. Buying a *Times* from the newsstand on the corner, watching the joggers on their way to Central Park. She had made her peace with the apartment, too. Though it puzzled her still, the strength of her reaction; she was tired but that didn't quite explain it. Poor Dana, she thought, aware that a part of what she felt had to do with the way Paul seemed to be treating her.

When Bill came back, with bagels and fresh orange juice, and babka muffins (he'd gone all the way to Zabar's), she looked in on Jean. But the girl was still fast asleep, lying with one leg hanging over the edge of the bed and the sheets twisted under her. Girl—she was twenty-nine years old. Her calves were stippled with small black hairs; she needed to shave them. And her toenails were painted bright green. Liesel could see them on the dangling foot, the little nails neatly colored in, like the drawing of a careful kid, the flesh surrounding them pink and perfectly clean. But green . . . it's a color you choose when you aren't very confident about your looks, and so make a joke of the whole thing.

Even when they were little, Liesel liked nothing more than watching her kids in bed. There's a personality in sleep, you can see it in the face, which is somehow a hundred percent likable—in the day, in their waking selves, the percentage drops a little. They resent you, they're busy, they show off. But at night, asleep, there's a kind of concentration or focus, and what's left is . . . regular breathing, REM. Liesel used to go into their rooms and look at them for a half-minute; it was part of her bedtime routine. The love she felt had a lot of pity mixed in. Poor thing, she thought, watching their eyelids flicker. It was like some kind of torture, subjecting these kids to a constant stream of images. I guess it happens to all of us. But Jean got nightmares, she often crawled into their bed, and Liesel let her, though she never let the others. Because Jean was the baby, probably. You had to be careful what she watched on TV. It was difficult to police, Nathan was nine years older, you couldn't expect him to put up with endless cartoons.

She walked out again and said to Bill, who was setting out plates and glasses, "We're meeting for brunch at eleven."

"That's okay."

"You won't be hungry then."

"I can sit there, who cares."

"I care. The point is eating together."

"But I got all this food," he said. And she let it go. She found a breadboard in the kitchen and brought it out—Bill cut the muffins in half and started eating.

"Aren't you going to wake Jean?" he said, with a full mouth.

"She was sleeping, I don't know. Let her sleep."

"What time did she get in last night?"

"A little after eleven. She woke me up. I was asleep in the chair."

"What time is it now?"

"A little after nine." Liesel poured herself some juice and went on, "I got an email this morning from a woman at *The Village Voice*—some woman my editor knows. She heard I was in town and wants to interview me."

"Okay."

"Just something for the blog; it doesn't matter."

"It doesn't matter if it doesn't matter. You should do it."

"Well, we have to make a time. I don't want it to be a distraction."

"It's not a distraction for anybody else."

"If I had this much money in New York," she said, "I would want a balcony."

"There is a balcony."

"I mean somewhere you can sit."

"You can sit on the balcony if you put out a chair."

"Maybe Dana can. I can't."

"Why Dana?"

"She's very small."

"She's six foot."

"Well, she's very skinny. All of Paul's girlfriends were always so skinny."

"What's that got to do with it?"

"Nothing."

"When were you planning on waking her up?"

"You go," Liesel said.

After Bill left, she took one of the muffin halves and walked to the balcony with it, opened the French doors and stood outside, eating. It had rained some more in the night, heavily at times; the parked cars looked recently cleaned. The air was heating up, but the sunshine, coming over the apartment building on the south side of the street, hadn't reached them yet. Bill thought that one of the reasons she wanted to move to New York was professional. She had an agent now and an editor, she had started to write a few pieces for *The Times Book Review*, there were parties she could go to. He didn't object, not at all, but he pointed it out as a reason she had that he didn't, for moving to New York. But she didn't like parties, she said, she didn't want to go to any parties, and was sure at least that that part of her explanation was honest. Why shouldn't you go to parties, he said. You might meet someone useful. Because I don't want to go. Somehow the argument always got twisted around.

But she didn't mind any of that, just standing there on the balcony, looking out over 83rd Street. She was basically very happy, she could hear Bill singing, *There she is, Miss America*, to wake Jean up. In his deep, almost comically deep singing voice; his mother thought he could have been a cantor. *There she is, your ideal.* One of her little reproaches, for marrying his son, when she wasn't Jewish. It didn't matter now. His mother was dead. They had made their peace with each other, all three of them, before she died. And the only thing that bothered Liesel, a little, was that thread of selfishness in her happiness, the thought of talking to the woman at *The Village Voice*, which very slightly offset her worries about Paul.

Jean was already half-sitting up in bed, with her hands behind her head on the pushed-up pillow.

"I'm up, I'm up," she said, but Bill kept going:

The dream of a million gals who are more than pretty,
Can come true in Atlantic City.

"I'm up."

"How are you doing? How'd you sleep?"

"I don't know. By the time I got in I had kind of pushed through the sleep window and come out the other side. So I just lay there reading. And then it was like, somebody knocked me out cold."

"There's babka muffins."

"That's what I came for, Dad."

Her accent had shifted slightly in England, and she overcompensated now by exaggerating her Jewishness a little—you could hear both London and New York. Austin was in the mix, too . . . she was hard to place.

"All right, I'll leave you alone. We're meeting the others for brunch at eleven."

"Who?"

"Everybody but Susie and the kids."

"When are they coming down?"

"Tomorrow."

"On her own? What about David?"

"Who knows," Bill said. "Nobody tells me anything."

Since leaving college, seven years before, Jean had become aware of a couple of things: that she was unusually close to her family, and that her family was odd. There was a quiet contradiction in recognizing both at once, which she dealt with by presenting a cheerful front whenever she saw them. It let them in and kept them out at the same time, but didn't always last very long.

"What do you think of this apartment?"

Bill looked around. "Cheap at half the price."

"If I were Dana, I think I'd have stuck it out with this guy."

"Well, there's something to what you say. I'm not sure it was her choice."

Jean pushed the covers off and swung her legs over the side of the bed.

"What time is it? Do I have time to shower?"

She was wearing boxer shorts and a T-shirt. Bill felt vaguely uncomfortable around his daughters' bodies; he felt a kind of shame, not for his own sake but for theirs. Something had happened to them since they were kids and used to climb on his lap. He didn't have the same reaction to the boys.

"You have time. Almost ten."

Jean wouldn't have taken off her shirt in front of her

father, but she wouldn't have asked him to turn around
either. She didn't have to, because he walked out. The bathroom was just outside her door, down half a corridor, and she
undressed and tucked a thick white towel under her armpits.
Barefoot, feeling first the tacky wood-stained floorboards of
the hallway, then the cool black-and-white tiles of the bathroom, then the faintly resonant cast iron of the tub, she got
in the shower. The pressure seemed good, especially after
England, and she closed her eyes against the heat. Her hair
went smooth and lank; she pulled the water through it.

Always the side effect of closing her eyes was that the
consciousness of other people began to press against her.
Henrik in England, though he was probably on a plane to
Split right now, or already there. His wife's family owned
a beach house near Vranjic, and Jean tried to picture him
going about his day. They had an old boat, Henrik was
good with his hands. The boys spent as much time as they
could in the water, he took them fishing. They ate their
meals outside and poured honey into empty wine bottles
to keep the wasps away. For whatever reason, he got on
well with his wife's Croatian relatives, the men at least.
Everybody relaxed.

Why he had told her these things, who knows. It was
his habit to explain himself calmly on all subjects, to make
no distinction between public and private, or personal and
impersonal. At least this is what Jean said to him. Instead
of expressing jealousy, she analyzed his character, but it
came down to the same thing. Eventually they both admitted this, and Henrik did his best to comfort her. In those
early days, everything, even guilt, could serve as an excuse.

Though now that she was here, in New York, trying to wash the jet lag away, and with her parents in the next room, she really couldn't tell how jealous she felt. It was like testing a wound; she seemed okay. And that worried her, too. Because in that case, if it didn't matter much . . .

Over breakfast she argued with her mother about the apartment. It started out as teasing and almost turned into something else. "Check out the real estate," Jean had said. Liesel couldn't keep out the disapproval in her voice, and Jean reacted against her mother's disapproval. Really she was taking Paul's side. But Bill eventually shut them up—he hated being late and waited at the elevator door for two or three minutes, pressing the button, until his wife and daughter were ready to go.

Out in the street, Liesel said, "I'm worried about Dana."

"What's wrong with Dana?"

"I don't think she has enough to do with herself. You go a little crazy."

"She has a two-year-old kid."

"That's what I mean. It's a lot of work."

"You're not making any sense."

"Tell me about it," Bill said.

"They've got Inez to look after him," Jean said.

"That's what I mean. She doesn't know what to do with herself. She goes to the gym, I don't know what she does. And Paul doesn't help."

"What's wrong with going to the gym?"

"Nothing, but you can't spend your life this way."

"What do you think Paul does for a living?"

"I'm talking about him, too."

"You're not making any sense."

Liesel looked at her daughter. "You're supposed to be my sympathetic child."

"I'm being sympathetic. I'm pointing things out."

"Well, I don't know," she said. "I'm just trying to talk, to say something. There's something I don't like going on."

"I'm sure it's fine. He always gets funny before a big tournament."

"I don't know."

"He's not the one I'd be worried about, if I were you."

"Who should I worry about?"

"Don't worry about anybody," Jean said, taking Liesel's arm. Bill was never physically affectionate with his wife; she relied on her daughters, and now that they were all grown up . . .

"I miss you in England."

"Don't say that," Jean said. "How do you think I feel?"

Paul and Dana and Cal were waiting outside the restaurant, MaBelle's on Amsterdam and 81st. The sky looked recently swept, the air felt cool and humid. It must have rained heavily overnight. The awning still dripped and the plastic surfaces of the outdoor tables and chairs were covered in beads. Cal was in his stroller, not quite asleep but glassy-eyed. Dana rolled him back and forth without thinking. Jean, when she saw the boy, went straight to him and crouched down. "Hey, kid. Remember me?"

"Maybe let him be." Paul was hovering. "He's almost asleep."

"It's okay," Dana said, but Jean stood up anyway and gave her brother a hug. She wore black jeans and black Converse, like a teenager. Her white T-shirt had a grid of numbers on it; they seemed random, but maybe they weren't. It looked like a math geek thing. Around her family she almost consciously regressed. It was a relief, it felt less like regression than a return to normality.

"Who chose this place? It's so Upper West Side."

"What does that mean?"

"Expensive and pseudo-homey."

"Dana," Paul said.

Dana made her not-really-offended-but-protesting face. "What, I like it. I like the jam. We needed somewhere that could seat a party of nine."

"Party party," Jean said. "I'm just being a snob. Ignore me."

There were two sets of glass doors leading in; a couple seemed to be waiting in the space between them, and Bill pushed his way past them and looked inside, then came out again. "Do we have a reservation?"

"So what kind of place do you go to in London?" Dana asked.

"I don't go out much, it's too expensive. I like English breakfasts, so I go to greasy spoons. But my friends have a thing for upmarket pseudo-American diners." After a moment, she added, "Pseudo seems to be my word of the day."

"We've got a reservation," Dana said. "But they won't seat us until we're all here."

"Someone should tell them we're here."

"What about Nathan?"

"He'll be late."

Liesel stood up for her eldest child. "He's gotten better."

"Shouldn't you be out hitting balls or something?" Jean said to Paul.

He was stretching his neck, turning his shoulders from side to side—motions that made him look relaxed but were really an expression of nerves. "I went for a run this morning. I'll hit some balls this afternoon."

"They're going to give up our table," Bill said. "Tell them your mother needs to sit down."

"I'm fine."

"Okay, then *I* need to sit down."

Jean put her arm around her father. "It's fine. It's a beautiful morning. We're all standing in the street, catching up, like a happy family."

"If we're waiting for Nathan, we might as well forget about it."

Jean said, "For five minutes, you can stop worrying."

Dana liked Jean—she often said what Dana wanted to say on family occasions. Of all the Essingers, Jean was the one she might have been friends with independently. This is what she told herself. Of course, a certain amount of intimacy had been given to them for free by their relation to Paul. But they had other things in common. Jean smoked socially, when none of her family was looking. She had lived in England long enough to pick it up, more as a social skill than a habit; and Dana had always belonged to the kind of rich fun crowds that treated smoking the same way. Sometimes, at very boring family parties, they snuck off and shared a cigarette. It stood for other things, too, an attitude to good times. Bill and Liesel hadn't taught their children to value pleasure. This is one of the things Dana sometimes fought about with Paul. She considered Jean an ally in these fights.

"How was your flight?" she said.

"It was a flight."

Bill bent down to stare at his grandson in the stroller. "Cal's gonzo."

"What about lunch? If he sleeps now, he misses lunch."

"Don't worry about it, Paul," Dana said. "Last night you weren't so worried about his sleep."

"I want him to see his cousins."

"That's assuming the cousins ever show up," Bill said.

He was in a better mood now, still pacing, but somehow pleasantly restless. Sometimes all it took was a joke to cheer him up—one of his own, to turn anxiety into good humor. He checked out the menus by the side of the door and watched the food being served at the window tables.

Paul noticed Jean's shirt. "Fibonacci sequence?"

"No. So how much money should I put on you?"

"You can't bet on sports in the state of New York."

"In London I can bet on anything."

"What odds are they giving me?"

"Who's got a phone?" Jean said. "I don't want roaming charges."

Dana looked in her handbag, but it was a mess—diapers and creams and bottles and little packs of cookies and fruit roll-ups. She began taking them out, one by one.

"By the way, I like American diner food," Paul said.

There were little frictions he forgot about when his family was absent. Not frictions, exactly, but you felt a kind of pressure to assert your own opinions. Which meant you had to have an opinion in the first place—you needed to come prepared. Dana sometimes complained about this fact. She said he idealized his family, nobody could live up to them, but then, in their presence, he went silent or picked stupid fights. Not stupid fights, Paul told her once, this is just what intimacy looks like. You wouldn't know, you're an only child. Which started off a very stupid fight.

"But you wouldn't spend ten pounds on a hamburger," Jean said.

"What do you think you spend around here? Fifteen, twenty bucks."

"But do they serve it in those cheap plastic baskets with check-tablecloth-style grease paper?"

"Sure, some places."

"I don't know, the whole thing bugs me somehow. The English have this ridiculous relationship with America, where they basically hate us for legitimate political reasons, and then they spend like twenty pounds for two small pancakes and some scrambled eggs and lox on the side. Which is not what you would get in any actual American short-order joint. They conflate diner breakfast with Upper West Side brunch . . ."

"Who says short-order joint anymore?" Paul asked.

This pulled her up short. "Assholes like me."

"Here's my phone." Dana passed it to Jean and started reassembling her handbag—she had spread the contents precariously over the cover of Cal's stroller.

"Okay, let's check out what Paddy Power has to say. Paul Essinger to win the US Open."

"Don't do that," Liesel said, sitting down. She had found a pack of tissues in her coat and used most of them on one of the plastic chairs.

"Paul doesn't care. Do you care, Paul?"

"I don't care."

"I care. Dana, stop them from doing this, please."

"I can't stop any of you guys from doing anything."

"Shades of former lateness," Paul said, because Nathan had arrived. He wore a dark gray suit, cut to hide an extra twenty pounds, and a pale green shirt from Gieves & Hawkes on Savile Row. Expensive clothes, but he didn't look after them. The old leather briefcase he carried under his arm had a broken handle. Maybe he was two inches taller than Paul, closer to six four than six three. Bill sometimes thought, if Paul had those two extra inches, who knows . . .

"What are you talking about?" Nathan said. "I was told eleven o'clock."

His kids, two girls, had been walking behind him. They came up and stood by their father's side, in the shade of his protection.

Bill looked at his watch; he had to shake out his arm, and pull up the sleeves of his sports jacket, and turn the strap around on his wrist. "Eleven seventeen and . . . thirty seconds."

"That's within the margin of error," Nathan said. He was a big man who didn't know what to do with his bigness. Yet at the same time it was an attractive quality and suggested force or gravitas and not only that but generosity. With his long arms, he could tap you on the shoulder from a distance; his hair, still full, waved in the wind. Almost forty, approaching middle age, he looked both younger and older—a little wild but also somehow well established, and very much at home on the streets of New York.

"Whose error?"

"I don't care," Liesel said. "Tell them we're here. I need another coffee. Where's Clémence?"

"Montreal. Visiting her sister."

"She's not coming?"

"You knew this," Bill told her.

"Hey, Julie. Hey, Margot," Jean said.

She bent down to her nieces, playing the jolly aunt. Jean hadn't seen them since Christmas and always felt a kind of reproach in the way they changed, as if she hadn't been paying attention. Which of course she hadn't. Margot at least was still Margot, five years old and someone you could read to, if you couldn't think of anything else to say, but Julie must have grown three or four inches in the past eight months. If you didn't know her you could almost see her as a teenager. Still just ten, but in a transitional state, she had responded to what she couldn't control by cutting her hair very short. A razor cut. Straightening up, Jean ran her hand through the bristle, and Julie flinched or shrugged.

"It looks good," Jean said, hurt. Her niece wore a flowery little-girl dress and big black heavy Doc Martens.

"What are you doing on the phone?" she asked.

"Seeing if your uncle Paul's going to win."

"You can't find that out on a phone," Julie said. She had learned to respond matter-of-factly to anything that resembled condescension and Jean felt (as she often felt around other people's kids) slightly foolish. Not quite a grown-up and not quite one of them.

"I used to wear that dress," she said. An old Laura Ashley design—pink roses with stems and thorns on a limeade-colored background. The material had faded like a photograph with repeated washings.

"I know." People were always telling Julie things they had told her before.

"I remember when I got it. It was so long I could stand on the hems and pretend I didn't have any legs."

"That doesn't make sense. Why did Liesel buy it if it was too big?"

Nathan's children called their parents and grandparents by their first names. It was a part of the way they were raised—to treat everybody as equals.

"I got it from Susie. It was a hand-me-down."

"Listen," Nathan said. "We should go in and eat. I've booked a couple of viewings for one o'clock."

The Essingers had reached the stage of family evolution when the oldest child begins to take charge. Nathan in full flow had a lot of energy, for work, for good times, for argument; for sympathy, too. There were so many things needing his attention, and he liked a full dance card, as his father put it.

Liesel called out from her chair: "What do you mean, viewings?"

"Apartments for you to look at."

Bill stopped pacing. "Who's buying a place in New York?"

"Maybe you are, Dad."

"Twelve hundred to one," Jean said.

"What?"

"The odds they're giving for Pauly to win the Open."

"Where are these apartments?"

"I have to look it up."

"Put me down for a dollar," Bill said. "If he wins, I'll buy an apartment in New York."

"You'll need to put down a little more than that. Let's say a grand."

Paul smiled and shook his head. "Those are not reasonable odds."

He helped his mother up; she had reached out both hands to him, and he felt how warm and wrinkled they were. Liesel looked at Jean indignantly. "I didn't want you to do this."

"What. They're better odds than I've got."

"That's not what I mean," Paul said. "There's no point in putting odds on something that's not going to happen."

"What's not going to happen?"

"I'm not going to win the Open."

"You don't know that," Bill said.

"I know it. What are the odds on my first-round match? That's a reasonable bet to make."

Dana broke in: "Has someone told the waiter we're here?"

"Let's change the subject," Liesel said. "What kind of apartments?"

"One of them is in a brownstone—"

"I'll tell them," Paul said, but Dana had beaten him to it and escaped inside.

Nathan kept going. "Two bedrooms, it's got a working fireplace. No real balcony, but there's a fire escape at the back, with a window in front of it. Maybe you can climb out."

"Your mother's not climbing out anywhere."

"The other apartment is less nice, but there's a door-man and the balcony is unusually large. You're high up, though. I can't tell from the website whether it's the kind of place you'd want to sit, or whether people just put their bicycles out there."

"We're not going to have any bicycles," Bill said.

"You know what I mean."

"I can't understand this." Jean was thumbing at her phone. "There's a plus minus number next to your names."

"What are the numbers?"

"He's plus 450. You're minus 200. Is that good?"

Nathan shifted the broken briefcase from his right arm to his left. He said, "That's not particularly good," and opened the case one-handed to take something out—a small blue academic datebook. He had to dig around. "The brown-stone is on 84th Street, between Amsterdam and Colum-bus. The other one's on 86th, closer to Riverside. What do you think, Paul, a five-minute walk between them?"

He put the datebook in his jacket pocket.

"Closer to ten."

Dana came back. Sometimes when she was around the Essingers, she started sounding like them, too—almost consciously. But then it became a habit and she couldn't help it. Her mother sometimes made fun of Dana for this.

"We can eat," she told everyone.

Nathan had been staring at Jean. "Recaman," he said suddenly.

"What are you talking about?"

"The number sequence."

"No."

Something about her older brother was pissing Jean off, she couldn't figure out what. The way he was late, just his general air of swooping in.

"How do you know?" Nathan asked.

"I know."

"Believe me, you don't know."

"There is no sequence. It's just random numbers. I bought it in Camden, from something called the Random Number T-Shirt Company."

"There's a sequence."

"Whatever."

Bill was already inside. Paul tried to hold open the door, for the stroller, but there were two doors, and they swung together, so Dana had to duck under his arm. There was nothing affectionate about the way she ducked, no physical contact. Both of them noticed this. Then Liesel, a little too late, took hold of one of the doors, resting subtly against it, and the girls, Julie and Margot, waited for her to go in first. "Go ahead," Liesel said, smiling at them, but they waited for their father. On the other side, Dana had turned the stroller around and was pushing backward through the next set of double swing doors. Bill came to help her.

"They've got us at the back," he said. "I'm not sure there's room to get the stroller through."

"I'll be okay."

She pulled the rain cover down to give Cal a little sound protection.

"Well . . ."

But people pushed in their chairs; it was all right. Jean said to Margot as the little girl walked past, "Are you hungry?" but the girl ignored her.

A waitress came by with a complimentary basket of blueberry muffins, steaming into a white cloth. Her face was heavily and cheerfully made-up; her skin had large pores, with the face powder caked in.

Bill said, "Can we get some water? We need menus, too."

"Sure can."

Her accent was Midwestern; she looked late twenties. Grad student? Nursing, maybe? Or just somebody working and having a good time? Jean thought, I wonder if she says she's from New York, when people ask her. Not here, of course, but on vacation—when she goes out of town. *Where you from, sweetheart? New York.* Jean had lived in London for five years, but she would never say she was from London.

"What's the hurry, Dad?"

"Nathan says we've got an appointment at one o'clock."

"But you don't want to buy a place anyway."

"Still," Bill said.

Julie pulled on her grandmother's sleeve. "Tell me a story."

The kids were on their own with Liesel at the end of the table. Nathan was happy to give them the space—as a matter of policy he treated his children like responsible adults.

Also, there was something he wanted to talk to Bill about.

"What kind of story?" Liesel asked, while Dana said to Jean, "Are you working on anything interesting?"

Jean sat next to Dana, opposite the girls. Cal slept in his stroller at the end. Dana worried that Margot would wake him up—she kept shifting his rain cover to get a better look at his face.

"That's okay," Dana said, touching the girl's hand gently. "He's all right."

The restaurant had exposed brick walls, with a few rough plank shelves unevenly spaced, propping up ornaments, most of which were for sale—small birdcages, wooden letter racks, and jars of jam. But the acoustics were poor, and the Essingers talked over each other.

"About Hitler," Julie said.

"I guess so," Jean said. "It's interesting, I guess. Everything's interesting, right? I don't know. All these fucking interesting documentaries, which nobody really wants to watch. I don't want to watch them either."

"Why do you want to hear about Hitler?" Liesel said.

"At Christmas you promised to tell me a story about Hitler."

"So why do you do it?" Dana asked.

"I don't know, it's interesting."

Liesel looked up; she was worried about Jean and sensitive to anything she had to say for herself. "I like to watch them. The last one you showed us, I thought—"

"It was excellent," Bill said.

"Well, I'm making another one with the same guy."

"Please tell me a story," Julie repeated.

Nathan turned to Paul, who was sitting across the table from him, next to their mother. "If you have a chance to win each match, you have a chance to win the whole thing."

"I have a chance to win my first-round match."

"Well, and then in the second round you play somebody else."

"That's how it works."

"Okay, and so you have a chance to beat him."

"Maybe."

"Immigration," Jean said. "There are all these people hanging out at Calais, trying to make it over on one of the ferries. Mostly from Africa—Eritrea, South Sudan. They sneak into people's cars, they swim after the ships, they'll do anything."

"That sounds—" Dana began to say.

Jean smiled at her.

"Well, we want to turn it into a kind of cheesy drama, where you root for the little guy. So we're trying to follow somebody the whole way, we're hoping to document it—through Africa, through Libya, into Tripoli, onto the first boat, hanging out with them in Lampedusa, and so on. But it's hard to just document these people, you want to step in."

"Are you going on location?"

"It's possible. Liesel and Bill don't like to hear this stuff."

"We can't hear you anyway," Bill said. "It's too loud in here."

"I don't really know any stories about Hitler," Liesel said. "I never met him."

"But you promised me."

"Maybe I meant the one about the postcard. But that's not really a story."

"Tell me anyway."

The girls both knew that their grandmother didn't play with children, she never stooped to their level; but Liesel was also like their father in many ways. If you asked her a serious question, she gave you her full attention.

"I'm basically a scaredy-cat," Jean said. "I don't do stupid stuff. I hang out at hotels. I watch rushes."

Nathan turned to Paul. "How many guys are there on the tour that you've never beaten?"

"There are a lot of guys on the tour I've never played."

"What's your record against Federer?"

"Oh for twelve."

"Okay, so don't play Federer. What about Nadal."

"I beat him once. He beat me, I don't know, seven or eight times."

"So let's say you have a roughly twelve percent chance against Nadal."

"That's not how it works."

"That's exactly how it works."

"If he wants to beat me, he can beat me. If he doesn't care, I can win."

Liesel said, "When I was a little girl, a little younger than you—and a little older than Margot, my school teacher asked us all to raise our hands if we had a picture of Hitler at home. She went row by row. We were supposed to talk about the picture, to describe it and say what it meant to us. She asked the first row one day, and the next row the next day, and I was worried that when she got to me I'd have to keep my hand down, because my parents didn't have a picture of Hitler on the wall."

"What did you do?"

"I told my mother."

"I just want to look at this on the numbers," Nathan said. "You don't have to play Nadal until the . . ."

"Semis."

"So let's assume that your chances of winning each round go steadily downward. What are the odds on you against . . ."

"Borisov," Jean said. "Seven to four."

"What did your mother do?" Julie asked.

"She bought a postcard of Hitler and put it over the fireplace, so when it was my turn, when it was our row, I could raise my hand with everybody else."

The menus arrived, printed on a piece of paper. Nathan started scribbling numbers on the back of one of them. "Okay, first round, eleven to eight, which translates roughly into a forty-two percent chance of winning. For you, I mean. Let's assume that in a general way your odds of winning each match go down, round by round. We can work this out, too."

Liesel said, "Please, stop."

"Paul doesn't care. Paul, do you care?"

"I don't care."

Liesel said, "Bill, tell them to stop."

"I'm going to tell them to order. Nathan, stop showing off."

"I'm not showing off. I'm interested. I want to know if I should put some money on Paul."

Julie said, "And what did you say about the picture?"
Liesel didn't understand her, and she had to repeat herself.
"When it was your turn, what did you say about the post-
card of Hitler?"

Liesel tried to remember—it was all a long time ago,
and she had told these stories many times. First to her own
children, and then to her grandchildren; she had put them
in her memoir, too. But the way Julie asked also brought
something out, a very faint feeling of what it was like to be
a kid again. Liesel's mother had had curly shoulder-length
hair, which she cut herself, and Liesel used to watch her
mother watching herself in the mirror and cutting it. There
was a red tiled floor and afterward she swept up the hairs in
a dustpan and brush and threw them into the wood stove,
where they suddenly crackled. The house had no mantelpiece—she must have put the postcard on a bookshelf.

"I don't remember what I said. I think I said, I was glad
when my mother got the picture, because it meant I could
be like everyone else."

"Nathan says there's no point in doing something just
to be like other people."

"Your father is very sensible," Liesel said.

Bill waved the muffin basket over his head. It was empty; he had eaten most of them. "The muffins are good."

"This is a good place," Dana said. "That's why I picked it."

She tried not to sound aggrieved, but in fact she found
the whole thing, the presence of so many Essingers, the
conversation about Paul, deeply upsetting—like the noise
of the sails whipping around when you rig a boat. A kind
of violence that you have to learn to ignore.

The waitress came back and Bill said, "The muffins are excellent."

"I know, right?" she said. "Can I get you some more?"

"I'll just eat them all."

"Well, that's what we make 'em for."

Nathan said, "This is very crude, but let's do it this way. Let's assume you face Nadal in the semis. And let's assume that the odds against Borisov are more or less accurate. Which means that you go from a forty-two percent chance of winning in round one, to a twelve percent chance of winning in round . . . six."

Meanwhile, people ordered and Nathan had to stop for a minute to find Margot something she could eat. Julie could order for herself. When the waitress was gone, Nathan said, "Let's further assume that the drop in your likelihood of winning each match is constant. That's a big assumption, but my guess is it's also pretty close to the truth. In which case your chances go down about six percentage points per round. Thirty-six in the second, thirty in the third, twenty-four in the fourth."

"I don't know why you're doing this," Liesel said.

"I'm trying to point something out to him."

Bill said, "Everybody gets the point."

"I don't think you do. Let me finish. If we carry this tendency over to the finals, that gives you a roughly six percent chance against whomever you face."

"That's a ridiculous calculation," Jean said. "You're just making this stuff up."

"Look, his record against Nadal and Federer is something like one and twenty, which is pretty close to six percent. It doesn't matter. I'm just interested in ballpark figures."

"You're not even parking at the ballpark. How do you know Nadal and Federer will make it that far?"

"I don't know. But my guess is, among the last twenty Grand Slam finals, the top four players have made up something like eighty percent of the finalists and top ten players account for most of the rest."

"What does that matter?"

"Paul, what's your record against top ten players?"

"I don't know."

"How about top four?"

"I can't believe you're asking him these questions," Jean said.

But Paul was smiling. "What I think is funny is that you really believe this is a meaningful way of assessing the likely outcomes. In spite of the total absence of any first-hand experience of what's involved in winning a Grand Slam tennis match."

"Let me finish. What are the odds on Paul?"

Jean said, "No."

"Just tell me. Don't be an idiot."

"Twelve hundred to one. I'm sorry, Dana."

"Don't apologize to me. You didn't make the odds."

"I mean, for starting this thing off. For making you listen to us."

"I stopped listening like five minutes ago," Dana said. But then she worried that this came across as angrier than she felt. "Let's talk about something else. Talk to me about London. Are you seeing anybody?"

"Not really," Jean said, blushing.

"What does that mean?"

"I don't know." But she was still caught up in the fight with her brother. "What are you doing?"

Nathan was still writing on the menu.

"I'm working out the probabilities."

Jean watched him for a minute, shaking her head. Eventually she said, "Just use a phone."

"I haven't got a phone."

"We've got like five phones here."

"I'm almost done."

Jean thought, there's no point in getting pissed off; this is just what he's like. You know this is what he's like. You lived with him long enough. But she didn't want to answer questions about her love life either—not to Dana. She turned to her nieces and said in her best camp-counselor voice: "When do you guys start school?"

"Next week." Julie answered for both of them. "I'm very excited. Margot's coming to my school for the first time."

"Look at you. Are you excited, Margot?"

"I don't know."

"A little excited, a little scared?"

"I don't know because I never went before. So I don't know if I like it or if I won't like it. I don't know."

She had large gray eyes and a round face. Everyone said she looked like Liesel, which was partly code for something else—her grandmother as a kid had the reputation of a good-natured bruiser. Margot's voice was deeper than her sister's, louder, too. She sounded faintly deaf, not just because of the volume but a faint tinniness or thickness in certain consonants. Also, an ability to ignore other people. In fact, her parents had twice had her hearing tested, but it was okay.

"But you might be excited or worried anyway. It's called anticipation. It means what you feel about something before it happens."

"I can tell you what your favorite day is going to be," Julie said.

"What." Margot looked up at her sister.

"Friday. Because Friday is fish day and you love fish."

"What kind of fish."

"It depends. Sometimes salmon. Sometimes fish sticks. I can tell you what my worst day is."

"What."

"Pizza day."

"Oh, I love pizza," Margot said.

"You won't like this pizza. It looks like somebody threw up."

"Julie," Jean said, but in fact she felt pleased. The girl looked so self-conscious, it was nice to hear her sounding like a kid.

"What? It does. It looks like somebody ate a lot of cheese and threw it up."

"That's disgusting," Margot said. She had recently lost her front teeth and never seemed to close her mouth completely. When she spoke, you could hear the spit in her voice.

"Julie, that's not how polite people talk about food."

"She needs to know. I'm telling her all this because she needs to know."

Nathan looked up from his scribbled-on piece of paper. "Well, that's not exactly the answer I was hoping for."

And then the food arrived, oatmeal and eggs, served in the cast-iron pan, pancakes and syrup and bacon, more muffins and bread. Everything seemed a little over-presented. Large sprigs of dry parsley decorated the eggs; there were a few token strawberries. The table started filling with dishes and glasses had to be shifted. Bill lifted a vase and set it down somewhere else—on another table, where a woman was dining alone.

"Madame," he said. She wore a gray jacket with shoulder pads; her red hair had faded. She was looking at her phone.

"What were you hoping for, Nathan?"

"I wanted to show you that you had a chance."

"And?"

Nathan's manner had changed, his voice, too. "I was stupid to start this. It's my fault. Jean, can you help Margot cut up her food? I can't reach from here."

"Look, it doesn't matter to me," Paul said. "I'm not a tennis player out of delusion."

"Fine."

"So tell me. You can't start all this and not tell me."

"I didn't start anything. I just wanted to prove to you that you've got a better chance of winning this thing than you think."

"So prove it to me."

Paul could feel the family sympathies ranging against his brother; it gave him a kind of pleasure but also made him feel sorry for Nathan. This is what his childhood was like— you can win a lot of battles just by keeping your temper.

"Well, these are very rough calculations."

"Which show . . ."

"Which don't prove anything."

"Listen, Nathan. I have a pretty robust and realistic sense of what my chances are. I just want to hear what you came up with."

Liesel said, "I don't understand what they're arguing about."

"Nothing. Nobody's arguing."

"Fine," Nathan said. "I'll tell you. "

But instead he took a bite of his food.

"We're waiting," Paul said, but in fact Liesel was right; he didn't want to hear. Not that he expected to have a reasonable chance, but he didn't want to talk about the odds in front of his father—he knew that Bill had unrealistic hopes.

Nathan finished his mouthful. "According to this, you're not a very good bet at twelve hundred to one." He looked up at Paul. "That gives you a roughly point oh eight percent likelihood of winning, whereas my calculations suggest you've probably got . . . a little less than that."

"If only someone here could have told you that."

"Can I say it again," Jean said. "That's a better chance than I've got."

"Can we just eat," Bill said.

He hadn't ordered any food for himself, but Liesel told him her omelet was too big and tried to give him half. First she offered and then she threatened—if he didn't take it, it would be thrown away. So he signaled for the waitress to bring an extra plate. Nathan also offered him a taste of his shakshuka. Jean gave him part of her short stack. The plate filled up. Only Paul said, "I need every calorie I can get."

"The girls start school next week," Nathan said, changing the subject.

"So they were telling us."

And then for a few moments the table went quiet. Jean broke the silence at last. "The Fressingers," she said, to no one in particular. To *fress* is to eat like an animal, to feed. "The one thing that can shut us up."

"Tell me another story about Hitler," Julie said.

Bill paid in cash—he always kept a large roll of bills in his wallet. On their way out, the waitress asked Paul, "Are you a tennis player?"

"More or less," Paul said.

"Are you playing in the Open?"

"Monday afternoon. Court 12."

"I'm sorry, I couldn't help overhearing. My brother plays for Emporia State, in Kansas. Can I ask your name? I was going to check the credit card but your dad paid cash."

"Paul Essinger."

"I know you," she said. "I know you. You used to do those tennis ball commercials."

Sometimes this happened to him, but not often; he felt pleased to show off his celebrity, especially in front of his brother. But he was embarrassed, too, because she would have heard their conversation. When you're an athlete your chances in life become public property. "I'd ask you

to sign something for him," she went on, "but he'd probably get mad at me for bugging you."

"It's no trouble," Paul said, but somehow he left without giving his signature; he couldn't really tell if she wanted him to.

On the street again, Nathan said to him, "I was sorry to
hear about Marcello."

"Well, me, too."

They walked in a long straggle toward the apartment
for sale on 84th. In the late August sunshine, which
came from almost directly overhead, the wide pavement
of Amsterdam felt uncomfortably warm, but as soon as
you entered the shadows of a side street, the temperature
dropped and the breeze kicked in. Paul put on his Long-
horn baseball cap—when he played, he had to wear Adi-
das, one of his sponsors. Dana brought up the rear; she'd
had a hard time getting the stroller out. Jean and Liesel
were waiting for her with the girls, though Liesel was
paying only distracted attention. She was looking ahead
at her sons: the younger one was also shorter and more
self-contained; Nathan had a way of crowding you on the
sidewalk. Bill stood a long way in front; he became impatient in large groups.

Paul said, "You go to these events and you realize
you've got a kind of public reputation or persona. People
expect you to be a certain way. And I realized last night
that I didn't much like mine. It's hard to put your finger
on it. I was thinking about it last night, lying in bed."

"What kind of persona?" Nathan asked.

"I don't know, a hanger-on. Somebody who's always

around at these things, but nobody knows who invited him or what his connection is. Somebody who joins other people's conversations."

"Well, these people don't know you very well. I wouldn't worry about it."

"That's what I told myself last night, but that's not quite what I mean. Maybe persona is the wrong word. Because it basically struck me that that's who I am. I hang around, I join other people's conversations. What are you supposed to do? As soon as you open your mouth, you turn into one kind of jerk or another. And if you don't say anything, then you're just one of those assholes who doesn't say anything."

"Not everything is a moral act."

"I don't believe you believe that."

"Put it this way. The stakes aren't always especially high."

"I'm not really talking about morality anyway. It's just that—I don't think of myself as a needy person or a follower or a hanger-on, but probably in this context that's what I am."

"This isn't an ordinary context, right. Your . . . mentor doesn't die every day."

"It's not just that, it's every time I enter a locker room or a press conference. Whatever, it really doesn't bother me much. But I was thinking about Marcello. He never made me feel this."

"You miss him. That's acceptable."

"That's not quite right, either. I used to see him once a year. Less, sometimes."

"There's a big difference between that and never again."

"I know, I know all this. But it doesn't feel exactly like grieving. It's more like—certain things becoming clear. You know, on the tour, there's a big difference between different kinds of events. There are the slams, there's the Masters Series, there's the Challenger Tour. That's what I was saying about Nadal. I can beat him in Basel or Atlanta, because he doesn't give a damn. If you win the first set, maybe he has a flight to catch. But I can't beat him at the Open. And you realize after a while that none of these games matters much. I'd like to think, from a healthy point of view, the whole tour is basically like the Challenger Tour. Nobody cares, it's not important. But, like, raising a kid, keeping up a marriage, these things . . . What's depressing to me is that I'm better at tennis than I am at anything else. Really, very much better—it's not even close. And by one perfectly reasonable set of standards, I'm not that good at tennis. You made that pretty clear at lunch."

Nathan didn't answer at first. They waited at 83rd to cross the street, while Liesel and Jean and Dana brought up the rear. In fact, they had stopped to look into a shop, and Julie ran up to her father to say that Aunt Jean had offered to buy them both a treat and was it okay with him?

"What kind of treat?"

"We don't know yet, we haven't decided. They have key chains in the window with little yellow cabs. Just New York stuff."

"Nothing sugary?"

"I don't know, maybe. They've got chewing gum too, Tic Tacs, things like that."

"Okay. Nothing expensive."

"We won't," Julie said and ran back, running not quite like a teenager or a kid, but slowly and almost dutifully. Her black heavy-soled Doc Martens boots felt like weights on her feet, but she liked them because they were waterproof—she considered them practical.

When the light changed, the two men crossed over, they wanted to keep talking. In some of the more obvious ways, they weren't particularly close. In high school, they didn't share clothes or get drunk together or chase girls, and Nathan stopped playing sports around the time that Paul turned ten or eleven and started beating him. But they had always been capable of interesting each other. When Paul dropped out of Stanford after two years, he committed himself to a lifetime of feeling intellectually inferior, especially around his brother. But maybe he would have felt that anyway. The only things Paul was better at were basically childish, knocking a ball around, playing cards, games you can win. But then they grew up—you're supposed to outgrow those games. As a kid, Nathan liked the company of adults, but he had an abrasive quality, he wanted to be taken seriously. Later, as an adult, he didn't have to fight for it anymore. The people he knew respected him, he could relax. But even around them, he missed something that he found in Paul's company. They had the same father. This seemed to matter more and more as they got older.

In 1961, Bill graduated first in his class at Port Jervis High School. He made Phi Beta Kappa at Stanford and got elected editor-in-chief of the *Cornell Law Review* a few years later. By most measures, he had lived a successful life, which had been comfortably rewarded by tenure, money, and healthy children. But at some point in his twenties the arc of his success began to dip or level, for reasons Bill only partly understood. While the kids were growing up, they had no sense of their father's professional frustrations: that he was having a hard time getting his articles published and felt himself institutionally passed over for the kinds of honors he used to take for granted in his grade-getting days. But later, as they entered their twenties, Paul and Nathan realized that these frustrations were a part of their inheritance—just as Paul began his own slide down the ATP rankings. Nathan had so far kept up the momentum of his accomplishments, from grad school to law school and from law school to tenure at Harvard. But he always felt the shadow of his father reaching out to him, intimately, almost honorably, which none of his colleagues could see. Paul understood this, which made possible for both of them a conversation about ambition and failure they couldn't have had with anyone else.

As they walked up Amsterdam, Nathan said, "You're clearly going through something right now. You don't have to take seriously every thought that honestly occurs to you."

"I don't know what I'm going through. But listen, there's something else I wanted to bring up. If you're looking at apartments on the West Side because of us—I'm not sure how much longer we'll be living here."

"I thought the plan was to move into television."

"That's Bill's plan. I've had enough of all of that. Maybe it's what Dana wants, too; I don't know."

"What do you want?"

"I've been looking at some real estate in Texas. Just land, really, outside of Austin, where I can build a house."

"I don't understand. What do you intend to do?"

"As little as possible. I don't know if you know this, Nathan. But I've made a lot of money—too much. More than I in any way deserve. Right after my first Open, Marcello put a few of his players in touch with this sports equipment start-up. I was one of them. This was in my rising star days. Weeks is more accurate. Anyway, it's very hard to break into the tennis ball market and that's what these guys were trying to do. Wilson and Head pretty much have the game sewn up. They couldn't pay us much, but my agent at the time negotiated some stock options."

"And they broke in?"

"No, they don't make tennis balls anymore. But they designed the soccer ball for the last two World Cups."

"So how much did you make?"

"It varies on the day, but I've been slowly selling up. After taxes, around six million dollars."

"Well, that will buy you some decent real estate outside of Austin."

"It's not just that. I'm clocking out. I don't want to do any of this anymore. I don't want to have any kind of contact. And I figure, with six million dollars in the bank, I don't need to. This will see me through."

"What do you mean, contact?"

"I don't mean you guys. In fact, that's something else I want to talk to you about. You must have done pretty well for yourself. We don't need this, right? We don't need any of this. It'll be like when we were kids again. I don't know, just riding our bikes, hanging out."

"You'll go crazy."

Paul looked at his brother, half-smiling. There was no fat on him, none at all, and when he smiled you could see the muscles in his face and guess at the skull beneath them. "Maybe I already am a little crazy."

"And that's not what we were doing when we were kids. You were playing tennis. I was taking classes at UT."

"Before that. Before that started."

"Well, I don't think you can live like that. I don't think your kids will want to, either."

"That's how we lived."

"What does Dana think?"

Bill was waiting for them at the corner of 84th, but they stopped outside a restaurant to look at the menu — Pickles and Biscuits, one of these up-market down-market foodie bars, with a cask in the window and naked light bulbs.

"Look," Paul said. "You can get a chicken-fried steak for twenty-two dollars."

"What does Dana think?"

He didn't answer at first, he was reading the menu. "When I first moved to New York, you could buy a beer for three bucks, even in this neighborhood. There was a little Polish bar that actual Polish people went to." After a moment, he added, "It's gotten to the point where I can't stand the way she loads the dishwasher. It's started to feel like a deliberate affront."

They walked slowly toward their father, who wa

watching them. Nathan said, "I think you need to back off from that point."

"Hey, Dad." Paul put his arm around Bill's neck. "Everybody's slow. I think I'm going to peel off and hit the courts."

"Knock 'em dead, son."

And Paul jogged on—up Amsterdam toward 86th Street. He had left his rackets at the apartment; he needed to get changed. Bill took pleasure from watching him. As a young man, he used to run the same way: almost flat-footed, with the legs bowed slightly at the knee, but lightly and easily in spite of these things, as if at any step he could change direction.

When the "girls" joined up with them, Liesel said, "Where's Paul?"

"He was late for his court time."

"Without saying goodbye?"

Jean turned to her brother. "Well played."

"He'll see us at dinner."

"Don't worry about me," Dana said. "I'm used to it."

"Did you guys have a fight?" Liesel asked her son.

"No, he was just running late."

"Speaking of which," Bill said; and, in fact, at that moment he noticed a woman in a pantsuit standing outside a set of brownstone steps, around thirty yards from the corner. She had a set of papers in one hand and was trying to type something into her phone at the same time. "Is that the place?"

"Probably." Nathan looked at his children. "So what did you get?"

"Different things," Julie said. "Margot hasn't learned yet that if you buy something like candy, after you eat it, you don't have anything."

"I don't care," Margot said, with a full mouth.

"Not now, but maybe later. Because I'll still have this." And she held up one of the yellow cab key chains.

"I don't want one of those."

"Well, you probably will," Julie said, but Margot's comment had already taken the shine off it, and she felt like a little girl holding a trinket.

Bill didn't want to move to New York but he liked looking at houses. He liked talking to strangers, too, and when the woman in the suit said to him, "Nathan, right? We spoke on the phone," he told her, "That's my son. I'm just an innocent bystander."

"Looks like we got the whole family."

She had a pretty, almost boyish face, though she didn't look young either—forty-something, dark-skinned and short-haired. Her accent sounded faintly South American. You could see her hips sticking out of the suit; the clothes hung on her like they would on a rail.

"Who is the buyer?" she asked, handing out brochures. They were made of stiff glossy card stock, with a photograph on the front, and contributed to the air of toy-store unreality.

"He is. They are," Nathan said, letting his mother go past him. She climbed slowly up the front steps, holding her brochure.

"These are the only stairs," the realtor said, and Liesel, annoyed, responded, "I don't mind stairs."

There was a tall bow window to the side, protected by a grille, which bent in front of the glass in flowing curves—the image on the photograph. Ivy grew up the bars, and a wide cratelike window box of chrysanthemums sat on the ledge in a patch of dirt. It all looked charming and expensive.

"Let me just say something quickly before we go in," the woman went on. "There was a little confusion with the owner. Mostly I talk to her daughter. I thought she was going out, but she isn't—the owner, I mean. She's there now. So maybe if we don't all go in at once."

"I don't care," Jean said, and Dana added, "I'm happy to wait outside. That way we don't have to carry the stroller up."

"What about the girls?"

"I want to see it," Julie said, and Margot wouldn't leave her so they came along.

Years later, her memories of that afternoon blended with other memories and Margot couldn't be sure if the old woman she saw lying on a sofa in the apartment was Liesel or not. It couldn't have been Liesel—they never bought the apartment on West 84th. But still the memory was associated with her grandmother. A woman lying on a couch, under a blanket, with thin gray hair. The television was on; it sat on a stack of big art books in front of floor-to-ceiling shelves filled with more books. The ceilings were high, too, and there were plants on the shelves; a pot of ivy trailed its leaves across the spines. The old woman was watching CNN, and the realtor said, "Mrs. Mitroglou, do you mind if I turn the sound down a little or turn it off?"

"Turn it off, turn it off. I wasn't watching anyway."

"I'm sorry to disturb you."

"What?"

"I'm sorry to come and disturb you. We thought you would be out."

"One of these stupid business shows, it doesn't matter. What? I never go out."

She tried to sit up; the room smelled of sleep. It was also very hot and a vase of lilies on the table in front of the big bow window had dried out. The rich dust of the stamens lay scattered over the cloth.

"Do you mind if I open the curtains?" Nathan said to the old woman.

"I keep them closed, otherwise I can't see the TV." And then, when he didn't move, "Go ahead, open them. You turned it off anyway."

Even when he opened them, the ivy on the bars outside kept out most of the light, but the leaves cast pretty shadows on the floor; there were edges of light that shifted slightly on the wooden boards.

Bill said to her, "These buildings have beautiful high ceilings."

"I'm sorry, they told me you were coming. I meant to get dressed."

She wore a pale blue nightgown, which might have been a dress, and a cashmere cardigan, which had pockets you could put your hands into. After sitting up, she adjusted

the blanket across her knees and smiled rather deliberately. "What's your name, little girl?"

"I'm Julie. This is my sister Margot."

"Do you like licorice?"

"I don't know."

"I always keep some Twizzlers for my grandkids."

Julie glanced at her father, who told her, "As far as I'm
concerned."

"Yes, please."

"Yes please what?" he said.

"I'd like to try one."

"Me, too," Margot said, and took the piece of sucked-
on candy out of her mouth. She still had the wrapper for
it, and carefully wrapped it up and put it in her jeans pocket and licked her fingers afterward and dried them on her
T-shirt.

Mrs. Mitroglou watched her until she was finished. "All
set? Well, give me that tin on the bottom shelf over there.
The one that says Old Soldier. I've got other things as
well—you can have a look."

"Do you mind if we look around?" Liesel asked her.

"Look, look," she said.

A wall used to separate the living room and kitchen, but
most of it had been taken down. There was now a wide
arch, and Liesel wandered through onto cracked linoleum
tiles. The kitchen hadn't been changed in thirty years—
the wooden worktops were rotting around the sink, there
were burn marks elsewhere, in perfect circles, where
somebody had put a pot down straight from the stovetop.
Everything looked sticky to touch. The contents of the

spice rack had discolored the wallpaper behind, and dried
needles of thyme lay scattered among the cereal boxes
underneath. A tall sash window over the sink showed the
backyard, which was paved with dirty yellow bricks. The
downstairs neighbor had put out a few flowerpots: begon-
ias and ivy, euphorbia, a few ferns. A bay tree. There was
a bench and Liesel could see the edge of the fire escape,
the characteristic rust-colored purple of the painted metal.

She felt surprisingly and deeply upset by the whole
thing, the smell, the lily stains on the cloth, the wet brown
wood around the sink, the sofa-bound old woman, who
probably had to move out because she couldn't look after
herself and her daughter didn't have the time. Maybe her
husband was dead and she needed the money. Liesel would
never buy the apartment, she knew that already, but she
wandered into the bathroom and checked out the padded seat, the freshener in the toilet, the faintly dripping
faucets, and the medicine cabinet, whose old-fashioned
mirror gave an almost green depth to everything in it,
including her own face. A study contained an exercise
bike, probably her husband's. They seemed to have a lot
of radios. Bill would like the rose kilim at the foot of the
bed in the master bedroom. Two big windows on either
side of the headboard let in some light, although one of
them was partly blocked by the fire escape. Some bach-
elor lawyer would buy the apartment and sit out there and
smoke with his girlfriends.

The difference between Liesel and this woman was five
or six years and maybe one serious health event. If they
moved in here it would be a short-term measure. Coming

back into the hallway, she heard Margot saying, "I don't like it."

"Just swallow it," Nathan said. "I'll get you some water."

"I can't. I don't like it."

"Well, what do you want me to do about it?"

She had scrunched her face up and was shaking her head from side to side, starting to panic, and Nathan put his hand under her mouth. "Just spit it out," he said, and "I'm sorry about this," to Mrs. Mitroglou. Margot spat the black purple mess into his hand, and he went to the kitchen sink to clean himself up. Julie followed him and whispered, "I don't like it either."

"Well, you can eat it anyway."

Outside, on the brownstone steps, Jean said, "I feel like I'm being pissy with everybody. Am I being pissy?"

"I don't know. I didn't notice anything." Dana looked surprised by the question; she had the clumsy and sometimes endearing habit of answering people honestly.

"You mean, because I'm always a bit like this."

"I don't think you are. I mean, you're not being anything." And then, in a different voice: "Don't confuse me. So who is this guy?"

"Which guy?"

"The one you don't know about."

"Oh."

The truth is, Jean wanted to tell her. In addition to everything else, she felt a very small amount of pride in the fact that she was having an affair with a married man. It

was like getting drunk for the first time or smoking your
first joint, it meant you were in the world. And she had
never had a serious relationship, not even in college. This
was the first one.

In college she sometimes made out with friends, guys
she liked who didn't want to go out with her, and she pretended to have the same attitude toward them. She called
them by their last names. In England, during grad school,
she had sex for the first time. It turned out to be easy to
get drunk at a party and go home with somebody. But she
was getting old for that, too, she wanted a real life. Henrik would turn forty-seven in October; he had a house
in Acton and three kids. It was like one of those cooking
shows—here's one I made earlier.

They met through Jean's supervisor at Oxford. She was
doing the BPhil, following in Nathan's footsteps; it was
partly just an excuse to stay in school. To avoid real life.
Jean complained to her professor, "Philosophy gives me
a pain in the head." That probably means you're doing
it right, he told her. But he was also one of these media
dons, who spent time posing as a public intellectual (this
is how he put it) on radio and TV—the kind of person
they call in to express prepackaged views, against the
backdrop of an Oxford study, with a gas fire in the grate.
Henrik was one of his contacts in the industry; he ran
a production company. After finishing her degree, Jean
wanted to stay in England and needed a job. Her supervisor put her in touch with Henrik, and she started working for him, first as a runner, then as a researcher. Later
she became his assistant; the whole thing took time, she'd

been with the company for five years.

In the early days, she also dog-sat for him at the weekend. They had a German shepherd named Tinker, and Jean lived about twenty minutes away by overground train. She came on Saturday, she came on Sunday, she changed Tinker's water, she took him for a walk, she filled his bowl and went home again. But she also saw the books on their shelves, she saw the kids' bikes in the garden, she saw the Roberts radio on their kitchen windowsill—she saw his life. They lived in a tall narrow house that backed onto the tracks; South Acton station was at the end of their road. There were five or six trains an hour, and Henrik once told her, before anything started between them, that his kids were so used to sleeping with the noise they found it hard elsewhere—a line that for some reason stuck with her.

The first time she dog-sat, he introduced her to the family—they were late getting away and in the middle of an argument. His wife couldn't fit the stroller in the back of their old Golf, which was filled with other bags.

"We don't need it," Henrik said.

"Then *you* can get him to sleep."

"There's nowhere to walk anyway. It's the countryside."

But she gave in in the end and made a very slightly exaggerated show of a wife's tired patience, blinking once slowly, with a little intake of breath, for Jean's benefit, by way of apology. She was tall, skinny, and small-breasted; her hair was light brown and growing colorless in parts. Jean knew that she ran half marathons and imagined she might look exactly the same at sixty.

After their relationship began, the dog walking stopped.

It was easy for them to find time and a place on location, but in London they used a friend's apartment. One
of Henrik's friends, an academic, who was himself in the
process of going through a divorce and had been teaching
at Boston University for the year. But he planned to come
back at the end of September; they were going to have to
make different arrangements. For that and other reasons,
the start of the school year seemed like a turning point to
Jean. Things could go either way.

Part of the problem with having an affair is that there's
no public record. It's like nothing is happening, even
though at the same time you feel caught up in the middle
of something incredibly urgent. So she said to Dana, "He's
my producer. He's married."

"Oh, one of those."

"What does that mean? He's not a bad guy—he's the
opposite of a bad guy."

"I meant, one of those complicated situations."

"I guess it is. Though it also feels pretty simple to me.
We want to be together, there doesn't seem to be any
doubt about that." After a minute, she said, "I'm sorry, I
probably sound prickly. I haven't told anyone."

"Nobody at all?"

"Nobody in the family."

They were sitting on the bottom of the brownstone
steps, so that Dana could push the stroller back and forth.
Cal was still sleeping—ambient noise often knocked him
out, and the restaurant had been very loud.

"He'll be in a bad mood when he wakes up," Dana said.
"He'll be hungry."

"Do you have anything to give him?"

"One of these mushy pots. Sweet potato and lamb."

"Fancy schmancy."

"Well, we'll see. Do you not want me to mention this to Paul?"

"Oh, I don't know. Maybe I should tell him myself, but I don't want to. You know, one of the reasons I almost didn't come, flights are expensive. Of course, Bill and Liesel offered to pay, but I don't want to take their money when I'm fairly certain they would disapprove . . . of how I'm living. Which is fine, which is their right, but if I want to be such a big-shot grown-up kid, making my own difficult life decisions, then I shouldn't take handouts."

"They wouldn't mind."

"They wouldn't mind about the money. They would mind about the other thing."

"They love you anyway."

"Of course, they love me," Jean said, a little testily, and then, more calmly: "I think Paul would probably be the most sympathetic."

She meant this in a general way, that he seemed the least likely to judge her, but afterward Jean wondered whether Dana might have taken it the wrong way—as if Paul would naturally be sympathetic to a married man's reasons for having an affair. Maybe she did mean something along those lines, who knows. Something else to beat herself up about.

"I don't know if you care about my opinion," Dana said, "but if you ask me, these things happen. You can't be too—I don't know—proper about who you fall in love

with. I think you sometimes worry too much about what
your family thinks."

"That's what I'm saying, I should stand on my own two
feet."

"I mean it's okay to live your life and still let them buy
you a ticket home." But Dana heard herself and added:
"Maybe I would say that. Isn't that what everyone says
about me? About my ex-husband, and probably about
Paul, too."

"What?"

"That I don't mind living off other people."

"Who says that? Nobody I know says that."

"That's not what your parents think? I mean, they don't
think it's weird to stay in Michael's apartment?"

"Of course that's not what they think." But Jean knew
this wasn't quite true and blushed slightly.

"Then what are we arguing about?" Dana said.

"Nothing. Nobody's arguing."

Dana had to push the stroller aside for a woman pulling
a suitcase behind her—a flight attendant, in matching blue
skirt and jacket. She had that artificial pretty look, which is
the look you can give yourself with prettiness-indicators,
like makeup and hair color, even if you aren't particularly attractive. She smiled at Dana, she smiled at Cal, she
looked tired. Her high heels seemed to wobble under her
feet; the wheels of her suitcase clicked over the sidewalk as
she strode away. Dana had never needed such indicators.

"It was sweet of you to buy those things for the girls,"
she said. "You're good with kids."

"I wanted to get something for Cal, too."

"Don't worry about that. I was just thinking, how nice it was to watch you with them."

"What does that mean?"

"Nothing, it doesn't mean anything. It was a compliment."

"Fine," Jean said. "Thank you."

But something about the way she smiled made Dana keep going. "Okay, look," she said. "I don't care about the right or wrong, I really don't. I just don't want you to get sucked into a situation that isn't going to give anything back."

"What does that mean—give something back?"

Dana wasn't good at this kind of game. Like all the Essingers, Jean could make you say things you didn't mean or take positions you didn't want to take. They pushed you into arguing with them. The worst of it was that sometimes you realized later, maybe these are your positions, maybe this *is* what you think. It was all pretty tiring.

"Nothing," she said.

But Jean wouldn't let it go. "You mean, like kids?"

"I don't know what I meant. Forget it."

"Because that seems like a very old-fashioned idea of what a relationship is." She added, in the silence that followed: "Just ignore me, I told you I was feeling pissy."

Bill spent the time talking to Mrs. Mitroglou. In his chinos and frayed jacket, with his untucked shirt, he looked presentable enough but also approachable. Nathan liked talking to strangers, too, he touched you on the elbow, he laughed at jokes, but there was a class difference between father and son—Nathan descended from the heights.

Whereas you could still imagine that Bill's uncle owned a grocery store, and that Bill himself as a teenager used to help out in the stockroom.

"Your name," he said to her. "Is it Greek?"

"My husband was Greek. But my father came from Silesia. I grew up in Milwaukee."

"Which part of Milwaukee? I have cousins who used to live in Sherman Park."

"It's all changed now. We lived in Lincoln Village."

"They were nice neighborhoods. Nice houses."

"Can you imagine?" she said. "When we were kids, we used to go to church at St. Josaphat's. For us it was like Notre Dame." She said it in the French way, with the short *o* and the short *a*.

"I apologize on behalf of my children," Nathan broke in.

"I don't care. Nobody eats licorice any more. My grandkids take all the cherry flavors and that's what's left."

"Should we turn the TV back on?"

"Yes, turn it on, turn it on."

And Nathan closed the curtains, too. He looked behind him, in the half-light. The place had good bones, a marble fireplace, high ceilings, original floorboards. There was plenty of space to walk around in, especially if you took away the rolltop desk in the corner, the side tables by the sofa, the piano and the plant stands and the extra chairs and the piles of newspaper. The kitchen was large enough for Mrs. Mitroglou to eat at a table pushed against the wall. If you tore down the ivy, you could have sunlight coming in from two sides, because of that window over the sink. It was a nice apartment. But Bill wouldn't want it, because he didn't want to move to New York. He was resistant to change, even the kind that makes you happier. And Liesel didn't have the energy to budge him anymore. They were both running out of energy. Which meant, if decisions were going to be made, it was up to Nathan to push them along.

On the steps outside, the realtor apologized. "I'm sorry, it's not good. She shouldn't be there. But what can you do."

"It's a nice apartment," Nathan said, and she gave him her card—her name was Bruna Pereyra and he watched her walk back to the corner of Amsterdam, where she stopped to look at her notes. Then she was on the phone again. There was something affecting about her, the pantsuit, her boyish face, her accent, with almost all of the foreignness rubbed away. So many apartments in New York, people showing them around . . . and for a moment he wondered whether giving out her card like that contained any kind of a come-on. Not because he thought it did, but just because these things occur to you.

She turned downtown and disappeared and Liesel said, "She's too skinny. The women in New York are all too skinny," and Dana couldn't tell if she was one of them.

Jean asked, "So how was it?"

"I don't want to live there."

"What was wrong with it?"

"There was nothing wrong with it," Nathan said. "It's a great apartment."

"It was depressing," Liesel said. "Lying there all day with the television on. And the curtains closed. No outside space."

"You can walk out the front door whenever you want."

Jean asked, "What are you people talking about?"

Bill, in his reasonable, explaining voice: "The old woman who lives there was lying on the sofa when we came in."

"I don't want to live like that."

"Nobody's saying you should," Nathan said. "These are two different things. There's the old woman who lives there, who by the way struck me as being perfectly on the ball. And there's the apartment. You're not buying her life."

Liesel shook her head in frustration, while looking down at her feet. "I'm not buying anything."

"If you don't want to live there," Jean said, "you don't have to live there. Nobody's going to make you."

Even she couldn't tell to what extent she was taking her mother's side to get back at Nathan for something. "I don't understand why you're angry," he told Liesel. "You're the one who wants to move to New York."

"Nobody's angry." Bill was in a good mood—somehow it cheered him up to hear other people arguing. "Okay," and he clapped his hands: "Where's apartment number two?"

It was one of those rapidly changing late summer days, more like September than August. Sunny one minute, and almost cloudless, but then the blue sky took on a pearly sheen, a kind of shadow fell on the air, and even though it didn't feel warm, you started to sweat. People in the street wore coats or T-shirts. The broad sidewalks had damp patches that showed up darkly on the yellowish concrete. Most of the stores looked busy, especially on Broadway, and the outside tables of the restaurants were half-full. But as soon as you crossed Broadway, heading toward West

End Avenue, the foot traffic thinned out, a kind of architectural quiet descended.

On the way Cal woke up and started to cry. Dana fussed over him, bending down so that you couldn't see his face, but the noise kept coming.

"Does he have a dummy?" Jean said, standing over them.

"He used to, but we took it away. About a month ago. We thought, maybe that was why he wasn't talking more." Dana stood up again, looking strangely at a loss; her son screamed almost passionlessly. "I don't know," she said. "I think I'm going to take him home. He eats better in his own high chair."

. But it wasn't easy saying goodbye—Bill had walked twenty paces ahead again, Nathan and Liesel were talking, and eventually Jean stepped in.

"People, people," she said. "Cal is hungry. Dana is going back."

Nathan looked at her humorously. "You don't want to see more real estate?"

With his dark Jewish complexion and high forehead, he looked like Paul, but older and heavier, taller and more expansive. Less inward. His mouth was wider, his lips were thicker, his hair was longer. The sleeves of his jacket rode up on his wrists; they were covered in dark curls. Sometimes Dana received from him a very faint indication of what it might be like to talk to him at a party, if they didn't know each other.

"I know," Jean said, "she's a pervert," and offered to keep her company.

"There's no need," Dana told her.

"Well, I want to. I can catch up with the others."

So they retraced their steps. Jean, with her head down, kept blowing the hair out of her eyes, or brushing it away. This wasn't a policy decision, but she disliked spending money on haircuts. It was like a tax on women, she couldn't believe how much some of her friends paid. Mostly she cut it herself, but the truth is, she cared a little more about these things since the beginning of her relationship with Henrik. And after she booked her flight, she thought, Liesel or Susie can cut it for me, that will be a nice thing for us to do.

Cal was still crying. It amazed Jean how long he could keep it up, and Dana confessed to her: "You get to a point where you think, maybe it's easier if you just admit that you've got a difficult child. But that's hard to do because you . . . because you love them so much."

"He's not so bad," Jean said. "He's just a kid."

"But in that case, the problem is you. It means you're just not very good at coping."

Jean didn't respond at first. It was like scratching somebody's itch, when they won't tell you exactly where the itch is. You do your best. Eventually, she said, "We're the ones who are dragging him around. None of this is for him."

"Sometimes I think he'd rather be with Inez. You know, she really loves him—she buys him presents about once a week. The thing he sleeps with is from her."

"I wouldn't put so much pressure on yourself. Of course, he loves you. I mean, that's a battle you're always going to win."

"Some of the pressure is just, you know, around your

family, I want to show him off. And then he's either asleep or crying. And because he doesn't see you very often, you think, that's what he's like. But maybe if you saw him with Inez." There was a pause. "These are the stupid thoughts I think."

"Don't worry about us." Jean was kicking the ground as she walked, scuffing her rubber soles. "I feel bad sometimes," she went on, "about the whole tone of our . . . what we get up to as a family. Like, what we consider a reasonable way to pass the time. Looking at apartments. Not just that but the way we talk about these decisions. I mean, Liesel has worked hard, she earns good money, why shouldn't she buy a place in New York, or not buy it, if that's what she wants. But even so, I sometimes feel like, none of us has a clue. They should see how some of my friends are living. Even I'm basically a lodger with a bedroom in somebody's house. It's a nice house, but still, I have a little corner of the fridge. And then you go around some apartment on the Upper West Side worth one point something million dollars, and you don't want to live there because there's an old woman on the sofa. I don't know."

Dana said, "Do you mind pushing the stroller? Cal might stop complaining if I carry him."

"Of course. I'm a jerk."

They stopped in the street and Dana took her boy in her arms, digging her hands under his sweaty back (he'd been sleeping for over two hours), feeling the hot skin under his T-shirt—while half in sleepiness and half in protest, he arched his back away and then bent so violently toward her he almost hurt his neck on her shoulder. But after that he quieted down and Dana felt like she had plugged into something. Heat and energy flowed into her again.

"Everybody I grew up with grew up in nice apartments or big houses," she said. "Nobody thinks about it."

"Well, it drives me nuts. Part of that is just stupid teenage embarrassment, which I should get over. But it's more than that, it's like we're totally out of touch . . . By the way, there's something else I want to make clear. If Henrik would have more kids, I would have his kids. I've got nothing against kids. I want to have them."

"You don't have to make that clear for me."

"I didn't want you to think I was trying to make any kind of a comment, about you guys or Nathan or Susie . . ."

"I didn't think that."

They were crossing 86th Street by the newsstand, but there were cabs coming in both directions, so they waited for the light to change. Even then, a few cars turning off Broadway pushed through the line of pedestrians.

"Does he want more kids?" Dana asked, stepping onto the sidewalk on the other side.

"I don't know. We haven't talked about it. We keep meaning to set like a date for talking everything through, but it always seems to both of us like a date from hell, so we keep pushing it back."

They had reached the awning outside Dana's building—an arch led through to the courtyard, and doormen stood by the gate to help and greet. One of them saw Dana and tipped his cap. He was eating a sandwich, and somebody said something to him from inside the office, which made him turn around.

"Do you want me to come up?" Jean said. "How are you going to push the stroller?"

"It's okay, Cal can walk from here."

"I don't mind at all."

"Go, it's okay."

She lowered her son to the ground, waiting for his legs to take the strain, and felt him adjust and release her. Sleepily, almost blindly, he stood on his own two feet. Jean bent down to him again, and noticed for the first time his plaid shirt and brown cords and basketball high-tops. He looked like a college freshman; his hair stood a little on end.

"See ya later, kid."

Cal stared at her quietly and then opened his mouth, to show her something. There were bits of what seemed to be strawberry jam all over his tongue.

"I gave him a fruit thing in the stroller to shut him up," Dana said.

"What are his words, what can he say? I live so far away and I don't even know him at all."

"He can say bye-bye, he can say bat ball. Which means, play tennis. He can say *gachas*, which means porridge in Spanish. Inez is trying to teach him, maybe this is why . . . They say bilingual kids speak later. Say bye-bye, Cally."

But he didn't say anything and just looked at Jean, who had to decide when to turn away. Walking back to join the others, she had the feeling that some expression of sadness or love was on the tip of her tongue.

At Broadway, waiting for the lights, she took out her phone and started writing a text to Henrik. As his assistant, she could text him risk-free, even if he was on vacation with his wife and kids—so long as she kept the tone semi-professional. Keeping that tone, and managing to sneak in something intimate, something she wanted to communicate, turned out to be difficult but not impossible. *Apartment hunting for my parents in New York. It's like going to the zoo for us*, she tapped out. But this isn't what she wanted to say, which was just *missing you NOW at the corner of 86th Street*, something standard and sentimental. And even what she had written struck her as wrong on two counts—a betrayal of her family, which she didn't feel; and also, for the same reason, too intimate, in a boring conversational way. Henrik was probably at dinner, or sitting in the garden, having a drink, and his wife would reach over and look at the text, and see that. The lights changed but Jean deleted each letter before crossing over.

She caught up with her family on West End Avenue, waiting for the realtor. They were a few minutes early. Liesel was sitting down on the low wall of a flowerbed outside the building and talking to the two girls. When Jean came over, she said, "Maybe Jean can tell you another story. You know mine already."

But Julie wouldn't be put off. "We want stories about the olden days."

Liesel looked at her in mock exasperation. "You know, there is a famous German play that begins like this. A son says to his father, *Aber ist Euch auch wohl, Vater? Ihr seht so blaß*. Which means, *But are you feeling okay? You look so pale*. And when I was a girl, older than you, Julie, but not much, we used to joke that instead of saying what he says, the father answers, *Not really*, and drops dead."

"Don't you feel well, Liesel?" Julie asked.

"I feel fine. Like a fish in water," she said. "*Wie dem Fish im Wasser*, but I have run out of stories."

"It doesn't have to be a story about the war. It could be a story about Nathan."

"Jean can tell you those."

"I can you tell those," Jean said, sitting down next to her mother. "He was a very annoying brother. He was always right."

The awning over the entrance cut out a wedge of shade, but at an angle—mother and daughter sat in shifting sunshine. The sky was clear and then filmy, the light kept changing, delicate shadows of branches and leaves brushed across the sidewalk, blurred and disappeared and then came into sharp focus. Dutch elm disease had recently struck and the trees were very young. But the building itself looked prewar: brownish yellowish brick, a vague kind of harvest motif cut into the stone over the doorway, stained glass windows on the ground floor. It took up the whole block. Jean could see her brother at the next corner, with a hand in his front pocket, walking and talking with Bill.

"How old were you when Nathan was a kid?" Julie asked.

"I don't know what that means. You're a kid a long time. Some of that time I didn't even exist."

"I mean when Nathan was as old as me."

Something about the question surprised Jean, the tone or mood. Her niece sounded childish again; their personalities go through these endless jumps and shifts. "How old are you, Julie? Ten? When Nathan was your age, I was like Cal. Maybe a little younger."

"And did he like you?"

"He was very angry with *me*," Liesel cut in. She made a face. With her brown skin and white hair, her expressions were very vivid. "And I'll tell you why he was angry, because up to that point the boys outnumbered the girls, and when Jean was born, it was two against two."

"That's not a good reason to be angry. That doesn't sound like Nathan."

"Daddies weren't always daddies," Jean said, and Liesel made a clicking sound between tongue and teeth—she had thought of something.

"I can tell you a story about him that isn't really a story, but it's about his name. It's about why we called him Nathan."

"Okay, tell us."

The girls sat on the broad front stoop of the entrance, at Liesel's feet. Margot had taken the old piece of candy out of her pocket and was trying to unwrap it. The wet sugar had stuck, and the foil made a sticky crinkling sound that annoyed Julie.

"There's a play called *Nathan der Weise*," Liesel said, "which means Nathan the Wise."

"Is that because you wanted him to be wise?"

"There are several reasons we thought of it, when we were thinking about names."

Liesel tried to explain the story but couldn't exactly remember it. The plot was over-involved, about a Jewish father and his adopted daughter, and the Christian knight who saved her, and the sultan who needed money. Everyone turns out to be related in the end but that's not what she wanted to talk about. She wanted to say something about cultural difference, and why tolerance could be difficult. Intolerance wasn't just a kind of mistake or a form of ignorance. Julie had been raised to think things through for herself; Nathan never held back when she asked him a question.

But she wasn't as good as Nathan at stripping a problem down to the bare bones, so that anyone, even a ten-year-old girl, could think about it. Liesel kept getting lost in tangents. She felt there was some connection between the play and their lives, her own marriage, for example, and the battles she had fought with Bill's parents, to accept her. This is what she wanted to talk about, but Julie made it difficult for her—she could be very literal.

"Why did you fight with Bill's parents?" Julie asked her.

"We didn't fight exactly, but we didn't get along. Bill's mother wrote my mother a letter, when we got engaged. She tried to persuade my mother to persuade *me* not to marry her son. But this is how she started it, My dear Mrs. Karding, which Mutti found very insulting."

"Why?"

The girl was digging in again, and Liesel felt tired. She had stayed up late the night before, waiting for Jean—dozing and waking on the sofa, listening for the elevator. Even when she went to bed at last she found it difficult to drop off. Bill always got up early. Also, you forget how exhausting it is, with kids, explaining everything from scratch; you lose the energy for it.

"It's very formal. In Germany, you would write something like . . ."

"But Bill's mother didn't know that. It's stupid to get upset about something like that."

"Well, she wasn't just upset about that. It was the whole letter. My mother thought, any woman should be pleased for her son to marry me." And then: "She thought I was a catch."

"So why didn't she want him to?"

"Who?"

"Bill's mother?"

"Want him to what?"

"Marry you."

"Because I'm not Jewish."

There was a pause while Julie took this in, and Liesel went on, "You have to see it from Essie's point of view. Bill's mother was called Essie, by the way, short for Esther. Which I always thought was very funny, because it's so German. Peter Petersen, Jürgen Jürgensen and Essie Essinger."

"Why is that funny?"

Julie never understood why grown-ups found certain things amusing; she tried to make them explain but they usually couldn't. Nathan had taught her a couple of Woody Allen jokes, and sometimes Julie repeated them, but she didn't understand these either. You see this watch? My grandfather sold it to me on his deathbed. You look so beautiful tonight I can hardly keep my eyes on the meter. Whenever she said these lines she watched eagerly for a reaction, and afterward, if somebody laughed, she said, what, what, pleased with herself but still puzzled.

"Oh, I don't know," Liesel told her. "But I can see it from her point of view, too. It was only twenty years after the war, and she thinks her son is marrying the daughter of a Nazi."

"Was your father a Nazi?"

"Of course not. But it's not that simple either. He was never a member of the Party, he never voted for Hitler. But he was an engineer, and when the war started, he worked for the German Navy. But I don't think Essie cared much about these distinctions."

There was almost no traffic on the street, and the neighborhood reminded Liesel of Berlin—wide empty avenues, tall apartment blocks, crowded with windows, mostly unadorned, so that the buildings seemed expressionless. In her twenties, as a young history student, she lived in Kreuzberg. In those days almost nobody owned a car, but her brother managed to get hold of an Opel Olympia and would pick her up and drive them to Wannsee. This was a few years before the Wall. They swam and lay on the beach; he brought a picnic. Sometimes their cousin came along. The idea of having this conversation then would have seemed incredible to her. You didn't talk about the war.

"It wasn't just her, it was Bill's father, too. They thought that if Bill and I got married, our children wouldn't be considered Jewish—that they wouldn't consider *themselves* Jewish. Bill said to them, we'll raise them Jewish, it's part of the deal. But in the long run, his parents were right. I mean, how Jewish do you feel?"

"How do I know? What does it feel like?"

"You're Jewish enough," Jean said. "You can be as Jewish as you want to be."

"But, of course, I gave up something, too," Liesel went on. "I gave up my culture, too. By living in America."

When Nathan was born, their parents met for the first time. Bill had a teaching gig at the LSE, and they were living in London for the year, in a two-bed flat on Denning Road in Hampstead. Liesel still remembered the argument she expected to have when they got home from the hospital, about who would sleep where when both sets of parents came to stay. It surprised Bill that his folks wanted to make the trip. My mother never flies anywhere, he said, this will knock her out, we have to offer them the guest room. But in fact she preferred to stay at a hotel. Liesel, underslept, anxious, in the first few weeks of motherhood, indulged in all kinds of crazy fantasies about what Essie was going to do, or what she would say. I feel like Rosemary in that movie, she told their friends. Only partly joking. At the very least there's going to be a scene, and accusations.

But in fact what happened was somehow even worse. Mutti had arrived the afternoon before and was already changing diapers, helping with the bottle and cooking meals. When Bill's parents came around, for tea and cake, they were extremely friendly and sociable, in what Essie considered to be a polite society kind of way, making conversation and complimenting everything—the cake (which Mutti had baked, an apple tart), the apartment and the furniture and the neighborhood, as if it were an ordinary social occasion. And Liesel could feel her mother's judgment against them. Especially against poor Essie, who came across as phony and insecure: with her heavily made-up face (it was Bill's face underneath), in her best dress. She wouldn't let go of

her purse and kept it on her lap, and then placed it carefully against her feet when the food arrived. They stayed for
an hour. Essie kept telling her husband, "We should go."
Mutti found the whole performance incomprehensible . . .
after they've come all this way. For much of their weeklong
visit, they saw the sights, Buckingham Palace, the Changing
of the Guard. "This is my chance to make him take me to
London," Essie said. (She thought she was being charming, in a wife-to-wife way.) "Isn't it wonderful?" Maybe
they spent four hours in the presence of their grandson.
But Liesel wasn't willing to join in Mutti's judgment—she
was bound to them, too. Sometimes, in company, Bill had
a tendency of going into details, at some length, when people asked him a question. Like his mother, describing their
hotel. How quickly these relations start to tear you apart. It
was a relief when everybody left.

"I don't understand," Julie said. "What's wrong with
saying nice things about the cake? Especially if your
mother made it."

"There's nothing wrong."

"And if they've never been to London . . . of course,
they should go to Buckingham Palace."

"When your father was small, we took him to see it, too."

"It's just snobbery," Julie said. And then, when nobody
spoke: "What does this have to do with calling him Nathan?"

"I can try to explain, but only if you want to hear."

"Of course, that's what I want. I just asked."

But this turned out to be difficult, too. There's a parable
in the play about a magic ring, which makes you pleasing
to God and man: *vor Gott und Menschen angenehm zu*

machen. A rather vague kind of magic, Liesel felt, even as she tried to explain it. Jean's translation, "It makes you popular," was clearer but also not quite right. And Julie anyway had a thing about popular kids; she disliked them. She wouldn't want a ring like that.

Her mood had changed—it was like walking through stiff high grass. Liesel brought back the idea of God, but that didn't help either. Julie said she was an atheist. The problem with religion is that it makes you believe in things like magic. And so on. Meanwhile, a couple of late summer bees started buzzing around the sticky candy wrapper, which Margot was still playing with—peeling and unpeeling it, for the sound. "Just throw it away," Julie told her. "You're being disgusting." But Margot stood up instead and tried to run from them. They followed her with lazy persistence; she almost ran into the street. Jean pulled her back. And then they walked to the corner together, where Jean persuaded her to throw the candy away. The trash can was overflowing; she had to balance the wrapper in the mouth of a Diet Coke. All of which took time.

Liesel by this point had almost had enough. Her knee hurt but it wasn't just that. The grandchildren asked for a lot of attention. She knew that her own grown-up children (Susie, too, but Nathan especially) didn't consider her particularly doting. They placed her on the "other end of the spectrum," as Nathan once put it. What's at that end, she asked. Nobody answered, but Liesel sometimes tried to work out what the opposite of doting was. Indifferent or cold? No, she wasn't either of those things. Just the idea that her kids could think she was . . .

It's also true that Julie reminded Liesel of the way she used to argue with Nathan when he was younger. She tried starting again. "The ring gets passed down from father to favorite son."

"Why just the son?" Julie asked. "Why not daughter?"

She had her father's broad forehead and was growing into the Essinger nose. Our half-Jewish nose, Jean called it. Straight and prominent, between deep eye sockets, where the color of Julie's skin paled—an effect that made her look serious and slightly sleep-deprived. Especially with her prison haircut, a kind of continuously broadcast public announcement: I don't care what you think. (Bill said to Liesel later, "Who lets a girl cut her hair like that?" Some of his views were surprisingly conservative.) Her complexion was generally olive-toned; she was likely to be tall and slim. If she turned out pretty, it would be pretty in an interesting way.

"In the old days," Liesel said, "to help the family stay important, people gave most of their property to the oldest son. Otherwise, if they had several kids, nobody got much of anything."

"But they could give it to the oldest girl."

"Well, if a girl got married, her husband took over her property, and the family lost control of it."

"That's not fair," Julie said.

"It isn't fair, but it's not what I want to talk about."

So she tried again. It was like remembering the names of rivers or the succession of kings—something you once studied for a test. One day a father has three sons, and he loves them all the same. At different moments he promises the

ring to each of them. What can he do? He makes copies, but
after his death, the three brothers realize what has happened
and begin to argue. They want to find out which of them has
the true ring. So they go to a judge, but he can't help either;
he doesn't know. Still, the judge gives them some advice.
The magic of the ring, he says, is to make you beloved by all
men. "This is the point," Liesel said. "That you should live
your life as if the ring you have is the true one."

"What does that mean?"

"It means that you should . . . make yourself beloved."

"But you don't need a magic ring for that," Julie said.

"Really it's just a symbol, for the three main religions.
For Christianity and Judaism and . . ."

"There are way more than three religions."

"It doesn't matter how many. The point is, nobody
knows which is the true one, but so long as you believe
in your religion and live well, the play argues, you will be
pleasing to God and man."

"But the whole point of a magic ring is that it's magic.
You want it to work even if you aren't . . . pleasing. That's
the point."

"There are problems with this story, but what it teaches
is basically a good thing. That we should be tolerant of
each other."

"I don't think that's what it says. It says we should all
just believe that we're right even when we're not."

Liesel was almost moved—by Julie's stubbornness and
self-certainty, her talent for arguing. Moved because it
seemed to Liesel like an inheritance you couldn't get out
of, that you were stuck with. You have to learn to live with

it. Nathan had gotten it from Bill and now Julie had it from Nathan. Some things at least are passed down. For much of her marriage, she had watched Bill paint himself into corners, winning arguments but also making himself difficult to agree with. Fighting fights. Nathan at least seemed to be better at getting his way; but maybe she sometimes resented him for that, too.

Jean had taken Margot onto her lap, even though the girl was probably too big. "I never get any cuddles," Jean said, which Liesel overheard and paid attention to. Margot had been trying to wriggle away, but then she turned around and put her arms around her aunt's neck.

"I can squeeze you," she said. Her fingers were plump and small; it was hard to imagine, almost, how they all fit on her hand.

"Okay, squeeze me."

Julie looked on with a patient smile; she felt happy again. "She's really very good at squeezing. It kind of hurts."

"It does kind of hurt," Jean said, a little breathlessly.

"Should I stop?" Margot asked.

"Don't stop. It's what I deserve."

Nathan had said to Bill, "Let's walk to the end of the block. I spend all day in my office these days."

So his father went with him. He couldn't sit still either or stand in one place. And he liked seeing the city. At the corner, if you looked toward New Jersey, you could almost make out the trees of Riverside Park—just an impression of greenness and space, the street opening out. On either side, apartment buildings loomed, and trees and parked cars narrowed the perspective. The truth is, he preferred this neighborhood to the other. He liked the quiet, and the proximity of the water. But it was probably a little dead for Liesel's taste. There were no stores.

"There's something I've been meaning to discuss with you," Nathan said. "I've had an offer."

"What kind of offer?"

So Nathan started to explain. After ten years of teaching, he was well aware, you develop a kind of classroom manner, which is hard to shake. Even if you're talking to your father. So there was something about his own tone that he didn't like. And not just the tone, a kind of thoroughness. Last year he was asked to contribute to a collection on the law of war. He said yes at first but didn't have time. There was a conference in Israel he ended up organizing, just because nobody else could get it done. It required a certain amount of delicate negotiation; they wanted to bring different parties together. Anyway, the publishers kept bugging him, and eventually he agreed to write a response to one of the pieces. On the illegality of drone strikes. The response he wrote was much more equivocal, he challenged many of the legal objections.

Well, a few weeks ago, someone from the Department of Justice contacted him out of the blue and asked him to lunch. A guy named Michael Labro—they used to clerk together for Judge Schuyler but hadn't kept in touch. Lunch was nothing fancy, by the way, just a brasserie in Penn Quarter, where you could go upmarket or order the burger. Nathan had the burger, which he asked for rare and they slightly overcooked. Anyway, he said again, hearing himself repeating the word, the offer on the table was for Acting Assistant Attorney General. But Michael also made it clear that they (whoever "they" was) considered it a stepping-stone to a judgeship. Probably in the First Circuit, after Mannheim retired, if they could get all their ducks in a row.

"What does that make you," Bill said. "One of the ducks?"

"It's an expression. It means . . ."

"I know what it means. I'm just being stupid." He added, "Well, it's nice to be thought of."

"It's nice to be thought of."

Nathan felt the awkwardness of this kind of confession. Often when you ask for advice there's an element of boasting. He wasn't really asking for advice anyway; he wanted to inform. Or rather, he wanted to talk through his thinking process in his father's presence, which can be a revealing exercise. One of the things it revealed, unfortunately, is that he took pleasure from saying in front of his father, Look, I have this opportunity, people with real power in the world want to get me involved. Not just to brag about it, but for Bill's sake, too. Because, like immigrants (even after all this time), the Essingers still felt or believed that any kind of advance or inroad you make, any kind of success, advances the whole family, brings everyone along.

"I'm not stupid either," he went on. "One of the reasons they want me at the DoJ is that any legal opinions I write for them will be protected by client privilege. They want me pissing inside the tent."

"I don't think they want you to piss."

"No," Nathan said. "That's probably not what they want me to do."

"Are you tempted?"

"We wouldn't be having this conversation if I weren't."

"Do you want my blessing or do you want me to talk you out of it?"

"I don't know yet. That's what I'm trying to work out."

They couldn't see the others by this point—they were halfway to Riverside Park, shady and full of trees, with the river behind it, and New Jersey behind the river. A weather front seemed to be coming down the Hudson, there was a lot of movement in the air, sunshine auras, dark vague clouds, and pockets of real heat in bright light.

"Shouldn't we get back?" Bill said.

He sweated in his jacket and kept pinching his nose. The close air was full of city dust and leaf pollen. He suffered from hay fever, and even when he had a stinking cold dismissed it as allergies.

"We've still got a couple of minutes. And if they're early, they can wait."

They crossed over Riverside Drive onto the wide pavement. A woman with a shopping bag sat on one of the benches. Or maybe not a shopping bag but some plastic bag full of belongings. Bill couldn't understand why you'd sit there, on the street, even with your back toward it, when the park is just five feet away—just on the other side of a low masonry wall. But in fact, as he and Nathan found, you had to walk quite a ways along that wall before a gap opened up. First they walked uptown and then they turned around.

"We really should go back," Bill said.

"You need to look at this park if you want to make a reasonable decision about the apartment."

"I know Riverside Park. I've been to Riverside Park."

"When's the last time?"

"Oh, I don't know. Fifty years ago. My father had an aunt who lived not far away, Aunt Ethel. She smoked, which my father didn't like, and had a small apartment, so he let Rose and me go out to the park by ourselves. We didn't visit often."

"Well, it's five minutes away from this place we're looking at. Less than that."

"Nathan, we're not going to buy this apartment."

"I want you to think seriously about it. This is a conversation you need to have with Liesel. She wants to retire soon—"

"Nobody's retiring."

"She wants to retire soon, and she thinks she'll be happier in a big city."

"Austin is rapidly becoming a big city."

"You know what I mean. Somewhere you can walk to the museums. She wants to see people passing by."

"She walks to campus every day."

"I'm not going to argue with you, Dad. But the sense I have is that you're not listening to her on this point. You're not really paying attention."

"I'm listening."

They entered the park, the path curved down; it was really just a stretch of grass with a few slopes. A dog run, there were a lot of dog walkers. Bill could hear the traf-

fic on the West Side Highway. Pleasant enough; many of
the dog walkers seemed to know each other. People were
having conversations. But you had to watch where you
stepped. Old-fashioned streetlights, black with a frosted globe on top, lined the walkways—a nice touch. And
looking back over your shoulder you saw, ten or fifteen
stories tall, the apartment buildings on Riverside Drive,
casting their shade. What a city. You could think of it in
family terms. He had raised four kids and knew what it
meant to give them somewhere to sleep and enough to
eat and things to do. And here you had occupation and
sustenance and shelter for almost two million. On a narrow island—you could feel it was an island so close to the
river.

"Okay, I've seen it. Let's turn around," Bill said, and
coming out of the park, he added, "It depends what your
ambition is. If your ambition is to have an academic life.
There are serious, smart people, you get to do your own
work. You can come home in time to see the kids. These
things mattered to me."

"There are some serious people at the DoJ. I've been
talking to them."

"Okay."

"Maybe you undervalue the kind of intelligence that
gets things done."

"That's me!" And he grinned at his son, through his
beard; happily enough, but it was also a smile he could
smile when he wanted to.

"You got things done," Nathan said. "Look at us." And
then, as they turned the corner on to West End Avenue:

"Think about this. Take this seriously. This is something Liesel wants."

"Well, we'll see if she wants it."

Clouds were advancing rapidly overhead, and Nathan and Bill ended up running the last few steps to the awning. The rain came down like somebody pulled the plug. Somehow it put them all in a good mood, three generations huddled together while their feet got wet in the sidewalk currents. It felt colder, too. Julie put her arm around her father. Jean held Margot.

A strong-man type, fat with muscles, in a too-tight black shirt and jacket, smoking a cigarette and carrying a very large umbrella, was crossing the street. He had to jump over the curbside stream; they could see his pink face now and his short whitish-yellowish grizzled hair. The umbrella advertised the realty agency (Corcoran) and he dropped his cigarette into the flowing drain. When he shook Nathan's hand, everybody could smell him—the sweetness of his aftershave, and the gray nicotine smell, which even in the fresh wet air filled the awning.

"So who am I talking to here, who's the boss?" he asked.

"This guy," Bill said, and put his hand on Nathan's shoulder.

———

On the way downtown, Paul kept up an angry conversation with himself. The bit about the dishwasher was just stupidity—it had nothing to do with anything. He didn't even get mad about it anymore. That was one of the things they had figured out. *He* loaded the dishwasher. But to parade it like that in front of his brother, like some precious detail, oh well . . .

With his racket bag and gym bag, he took up a lot of room on the subway bench. People got on at 72nd Street, and he shifted the bags between his legs, feeling cramped. Like a kid, he wanted to make himself small. Part of the reason was . . . (the conversation kept going in his head) that he had mixed competitive feelings about his brother's marriage. Nathan's wife, Clémence, was French-Canadian, with an Egyptian father, and white and black hair she didn't bother dyeing. She was eight years older than Nathan, a journalist who had covered the White House for *The Sunday Times* (her first degree was from the LSE, she studied with some of Bill's old colleagues). Nathan met her when he was clerking in DC. When he got the Harvard job, she commuted from Washington until the kids were born. Recently, she had started teaching at the Kennedy School, but she had also written books and was an occasional talking head on *The NewsHour* and *All Things Considered*. Nathan was like the junior partner in a Cambridge power couple.

Paul liked Clémence. She was lively and an excellent cook, she asked questions, she had endless energy, but there was also an undercurrent of family opinion (which he sometimes tapped into) that reacted against Nathan and Clémence's air of "successfulness." This is what Jean called it. What's the difference between that and success, he asked her once. "It's like *fullness* of success," Jean said. "It's like the style that goes with it. You can't stop by their house without Clémence whipping up saffron chicken and palm artichoke salad and five other dishes, and everything served in beautiful bowls, and Nathan brings up a bottle of wine he's been keeping for ten years in the cellar."

"That sounds terrible," Paul said.

"But you know what I mean. When the phone rings, it's a producer from NPR."

"You're just jealous."

"That probably *is* what I mean."

Maybe they all were, a little bit. Sometimes the jealousy got in the way of their natural love but mostly it didn't. There was a kind of protection he sometimes felt in Nathan's company. Nathan had thought of most things; he had expert views—on real estate prices and pension plans, on the veil of ignorance and the categorical imperative. And partly what Paul wanted to communicate to him was just that you can't understand my life as the end result of a lot of careful choices. That's not the way it makes sense. Look at my relationship to Dana. The explanation for many things is what does it do and how does it work. But for some things the explanation is, this is where it's breaking down. It's a mess and maybe you don't even have to understand it, you just have to get out of the mess.

No, it's not a mess, it's not that bad yet. It's just that you're coming to the end of one career and have to figure out what to do next. These are perfectly reasonable and predictable feelings. Also, you're basically misunderstanding Nathan if you think about him the way he presents himself to other people. You should know better than that.

After 72nd, the local stops kick in. The train screeches picking up speed and screeches again, a minute later, metal on metal, fighting to slow down for the next station. The cars fill up, even on a Saturday afternoon. At Times Square, everyone gets off, everyone comes on. Paul stepped out at 28th Street, pushing his way awkwardly through the high turnstile, climbing the steps. It was good to get out in the air again, even in the shadow of high buildings. He could have taken a cab to the Club, but he liked to think of himself as a regular New Yorker. Also, he was his father's son, he hated spending money on perishables, a category that in Bill's mind included taxis.

Almost three years ago, Nathan and Clémence and Paul and Bill and Liesel had sat in a bar overlooking West 27th, one floor up from a high-end travel and art bookstore. Paul walked by this bookstore every day on his way to the Club, the kind of place with antique globes in the window, restored mosaic floors, stained glass panels over the doorways, odd bits of old leather hanging from the walls. To get to the bar you had to pass through a shared corridor, go up some dark steps, covered in schoolhouse linoleum—one of those secret-style places you can find even in the middle of Manhattan. It was Nathan's choice. Bill and Liesel were coming back from London, staying with Paul for a couple of days after visiting Jean. Nathan had a conference in New York, about technology and the law, sponsored by Cornell. Let's all meet up, he said. I've got an hour or two presently unaccounted for on Saturday afternoon, before I have to catch my train.

Dana was pregnant with Cal at that point and feeling too out of it to come downtown. But it surprised Paul when Clémence turned out to be there. It meant their nanny would have to put the kids to bed—they gave her the weekends off, and Nathan was usually a stickler about these things. Bill rarely drank unless you offered him champagne, not for any snobby reasons, except that he wasn't much of a boozer but really liked champagne, even the cheap stuff. Nathan ordered a bottle of Pol Roger. What's the celebration, Paul said.

But there wasn't really a celebration. Clémence said something like, I'm afraid we have some news, or there's been some bad news. Afterward, Paul couldn't remember the word choice—he argued with Liesel about it. For some reason it bothered her. Paul's first impression was, they were getting a divorce, it was amicable, and they wanted to go about it in a civilized way. He couldn't explain why this occurred to him and it bothered him, too, in the aftermath, like a thought betrayal. In fact, as Nathan explained, a few months ago he woke up functionally blind; he could see light but he couldn't focus, and in one of his eyes he couldn't even really see light. When he tried to get out of bed he also felt some resistance in his left leg, like waking up with pins and needles, but it didn't go away. Nathan, it should be said, had a mild tendency to hypochondria; in low moods, his restless energy got redirected inward and turned into anxiety. But whatever had happened was serious enough that he canceled classes, and when the kids were in school, Clémence drove him to the emergency room at Mount Auburn.

"Why didn't you tell us?" Liesel said.

"We didn't know what it was, and I didn't want to worry you."

"For what it's worth," Clémence said, "I told him he should call."

They were sitting on high stools pushed up against a long narrow table, everyone facing the same direction, which had its advantages. Nathan continued. The doctors put him on a drip and afterward (he went home the next day) gave him a course of oral steroids; it was a Thursday morning when he went in, and by Monday he was back in class. The blindness was caused by something called optic neuritis, an inflammation of the optic nerve, but what the doctors were really worried about was MS. He was more or less in the window where people first get diagnosed. The fact that he had had what's called a multi-focal episode, with impairment in two separate areas of the nervous system, the problem with his eyes and the numbness in the legs, made it a pretty obvious call but MS is still not easy to prove, it's really a collection of causes and symptoms. So they gave him an MRI to check for evidence of previous attacks — it doesn't get called MS until they find some kind of history, they're looking for progression.

His tone was dry and neutral, he was trying to explain himself, to get the facts across. Paul thought, I guess all of these are coping mechanisms and for some reason the phrase came into his head, If you prick us, do we not lecture? Another minor thought betrayal, but sympathy itself is a kind of heightened response. It's a strong light that shows up little things, including details of your own reaction. What I would do is probably go out and hit balls.

Bill said, "There's nothing like this in the family, I mean, no history. Not that I know of. If that turns out to be relevant."

"The MRI looked pretty clear, the doctor said, in the top ten, fifteen percent of expectation. It's technical, I don't really understand, but what they're looking for is damage to a kind of fatty sheath that protects the nerve fibers. The fat keeps out water, so they're looking for water on the brain. This is how he explained it. I talked to him yesterday, that's why we're drinking champagne. That doesn't mean it won't happen again, it doesn't really change the diagnosis. What they're calling it is CIS, which basically means a single episode of MS. The relevant question is likelihood of progression. Some of the doctors you talk to seem to believe that more or less everybody progresses, we're just not that good at reading the footprints yet. But I thought you should know anyway. Maybe it's nothing, maybe it goes away, but if it doesn't there will be real repercussions for the kids, for Clémence—"

"Just to be clear here," she broke in, "I'm not worried about me."

"There will be things you can help us with, which may involve some sacrifice."

"We don't have to talk about this now," Clémence said. "It's a good day. This is good news."

She had a very striking face, miscegenated, dark-skinned under the white and black hair, narrow and eager and pretty. She used to smoke and after giving up never stopped fidgeting—her hands tapped, she shifted her posture, she leaned forward and threw her head back, laughing. She picked at beer-bottle labels; she stacked coasters, she ate nuts. The bar table ran the length of the front window. Below them, at their feet, taxis slipped through the traffic, the streetlights came on, the apartment or office building across the road presented the usual front of lit and unlit rooms. It was the Saturday after Thanksgiving, dark at half past four. Paul had just come from the gym and felt drunk quickly, light-headed and somehow hard of hearing—like a radio with tinny reception.

Liesel asked, "What can we do?"

"Right now, nothing," Nathan said, and Clémence looked her in the eyes. With her white hairs and smoking wrinkles, she might have been Liesel's contemporary, almost. They both spoke English with a faint accent; but there was also something else, something European, they had in common. "There's nothing to do. But we wanted to let you know."

Paul stood up and put his arms around Nathan, leaning in from behind. As kids, they used to be very physical; they sat in the bath together, Nathan and Susie and Paul, and took turns rubbing each other's backs. Not Jean—she was still too young. Nathan briefly rested his hand on Paul's fingers.

"How's Dana feeling?" he said.

"Okay. Pretty big."

Bill said, "Stan Murnau has a part-time arrangement at Boston College, where he teaches there one semester. I can talk to him."

"You don't have to do anything now."

"Well, let me know."

"Right now the decision we have to make is some of the doctors want to put me on medication, the kind they give you if you've got MS. The theory is you want to start early. But the treatment isn't costless. I mean, there are side effects, these are strong drugs."

"So what are you going to do?"

"A colleague of mine knows somebody at the Mellen Center. His background is really in statistics, he looks at the evidence base. We're going to talk to him."

Afterward, Clémence and Nathan took a cab to Grand Central, and when its taillights disappeared around the corner, Liesel said, "We're getting a taxi, too." Bill didn't argue; Paul stood in the street to flag one down, and as soon as they slid inside it became clear to him that Liesel was extremely angry. Angry and upset, by the news and the fact that Nathan had kept it secret for more than two months. The way they were told—opening a bottle of champagne, sitting in that fancy bar, the whole business. Bill said, "The champagne was because there was good news from the doctor," but he didn't really try to talk her out of it, he let her go. Paul, sitting in front, wondered why he thought at first they were getting divorced, whether this was because on some level he wanted it to happen, and whether on balance, if they *had* been instead of . . . but you don't have to make these kinds of choices, thank God. What you feel doesn't really matter. And also, he felt all the usual things, too. Watching his brother go off, bending his long body into the taxi, a successful young man in a suit, you don't think . . . but even the way he moved now suggested something . . . his clumsiness, which could dominate a room, the way he leaned into you when he walked. Paul thought of these as symptoms of . . . what his grandmother used to call a forceful personality. But maybe what they meant was something else. Frailty, his body didn't always do what it was told. You're reading too much into nothing. Nothing has happened. Don't mention it to the kids, Nathan had said. I don't want them worrying.

And somehow, since then, nobody talked about it— it didn't come up. Nathan was good at . . . not keeping secrets, but acting on his own recognizance. You are, too. He informs when necessary, and Paul didn't expect whatever he had revealed to his brother that afternoon to go any further.

Somebody said to him, standing outside City Gourmet Market, "Hey, you." One of those come-ons that makes you think a sales pitch is coming next—or a Greenpeace leaflet from a college-age cutie with an army backpack. The woman was pretty but closer to forty-five; she wore a Burberry trench coat loosely over a dress. A fan, or maybe somebody he should know from the USTA. A sponsor's wife; somebody. He couldn't think.

"Hey," he said. They waited for the light to change. She had dyed-blonde shoulder-length hair and looked a little too skinny—a woman who kept herself in shape. She gave him a smile, which either meant you don't remember me, or can you believe what we got up to last time?

"This isn't your neck of the woods."

"Well, my club's around the corner. How about you?"

"There's a Sporting Life exhibition at FIT." She said it with quote marks in her voice, good-humoredly. "I don't

know, like tennis shoes and Lycra. You should check it
out. How's Dana?"

So it was one of her friends; another mother, maybe.

"Fine," he said. "Great. Well, stuck with Cal, while I . . ."
And he lifted his racket bag. "Actually, I'm running a little
late . . ." And when the traffic cleared, he jogged lightly
across 8th Avenue.

Afterward, he felt faintly guilty and annoyed. The kind
of all-purpose intimacy of "hey, you"—no doubt she had
forgotten his name. And the way he ran off, like a guy.
Was he supposed to want to flirt with her? Who knows.
All of these vague protocols and semi-relationships. Once
you reach a certain point, everything adds pressure. Even
the kid at the front desk, who knew Paul by name and
called him Mr. Essinger, meant you had to act out the role
of minor celebrity. At a tennis club, a guy ranked 82nd in
the world occupies a position, which has little to do with
who you are or the kinds of interaction you feel capable of
having on any particular day.

The kid had a textbook out in front of him, big as a
phone book. He was studying for his MCATs. "Good
luck with that," Paul said, stupidly.

On the way to the changing room, down the window-
less corridor (there were arty, cartoony pictures of famous
tennis players on the wall, though not one of him), Paul
remembered the woman's name—Ireney. "My mother is
Russian Orthodox," she had told him. "If you know anything about that, it makes a kind of sense." They were at
some party at somebody's house; Dana was there, too, Cal
was a baby, very small, and they were still trying to pre-

tend they had a normal life, toting him around. A friend of Susie's husband had invited them along, a writer. Susie was there, too, and spent most of the evening with Cal asleep in her arms. And Paul had this intense conversation with Ireney about kids—she was very sympathetic, she had three boys, in their teens. Maybe she was older than forty-five now. He talked to her about what he felt like when Cal was born, the instant identification. Cal was long and skinny, wide-eyed, and Paul thought, this happened to me, too. "I mean, like, what a thing to wake up to." That's what he said to her, slightly drunk. "I thought, he's me. What's happening to him is happening to me." The apartment had a balcony and they went outside so Ireney could smoke. Dana came out after a while and took over the conversation, and Paul went inside and sat next to his sister on a sofa. You have these dim memories. It doesn't matter what you say, you forget it anyway. But for Paul, getting changed, laying his bags across the wooden bench, smelling the old shower smell, sitting down, taking off his shoes, changing his socks, the vague feeling of guilt intensified, like he had let someone down.

Luigi was already on court, warming up. That fat fuck—this is what he sometimes called himself. Another one of Marcello's protégés, though Luigi had retired from the circuit a few years before. Even in his playing days, he was a little chunky; one of these bouncer types, thick-legged and built like a lampshade, very heavy on top. A beer belly. But he hit the ball a ton, and cleanly, too. At his best, in the early aughts, he was ranked number twelve in the world and once reached the semis of the US Open.

Since retiring, he had moved to New York full-time and let himself go—he ate what he liked, he got drunk. (He did all these things before but used to run some of it off.) Now he was trying to turn himself into a television personality, the colorful ex-player. But the transition wasn't easy. On air he came across like somebody trying too hard. He hammed up the Italian thing, they showed him cooking tomato sauce in his kitchen before a match: "This is what you need to eat-a the night-a before." But it all seemed staged, the kind of thing a producer would dream up. Which was odd, because in life Luigi was knowledgeable and smart, a very self-aware player—funny, too. And good to practice with, because he hit the ball so hard.

He wore cut-off jeans shorts and an extra-large Iron Maiden T-shirt, with the band name stenciled in bloody red. His hair, what was left of it, was tied back in a ponytail; there were freckles and flakes of dried sunburn on his scalp. When Paul came in, he was practicing his serve. Never one of his strong points; Luigi was only five ten. An outsider would think, looking at the two of them—Paul, slender and handsome, strong-armed, light-footed—that the fat guy didn't have a chance. But in fact their practice sessions were extremely competitive.

Partly because they played without serve. One of them would knock the ball across the net, they rallied a little, and then started going at it. Games to seven, like a tiebreak, win by two. And when Luigi saw Paul, this is what he did, flung a ball at him and said, "Come on, prince. Let's go." (He called people prince, count, *jefe*, *capo*, boss.)

"I need to warm up a little."

"You want to warm up, you come early, like me."

And so they started knocking it around. It was really almost unbelievable, how hard and low Luigi could hit the ball. He caught it rising, in the fat of the racket, and never seemed to move his feet. Wherever he happened to be, that's where the ball came back at him. Boom boom boom, like banging in a nail. If the first knock didn't get the job done, the next two would. And, in fact, Paul felt his wrist give slightly, and he feathered a forehand into the net.

"One love," Luigi said. And then two-love and three-love.

But if Paul could stay in the point, if he could move Luigi around a little, wear him out, Luigi hit too hard and flat not to make mistakes.

Under the big bubble of the canopied roof, echoes flattened out and ran away from you, sounds came back after a slight delay. There were half a dozen courts around them, people hitting balls, chasing them down, talking a little; and for a while Paul felt faintly underwater. There was too much space around his head. Everything seemed small and random, his own head included, the balls doing their math against the green of the hard court and the white of the roof. You felt lucky just to make contact, and Luigi took the first game seven–two.

Afterward, they met at the net and shook hands.

"Come on, big man," Luigi said. "I don't want to feel sorry for you."

Luigi had been at Marcello's memorial, and they talked about that, too. "Fucking beautiful," he said, and Paul couldn't tell if he meant it. But Luigi went on, "Beautiful beautiful, fucking fucking, blah blah blah. Everybody says

what they have to say. It don't mean nothing." Luigi liked
Marcello but didn't have any illusions about their relation-
ship. "For me, in my mind, I am number one guy, simple.
But for Marcello, number six, maybe number seven. You,
maybe number ten or twelve. Everybody knows this.
Nobody says it."

"I never felt that with him," Paul said.

"Because you don't want to. But that's not his problem,
that's yours."

By the time they started up again, Paul's head had
cleared. He was breathing without thinking, moving his
feet. And he felt good. Sometimes your body sends back
physical reports, delivers its news, and the weather is fine.
Hit and move; hit and move; follow through. Come to net
when you can. Hit and move.

When he was playing well, he often thought about something else—something stupid or important, which kept his
brain busy and let the rest of him get on with the job. The
music that was playing at that party: *They tried to make me
go to rehab, but I said no no no.* His sister Susie, sitting on
somebody's sofa with Cal asleep on her arm. Sometimes it
annoyed Paul, the way she took on the mother role. "Go
have fun," she told him. "You need a break." But it pleased
him, too. You get these glimpses of continuities—when
they were kids, she made him play tea parties, they pretended to drink from tiny china cups. A few weeks ago
she had told him she was pregnant again. "Oh God," she
said. "I haven't told Mom yet. What am I doing with my
life." Susie was the only one who referred to their parents
as Mom and Dad. They were worried about her career.

The ball flashed at him and he struck it. Sometimes it amazed him afterward, watching videos of himself. Did he mean to hit it there? On the line or a few inches inside. The ball as it touched the surface left a print in your mind's eye, yellow on green. And sometimes only then did you realize, yes, that's where. Or no, it was long or short, and you had to adjust.

He won the second game handily, seven–three or seven–four. There was some dispute about a line call, and later they couldn't remember the score. But it didn't matter. Paul gave him the point and won anyway.

The next was closer; they traded leads. Luigi still had a certain amount of pride at stake. Their relationship was based on various facts—one of them being, that he was a better player than Paul. At least, his own view of their relationship was based on this fact. And there was a lot of evidence to support it. You could measure his superiority in different ways: career prize money, for example, or highest ranking or head-to-heads. But Luigi was also older and fatter, a little rusty. The way he thought was, I'm better, but out of shape, I can't keep it up. But if I want to win a point, I can win it. So sometimes he really wanted to win. At seven–six down, he hit a backhand down the line that touched the line, and he skipped a little afterward, out of pleasure. "Hey," he said, "not bad, huh? For a fat fuck." But then he dropped the next two points on stupid errors: a crosscourt forehand, which almost climbed the tape but didn't; and an overhead, which he lost in the lights. When it bounced behind him, he laughed. Maybe when he was younger, he would have chased it down.

This was Paul's style. He hit everything back and made
you work until you screwed up. If you don't screw up,
you beat him, but even good players screw up. And afterward ask themselves, how'd I lose to that guy?

By this point, Luigi had started to puff a little. When he
was tired he tended to jump the gun, over-anticipate, reach
out and swat; his feet couldn't keep up with his hands.
He caught the ball too early on the rise and sent it long,
or flat into the net. And so they worked it out between
them, this argument about who was better, hardly talking
much, except to report the scores. Four–three and five–
three. Six–four, six–five. Game. And so on. One game
after another. Luigi said, "Too much good living." He was
sweating it out, enjoying himself, feeling his legs again,
which would ache in the morning. But the system started
producing errors. He hit short and Paul could move him
around, force him to the net and lob or pass him. After a
while, it didn't matter. It's hard work, concentrating. Your
brain gets tired quicker than your feet, and Luigi wasn't
used to it any more. You have to care, and he stopped car-
ing—there's even a muscle for that, which gets tired.

Just to keep the points alive, Paul planted himself in
the middle of the baseline and traded shots—pound for
pound, forehand to forehand. They stopped counting
score. A couple of high school kids in Dalton Tigers
T-shirts, playing next door, started to watch, and Paul
could feel them watching, or feel something watching, his
life's work condensed into these repeated motions, muscle
memory serving as a kind of history. (Sometimes, when he
couldn't sleep, Paul tried to work out roughly the number

of forehands and backhands he had hit in his life and the hours he had spent hitting them, thousands and thousands and thousands.) Afterward, when Luigi, laughing, rimmed skyward, the boys turned back to their game.

In the showers, he kept thinking about Susie. That phrase, "I haven't told Mom yet," had been running through his head. Every time he hit the ball it came back to him. I haven't told Mom yet—bam. I haven't told Mom yet. Susie complained about the smoke smell when he came in from the balcony. Ireney's cigarettes. "It'll wake Cal up." Give me a break, he said. He's out cold. Anyway, I remember when you used to smoke. I never really did, she told him. God I miss babies. Her two boys were five and eight at the time, a little older than Nathan's kids. She was younger but had started earlier. It's like, she said, their whole childhood you're in this period of slow mourning. For what, he asked her. For their childhood, because they keep getting older. I really want another baby. And now she was pregnant again. He didn't know who knew.

One of the Dalton boys stopped him in the lobby. "Can I have your autograph?" he asked and handed Paul his sweaty shirt, so Paul signed that. He had worked hard in his early twenties to make his signature legible, when he thought he might become famous. Now it amused him to think that sometimes the kids who asked him for it would have to look him up afterward, with no other information on hand but that bit of scrawl. Did the Dalton boys know who he was, or did they just figure, you must be some-body? Luigi was standing back, waiting, probably feeling annoyed. Usually it was the other way around. People recognized Luigi from New York One; he was sometimes a guest on *The Last Word*. Maybe this was another good sign, and Paul remembered catching his razor cleanly in the bathroom, by the handle, and putting it back in the toothbrush cup.

Not that he believed in signs but he believed in something—hard-to-pin-down alignments of certain facts, biological and other. Outcomes are the products of complicated multi-systems. Every athlete knows that. Some of them you can control, and some you can't. But either way you try to tune in to what's going on.

Afterward, they went for a drink; Luigi wanted a slice of pizza, too. They could tell from the air and the streets that it had been raining, hard. The drains were still making their happy noise, the awnings dripped. There was a divey kind of place near Times Square that Luigi liked, on 8th Avenue. Paul was happy to walk, to break down the lactic acid in his leg muscles. Maybe that was just another myth, he didn't care. The rain had stopped and some of the streets were steaming. He felt good and just slightly sore, with the racket bag bumping against his hip.

Paul asked Luigi about Borisov, his first-round match-up. But Borisov was too young—they had never played. "You got that guy, easy," Luigi said. "He's nothing special, just another one of those Russian guys."

"Bulgarian."

"Same difference."

But Luigi was never reliable on this front. He picked whatever attitude amused him most. Now it amused him to pep Paul up. "That guy does everything okay," he said.

"Like I said, nothing special." At the back of his mind, Paul also thought, you're getting back at me this way. Everything you say about Borisov, you can say about me, and you know that. Luigi was savvier about his own career, much more interesting. And over his slice of pepperoni, which stained the paper plate with oil, he talked about that US Open when he reached the semifinals, more than a decade ago now. As the sugar hit his blood, he seemed to calm down a little, he lost his edge. Paul drank an O'Doul's.

"I was lucky," Luigi said. "I think about this a lot. I was twenty-three years old, number forty-four in the world. But I didn't think I was lucky. I thought, maybe I'm good. Nobody worried about me, nobody heard of me, so they wanted to make it into a big story. This fat Italian guy, look at him. But who did I play? In the first round, nobody. Todd Singler. Guys like that I beat every day. In the second, Marcel Kunick—a qualifier. In the third, Portas, who was number eighteen, nineteen, something like that. But you only got to worry about him on clay. This guy never gets past the third round in the US Open his whole career. So I beat him, too. Then I play Todd Martin. The year before, he lost to Agassi in the finals. So this is a big deal. But he's getting old, his shoulder is bad. People don't know it, but the downhill has begun. And then in the quarters, Tommy Haas. Number five in the world. But, who knows why, Haas—I can play Haas. Our whole careers, the record is something like, eight and twelve, eight and thirteen. Usually he wins. Sometimes I win. This time I win. And then, against Sampras, like this." He makes the knife sign across his neck. "Six–one, six–three, six–two. No chance. But everybody thinks, something is beginning. Me, too."

He stood up to order another slice then went to the bathroom while it was heating up. Paul thought, watching him go, sometimes when we play it's evenly matched, and sometimes it's like today, and the outcome is really pretty clear. It was bad he didn't know who else knew about Susie's pregnancy. Everybody probably, but nobody had said anything to him. The family network of communication sometimes broke down; people assumed. But he was also being a little self-involved at the moment. Not noticing things. I bet Ireney didn't remember my name. *Hey, you.*

When Luigi came back, the slice was ready. He bought another beer and another O'Doul's for Paul (which Paul didn't drink) and carried everything back to their table.

"How come you don't got a coach?" Luigi said. "Guys these days got so many people."

"I don't know. I've got as many people as I want."

"You don't got nobody."

"Well . . ."

The kind of look he gave Luigi, modest and wry, was the kind he couldn't tell if Luigi understood. But Luigi didn't care; he was already talking about something else.

On the way uptown (Paul caught the subway again), he replayed in his mind many of their exchanges. Luigi won some of them, but Paul won more. The drop shot worked well for him, the lob worked well, he had a lot of success with Luigi at the net. Borisov was taller by a couple of inches. He was certainly in better shape. But I don't think he's comfortable at the net. If you hit some of your rally

shots short, maybe you can force him in. Something to
think about in the third or fourth set. Guys take the easy
way out when they get tired. And they think, if I can get
to net, maybe I can kill this thing off. It's funny, sometimes, when you're not in the mood, you've got things on
your mind, you play better. Sometimes when you really
don't care, you start winning. But you can't fake not car-
ing. You have to not care. And for some reason he remembered Cal trying to fling himself out of his arms the night
before. Until Dana took him away, while Liesel watched.
66th Street. 72nd Street. 79th.

———

E verybody came together for an early dinner at Paul's
place. Early because Julie and Margot, Margot especially, had to get to bed. They brought in pizza, but
Paul ate a big plate of spaghetti instead, with Zabar's mar-
inara sauce and a little parmesan. His pasta was ready
before the delivery arrived, but Paul didn't wait, he sat
down by himself and tucked in.

"I'm sorry," he said. "Otherwise I get the shakes, and
later I can't sleep."

Bill watched him approvingly. "The kid can eat. The kid
always could eat."

Dana tried her best to seem intimate with Paul. She
wanted everyone to think they were getting along. This in
itself was the kind of thing that sometimes annoyed him.
He figured, if we're fighting, they can see us fight. But
tonight he didn't appear to mind; or maybe he just wasn't

paying much attention. She brought him a glass of water before he asked for it; she brought him the cheese grater and the pepper mill. She leaned over the table and kissed him on the head.

Cal and Julie and Margot were watching TV. The living room shared an arch with the dining room, and Paul could watch them watching while he ate. Julie had taken Cal onto her lap, between her legs, holding him by the belly, and for some reason he thought about Nathan and Susie sitting in the bathtub with him, exchanging backrubs, the kid in the middle giving and receiving at the same time.

He wanted more children, but Dana wasn't so sure. She needed to get her career on track. Lately he had stopped bugging her about it, and she didn't know why.

The doorbell rang and she and Nathan decided to let the kids eat in front of the TV. She brought in three small chairs from Cal's bedroom and laid out plastic plates on the glass coffee table. Paul didn't want them eating pizza on the new couch.

"Well, anyway," Dana said. "This way the grown-ups can talk."

Sometimes the Essingers talked at meals and sometimes they didn't—sometimes they just ate. Bill could be extremely quiet. Paul had finished and kept wandering in and out. He stood in the doorway, leaning against the jamb. Then went back into the kitchen to make a fruit salad, which was one of the things he made. Jean and Liesel seemed to be arguing about something in an underground way—they weren't talking much. Which left Dana to make polite conversation.

"How was the other apartment?"

But Jean wasn't in the mood for politeness. "Anybody in their right mind would be lucky to live there."

Bill said, "His right mind. Her right mind."

Liesel had the gift of not always paying attention to her children's tones of voice. "The balcony was too high. I don't know if I would sit out there."

"The views were too spectacular," Jean added.

"The neighborhood was also a little quiet, for my taste. Bill liked it."

Nathan turned to Dana. "They don't have a realistic sense of what it takes to get an offer accepted in Manhattan."

And Liesel said, "It was very dramatic, in the rain. I love this kind of weather—we all had to stand under a bit of awning. My shoes got a little wet. They were supposed to be waterproof. I had a very nice afternoon."

When the pizza was finished, Paul brought out the fruit salad—in a big china bowl covered in bright flowers, which Bill and Liesel had given them for Christmas. He tried to get the kids to turn off the TV. But they refused to come, and Margot just picked up the remote control and turned it on again.

"Come on, kids," he said. "I want us all to sit down at the table for a part of the meal, like a family."

"It's the middle of a show," Julie said. She sounded very sensible, grown-up and matter-of-fact.

"It's always the middle of something."

"Well, if you waited until the end, it wouldn't be."

Paul watched for a minute. It was a cartoon—there was some kind of ship, people were singing, one of the figures, a bright red squirrel in a pirate bandana, played guitar. "When does it end?"

"I don't know."

"Look, I'm not discussing this with you. It's over." And he took the remote forcefully from Margot (who started to cry) and turned it off again. "Come and sit down," he said. "Eat dessert. If you finish your dessert, maybe you can watch a little more TV."

"I don't want dessert, thank you," Julie said. "Anyway, it will be over then."

"Julie," Nathan called out from the dining room. "Come. Now."

In fact, he resented Paul for intervening with his kids and redirected those feelings toward his children.

"What about Margot?"

"Margot, you, too. Stop crying."

"But he snatched."

Paul felt strangely heartbroken by that *he*. He remembered, when he was a kid, what adults were like, foreigners. Even people your parents loved. There was something showy about all their friendships and relations, something not quite real. You knew this; and then you grew up and realized, you were right.

Dana got up and started clearing their plates from the coffee table.

"Paul, is it worth it? Everybody was enjoying themselves."

"There was something I wanted to say."

"To the kids?"

"Forget it."

"Do the kids need to hear it?"

"I wanted them to hear it, yes."

"All right, kids. Come on."

She picked up Cal from his little chair but he didn't want to leave his cousins—she had to put him down again, he was wriggling so much.

Julie said, "Uncle Paul ate before everybody else did anyway."

Nathan kept his voice deliberately level. "When I say something once I don't expect to have to repeat myself."

"Fine." Her chair was much too small for her, and when she stood up, it fell over. She left it like that and walked into the dining room.

"There's nowhere for me to sit," she said.

"Pick up the chair you knocked down. I said, pick up the chair."

Jean made a noise and Nathan looked at her. "What?"

"Nothing," Jean said.

"What?"

"I just don't understand why everything has to be a fight."

"Because everything's a fight."

"Don't say it like that. Don't say it like, when you have kids, you'll understand. I grew up in a family, too."

"And we fought all the time, you just don't remember. It's not a big deal."

"Well, maybe that's where we disagree. It should be possible—"

"And, listen," Nathan broke in. "Two minutes ago, you were the one picking a fight with Liesel."

"That's for the same reason. You have no idea how spoiled we all sound."

By the time Julie returned, Dana had brought more chairs from the kitchen; everybody made room. Cal sat on her lap, but wouldn't touch his fruit salad, so Dana ate it for him. Bill said, "Very nice."

Julie picked out the grapes. Margot said, "I don't like bananas."

"So don't eat the bananas," Nathan told her.

"It all tastes like bananas."

Jean said, "Maybe you're right. I don't know. I'm probably part of the problem."

Paul was starting to regret the whole thing. He felt angry before, but most of the anger had gone, and he now just felt embarrassed and upset. "Would you like something else?" he asked Margot, trying to make it up to her. "We've got different kinds of yogurt in the fridge. Strawberry. Raspberry. Yogurt and honey."

"No, thank you," Margot said, politely.

"Cal might like a yogurt," Dana broke in. "I'd get it, but I'm kind of stuck here."

In the kitchen, by himself, Paul ran the hot water and let it warm up his hands, which were still a little sticky from the fruit juice. He stood like that longer than he needed to, trying to control himself. Start again. There are things you can only say in a certain mood, but the mood was broken, and he didn't know whether it was better to wait or just go through with it. But if you waited, people acted like you were making a big deal. So either way you were screwed. It didn't really matter.

When he came back in, he had forgotten Cal's yogurt. So he went out again and mixed plain yogurt with honey, using two spoons, and licked the honey spoon afterward and left it in the sink. Just to sweeten my disposition, he told himself. So that when Nathan said, "What's the big announcement?" Paul could push through his reluctance.

"I just wanted to say thank you for coming. I know it's a schlepp, and you've been doing it for years. It can't be much fun for anybody. Especially for the kids. You get dragged down here. And I don't even let you watch TV. Anyway, and all of this happens at a moment when I'm particularly caught up with myself and not really paying attention. I feel like there's something kind of disproportionate about all of the effort people make to be here." He looked at Jean, who looked back at him with her younger-sister eyes, very wide and registering already the emotion he had begun to feel, and which seeing her brought out. "Especially you, Jean. I mean, it's a long way to come. And for what. Mostly to watch me lose. Look, I'm not asking for a pep talk. I'm just describing facts. Maybe I say this every year. But the other thing I wanted to say is, this is the last year. Nobody has to do this again. Which makes it seem a suitable time to—register my appreciation. You know, I want to go into this thing with my eyes open."

"You don't have to make up your mind now," Bill said. "See how you feel when it's over, in a couple of weeks."

"To prove to you that I've thought about this I'm not going to pick a fight about it now."

Dana looked at him, a little stunned. This was the first she'd heard of it. But her instinct with the Essingers was always to resist getting involved. And part of what upset her was just the idea that Paul's retiring was their business first and not hers. The other part was, how easy he found it to keep these things to himself. Every night they shared a bed, they kissed each other before turning over. I mean, what else is he keeping back? I could understand it if he were having an affair. But what's the point of not talking to me about this? She still had Cal on her lap, eating his yogurt, and she couldn't help it, she kept thinking *mine, mine, mine.*

After supper, Nathan took his kids home—they were staying in Columbia housing, near Morningside Park. A friend of his at the law school was on sabbatical in Rome; his apartment was empty. The guy wasn't married, but he had a study/spare bedroom, and a fold-out double bed where the kids could sleep. They would be perfectly comfortable—it was a nice apartment, with a corner view over the park on one side and downtown on the other. High enough you didn't hear much of the traffic noise. The kids should be tired enough to sleep anywhere.

"How's Clémence?" Paul asked, while they gathered in the hallway. Nathan had dropped their overnight bag at the apartment, after driving down. Now it was just a question of remembering his briefcase and any stupid little things the kids had brought with them or picked up during the day.

"Sorry not to be here. She sends her regrets. But her sister is going through a tough time, IVF, the hormones make you a little crazy, and this seemed like too good a chance to miss, going to see her without the kids. Anyway, I like having them on my own. You just deal with it."

"What do you deal with?" Julie asked.

"You," he said, and Nathan picked her up—even though she was big, as tall as some grown women, and she seemed a little uncomfortable in his arms. But she liked having a tall father. He put her down again; she was red-faced.

"Are we going to get a yellow cab?" she said.

"We're getting a yellow cab."

And Julie pulled at her sister's arm. "Margot, Margot. We're getting a yellow cab."

"Do you want me to come? I can help put the kids to bed." Jean was conscious of not getting along with Nathan very well and wanted to compensate.

"It's fine. It's really not a problem anymore. But come if you want to. That'd be nice."

"It's not a question of what I want."

"No, come. I was just thinking, there's some work I was hoping to get done when they're in bed. But I'd rather talk to you. Come."

"Look, I can hang out here as well. It's not a big deal."

But Julie started pulling at her T-shirt. "We never get to see you." She could act the kid when she wanted to, she could be very dramatic. Margot joined in, tugging at her shirt, and Jean had to tell them, "Not on my clothes."

"Done," Nathan said. "It's decided. And we can pay for the cab to take you home."

"I can pay myself. I can take the subway. I can walk. I'm like a grown-up."

But she came anyway. Bill was in the kitchen doing the dishes, but Jean said goodbye to everyone else and followed Nathan and the kids into the elevator.

Suddenly the apartment seemed much quieter, almost

empty. Bill finished up in the kitchen and asked Dana if
he could use the phone. Paul and Dana retreated down the
hallway to put Cal to bed. Liesel couldn't hear them—her
hearing had gotten worse. She sat on the sofa and thought,
maybe I should help them, I should go see Cal in his
bath. But she also wanted to leave them alone. She was
also tired. Bill kept pacing back and forth, talking to his
sister. He was always restless physically and with cord-
less phones could talk happily for hours, which he never
used to do. Liesel felt mixed emotions—not just mixed,
but stirred up, unsettled. It pleased her to see Jean going
off with Nathan, two of her kids living their independent
lives, accommodating each other. But she also thought,
when they were little and fought, it didn't seem to matter
so much. Everybody laughed more.

In fact, Jean turned out to be very helpful. She was a deeply competent person; her job required her to coordinate
lots of different people and bring various unrelated skill
sets to bear on complex tasks. In other words, as Nathan
reflected, she would make an excellent parent. When they
arrived at the apartment, the beds were unmade and the
sofa bed in the study was still a sofa. Nathan couldn't find
sheets or towels; Jean found them. She managed to work
the TV, which seemed to involve several competing remote
controls, so the kids could watch while Nathan prepared
something for Margot to eat, because she hadn't eaten
much at dinner with nobody looking out for her. Some
milk and dry crackers (Ryvita) with jam spread over them.

Julie had a bowl of cornflakes, a habit she had picked up from her father. All of the Essinger men liked eating cereal before bed.

The apartment had a dining table in the living room— some of the chairs faced the TV. While the kids were eating, Nathan and Jean pulled out the sofa bed together and fitted the sheets, filled the pillowcases with pillows, and laid a woolen blanket over the top. Nathan rifled through their overnight bag to find nightclothes and toothbrushes and sleeping toys. Margot had a little shark; Julie slept with a Raggedy Ann doll, which used to belong to her mother.

Jean said to him, "You're a good daddy," because she was touched to think of him remembering these things for his kids' sake. As a brother he had much less tolerance for the insignificant.

"Julie," Nathan said, when she had finished her bowl. "No reading tonight. It's late, and Margot needs to go to bed."

"Can't I stay up with you?"

"It's a strange house. I don't think she'll want to go to bed alone."

Margot was watching the television; it was sometimes hard to tell how much she listened in. She had large round gray eyes, like Jean.

"Well, we can ask her."

"You can ask her."

"Margot," Julie said, in her sweetest voice. "You don't mind sleeping in that big bed alone."

"I do," Margot said, still watching. "I want to sleep with you."

"I'll give you a present."

"What present?"

"I'll give you money."

Margot had a dim sense of the value of money, but she liked the thought of it. Julie figured she could probably get away with offering a nickel.

"Not like that," Nathan said.

"Like what?"

But it didn't matter. Margot agreed, but then when Nathan tried to put her to bed, she refused and called out for Julie. The long narrow room was full of books, on all sides—they seemed to lean out of the walls. There were pictures, too, large Victorian prints, vaguely Hogarthian, of drunken men and loose women, brightly colored in. The window over the desk had no curtains; the night looked very black outside, with gleams of city light. And Margot could smell something intimate and unfamiliar in the woolen blanket, not just a wool smell, but something else. Some of Mommy's friends smelled like that. The guy whose apartment it was used to nap on the couch. He smoked, not at home, but enough for the smell to come through. It was scratchy too; Margot was used to duvets.

An African mask, a man's face with an open mouth and sharp pointy wooden hair, hung over the doorway.

"Julie," Nathan said. "Come on. Help me out here."

"But we had a deal. It's not fair."

Nathan considered this. "I don't know if it's fair or not. I'll have to think it through. But I'm perfectly willing to talk it over." He had to repeat himself, more loudly: "I said I'm willing to talk it over."

Julie, in her nightgown, which swept almost to the floor, came into the bedroom. She had been shouting her end of the conversation from next door and looked up at her father now with a kind of sarcastic meekness or air of dutiful constraint.

"Have you brushed your teeth?" Nathan asked.

She nodded.

"The deal you made with Margot is neither here nor there," he went on. "It's not a binding contract. She doesn't understand the value of what you're offering, and you know that. She isn't competent to judge."

"But she agreed."

"That counts for less than you think. But I don't really think you expected it to count for much. You knew she would change her mind. The contract argument isn't your best bet."

"What is?" she asked.

Jean, who was standing in the doorway, watched them. She could see how much Julie loved her father, she had softened already. Nathan was giving her his full, adult attention, the attention he would give one of his students. He was a very good teacher.

"Well, you could say, for example, that at home you get to read in your room, while Margot has to have lights off by eight o'clock. And there's nothing in itself about sleeping in another house that should affect these relative privileges. Especially since my reason for curtailing them has nothing to do with you—with anything you've done or didn't do. It's just because Margot is scared to sleep alone."

"Okay, that's what I want to say."

"The argument is complicated, because one of the things this arrangement makes clear is that the principle of equality doesn't really operate here, in the family. You've got rights and responsibilities that Margot doesn't, and I've got rights and responsibilities that you don't have. We're not all equal before the law, which makes it difficult to argue from first principles. Or rather, the first principle is the family—everything's for the state. From each according to her ability, to each according to her need. And your sister needs you to go to bed now, so go to bed."

Jean said, "Can I read a little to both of them? I never get to read out loud any more without feeling weird."

"Do you want Jean to read to you?"

"Okay," Julie said and got into bed. Jean took off her shoes and climbed in between the girls.

"What should I read?"

But they had an argument about that, too, which Julie won. Nathan said she could choose the book, it was only fair. Julie had read *Little House on the Prairie* when she was eight, and loved it. Now she was going through the backlist. Jean picked up her novel and started from the bookmark, in the middle of a chapter. She read very well, very naturally, while Margot stroked the side of her face, without saying anything. Jean kept going. It tickled a little, but she didn't want her to stop.

Afterward, feeling a little softened up, Jean told Nathan about Henrik. Margot was sleeping, the lights were out. Julie lay wide-eyed in the dark, and if you put your head around the door she gave you a suffering look. But she didn't stir or call out, and Nathan found some red wine in a cupboard and took it out on the balcony—there was a small balcony running off the kitchen, and a couple of chairs outside. In the coolish summer night, under low-pressure clouds, sitting ten stories up over Morningside Park, they drank half the bottle. The chairs were still wet when they sat on them. Jean sat down then got back up and wiped them with a dish towel, but she could still feel the damp patch on her Levi's. Nathan pretended not to care. He stretched out his legs and crossed them, he gave her his full attention, too. This was a very attractive quality, women liked him for it. Jean was much younger than her brother, nine years younger, and sometimes she still felt like a kid around him. She wanted his approval and advice. But for the first part of her story, he just listened.

"Of course, if he were happy," she said, "none of this would be happening. But he's not happy. I don't like any of the phrases that you use, I'm suspicious of them, too, but they've grown apart. In almost twenty years of marriage, he's never seen her cry. He told me that."

"That's not growing apart. You don't strike me as much of a crier."

"I don't know if that's true. He can make me cry if he wants to."

"I'm not sure I like the sound of that."

"Maybe it came out the wrong way. I mean, I let myself go around him, which I don't really do with anybody, outside the family."

Nathan didn't know what to say. He had opinions, strong opinions, but he needed to be careful about measuring them out, in manageable doses. Jean could get prickly, everything was pissing her off today, and for the moment at least, he wasn't. He was also fairly upset and already on his second large glass of wine. Not that he felt the least bit drunk. But whatever he felt seemed a little deeper and more meaningful than it usually did.

"Look, if it makes you happy," he said, "then I'm happy for you."

"He makes me happy. You know, one of the things that neither one of us has any doubts about is our feelings for each other. I've been in relationships where you spend the whole time wondering if it's real. This isn't one of them."

"Everything's real, in one way or another."

"You know what I mean. You dated, too. There were people you had nothing to say to, and people you did."

She felt awkward having this conversation with her big brother. Showing off. Look at me, I'm a grown-up, too, like you. When I'm really not. Also, she didn't like red wine—it gave her a headache. In London, she usually ordered a gin and tonic. She didn't drink at all in college, and then when she got to England it was the first thing she tried. Since it tasted okay, she stuck with it. At dinner parties, she sometimes drank wine with food, but even then not much.

"I remember in grad school," she said. "You went out with somebody's girlfriend."

"That ended well."

The wine was nicely cool and left a little resiny taste on the tongue. He looked out over the view—blackness broken up by irregular lights. Maybe you could see the trees, maybe you couldn't; but you could feel the greenness, a different kind of darkness below, coming from the park.

Traffic sounds floated up, sometimes even conversations. The night air had a loose quality, it seemed to echo a little, to retain sound. Your own voice carried. He wanted to get the phrasing right. Keep it simple, he told himself, so it doesn't look like you're thinking too much about it.

"It's different when kids are involved," he said.

"Believe me, I know that. He knows that. But even at his age, you have a right to live a life you can put up with. Don't you, I don't know. I mean, the way he talks about his marriage it's basically a professional relationship. It's like a business arrangement. They share office space or something. There's no tenderness. He said to me, if we were choosing now, who to be married to among our circle of friends, if we all got to choose again, at this stage I would pick her fourth or fifth."

"That's a charming thing to say."

"According to Henrik, she feels the same about him. He's very honest like that, he's totally straightforward. It's one of the things I like about him. He also said, if you want to know, that this is part of what makes family life so sad. Because for the kids even the idea of choice is ridiculous, it's like blasphemy, you don't want to choose your mother. But then at the heart of the whole enterprise is this weird decision, which your parents made twenty years ago, for reasons that don't make much sense to them now."

Nathan let this go for a minute. Then he said, "You have to realize that these people have a depth of relationship you can't really begin to scratch the surface of."

"Which people?"

She was just wearing a T-shirt and beginning to tremble a little. She felt the cold easily.

"This guy and his wife."

"I don't understand what you're saying."

"You present their relationship as a business arrangement—"

"I realize it's more complicated than that."

"Maybe not. But if you think about a business as somebody's life's work, if you think of these people as colleagues in that work . . . People care about their business."

"I don't understand what you're getting at. They don't make each other happy. You should hear them talk about each other—I mean, I've heard it from both sides. I know that he has a choice to make, and that if he chooses me, it's going to cost him. It will cost him money, for one thing. But it's also going to damage his relationship with his kids. You don't have to tell me that. But if you're trying to say that their marriage is much more meaningful and real and deep and important than I can begin to understand, then you don't have a clue what you're talking about."

"Look, I'm on your side here . . ."

"I'm not sure I'm on my own side here. Don't think I'm happy about any of this. I'm not. I feel like shit half the time. And the other half I just feel insecure."

"Jeannie."

"What?"

"This isn't like you."

"Well, that turns out not to be true." Then she said: "Don't tell Liesel and Bill."

"Who have you talked to about this?"

"I told Dana. I'm talking to you."

"I feel I have to say something you're not going to like."

"What?"

"There's a moral responsibility here. The primary obligation is not yours, it's his. But there are people who will be affected by what you do. Not just the wife, who can take care of herself, but the kids. You have a minor but not insignificant duty toward them. This will have a real effect on their lives. And by real I mean measurable, in terms of expected future income, educational attainment, even marriage prospects."

Jean was crying by this point, partly from the cold. "If it wasn't me, it would be somebody else." She was also unbelievably tired—in London now the time was three in the morning.

Later, when they were waiting for the elevator in the hall (Nathan had left the front door propped open), he said, "There's something else I want to talk to you about. Liesel hopes to retire in a few years. Bill has no intention of retiring. They are going to argue about this, because it affects where they can live. I think there's a compromise solution, which may or may not involve buying an apartment in New York. But Bill doesn't want to think about any of this."

"What should I do?"

"Well, you're staying there. See if you can talk to them about it. Separately maybe. You're the good kind loyal loving kid. That's your position in the family, they listen to you."

Then the elevator came and she got in and turned

around and looked at him. In her jeans and Converse All-Stars, she seemed very young. Her hair looked bedraggled from the wet air. Her face was still a little red; she had Margot's complexion. With Margot you also had to worry about allergic reactions. She had sensitive skin and often came out in hives. When Jean was a baby, she couldn't drink cow's milk, but she grew out of it and Nathan was hoping Margot would do the same.

"Do you need any cab money?" he said.

"No, I'm fine."

He watched the door close on her and went back inside.

Bill and Liesel didn't stay long. After getting off the phone, Bill told his son that he had arranged to see "your Aunt Rose" in the morning and probably wouldn't get back to Manhattan until after lunch.

"I figure you got things to do. And Susie doesn't come in till the afternoon anyway."

"Where are you going now?" Paul said. Bill often carried a canvas bag with him, which he had left in the hall and now went to pick up. Liesel was in the bathroom.

"Your mother's tired. We're heading back to the apartment. You guys could probably use a break."

"Well, do what you want to do. But once Cal's asleep, there's nothing to do here. We can put a ballgame on, it doesn't matter to me."

Paul felt the old reluctance to see his parents leave, even for a few hours, to watch them depart, looking older and more vulnerable than he imagined them to be, on the other end of a phone line. But it's also true that he didn't want to talk much. He wanted to turn on a baseball game and not have to think of things to say, which is partly why he hoped they would stick around.

"I think Dana can use a break," Bill said.

When Liesel emerged from the bathroom, with wet hands, they went home.

The front door slammed, it was heavy and old-fashioned, with a kind of metal rim at the bottom, difficult to shut gently; maybe this is why Cal woke up. They both heard him crying, a sound so faint down the long corridor, it sounded like a memory of someone calling you, not quite real.

"I'll go," Paul said.

Dana was still standing around, to say goodbye. For some reason, she had an apron on.

Paul sat with Cal for a few minutes, in the nursing chair. By the time he reached the kid's room, the crying had stopped. Cal lay on his side, with his head tilted back awkwardly and his mouth open. His blanket of knitted white cotton had become tangled in his legs. Every time you bent over to adjust something, or to pick him up, you banged your head on the mobile attached to his crib. Paul sometimes argued with Dana about whether or not to intervene if Cal looked uncomfortable. She always wanted to, he didn't. "You'll wake him," he said, and sometimes he was right. "Otherwise, he'll just wake up later." And sometimes she was. But this time, for whatever reason, he pulled at the blanket until it came free, then laid it gently over his son. The summer night was on the cool side, and the heating was off all over the building.

She was in the kitchen handwashing clothes when he came out. The sink was full of grayish water and bubbles.

"Give me a hand with this," she said. "You're stronger than I am."

So he wrung out a thin wool cardigan he had bought her at a Barneys sale and that she wore all the time.

"Well, that was quite the bombshell," she said, a turn of phrase that had always irritated him. Just the grammar of it—quite the this, quite the that, the kind of English-sounding idiom only Americans use, and only certain kinds of American.

"I don't think anyone was surprised."

"I was surprised. I was surprised you didn't tell me before."

"I didn't have a chance. I made up my mind this afternoon."

"That's not what you said to Bill."

"Look, if you want you can have an argument with me about how I told you, we can argue about that. Or we can talk about what I said."

"I don't want to argue with you."

"Okay, then don't," he told her and went into the living room to watch TV.

There was a ballgame on, the Mets were playing, and even though he didn't much like baseball, he liked the background noise. His knees hurt him, a little; his feet, too. He took off his shoes and lay on the couch. Almost in spite of himself, his body put him in a good mood. It was tired; it had worked hard. Some of the shots he played against Luigi came back into his mind—a flat forehand down the line, no topspin. Something he was working on, just to vary the bounce. But it's difficult to keep in play. Luigi could hit it hard and low like that. Paul needed work on his drop shot, too. He wanted it to look like an ordinary backhand slice, a rally shot. Once or twice it came off today, but with Luigi, who knew. The guy gave up running when he retired.

When Dana woke him, the score was tied, four-all in the seventh, Jose Reyes was at the plate. Two–one count. "Go to bed," she said. The night sounds, the game sounds, had gone through their subtle alteration; you could tell it was getting late. He felt a little feverish, not feverish exactly, but shivery, childish and intimate, but maybe just because the apartment was cold.

Putting on his pajamas woke him up again. He washed his face in the bathroom sink. Already he felt slightly panicky at the thought of not being able to get back to sleep. This is the sleep that counts, two nights before his first match. He shouldn't have washed his face, but you need to stick to routine, you need to read a little. Books put him to sleep, especially since Cal was born. Susie had recommended *Lord Jim*, and he was fighting his way through it, a few pages at a time. He hadn't read any Conrad since *Heart of Darkness* in high school, when he used to have opinions about books. Now he just read what people he respected recommended to him. That's not quite true, but sometimes you tell yourself these things when you feel low. His announcement hadn't gone to plan, it hadn't made him feel what he wanted to feel. That retiring was the right thing to do, for example. Sometimes he had the uncomfortable sense that all of his big decisions were made at the same basic level of emotional maturity you have when you're in the department store, looking in the changing-room mirror and picking out a shirt.

Dana said, "Jean told me something today. I don't know if you know or if I should tell you."

"What?"

He had almost forgotten she was there. They had grown so used to each other in bed that her physical presence didn't always protrude into his thoughts. Sometimes they turned the lights out without speaking or kissing.

"She's having an affair. With her boss. He's married." Dana felt a little guilty, passing on secrets, especially since it involved a kind of boasting. "I think she expected me to tell you."

"Why didn't she tell me herself?"

"I guess she thinks you guys will judge her."

"What do you mean, *you guys*? So what was your reaction, congratulations?"

"I told her she's old enough to do what she wants."

"Well, maybe she should want better things."

"She wants a love life."

"There are other ways of getting it."

"Yeah, well."

He was hurt that Jean had confided in Dana but not in him. "I need to sleep," he said and turned off his bedside light. She put her book facedown on the floor and switched off her own. They lay like that, in the half dark. For Cal's sake, they left the hall light on, and even with their door half-closed, the light leaked in. The curtains over the windows also let through a kind of city grayness. As his eyes adjusted, the room around him looked clear enough, the outline of the dresser, the mirror on the wall (which gleamed faintly), the chair with their clothes piled on it, the sliding door of the built-in closet. Dana's pretty dresses on their hangers. Only the color was gone. But he also thought, if Jean is confiding in her, it's because she considers Dana a part of the family, like everyone else. Somehow this affected his view, so that when she said, into the air, "What do you want to do next?" he wasn't angry.

"I don't know. Something different."

"Like what?"

"I have this idea of buying some land outside Austin and building a house."

This wasn't the answer she expected, and she laughed — she couldn't tell if he was being serious.

"Is that funny?" he asked.

"I'm sorry. It's just that it doesn't sound like you." She added, trying to keep up her tone or air of amusement, "You can't even drill a hole in the wall without making everybody watch."

"I don't want to build it, I want to pay people to build it."

"Okay."

But it wasn't easy, pretending to be amused, and she felt the dishonesty in her own voice. This is something Paul occasionally accused her of, that she didn't confront him with her real opinions, she always seemed to be playing an angle. Because I don't always know what they are every minute of the day, she told him. I'm not an Essinger.

But even that line struck him as a kind of ploy. What do you expect, she said. This is how the women in my family operate, this is how we get what we want. Do you get what you want, he asked her. Not with you.

"You think it sounds stupid?"

"I don't know, Paul." She was trying to do better. One of the reasons she loved him—this is what she used to tell her friends—is that he forced her to be honest. But maybe even this was an example of the way she had given in to him, to his version of events. It was so hard to tell. When you're floundering, whatever people say about you seems true. "It sounds to me like you're going off the rails a little bit. First you announce that you're retiring, and then you tell me you want to build a house in Texas. I don't get it."

"What don't you get?"

"I don't get how it fits in with us."

That was as close as she could come to saying what she thought they were talking about. She was doing her best.

"Who is us?" he said.

"You know who us is. Me and Cal."

They were both still staring up at the dark ceiling. Always you had this sense in New York of carved-out life. The pipes made noises, you could hear your neighbors' footsteps overhead, suggestively moving around. Going to bed? Making something in the kitchen? And behind their heads, just two or three feet away, on the same level, there was another bedroom, a couple they knew, Bob and Linda; she was expecting a baby any minute. Dana kept meaning to pop by with a few things they didn't need any more. Boxes of baby diapers. Cal had gotten too big for his BabyBjörn.

She broke the silence first.

"I'm happy. I thought we were happy," she said.

"Can we have a serious conversation about this? Without make believe?"

"I thought we were."

"You can't have thought that, you're not being honest. You keep telling me, you're going crazy, stuck around the house all day."

"We have a small kid, that's what it's like."

"I don't see why it has to be like that."

"Well, try looking after Cal a little bit more."

"I just don't understand. You've got Inez five days a week."

"You don't understand what?"

"What you do all day. What you want to do with your life."

"You mean, like, move to Texas?"

"Don't take that tone. I hate that tone. If you want to disagree with me, fine, but don't make a joke out of everything."

"I'm not trying to, Paul. I'm just trying to understand. Are we supposed to come, too?"

He turned over and looked at her—he was only a few inches away. With his brown skin, a little sun-damaged, his stubble, his large brown eyes, there was something almost evangelical in his face. He picked at his eyelashes, too, a nervous habit. As a kid he suffered from blepharitis; he often woke up with heavy sleep on the lids. Cal did, too. It wasn't a big deal, but she took him to the doctor anyway. She learned about it. Paul's lashes grew back but they weren't very prominent. Maybe this is why his eyes seemed bigger, more open and earnest. The Essinger earnestness, she used to think, but in fact, Paul had it worse than any of them. She found it very attractive, when they first dated. He was a serious guy, he took her seriously. Just now he seemed to her a little crazy. Not exactly happy or unhappy, but in one of those moods where it's like everything has just occurred to you and makes complete sense.

"Why don't you talk to me about this stuff?" she said, when he didn't answer.

"I'm talking to you now. Because you don't want to think about it."

"Think about what? I still don't understand."

"We can get out of the whole business. We don't need careers, we've got enough money. Cal could have a big backyard, he could run around. We don't have to go to dinner parties or make contacts, or *chase* anything. We don't have to surround ourselves with people we *quite* like. We don't have to do anything we don't want to do."

"I don't want to move to Texas."

"Forget Texas, you're not really listening to me. At Marcello's thing, it basically came home to me that ever since I quit Stanford my life has involved hanging around people I don't know very well and who don't know me."

"Am I supposed to be one of those people?"

"No," he said. "Of course not."

"You always get this way when your family comes to town. But then when they come you do everything you can to avoid seeing them. I mean, you can't pick them up from the airport, you sneak off to practice."

"I don't sneak off."

"Even when they come to dinner you eat beforehand. You don't see it—I do. You go into yourself, you basically stop talking."

"That's not true."

"Paul, I live with you. I know what you're like when you're shutting down."

"You don't understand. This is what it's like to have a big family. You don't always have to participate."

"That doesn't sound at all like shutting down."

"I'm not talking about my family here. My family is part of the problem. The way Julie is growing up. Nathan told me she gets two hours' homework a night. She's ten years old. They've got a tutor for her, too. They want her to get into Boston Latin. We all went to shitty public schools in Austin. I mean, we turned out okay. But beforehand we had this thing called childhood. I don't want Cal growing up in New York."

"I grew up in New York. Let me tell you something, if you move to Texas, Cal is growing up in New York."

Afterward they lay in silence for a while. Paul's heart was beating audibly, he could hear it in his ears. He thought, neither one of us will be able to sleep now, and the stupid idea crossed his mind that maybe if they had sex they could get to sleep. Not that he wanted to much, but he really needed to sleep. He didn't know how deep the argument went, you couldn't always tell at first. But then after a few minutes Dana's breathing got louder and he had to listen to her, hating her a little. Someone who could sleep like that didn't care about anything.

But it calmed him down, too, after a while, looking at her, the way it calmed him down to watch Cal in his crib. She was just who she was, she couldn't help it. When you're a teenager you can't believe that when you grow up you'll spend every night like this, lying next to a grown woman. There's a familiarity there you don't have as a kid, with anybody else, after you stop sleeping in your parents' bed. Familiarity combined with latent strangeness, because you can both walk away from the deal at any time. Sometimes when he spent the day with Cal he tried to imagine that he was looking back at himself from some future date, watching with envy, while he cleared up a spilled drink or put away wooden blocks, crawling on the carpet on his hands and knees; or put fish sticks in the oven and ate Cal's leftovers while Cal sat in front of the TV. Enviously because Cal was now grown and married, a little distant from him; because Paul's hips hurt, and so on. The envy gave a kind of spice to the day. Some day, looking back, you'll wish you were here and he wondered whether in the future he would feel the same about lying here now.

SUNDAY

Jean woke up early, with jet lag. It was gray outside, not black, and she could already hear regular traffic along Central Park West. The streetlight outside her bedroom window glimmered vaguely. Birds made noises.

Recently, she had started jogging in London, and she had brought her running shoes with her. Lying in bed, wide awake but at the same time completely tired, feeling hollowed out and hungry, she imagined putting on her sneakers and running in the park. Like some crazy person, she told herself, but got up anyway and pulled on her shorts. She peed and spat in the toilet and brushed her teeth. Sneaking out, she was startled to hear her father say, "Couldn't sleep?"

He lay on the sofa, with a blanket across his legs and a book open on his belly.

"I figure I may as well go for a run."

"Good girl."

"What are you reading?"

"I don't know." He turned over the cover. "Your mother bought it for me for the plane."

It had rained overnight again, there were puddles on the sidewalk, and she shivered in the early morning air. I wonder how much of this is a kind of punishment. But as her blood warmed up, she began to feel better. The park was only a block away, and she ran past the playground and across the curving roads, toward the gritty track around the reservoir. She didn't go far or fast; even in the cool air, she sweated. The salt blurred her eyes, but she could still make out the sunshine climbing the skyscrapers on Central Park South, astonishingly yellow. There were people out walking their dogs, old men, a few women, many of them in overcoats or college sweatshirts. The breeze was brisk enough to raise a few waves, and foam built up on one side of the rocky shore—soda bottles bobbed among them. But it wasn't properly cold, either, and with the blood warming up inside her, she started to feel pretty good.

Various thoughts went through her head, to the rhythm of her feet, but after a few minutes she realized she was composing something for Henrik, probably an email or a text, and at the same time carrying on the argument with Nathan from last night. I told my brother about you. I thought it would make me feel better but it didn't, it just made me miss you more. Her shoelace came undone and she sat on one of the benches to tie it up—breathing heavily, feeling her heart rate in her ears. When she started running again, the conversation started again. I told my brother about you. He read me the riot act. I don't know what you would have said. Probably agreed with him. He's very persuasive. All of this got mixed in with something else, a kind of ongoing voiceover or description of her day, which she was preparing in advance, in case Henrik called later or she called him. I went for a run in Central Park at some ridiculous hour, but it made me feel kind of virtuous and glamorous at the same time. Maybe I've been in London so long that I've developed

a Londoner's sense of the glamour of New York. East
of the reservoir, she ran alongside Fifth Avenue. There
were thick green trees lining the park walls, but through
them she could also see, in the rising summer morning, the
Neue Gallerie, built like a bank, the vista of 86th Street,
traffic going both ways, a bus turning, and then the Gug-
genheim, like a parking garage, more trees. By this point
she wasn't talking to Henrik, she was talking to Nathan. I
know it's wrong but it's not even like it feels right, because
it doesn't. But it's like I'm being presented with two different kinds of reasons for doing something, and one of
them matters more than the other, it's not even close. The
track curved around, she was heading west again, into the
park, there were tennis courts below her, an implausible
number, stretching out green and empty and patched with
last night's rain. One of them is, you don't have to tell me,
he's got a family, there are kids, people will get hurt and I
don't like to hurt people. That's one kind of reason. And
the other is just this overwhelming feeling of excitement,
to be at the center of something, or just for something to
be happening. When I got to New York I was also thinking to myself, like a kind of test, let's see how much I miss
him. And at first I didn't, which made me feel guilty in a
funny way, but then I did. I mean, let's imagine, he leaves
her and it works out and we have kids together and ten
years from now they're seven and four, or something like
that, and it's all pretty conventional, and they owe their
life to what I'm doing now. Can that be a justification?
There's nothing you could say to them that would make
them really believe I shouldn't have done what I did.

Sometimes she had to watch out for dogs, they moved unpredictably, and there were puddles on the running track—she didn't want to get her shoes wet. People dressed in extraordinary ways. There was an old gray-haired woman, wearing neon yellow leggings and a pink headband and a Lakers jersey over a long-sleeved T-shirt. She had earphones on, you could hear music coming out of them. She moved at a snail's pace, but sort of lifted her legs as if she were running. Jean passed her, feeling, at least I'm fitter than she is, I'm younger than she is, I'm in okay shape. What? I am. By most human standards. She was thinking of Paul, talking to him. She knew that when she jogged she looked very red in the face. Poor Paul. It worried her how little she had thought about what he said. Even with Nathan, she didn't discuss it. And yet when he gave his little speech, she was almost in tears. He always seemed so physically healthy and well, it was hard to imagine—but that's stupid. Everybody has problems. I wonder if Dana told him. She probably did unless they aren't talking very much at the moment. I guess they have other things on their mind.

Emerging again, into the ordinary city, with its traffic and tall buildings, she crossed the 86th Street entrance to the park, busy with cabs, and ran along Central Park West for several blocks. The concrete hurt her feet a little; she had to dodge commuters making for the subway, but the sidewalk also felt vaguely downhill. She was winding down, she started walking. On the corner of Michael's street, she noticed a Greek-looking guy setting up his food cart—he sold bagels, muffins, and croissants, hot coffee and tea.

A stainless-steel booth, not very clean-looking, unfolded and provided shelter from wet weather. But the sky had cleared up; there were just enough clouds to make the sunshine pink, spread out like paste. She had a twenty-dollar bill in her pocket, she wanted to bring back something for breakfast, but ended up walking to Broadway and waiting for Zabar's to open. There was already a line outside the door, people who knew each other, shift workers, old guys with newspapers. Later, she sat at the café counter, drinking grapefruit juice and listening in, and feeling (as she told herself a little self-consciously) the things you're supposed to feel as a young woman in the middle of a big city with a lot going on in your life.

She had more or less stopped sweating by the time she walked back to the apartment, carrying a paper bag. Bill was in the bathroom. Liesel was trying to make coffee in the kitchen. Jean said, "I brought some breakfast stuff," and left the bag by the sink, then went to her room and wrote an email on her phone, tapping it out clumsily with cold fingers,

> Hey, I told my brother about you. He was worried about me. I miss you and want to talk to you, but I know you probably can't oh well. Consider this just a hello. Hello x

and sent it. Afterward, she sat on her bed in her running shorts, with her hands on her knees.

A minute later, she heard her name being called. The apartment had thick walls and heavy doors. Voices traveled unpredictably, everything sounded muffled or far

away. But it was her mother calling her, and Jean shouted out, "What, I'm here. I'm here," then stood up, a little
stiffly, and went to find her.

"What," she said.

They were standing by the door to the elevator, waiting
to go out.

"We're going out," Liesel said.

She had a date with some woman from *The Village Voice*.
They were supposed to meet for coffee at an Italian place
by Washington Square, and Bill had to get to Grand Central—he was taking the train up to Yonkers to see Rose.

"Send her my love," Jean said.

"I'm sure she would love to see you," Bill told her.

"I'm kind of worn out."

"Okay."

"I'm a little disgusting right now."

"Okay. I just didn't want you not to come if you wanted to come."

"I want to see her but not now."

"Okay," he said.

It broke her heart a little, the way she could disappoint
him; but the truth is, he didn't really mind that much, Jean
knew that. She was just being sentimental. And when they
left, Jean had the apartment to herself. Susie was coming
in that afternoon, which left Jean three or four hours to
kill. She showered and checked her phone, to see if Henrik had replied. When he hadn't, she went back to bed,
thinking she could read at least. In fact, she started falling
asleep and put her book facedown on the duvet cover and
closed her eyes. Today was supposed to get warmer, you

could hear it outside, in the traffic and birdsong, and she lay listening for the sound her phone made when an email arrived, then she was out cold.

———

The nearest subway stop was at 81st Street, by the Museum of Natural History, where they could take the C train downtown. It went to Washington Square and Bill could get out at Bryant Park and either take the 7 to Grand Central or walk. He would probably walk, it looked like a nice day. Bill worried that Liesel would get lost. Her sense of direction wasn't terrific, but she had a map in her handbag, she had plenty of time. He teased her in the subway, for dressing up a little—she wore a silver necklace, which he had bought for her at a market in Berlin, and her less comfortable shoes. "Look at you, big shot," he said.

"I'm worried about Jean," Liesel told him. She sat with her handbag on her lap. The plastic seats were too narrow. Bill had left a space between them; the car wasn't busy on a Sunday morning.

"What are you worried about? She went for a run this morning, she's lost a little weight. She's taking care of herself. She looks good."

"She's keeping something in, she was snapping at people yesterday. It's not like her."

Bill had his own canvas tote, which he rested on the empty seat. He planned to pick up something for him and his sister to eat at Polanka's on Nepperhan Avenue, where she took him once a few years before. Rye bread and sausage, pickles, a little cheese. Rose wasn't very mobile, and she also got embarrassed, eating in restaurants.

"She's not a kid anymore," he said. "You can't expect her to open up at the first opportunity. Of course there are things going on she doesn't want to tell us about."

"You say it like that, like it's a normal thing, but it doesn't make her happy."

"She looks happy enough to me."

They sat in silence for a couple of stops. At 59th Street, the car started to fill up and Bill put the bag between his knees and shifted over. Liesel said, "Do you think you would have had a different career if we didn't have so many kids?"

"It's possible."

"Do you regret it?"

"No."

More silence, which Liesel broke. "Yesterday, for some reason, I was talking to Julie about your mother."

"Huh," he said.

After he left her, at 42nd Street, she went over the conversation in her head, thinking of Julie but thinking of Essie, too. When Bill's father died, Essie came to live with them in Texas. She was mostly blind by this point, because of a botched cataract operation; she had had several strokes and struggled to find the right words. It was like watching a woman look for something in her handbag, perfectly reasonable and exasperated. Liesel was friendly to her, in a distant way. The sad thing about all these fights with your in-laws is that in the long run you always win. Essie had refused to show up for their wedding, but for the last four years of her life, she lived with them. Bill fought with her, he couldn't help it; she made demands on him, but sometimes he reacted to her as if they were still . . . You don't always have to listen to your parents. Sometimes you have to ignore them. She said this to Jean, too.

Because of the bright Texas sunshine, Essie wore heavy brown sunglasses that pinched the bridge of her nose and left permanent marks. She kept her arms toned by exercising with running weights, pacing back and forth in the kitchen, lifting her knees. Even at her age, blind and incontinent, she had her vanity. Paul sometimes read to her; he was fifteen years old when she died, for some reason they had an affinity. The way he hit that ball against the wall, over and over . . . But Liesel liked to listen to him read, more than she liked to watch him play. He had a nice voice, naturally serious, and Essie was obviously proud of him. She said things like, let me see your beautiful face, and Paul always said, not minding, how do you know it's beautiful, you can't see it.

Thinking of this put Liesel in a good mood. She was looking forward to her meeting. The book had done well, she knew that for a fact—her editor wanted her to write another collection. The first was called *War Stories* and had a subtitle: *Growing up in the Third Reich*. But really it was about a happy childhood. She had had a very happy childhood. Her mother was loving and fair and sometimes fun, she was very resourceful, even in the difficult years after the war, they had enough good things to eat, very simple food, some of which they grew themselves, and

anything else was a real treat, packages from her aunt, for
example, who lived in Canada. That was really the point
of the book. These terrible things were happening, not just
far away, but around her, in her own family—for more
than a year, her father lived at the Eastern Front, they never saw him, never spoke to him, sometimes they got letters, which Mutti read out to them, where suitable—but
in spite of all this, Liesel had a very happy childhood, and
nothing in her afterlife could live up to it until she had
children of her own. Because family life protected you
against these things, though maybe that wasn't really the
right way to think of it. Family life made none of the other
things matter.

The stories she told about the war were often funny.
Her mother once found a sausage in a hedge. A soldier
must have left it there, who knows how long it had been
stuck among the twigs and leaves. *Saucisson*, Mutti called
it; it was the first time Liesel had heard the word. Her
mother's family had been very well-to-do—Mutti spoke
excellent French and as a young girl spent her holidays
near Abbeville. She unwrapped the sausage from its skin
and laid it on the kitchen table. Everyone gathered round.
Nobody wanted to taste it, and eventually Mutti cut off a
little slice and fried it in a pan and cut it in half again. She
ate one half and her brother, Onkel Torsten, ate the other.
For the rest of the day, the sausage just lay there on its
board, on the kitchen counter—even though they were all
hungry for meat. Mutti and Torsten kept asking each other, "Aber ist Euch auch wohl, Vater?" like the son in the
play. They weren't really worried, it was a big joke, and

the next day everyone tucked in. This is the kind of story she told in the book. Liesel talked about Abbeville, too. Years later, as a foreign-exchange student, she lived for six weeks with a family in Dieppe, and spent one Saturday negotiating the trains and buses to visit Abbeville, to see if she could find the hotel where her family used to stay. But it had all been bombed beyond recognition.

Liesel got off at West 4th Street and stepped out of the subway onto Sixth Avenue. It's true, the city was very bewildering. Her knee hurt her, the subway steps were difficult. Instead of checking her map, she asked a woman pushing a stroller how to get to Washington Square. Police-men and women with children, she thought; that was the advice she used to give her kids, when they were lost. Ask a policeman or a woman with a child. The woman pointed—the leather bag on her shoulder slipped down to her elbow, but she held her arm out straight anyway, and the fact is, Liesel should have been able to guess. There was a little concentration of green at the end of the block. She walked toward it, and then, when she reached the square, found a bench under one of the trees and sat down. She was a little early, Bill had to catch a train, which is why she left the house when she did, to keep him company. And she liked Washington Square. It was like an American version of a European square, bigger and greener, but the idea was the same. So that people should come and run into each other, so that there should be some common life. It was only half past nine but already a group of kids with backpacks were kicking something small, like a little bean-bag, in the air. When it fell on the ground, they shouted good-naturedly and complained to each other. Old men played chess, three women in spandex stretched themselves against a lamppost, talking, someone read a book. A man in a suit sat with a McDonald's paper bag between his legs and drank coffee. Liesel liked looking around. Again and again the sense of how far she had come in the world, without having to change too much, comforted her. Some people didn't have to change much to get along; she used to think Paul was like that.

But maybe she also underestimated what she had gone through. The prospect of her interview made her begin to go over old stories, to narrate them. That first year in America she cried herself to sleep every night. In those days, you had to take a boat to get back home; four thousand miles meant something. And everything in America seemed unreal to her. The air, for example, which over the winter was piped in from heating vents and made her skin dry; she got into a lot of arguments about opening windows. The bread tasted like cotton. Even the money looked fake—she couldn't believe it when she saw, written above that image of the White House on the twenty dollar bill, the words, In God We Trust. But she liked American Jews, right from the beginning. Who knows why—some cultural attraction. Mutti once said to her, I wish I could say Jew the way you do. Without a kind of special consciousness, she meant. Liesel didn't know what to tell her. Now here she was, almost fifty years later. Her husband was Jewish, her kids were vaguely Jewish, and she was sitting in Washington Square on her way to breakfast with a reporter from *The Village Voice*. To talk about her German childhood.

In a long life, everything gets used.

She found the café easily enough—one of these places with small round tables and ornate metal chairs, all crowded in together; black and white tiles on the floor, brick walls with plants hanging off them, old-fashioned mirrors. There was a bar running along the side, and it looked like they were just opening up. A woman with a nose ring emptied a dishwasher. She looked tired or hung over and dried the glasses with a dirty dish towel. She had some acne on her nose, which made the ring, a small diamond stud, appear painful, but she was otherwise pretty enough. There was only one other person in the café, a student type, eating eggs; his backpack was on the floor, he was playing around on his phone. Maybe he worked there, too. Liesel asked for an Americano and sat down near the window. The woman was late, and Liesel began to worry that she had the wrong place or the wrong time. For some reason she was feeling nervous or unsettled; it was hard to pin down. Maybe she was just anxious about the interview. You have a coffee with someone, you talk about yourself, you seem to get along fine, and then they write what they want, and it seems to bear no resemblance—to what you think of yourself or even to the tone of your conversation. But she was also worried about her kids. About Jean, who seemed to be dealing with something privately, about Paul, who was fighting with Dana, about Dana, who didn't know what to do with herself, about Nathan . . . Her worries about Nathan were complicated and somehow not entirely disinterested. She had too much at stake, you get overinvolved with your first child. Or under-involved. It's like a kind of wrestling match that neither one of you ever completely grows out of.

But even this didn't bother her very much, sitting in the café—the coffee had come, surprisingly watery, dirty-colored, but perfectly drinkable. There was a little wrapped biscotto in the saucer, which she ate. Bill hated stopping for coffee; he hated spending money on what you could make more cheaply at home.

She had finished her first cup when a woman came up, carrying too many bags, looking breathless and putting on a smile of apology or anticipation. "Liesel, can I call you Liesel?" the woman said. "I'm late, I know. It's very unprofessional, and I'd like to say it's totally out of character, but . . ."

Even sitting down seemed to require intricate maneuvers. She had a handbag and a computer satchel and a water bottle and a coat, which she didn't need. Her name was Karen and then something Polish-sounding, maybe Bartkowski, and she wore a button-up white shirt (wide open at the neck) and a dark skirt and tights and high boots. Her hair was blonde but streaked and not quite curly or straight. She gave off a kind of heat, of exertion or entropy, you could almost feel it, which explained the undone buttons and the untucked shirt and the breathless manner. Her face, in repose, might have been pretty, but she smiled too much, apologetically, and her teeth weren't particularly good. She looked about forty-five years old and Liesel basically liked her.

Karen ordered an espresso then took a long pull from

her water bottle. "Okay," she said, "I'm here, you're here. Okay. Breathe," and laughed.

She put her phone on the table and asked if Liesel minded being recorded. She did, a little, but said, no, of course. The espresso came, it was the guy with the backpack who brought it; and then the woman with the nose ring refilled Liesel's cup from a coffee carafe. Karen began by saying "how much she loved" the book, which annoyed Liesel. She had a theory that it was one of those things Americans have to say, like *have a nice day*. Sometimes they even believe it.

But it didn't get better from there. Karen asked a lot of questions but didn't always wait for the answers. It amazed Liesel (this wasn't the first time she'd been interviewed) how often people interrupted her. They had their own ideas about the book, and the interview was really just a chance to run them by you. Again, Liesel minded a little but not much. Most of what she had to say she had said before—some of it she had even written in the book. There was something depressing about repeating yourself in this way. At least if they talked, you didn't have to. But she also had the sense that they were wrangling about events that had actually happened to her and which this woman had clearly misunderstood. Karen wanted to argue that the book showed how children of the Third Reich were deceived and implicated along with everybody else—that the book was Liesel's attempt to wake up to that deception and acknowledge it. But this wasn't Liesel's point at all. She had had a happy childhood and a wise, loving mother. There was no deception, at least, nothing that would have mattered to her as a child. Even in the middle of terrible political events, pockets of ordinary, innocent and happy family life remain possible.

After half an hour, the phone started to ring, and Karen looked at the name and said, "Oh, shit," and picked it up. "Give me ten minutes," she said to whoever was on the line and clicked off again.

A friend of hers was coming to stay from San Diego and Karen had totally forgotten about it. She had had a kind of feeling all morning that there was some reason she shouldn't go out but couldn't remember why.

"It's only ten minutes away," she said. "Do you want to wait or you can come too and we can do this in my apartment."

"I'm afraid, with my knee, I can't walk very fast."

"I meant ten minutes in a cab."

So that's what they did and somehow Liesel ended up paying for the taxi. Karen ran out of hard cash settling the coffee bill. It didn't matter, Liesel said, and really it didn't matter, but you resent it anyway. You want things done right. Not just out of respect, though that was part of it. Out of respect for the whole business, Liesel thought. It wasn't personal, but you want to be involved with serious people, who do things the right way, so that you can tell yourself, this is the world I belong to. Whereas in fact she ended up asking for a receipt from the cab driver, a black man with a friendly, very quick foreign accent, who scribbled something illegible onto one of his cards. Liesel put the card in her purse, even though Karen tried to take it from her.

"I can probably get it back from the magazine," Karen said.

But by this point, Liesel was annoyed and insistent. "My husband would say, it's a tax deduction." Later, on her way uptown, she threw the receipt into a trash can next to the subway entrance.

Karen lived quite far east, past Avenue A, on a side street, in an ugly but not very tall apartment building, which looked recently built. At least the scale was human, there were only five floors. But the hallway was depressing, there were municipal-looking tiles on the floor, which showed footprints of dirt; the lighting was poor. And there wasn't an elevator. Liesel, with her knee hurting, had to walk up three flights of stairs. Their steps made a loud, hollow sound underfoot, everything echoed. There were galleries or corridors running off the stairwell, with four or five doors on each floor. A woman was sitting on her suitcase outside one of them. She appeared to be roughly Karen's age but dressed like a much younger person—she had heavy boots on, and black jeans, and a man's plaid shirt. She was slightly overweight but also looked strong and well, even after her long flight, and had made herself comfortable on the suitcase and didn't seem impatient or annoyed.

"Somebody let me in, so I figured I might as well lug this stuff up here," she said, pushing herself up, with her hands on her knees.

"I'm a jerk," Karen told her and gave her a hug. "This is Liesel, she's a trouper."

This annoyed Liesel, too, but she got over it.

In fact, she was curious about the apartment, she was curious to see how someone like Karen Bartkowski lived. By which she meant a journalist for *The Village Voice*, a freelance writer in New York—a youngish or middle-aged woman without kids, who had made a life for herself in the city, doing more or less what she wanted. There was a kitchen with a dirty linoleum floor and a gate-legged table pushed up against one wall. On the other side, the window over the sink stood half-open, with pots of herbs ranged across the sill. Their leaves pushed against the dirty screen. Everything was dirty, but homey, too. The living room was crowded with plants and furniture.

Karen said, "It doesn't normally look like this. My aunt died and I'm the only one left in New York, so I guess that makes me the big winner. I couldn't bring myself to give this stuff away."

"Which is my couch?" her friend said.

"You can have the bedroom."

"Don't be silly, I'm not kicking you out."

"I don't mind, let's talk about it later. I don't mind sharing either."

Liesel had to admit, they were good friends, nice people.

The woman's name was Pam, she was a photographer. Karen made tea and then they carried it outside, which meant going up more stairs, and onto the roof, which was split into different sections. There were deck chairs and grills and bicycles, Astroturf carpets, a metal coffee table, rusted and peeling, and all kinds of pots and plants. It was turning into a nice day, getting warmer; you could hear the traffic passing on the streets below, but you could also hear birds, a plane went by overhead, and Karen pointed to the wide brick wall of an old apartment building next door and said that sometimes in the summer they projected movies onto it.

Pam worked with video as well and had brought her camera along. Karen started the interview again. Pam filmed them. Liesel felt self-conscious at first, but she also found it pleasant, sitting on the cluttered rooftop, drinking tea and talking about herself, about her childhood. But she also felt excluded from something, she felt like a visitor. She thought maybe Pam and Karen had things to catch up on and she was in the way. But they assured her, no, they were very interested in what she had to say, Pam, too, and somehow this made Liesel feel old as well as flattered. She kept talking.

Afterward, on her way out, they stopped by the apartment again, so that Liesel could use the bathroom and pick up her purse. "So what do you do when you come to New York?"

"I don't know yet," Pam said. "We'll think of something."

She had a gallery in New York, she had an agent, there were people she needed to see—people she liked, but these were also business relationships. She looked forward to seeing them but she looked forward to seeing people like Karen more.

"What do you mean, people *like* me?" Karen asked. "How many are there?"

"Just you," Pam told her. Also, she wanted to visit the museums. San Diego had some great museums, too, but not like New York.

Karen walked Liesel down to the lobby. She checked her mailbox and held the door. She said, "I don't know whether to hug you or shake your hand. I'm going to hug you," and Liesel had to respond with an arm to her embrace. She had never much liked the confident way women claim each other, especially American women.

She said, "Do you know when the piece will come out?"

"Hard to say. My editor there can be a little tricky to pin down. I'll let you know. The video is great, by the way. That really helps."

And then Liesel was in the street, on her own again—she had forgotten to ask directions to the subway. She looked up and down and decided to walk toward the busier intersection, toward the traffic. But that doesn't always work in New York, the subway stations can be hard to find. Part of her thought, just get in a cab, but she knew Bill wouldn't like it, and she also wanted to prove to herself she could get around New York. Somehow the flavor of the women's friendship, Karen's apartment, the sense she had of the day ahead of them, with nothing to do and nowhere to be, maybe they would talk about men or go to a bar in the early afternoon, made her want to find her own way home. Something about the whole experience had unsettled her, she couldn't tell what.

She reached the corner and looked around—she could never distinguish north from south in Manhattan. Bill would correct her and say, uptown or down. Anyway, the cross street signs were too far for her to see. But she started walking and told herself, it's nice to be in a city, there are things to look at, shops and people. This is the reason you want to move here. If the numbers go up, it's up. She passed East 4th, and thought, at least I'm heading in the right direction, but she didn't notice any subway signs. It amused her always, the way corner stores in Manhattan called themselves delicatessens, when all they had were a few big slabs of dry cheese under a glass counter, and some sliced bologna. She came to a park or square, one of these New York parks made up mostly of tall trees and stony paths, and fenced-off bits with flowers. But there were grassy areas, too, people were sunbathing. By this point it was half past twelve, she was tired and hungry, sweating lightly, which made her eyes sting, so she took off her glasses and put them on again, feeling both anxious and slightly exhilarated.

There was nothing to stop her from getting something to eat, and, in fact, several cafés and restaurants overlooked the park. Some of them even had tables on the sidewalk. Bill disliked eating outside, he felt the cold, bugs bothered him, he wanted to concentrate on the food. She crossed over the street and walked past a pizza place and then a kind of brunchy place—someone had put flowers in jam jars on all of the tables, blue and yellow irises, but the flowers turned out to be plastic. It didn't matter, she sat down. Whenever you do this kind of thing, talk about yourself, about a book, for publicity, afterward there's a kind of letdown. Not a letdown exactly, but you get a little wave of performance anxiety, you want somebody to say, well done, you were great. But even if they do, you don't believe them; and even if you do believe them, you feel a kind of distaste for your own self-presentation; a self-distaste. Just the way Karen had said, at the end, my editor can be kind of tricky—as if you were asking *her* for a favor. When really, she had contacted *me*. And suddenly the notion occurred to Liesel (she couldn't tell how crazy it was) that Karen was working on spec, without a commission, hoping to place her interview in *The Village Voice*, or somewhere else. Which is why she also said, the video would "really help." Even when she said it this struck Liesel as odd.

A waiter should have come by now. But then a girl stopped at her table with a sweating plastic pitcher full of ice water and poured her some, and Liesel said, "Can I have a menu?" and the girl took out a dirty sheet of paper from her apron.

"Wait a minute," Liesel told her, looking in her purse for her reading glasses. "Don't go anywhere."

She ordered an omelet and a glass of apple juice, for the sugar. The apple juice arrived very quickly. There was a fair amount of traffic in the street, it was quite loud, you could see the park only between moving cars. People going in and coming out of the gates, a few of them on rollerblades, others carrying musical instruments or their lunch in a bag. But still it was very pleasant to sit on the sidewalk and watch them. Especially when the food came, an acceptable omelet. Bill hated eating at this kind of place. But he was getting better. Sometimes he sat with her and didn't order anything, and then he finished her food, when she said that she'd had enough. In fact, she was hungry now and ate everything, even the little salad on the side. It didn't matter much about the interview. You thought you were going to have a glamorous experience and instead what you had was . . . But actually there was a kind of glamour. The two childless women in their forties, the roof garden, Karen's apartment where she lived alone, only four or five blocks from this pretty park, in the middle of a lively neighborhood, and maybe what Liesel felt was left out of it.

Afterward, she had a coffee and took out her map. The nearest subway was on 14th Street, about ten blocks away. She could make it that far, she felt okay. And when she reached the station she took the cab receipt out of her purse and threw it away—a gesture toward something, who knows what.

But when she got home, over an hour later, Liesel almost burst into tears. Her eyes filled. It always surprised her, it struck her afresh each time, the pleasure she got from seeing her children. The pleasure it seemed to give them— Susie especially, who had sentimental feelings about family. She was sitting on a sofa with her son Ben, a likable kid with glasses; they were doing *The Times* crossword together, with the newspaper spread out across the coffee table, over the art books. Both of them stood up when Liesel came through the elevator doors. "The first thing I need is the toilet," Liesel told them, setting her purse on the floor. When she came out again, Susie put her arms around her mother, and then Ben, rather dutifully, took his turn. At ten years old, he was tall for his age, and a little too old to hug her childishly. But he tried and Liesel was touched. She didn't see him often, they didn't know each other well.

"Where are the others?" Liesel asked, but didn't listen to the answer. She meant David, Susie's husband, and her younger son, William. Maybe they had gone out already.

Jean stood in the background awkwardly, barefoot with crazy hair. She had gone to bed after a shower and just gotten up.

"Are you okay?" she said to Liesel. "How did it go?"

"I'm fine, I'm tired. It went fine. I got a little lost, that's all. I need a nap."

"How did what go?" Susie asked.

But explaining herself was more than Liesel had the energy for. She started and then stopped. She said, "I'm really very glad you're here, but I'm going to bed." She went to the kitchen and poured herself water in a mug—the glasses were on a higher shelf. She drank some and took the rest to her bedroom. Susie sort of followed her around, Ben followed Susie. In the doorway, Susie said, "Sleep tight. Do you want us to wake you up?"

"In an hour, maybe. If you don't hear from me."

But she couldn't fall asleep right away. Normally at home she napped on the rug outside her study. The hard wood floor underneath made her feel that sleeping in the middle of the day was an act of virtue. But she didn't feel comfortable in someone else's apartment, lying on the floor. And climbing into bed with her clothes on felt dirty and sad. So she lay on top of the sheets, with her shoes off. Daylight streamed in through the opened curtains. She stood up to draw them but that turned out to be worse.

Light glowed around the edges, it was like sitting in a closet. She opened them again, pulling on the curtain cord,
drawing back the radiance from the pillows where she
wanted to put her head—a tug and the light shifted, creak-
ing. A little more. Sunshine on her lap she didn't mind.

But if you can't sleep, you can't sleep. You can't think
yourself into sleeping. There were things she had said to
Karen that she wished she had said differently or not at all.
Now on the video she would always repeat them, exactly
the same way, like a dinner party bore. Mutti used to grow
her own tobacco, to save money. She was very resourceful
but also suspected it wasn't good for you, and gave her
children extra pocket money if they could tell her honestly they hadn't smoked at the end of the week. I suppose
we thought it was glamorous, we were dumb kids. She
told this story in front of her grandchildren, and afterward
Susie took her angrily aside. What were you thinking, she
said? Liesel felt angry, too, and a little embarrassed. Smoking is a very bad thing to do, I made that clear. For some
reason she mentioned this incident to Karen on camera.
She meant, it's funny, the different things different generations get worked up about. Americans are very attached
to the idea of purity, there are no half measures, you're
either a smoker or not, everything is a potential source
of identification. When she was a young woman it was
much stranger not to smoke at all. People didn't worry
so much about what camp they belonged to. She realized
later, this was a stupid way of putting it. That's the trouble
with interviews, you can't edit anything out, you have no
control.

Also, they stir things up and it takes a while afterward for them to settle down again. You keep talking in your head, intimately, to a stranger. You say things like, it's upsetting, none of my children knew my mother very well. Lying on top of the strange sheets, in the strange bedroom—in your son's girlfriend's ex-husband's apartment.

Mutti died when Nathan was nine or ten. She had been ill with colon cancer for over a year, and Liesel flew out at spring break on her own to visit her. It turned out to be an extremely important trip, a kind of turning point. She was thirty-eight years old, she still spoke English with a German accent. Her parents had retired to Bonn, to a nice suburban house, near some woods, with a large garden of its own; but it was not the house she grew up in. Mutti had bought a new dog, to keep her husband busy after her death. But the dog was young and difficult—you forget how much trouble they make in the first few years. It was a mistake. Mutti was mostly bedridden by the time Liesel left, but they could still talk optimistically about seeing each other again over the summer; it wasn't completely out of the question.

When Liesel landed at the Austin airport and stepped outside into the wall of Texas heat, she felt an almost overwhelming sense of being a stranger, which persisted in the presence of her husband, and even her children. (Later she took some comfort from these feelings.) The temperature outside, even in the shade, was ninety-five degrees—humid heat. Just walking from the airport terminal to the car put you in a sweat. Bill picked her up in the old Volvo, which didn't have air-conditioning. He had started growing his beard by that point and kept scratching his neck. The leather of the car seats was almost too hot to sit on. Germany seemed a long way away.

Two weeks later Mutti died. When Liesel broke the news to her children, only Susie cried. Nathan tried to explain to her that he didn't want to pretend to be upset, because that would be worse; but he didn't really know his grandmother well enough to feel much. Paul was just a four-year-old boy, you couldn't explain anything to him, you couldn't force his attention; and anyway, at that stage, he took his cues from Nathan. Jean was just a baby. But Susie cried and cried. Of course, this was also a bid for attention—the second child, pushed out by two more babies. Wanting sympathy. Eventually even Liesel lost patience with her. She wanted to say, she *did* say, it was *my* mother who died. Yet it meant something to her, see-ing Susie in tears, having to console her, and thinking, this is what gets passed on, the role gets passed on, you have to do for them what she did for you.

Of all her children, Susie resembled Mutti the most. She had Mutti's large eyes and brittle, slightly curly brown hair, down to her shoulders, and Mutti's pretty-enough face. For a woman of her time, Mutti had a very modern outlook, she was forward-thinking; but somehow, in their resemblance, Susie sometimes came across as old-fashioned. She was a good cook, she was a good mother, they had a nice house, tastefully cluttered, but Bill worried about her career. Liesel did, too. When Susie met David they were both junior faculty. David made tenure but at some point between the births of Ben and William, Susie had taken herself off the clock. She said it made everybody's life much easier. She could still teach if she wanted to, and she did teach, on an adjunct basis. A few courses each year, for the money and something to do, now that William was in school full-time. But you reach a point in your life when you realize that some things matter more than others. She just didn't want to do what you have to do to get tenure. Let David spend his time at conferences. If it's a choice between that and seeing the kids . . . then it's not a difficult choice.

The house is what she put her energy into, a barn-red saltbox about half an hour outside of Hartford. It was almost three hundred years old and needed endless work. The chimney leaked, some of the windows were original, only certain skilled people could restore whatever went wrong, and Susie had developed relationships with local tradesmen and craftsmen, often interesting types, but the kind who need a lot of management. The plot was over three acres; she had turned it into an English garden, with tulips in the grass, wild borders, everything always on the verge of overgrowing, a vegetable patch, staked and veiled with nets, a dirty greenhouse. When you came round for lunch, she put cut flowers on the window ledge and on the table, the salad was from the garden, there were home-made jams and breads. She sent the boys out to get logs from the woodshed, she lit the fire. All of this took work. The fact that she made it seem natural, the overproduction of benevolent neglect, this was part of the work; and the time that Susie spent on the house was time she couldn't spend on other things.

When she was younger, she wanted to be an artist, which Bill had discouraged. Now she talked about writing children's books. It seemed to Bill the kind of thing you do when you don't know what to do. When you're restless and bored and your kids are growing up. But okay, let her try it, he thought. Let her do something. We should do something. People were talking next door, everything blended together. Liesel felt happy enough just listening to them. I mean, it's a sunny day, we've got all afternoon, we're in the middle of New York. When Mom wakes up. Someone in a parked car outside was playing their stereo with the windows open, loud enough Liesel could hear the melody, but the words were just noise.

—

It's about a half-hour train ride to Yonkers, much of it along the river. You come out of the city, off the island, and countryside appears, green strips of landscape, woody bluffs, brown water, telephone lines, you can see New Jersey. Stacked up behind you, northern Manhattan fades away. Liesel liked the train, she liked looking out the window, but Bill felt the confinement. He got bored. In Texas you get used to driving everywhere, you live in the car. He tried to play a game of solitaire on the empty seat next to him, but the train shook too much. He tried to read a book but felt distracted by various things, including the view. By other things, too. The sound of the wheels on the tracks, metal on metal. It's true, though (he was talking to Liesel in his head), you get these young-man feelings on a train, you could go any-where. Or see your sister.

At Yonkers he picked up his empty bag and emerged into warm late-August sunshine. The station was on a bridge. A river ran under it, or hardly moved, covered in rocks and reeds. The city had recently invested in its municipal spaces. There was wide clean pavement with bicycle racks and benches lined up against the river railings. The blind windows of a new office building reflected the sunshine; you had to squint against them. Bill stood for a second on the sidewalk, sweating lightly. Rose had taken him to Polanka's deli before, but that was three years ago, after picking him up from the station. She offered to pick him up again, but he said, don't bother. I like walking. But you don't know the way. I remember, I'll figure it out. And he set off in a good mood, with just enough low-level anxiety to keep it afloat.

Ever since Rose's divorce she had been in decline. She had put on weight. For years he argued with her about this. You can't eat your way out of loneliness. But, of course, she told him, what do you mean, eat my way. I'm always on some diet or other, you've seen that for yourself. Which was perfectly true. And later, when the doctor diagnosed her with a thyroid problem, she felt vindicated—she called him up on the phone. It's a condition, she said. It's got a name. Then she read it out to him: Hashimoto's thy-roiditis. Bill believed her, but he also didn't totally believe her. He also thought, whatever you've got, weakness of will played a part, unhappiness played a part. For none of which he blamed her. When he used to watch Paul playing

tennis in junior high he couldn't stop thinking, come to
net, come to net. As a father you have to repress certain
insights. It was the same with Rose—there are preventable
mistakes, there are correctable habits. You want to be able
to control what you can't control, out of love.

But you can eat your way *into* loneliness, that you can
do. You can surround yourself with fatty tissue. They
treated her with levothyroxine, a little pill like an aspirin,
which she took once a day. Her TSH levels were under
three, the doctors seemed satisfied. But still she kept the
weight on, she felt slack and slow and had a hard time
getting out of the house. They spoke on the phone once a
week and most of what they talked about was their kids.
Rose had a daughter, who lived in Evanston, Illinois. She
had wanted a large family but never expressed the slight-
est envy of Bill and was endlessly interested in all his
children, in Jean and Paul and Susie and Nathan. She was
a warm curious person and complained very little. When
they were kids together (Rose was three years older),
Bill would lie in her bed on Saturday mornings and she
would read to him. Whatever he wanted, comic books,
even the sports page. He loved her body—they bathed
together, too. She used a bar of soap or a toothpaste tube
and pretended to have a penis. So they could be alike, it
was all a big joke. She had sensitive skin, like Jean, and
turned red in the hot bath. When he lay across her lap he
slipped off in the soapy water. And now just the thought
of her body made him physically turn away or avert his
gaze, out of sympathy. He actually lowered his head.

When he first told his father about his engagement (they

knew about Liesel and had met her and disapproved), his father and mother drove him to Pittsburgh to see one of his cousins, who was a rabbi. This cousin was a persuasive and sympathetic man. He was supposed to talk Bill out of it. He was supposed to say, how can you marry a woman who is not only Christian but German? As if these things don't matter, history doesn't matter, religion doesn't matter. As if you're above all that. Bill said, okay, I'll go along. He was willing to do whatever his parents wanted him to do, apart from the one thing they wanted him to do, which was break it off. So they drove up together in his father's Lincoln Continental. In those days, in that car, it took them eight hours. They set off after breakfast and stopped for lunch at some Penn State student diner. They ate supper with the rabbi and stayed the night, and the next day drove back—watching from the window the Pennsylvania farmland and listening to a Dodgers–Phillies double-header on the radio. Bill had kind of a good time. He was twenty-seven years old and about to go on the job market, after finishing his PhD. He was about to get married. Who knew where they might end up (Texas!). This was the last extended period of time he spent with his father, who was hard-working, patient, self-disciplined, and shy. Later, after he died, Bill's mother had a stroke and came to live with them for several years. But all of that was in the unimaginable distant future, which you don't have to imagine because it happens anyway.

Rose probably suffered most in the fallout. She hated any kind of family strife. Once she admitted to him, I hoped Cousin Seymour would talk you out of it. I don't know why, because I always liked Liesel, but I didn't think Mom and Dad would forgive you. But she came to the wedding anyway, at The Statler Hotel in Ithaca. Wedding isn't quite right; Bill and Liesel walked in and they walked out married a half-hour later. Two of their Cornell buddies signed the registry. (Both Jews, as it happens, a couple who later married and then divorced, after which everybody fell out of touch.) Rose got all dressed up. She was the only family on either side and wanted to make an effort. Bill wore what he wore to teach in, chinos and shirt and jacket, but he took off the jacket, because it was a hot day. Liesel had on a long, pleated skirt. But Rose did the business, pink dress, flowers in her hair, and felt silly the whole time, emotional and uncomfortable, because it showed she didn't know her brother as well as these other people, who got the tone right without trying. On the long Greyhound bus ride back to New York the next day, she broke down in tears. Her little brother. She told Bill that part, too.

Nepperhan Avenue is a busy, undistinguished street, with a highway frontage road curving off it on the far side, pushing traffic in the opposite direction. A concrete-block wall, growing with the access lane as it peels away, separates the higher ground above it from the street level, where Bill was walking. He could see the cheap houses and apartment buildings above him, while sycamores grew out against the chain-link fence. Maybe there were kids whose backyards ended in that sheer drop, kicking their balls against the fence. And everywhere, the sound of cars, which bounced between the frontage wall and the buildings on the other side. Not pleasant walking, and Polanka's wasn't the kind of place you'd look at twice unless you knew about it—two cheap storefronts under a fifties block of apartments at the beginning of a commercial strip. His kids always told him, you're a little crazy, but this is the kind of place he liked. As a teenager, he used to help out in the stockroom of his uncles' store. That's what the Essingers did when they came to America. Sell groceries.

The signs were in Polish, but the staff looked Latino. At the back of the shop, through an open door, Bill could see metal racks hung with pale sausages. Hundreds of them, like loose fingers. Under the counter, there were metal trays of food, potato salad and something oily with carrots, goulash, meatballs in tomato sauce, a party platter with fanned-out cold cuts, wrapped so tightly the Saran Wrap had pulls like runs in pantyhose. On a warm afternoon, the shop had a smoky locker-room smell. Various breads, dark and white, lay on the countertop, and there were more loaves stacked in floury baskets sitting on shelves behind. One of the guys was busy making a sandwich for somebody, thickly slicing the tomatoes and laying them flat. "Not too much mayo," the customer said—a fat kid with his first mustache, unshaved. "That's what my mom said. But, you know."

He had a yarmulke at the back of his head, almost falling down, shiny blue with a Mets logo stitched into it. Bill ordered a mix of things, including two pieces of crumb cake and a bag of powdered cookies. Then he walked out, blinking, into the sunshine.

Rose had a house on Prescott Street, overlooking a park. About a fifteen-minute walk through residential neighborhoods. By this point Bill was tired and hungry – he ate a cookie as he walked, and then another. Really it was too far to walk, he should have taken a cab; he was putting something off. The houses depressed him. Some of them were boarded up. Around Nepperhan, among the shopping streets, there were handsome pale brick apartment blocks, turn of the century. But leaving these behind, he saw crowded row-houses with cheap siding. Most of them looked lopsided, they had weak foundations. The roads needed fixing, too, the asphalt was cracked, even the repairs looked temporary. You could hear highway noise from the sidewalk, all those junctions between Saw Mill and Yonkers Avenue. He couldn't help it, it upset him, the thought of his sister, spending her life indoors, while everybody she knew moved to White Plains or Rockland County. Or Florida. The only person she saw regularly was her cleaner, Rosario, a wonderful woman, who also assisted in other ways – she sometimes did a little shopping for her, she changed the sheets. Rose and Rosario. People adapt, what else are they going to do.

Sometimes he got on her case to sell up, too, and move somewhere with a bit of street life. Something to look at from the window or just so that walking out the door gave her places to go. Restaurants and supermarkets. So she didn't have to get in the car. But this was the house of her marriage, it was the house where Judith grew up, if you took those things away from her, she said . . .

What, he said.

I don't know.

She was sitting in the front room when he walked up the driveway, sitting in the window, and he waited for her to get up and come to the door. He didn't need to ring.

"Billy," she said.

The way she stood, leaning back slightly, thick-legged, you could tell she had trouble with her knees. Nobody called him Billy anymore. He put his arm lightly across her shoulder. The Essingers were not a physical family, they were talkers not touchers. And then he waited again for her to turn around—it was like watching a vehicle turn—and followed her slowly down the dark hallway, checking his stride. She sat at the kitchen table while he laid out the food. He took plates from the dishwasher (which had recently been run), he filled glasses from the faucet, waiting for the cloudiness to resolve itself and then filling them again. He put two kielbasas in the oven, and while they were baking he emptied the rest of the dishwasher and stacked what he couldn't find places for on the counter.

"I like this kitchen," he said.

There was a view over the sink of the boxed-in yard, which had gone to seed, but not unattractively. Rose just didn't have the energy or money. Blighted roses grew against the wooden fence. The grass looked long and thin, like thinning hair; it was seeding, too. Dead ivy, still clinging to the windowpanes, blocked some of the sunlight but also cast pretty shadows. Linoleum counters, milky with age, a few burn rings. The faucet dripped, onto the metal sink. On the shelf with her cookbooks, next to them, Rose kept her cereal boxes, which were also bright and decorative in their way—yellow Cheerios, purple Raisin Bran, Frosted Flakes, sky blue. Judith, her daughter, had a four-year-old boy, and when she visited, Rose liked to spoil him with sweet things, but after he left the boxes went stale and she couldn't bear to throw them away.

It looked like their mother's kitchen at home, in Port Jervis. In their first house, the one they were born into. When Rose was thirteen and Billy was ten, they moved. The new house had a funny position, on the corner of Roosevelt and Watkins—its yard backed onto Roosevelt, while the front door opened onto Watkins. But they listed their address as Roosevelt, which was a well-known avenue, with grand houses, a very good address, and for the rest of his childhood Bill had to suppress a slight embarrassment whenever he told someone where he lived. He never liked the new house as much as the old one. For one thing, he loved the old kitchen, which had a hanging lamp in the middle and a table for four underneath, where you could squeeze six people, especially if the extras were kids. Kids like Lisa Liebowitz and Kelly Hanes, Rose's friends, and Mike Schultz, who played shortstop on Bill's Little League team. In the evening, under that lamp, his mother taught him to read. He did his homework while she washed clothes in the sink. The new house had a laundry room and a dining room.

Rose, peeling the lid off the potato salad, said, "Judith's going through something right now, I don't know what to call it. If we were Catholics maybe you'd say a crisis of faith. But it's hard for me to do anything. She's too far away."

Her daughter had moved to the Midwest for college and never come back. At Northwestern, she studied biology. Judith wanted to be a doctor and got into med school in Chicago. Three years later, she changed her mind and dropped out. The coursework involved a lot of memorization; it was like a factory, she said. You pick your little part of the process, you do things over and over. This isn't why she went into medicine, to be a cog in the machine. After that, she bummed around for a while, living with friends, working as a secretary at a medical clinic in Jefferson Park. Wasting her life, as she said herself. She also had a lot of unhappiness with men, some of them Jews, but mostly not. Eventually she applied to law school. I miss getting grades, she told her mother. Northwestern accepted her, and she even made it through two and a half semesters, before dropping out—to get married.

Somewhere along the way she had decided that the cause of her unhappiness was religious, that she had drifted away from her faith. Northwestern had a strong Hillel community, and one thing led to another. She changed her diet and lost weight, she started covering her head. Whatever Judith did, she had to be the best, and that also meant being the best Jew. She let herself be persuaded to try a matchmaker. Two dates later, she was in love. For months this was all she could talk about. How she had spent ten years on the dating circuit and never met an intelligent, decent, clean American man. Rose found the whole thing extremely upsetting. But for a while, it's true, Judith seemed happier. She married the guy, a doctor, as it happens, who seemed perfectly nice, with predictably old-fashioned views; but patient and gentle. They bought a house in West Ridge; they had a beautiful boy. For the first few years, Judith said, she was busier than she had ever been in her whole life, including med school.

But now her son was four and she was getting restless again. She didn't like the school they were sending Michael to—she didn't like what they taught him. A very restricted education. This is not how she'd been brought up.

"I could have told her that from the beginning," Rose said to her brother. They were picking at the food while the sausages blistered in the oven. Pickles and potato salad, with hot mustard. Wiping the dressing up with the soft rye. "Really the trouble is, she's bored. They wanted a large family, but it's not happening. If there's something she should pray for, it's a baby, but even that is only a short-term solution."

When Rose stood up, to get salt, she pushed at the table with both hands. Bill could feel it in his groin, watching her move; that's how it hurt him. A sharp, very intimate pain.

"I put on a dress for you," she said, sitting down again. It was blue with white shapes on it, like little moons. She wore it over thick dark tights so you couldn't see her legs. He stood up to turn off the oven and used a dish towel to lift out the pan of kielbasas.

"There are more condiments in the fridge. Mustard is fine with me. I shouldn't complain—you listen to her talk, and everything she says is very reasonable. It always has been. She starts something and it turns out to be not what she wanted. So she quits and starts over. After a while, like this, you don't get anywhere. You just get older. But this thing she's started now is a little harder to quit than the others. You can't drop out of motherhood. There's something else, too. Alex keeps bugging me." Alex, her ex-husband, worked in pharmaceuticals and lived in Santa Fe. He had married again, a schoolteacher named Guadalupe, and they had two girls, twins. "He wants Judith to have some kind of contact with the girls, he wants them to know Michael. It doesn't make sense to me but all these kids are roughly the same age. What can I tell him, she doesn't want to. But it puts me in a strange position, especially since, on this front, I think he's right. Kids are just kids. I'm pissed off with Alex but that's his fault not theirs. I like to think Judith is taking my side, but that's not why. He's raising the girls Catholic, like their mother. Judith thinks it would be confusing for Michael. What can you say to that? It *is* confusing."

The kielbasas were good, but he should have left them in longer. Bill liked the fat too hot to eat and the skin almost burned. But he couldn't just sit there listening, he had to do something. Also, otherwise you fill up on potato salad. He cut a sausage in half and folded the meat in a slice of rye, where it stained the bread. Before each bite, he dipped the end in mustard. He said, "So what do you tell him?"

"I tell him she's thirty-five years old. You can't make her do anymore what she doesn't want to do. Go out and see her yourself, show up at her door. But he's right. Judith's husband wouldn't like it. I think there's a very real possibility he wouldn't let them in."

"She would let him in."

"I'm not so sure. But it doesn't really matter. Alex is lazy. He complains but he doesn't . . . I don't mean to sound critical. The truth is, I like talking to him these days. How's Paul?"

"Nervous, a little on edge. He wants to retire, but he's not thinking straight. A tennis player has a long life to be retired in. I mention this in case you want me to see if I can get you a ticket. Tomorrow could be his last match."

But Rose only looked at him and looked down. She had a fat bottom lip; when she was younger, a teenager and a young woman, boys liked her mouth, which was full and sensual. Now, with her heavy chin and thick nose, her cheeks, pale and red, her soft thin hair, her mouth expressed apology, shame, pity, and good-humored self-deprecation.

"I'd like to, Billy. But it's a long way. I don't like sitting on those narrow seats. My legs swell up. If I can get it on the television, I'll watch it here."

"I don't think it will be on TV."

For some reason, this killed the conversation, at least temporarily. They sat like that, eating. Bill refilled his water glass—he drank a lot with meals. He had shaved that morning, under his beard, and his Adam's apple looked a little raw. When he drank, it moved. There was mayonnaise in his mustache; he wiped his mouth. Eventually Rose said, "I didn't tell you, but Nathan came to visit me, with the girls. All of your children are very attentive. Some friends of his with a big house in Brooklyn were throwing a Fourth of July party. He said I was on the way, he was just stopping by. He's a good kid, coming to see an old woman. That Julie has a head on her, right? Though what she did to her hair, I don't know. Everybody wants to grow up. The way she talks, like a professor. Nathan, I remember, was just the same. Always looking for somebody to explain something to. It runs in the family."

Bill said, "I'm worried about him, too."

"What for?"

"I don't know. Nothing maybe. But he's getting mixed up in something political, which I don't much like. There are people from the Justice Department trying to woo him. He wrote an opinion, which they think lets them off the hook. I disagree—with the opinion, I mean, but it's hard for us to have these conversations. He thinks it's personal for me. Professional jealousy. Maybe he's right."

"All of this is beyond me," Rose said. "You know what I hear when you talk like this? Success, that's what I hear. I'm proud of all of you. My little brother and his many children."

Bill had told himself beforehand not to mention it, but somehow the association set him off. Also, with Rose in front of him, just across the table, he couldn't pass up a chance to give her pleasure.

"Nathan went with us to see a couple of apartments yesterday," he said. "Liesel, when she retires, wants to have a place in the city. She says Texas gets too hot, she wants to be able to walk outside. And then there's Paul in New York and Nathan in Boston. Susie in Hartford. The grandkids."

Rose stopped eating. Her wide eyes could still look girlish—she made vivid expressions.

"Well, we looked at them," Bill said.

"Where were they?"

"Upper West Side. One of them around the corner from Aunt Ethel's."

"I'm not going to say anything," Rose said, and Bill averted his face. When they were kids, they talked about opening a shop together. This was Rose's idea, it was one of their games, and she dressed him in an apron and bossed him around. He loved it. They stuck prices on their mother's cans of food, five cents, ten cents. The coffee table in their living room served as a shop counter. Mother came in and pretended to buy things from them, handing over real change. She sometimes had to fight to get it back.

"It's something Liesel wants," Bill said. "I don't know. She wants to retire, I don't. She likes big cities. It doesn't make sense to me how much everything costs. For four rooms, five rooms. But I guess these days we don't need much more."

Afterward, he cleaned up, rinsing the plates thoroughly and lining them up in the dishwasher. There was half a kielbasa left on Rose's plate, and Bill asked her where she kept the aluminum foil. But Rose shook her head. "For this kind of thing, at Yom Kippur, I add a few lines to the Al Chet." And she recited, in her synagogue voice, *"For the sins we have committed by throwing away leftovers. For the sins we have committed by not making stock from the chicken carcass. For the sins we have committed by opening a new jar of jam . . ."* Meanwhile he scraped the sausage into the trash can and took a piece of steel wool to the baking pan—some of the fats had burned into a crust. Rose watched him, sitting down with the chair pushed away from the table. "You're a good brother," she said. "I'll drive you to the station."

"That's okay. I don't mind walking."

"Otherwise I don't get out of the house, I sit around all day going crazy."

"What should I do with the crumb cake?"

"Take it."

"There's no hurry. I can make a pot of tea."

But Rose said, "I'll drop you at the station and come home and have a nap. It's something to look forward to."

Before they left, he used the bathroom. Bill had had prostate surgery a few years before, and every time he went on a trip, even a short one, he took a preemptive leak. The toilet had a padded seat; the skin over the cushioning was cracking. Rose used an air freshener, Woodland Escape, a little lime-green unit attached to the wall, but the liquid inside had run out. He looked at himself in the mirror (he looked like his father) and then tugged at the edge to check the medicine cabinet. But there wasn't much there—it was the downstairs bathroom. Just an open bag of Bic razors and a toothpaste tube. As if she sometimes entertained male guests, people who stayed the night but slept in the spare room. Maybe he had left them there himself.

In the Buick, he said to her, which he always said, "How are you for money? Can I give you something?" And she said, "A little would help."

With Judith unhappy, really in bad shape, Rose wanted to fly out to see her. But flights cost money, and everything ended up costing a little extra for Rose. A cab to the airport, porters. She could only travel in a business-class seat.

She worried about thrombosis. Before you know it, just to see your daughter, to see your grandson, costs two, three thousand dollars. That's the price of admission. Judith was trying to get Michael into a different school—she wanted at least to check out the alternatives, but there was resistance from his father. If Rose was around, it might make a difference. Everybody resents their mother-in-law anyway, she said. I can take the heat, I got nothing to lose.

"I'll call Bryce Newman tomorrow," Bill said. "Tell him to wire it over."

Rose blushed. "Thank you. I don't know what I'd do . . ."

The car was full of those coupons you get in Sunday's *Times*. There were newspapers on the rubber matting at his feet, along with muffin wrappers, empty juice bottles, even a box of Kleenex. When he got in, she reached over and swept everything onto the floor. "Excuse the way I live," she told him. Climbing out, he took some of the junk with him—there was a trash can by the station. "It's no trouble," he said, and Rose waited by the curb for him to come back. They didn't kiss, but she reached over and took his hand; her palm was soft and very warm. Traffic built up behind her, but she didn't seem to notice.

"Okay," he said, and squeezed her hand and let go.

She leaned across the empty seat. "Tell Nathan to send me the links to those apartments."

He pushed the door shut and watched her drive off. Then he was alone again—at the hot point of the afternoon, around three o'clock. People were coming out of the station, a train must have arrived, and he waited for the concourse to clear before going in.

On the journey back into Manhattan, he watched the view reverse itself—the green strips of landscape, the woody bluffs, the river, following the telephone lines, running toward Inwood, where the architecture greeted you like a postcard. He had forgotten to leave Rose the bag of cookies. From time to time he ate one, and licked the powder off his fingers. He needed the sugar hit; he felt low. And in his head, he kept up the conversation with Liesel he had started on the train ride out. You have to understand that for me moving here is like going backward, it's not a simple thing to do, it stirs up various associations.

But he also withheld from Liesel a part of what he meant, he didn't explain himself completely. Seeing Rose, wandering through her neighborhood (the houses in need of repair, the roads pot-holed, everything scraped at and knocked around by the long Northeastern winters), he also saw Texas in a new light. As an escape from all that. From the narrowness of his childhood. From the two sets of plates and the Friday night dinners, from the Hebrew you could speak but not really understand. But also from something else, something like bad luck, which was connected in his mind to Jewishness. Immigrants working hard to climb up the ladder. The grocery business his uncles started had expanded. There used to be Essinger Brothers stores all over the state, selling Astor Coffee and Pillsbury Flour. Their kids became lawyers and doctors and accountants. But the ones who stayed, the cousins who stuck around, in Middletown and Port Jervis and Yonkers, had retained somehow an air of struggling against harsh conditions. There were medical issues; they put on weight; they got divorced. Maybe he still suffered from it, too, immigrant's luck. But in Texas, raised the way his kids were raised, the effects seemed diluted—and Nathan, if that thing doesn't . . . if his health holds up . . . might yet emerge clear of it altogether. Anyway, he didn't want to go back, which is what upset him, saying goodbye to his sister. It was a relief to get away.

—

S usie had no special love of Manhattan, but she liked the idea of spending the day with Ben. Even just sitting on the train with him, peeling an orange and sharing it while he read his book—this is something she had looked forward to. Maybe she should have pressed David harder to come along. In fact, he offered to come, he was good at offering, but for some reason, she said no, stay home with William (who had a slight cold). I want him completely recovered by the time school starts. What he doesn't need is a late night in New York.

But that wasn't the only reason, and the train ride gave her a couple of hours to think through the others. Ben was her firstborn, and you never really recover the concentrated, isolated intimacy of those early years. (Though you try. Sometimes, when he was in school, if she didn't have class, she napped in his bed; as the months wore on she got more and more tired.) In a week, he would start middle school. He still seemed to her very innocent, he *was* very innocent, but there was a kind of—not slyness, exactly—a kind of pleasantness, which he had inherited from his father and might later on conceal any number of thoughts and feelings. She didn't think it concealed anything yet; he was just good company. Even though he was reading, and absorbed in his book, he looked up from time to time and told her details about the plot. He wanted her to laugh at the bits he found funny. So she laughed, feeling false and friendly. It seemed to her like a game they were playing, where he pretended to want her approval, and she pretended to give it.

Outside the window, the view kept changing. Susie had a book along, too, one of her freshman English texts, but she didn't read it, she watched the view. And sometimes interrupted Ben to point things out. A school bus depot, all of them lined up like yellow pencils. When she was a kid somehow it seemed tremendously important for everyone to use number two yellow pencils. I don't even know what that means anymore. They passed a harbor with houses strung out along the shore, and she touched her son on the knee. "I think one of those is the Edelmans' place. Over there. Isn't that the island they rowed us out to last summer?"

There were waves in the bay, which reflected the sunlight and clouds, fighting it out above them; you could feel the wind in the trees, too. The houses looked like summer houses, not in great shape—their paint was peeling, you could see sheds and disused greenhouses in the backyards, which straggled and fell to the water.

"No, there wasn't any building on it."

"I don't remember. I thought there was."

What she really wanted to tell him, the way you might

tell an intimate friend, was just, I'm going to have a baby. Maybe you'll have a sister, but I don't really care. Boys are good, too. This is another reason she didn't want David along. She expected to have the conversation with her parents that weekend and thought it might be easier without him.

Ben's backpack, an army-green JanSport, was a present for starting middle school. (It was also his birthday the week after, but they wanted him to have it on the first day of class.) She had let him pack it himself, with toothbrush, toothpaste, underpants, socks, a spare T-shirt, a pair of shorts, a pair of sandals, and the AIA Guide to New York City, the fifth edition, which David had bought for him. When the train pulled into Grand Central, he hoisted it over his shoulders and waited swaying by the doors—he liked being first out. And she let him lead the way, her baby boy, about four foot eleven inches tall, pushing along with everybody else like a commuter. But then, under the great domed roof, with its deep tile-green night sky, they both stopped to look up; she wanted to hold his hand but refrained.

Afterward, they caught the shuttle to Times Square and wandered through more underground tunnels— unfinished-looking spaces, not quite for the public eye, but full of people—before beating the crush and pushing their way onto the uptown local. She watched Ben holding onto the pole, trying not to move or make eye contact, anonymizing himself, but at the same time taking everything in. So that you see your kid the way a stranger might see him, but with this double vision, knowing him, too, but seeing him somehow more clearly from the outside, a ten-year-old boy. When they stepped into the open air again, into the changeable summer's day, with Broadway at their back and the buildings rising everywhere around them, she said, "Sometimes I don't understand how people can live in this city."

"I guess a lot of people do."

He didn't want to say it but he was very happy to be there, in Manhattan with his mother. Just getting the subway with her, walking around. A doorman greeted them from the lobby of Michael's apartment. He was actually standing outside, under the awning, in cap and uniform, and moved aside to let them pass. The elevator opened straight into the living room. Ben loved the apartment, too, the parquet floor, the marble fireplace, the little balcony with its potted trees. Even the Tiffany lamps and claw-footed silk-upholstered furniture appealed to his sense of strangeness, of big city grandeur, though he had to fight the vague suspicion that his mother's taste didn't approve of these things. And he felt shy of his aunt, who was fresh from the shower and wearing a towel. "Come here," she said. "Give me a hug." Afterward, when she was dressed, Jean brought out the leftover babka from the kitchen and cut a few slices, one of which she offered to Ben on a plate with a glass of milk. Nobody had had any lunch.

"Is it all right if I read my book?" he asked his mother, who sat with a copy of *The New York Times* on her lap.

"You've been reading all morning," she said. "Jean is here. Let's talk."

But in the end she agreed to help him with the cross-word, something he had started to do with his father on weekends. From time to time he reached for a bite of the cake, stretching and leaning carefully over the plate, so the crumbs didn't leave a mess.

When Liesel came in, limping through the elevator doors, her brown face flushed and slightly sweaty, Susie felt a pang of something, conscience or sadness or love, she couldn't tell. Every time you see them they look older. You feel like, it's not your job to notice certain things about them, but you do it anyway. Also, she didn't know what Liesel would say about the baby. Her parents blamed David for the fact that her own career had taken a back seat. Somehow you have to protect yourself against their opinions. In the presence of her family she became aware of the existence inside her of ancient defenses—like the remains on a hillside of Roman fortifications, which you can just about make out from the lay of the land.

Part of what upset her is just how quickly Liesel went to bed. They talked for a few minutes, while her mother filled a mug of water at the kitchen sink, and then she retreated to her room. I haven't seen you since Christmas, eight months, Susie thought. But it's always like this, there's no point in minding it.

Instead she spent the afternoon arguing with Jean.

First they argued about calling Nathan—Susie wanted Ben to have someone to play with, someone his own age. "He never gets to see his cousins."

"What about me?" Jean said. "He never gets to see me. And I've been cooped up in this apartment all morning." Waiting for you, was the implication. "If we call Nathan, it's going to be another hour. Let's just have lunch."

But then they spent forty minutes wandering around the Upper West Side, looking for somewhere to eat—Jean had ideas about what was and was not acceptable. "I've counted them out," she said. "I've got twelve meals in New York before I fly home. The truth is, we should really go downtown. There's nothing here."

Finally Susie put her foot down. She was hungry, too, tired and pregnant (though Jean didn't know), frequently on the edge of tears. "Ben has to eat, he's ten years old, it's almost two o'clock, he has to eat," and they got bagels from Barney Greengrass and took them to the little park outside the Natural History Museum. Another six-block walk—more delay. But they had a nice enough meal, under the trees, and scattered some leftover bagel for the birds. Sparrows pecked at their feet, leaf shadows shifted in the wind. Afterward they had an argument about when Liesel would wake up, and if they could stop in the museum quickly, before going back to the apartment.

"She'll be upset if she wakes up and we're not there," Jean said.

"So why don't we call the apartment. Do you have the number?"

"I don't think she'll pick up the phone. It will just wake her up."

"You're not making sense. If she's still asleep, then what are we arguing about?"

"I don't know if she's asleep," Jean said.

"Well, why don't you go back, and Ben and I will just have a quick look."

"There is no quick look. It's a big museum. And thanks, by the way. It's nice to see you, too."

For some reason, they weren't getting along, and Susie couldn't figure out why. Maybe Jean was being defensive with her, maybe it was the other way around. Somehow it seemed that Ben was part of the problem. Jean was very nice to him but you also got the sense that organizing her day around Ben wasn't what she had in mind. "Liesel has my cell phone number," Susie told her. "If she wakes up and nobody's home, she'll just call me."

"She's not good with that kind of thing. She won't think of that."

"She calls me on my cell phone all the time."

Susie could wield the implications, too. You don't know what goes on, she was saying; you live in London. At least, this is what Jean heard.

By the time they got back to the apartment, hot and bothered and even a little sunburned, it was three o'clock. The sun had finally burned away the clouds, the air felt thick and close, like a laundry room or public showers, the hair on your skin responded to the moisture. But the lobby was air-conditioned and the apartment itself was pleasantly cool. Liesel sat at the dining table, tapping away one-fingered on her computer, answering emails. The reporter had sent her a thank-you note, with a few more questions, and Liesel wanted to answer them while the meeting was fresh in her mind. But after a minute she closed the laptop.

"Has anyone called Nathan?" Liesel asked, and Susie felt a little of Jean's irritation. Why should everything revolve around their brother. But she said, "I tried to call him earlier but Jean wouldn't let me."

"That's right," Jean said. It was all childish and petty, and somehow put them both in a better mood.

As children, the Essingers aligned and realigned themselves constantly. Let the boys do it, Liesel might say. Or, I need one of the girls. But they also divided according to age: Nathan and Susie; Paul and Jean. As the youngest, Jean had her pick of models to follow, which gave her a funny kind of power. Whoever she decided to like or imitate often got his way. Or her way. But even though Jean grew into Susie's old dresses and read her old novels, she also liked watching sports with Paul and arguing with Nathan. Maybe Susie sometimes felt a little betrayed, she wanted more from her kid sister. After Jean graduated, they sometimes talked to each other about men, but not much. There was an age gap, six years, and by the time Jean was comfortable enough in her skin to joke about dating, Susie had already started having kids.

When Ben was born, the first grandchild, Jean flew out to help. It was September, she was about to start her junior year abroad. But the Oxford term didn't begin until October and her parents paid for the flight. She changed diapers and took the first nightshift, until one or two, before bringing the baby to Susie in bed, so he could feed. Jean and David got along well, they talked about English things, frustrations, the kind of thing he had escaped to America to avoid, but also what he missed: Southampton FC, flat beer. But he was less good at changing diapers. He liked talking. When guests came to admire his son, he kept up his interest in the outside world, he asked questions and invited them for dinner. When what Susie really needed was for people to leave her alone. Jean stayed two weeks. She cooked, she cleaned up, she went shopping— and bought a cabbage for the fridge. One of Susie's nipples had started to bleed, Ben was coughing up blood, someone had said that cold cabbage leaves helped. And every night, Jean lay on the sofa in the dark of the house, watching TV, while Ben slept on her breasts. (Sorry, buddy, she thought. No milk.) You don't forget these things. But already she had the sense of a shift, a crack in the ground, growing wider; Susie had ended up on the other side.

Julie came next, the following summer, three weeks early, jaundiced, long and skinny, and Jean offered to help again. But Nathan told her, listen, this is our mess, we got ourselves into it, you have to live your own life. Which suddenly seemed to her a different kind of life. Then Paul "fell." You were my buffer, she told him. Now when she flew over to hang out with her family, she ended up hanging out with their kids.

Which is what she did for the rest of the afternoon. When Nathan came by, Ben and Julie disappeared together (they were exploring the apartment), but Jean ended up on the floor with Margot, playing pickup sticks—there was an old-fashioned antique set on one of the bookshelves. Then the big kids joined in, Jean got everyone involved, they had to push the coffee table aside. The carpet underneath, a Turkish kilim, was old and rough to touch; Jean, in her short dress, got red knees. Her ankles started hurting. Approaching thirty, she had started experiencing low-level physical discomforts, which only bothered her because she was a mild hypochondriac. Even little things could contribute to her anxiety levels. Once her back gave out, she could hardly walk for a week, she didn't want that happening again. But she also didn't want to stop the game, the kids liked her and deferred to her, it's amazing how quickly you can make up lost ground; she just wanted their parents to notice a little more. They acted like she was having fun.

In fact, Nathan was in one of his good moods. His dark hair, uncut, uncombed, expressed energy and enthusiasm. Everything is terrific, everyone is wonderful. He opened the French windows and stood out on the balcony and came back in. His physical restlessness took up a lot of space. "This is an incredible apartment. I'm not sure I would have ditched this guy for Paul." He was looking at the bookshelves and touched a book with his finger and lifted it out.

"Other people have had that thought," Jean called out, from the carpet.

"It's awful," Liesel said. "It's all for show. A man who has an apartment like this, the way he treats women, there's no private life, it's all public. You don't want to live with a man like this."

"What are you talking about," Nathan said. "It's an apartment on West 83rd with a view of the Park."

"Only if you stand out on that balcony and lean over."

"This is what I like about you," her son told her. "You

think that you're standing up for the people, but really what you're saying is, none of this is good enough for me."

Susie kept quiet. She knew that she couldn't compete with Nathan in this mood. His cheerfulness refused all contradiction. But she liked watching her son, who was sitting Indian style on the floor, next to Julie, with the crossword on his lap, so he could work on it between turns. He looked like his father. They had the same vague friendly face (though Ben's was paler and not so fat), with blue eyes and a weak nose, the kind you like somebody for, because it suggests modesty. But, in fact, in both father and son it meant something else, indifference, or a willingness to reserve opinions. People kept saying to Ben, "It's your turn. Come on, are you playing or not?" He was trying to think of a word and read out the clue. Julie took the newspaper away. "Either you play or you don't," she said, and Susie saw him lift a stick from the pile. But no one was watching. It moved a little, she saw him see it move, but then he started addressing himself to the pile again, using the stick he had just picked up to lever another one away from the crowd. Julie said, suddenly, "What are you doing?" and Ben said, "I thought it was my go."

"It moved."

"I haven't even touched it yet."

"No, the last one. I saw it move."

"Did it?" Ben said. "Okay. I didn't notice."

And Liesel said, "You have much more appetite for this kind of place than I do. You're more of an aristocrat than I am."

"No, I just know these people better than you do."

Nathan had found one of the armchairs and started to flip through the book. "The people who make this kind of money usually make it for a reason, because they're smart, serious people. Whoever bought this apartment is somebody who knows what he's doing."

"That's what I mean. You have more respect for success than I do."

"Maybe, but that has nothing to do with being an aristocrat. Quite the reverse."

Susie wondered if she should intervene, but the kids seemed to be playing happily together. And even noticing something that upset her, Ben fudging or lying or cheating, involved her with him in some way that also offered a retreat. From Nathan and Liesel and Jean, from her old family, whose problems weren't quite her problems anymore.

Bill came in shortly after, with one side of his shirt untucked. "What's the plan?" he said. "Has anyone called Paul?" He was carrying a bag of groceries from Fairway Market—mostly fruit, a watermelon, which he cut up in the kitchen, some cherries and grapes, which he washed and put out in whatever bowls he could find. For the next few minutes he had juice on his fingers and beard, he kept eating slices of melon, and spitting pits and seeds into his hand, walking back to the kitchen to throw them away.

Jean said, "How was Aunt Rose?"

"The way she lives, the way she's forced to live, it's depressing. Everybody she knows has moved up and away around her. The people who come in are people she's never going to be friends with."

"What does that mean? Is that some kind of code?"

"It means what I said. People she won't become friends with. At her age. When she can hardly get out of the house. Unless she drives. And even getting into the car and out again is no picnic for her. How is she going to meet these people, I don't care who they are."

Liesel said, "I'll call Paul now." She put her hands on the table but didn't move.

"I don't want him under any pressure to come out to see us. He's got a match tomorrow, he doesn't need any obligations."

"I don't think he thinks of us as obligations," Jean said. She was still on the floor with the kids. "Someone help me up." And she reached out her hand. "My back gets stiff." Ben stood up and started pulling.

"He's quite strong," Susie told her, but in fact Jean had to shift onto her haunches, he couldn't lift her.

"I've put on weight."

"Not that I can see," Liesel said.

"At a certain point, everything becomes an obligation."

"I want to see Paul, I want to talk to my brother," Susie said, her voice rising slightly. "You guys saw him last night. I want to see him."

In fact, Paul stopped by with Cal around five o'clock. He gave the kid something to eat in the kitchen, just one of those jars of baby food. Dana had a gym thing she liked to go to. Maybe she'd join them later for dinner, depending on where they went. He planned to stay home with Cal and watch a baseball game.

Nathan said, "Do you want somebody to hang out with?"

"I don't think I'll be much company tonight."

He felt strangely excluded from the clutter he saw around him: Bill's bowls of fruit on the table (the paper grocery bag, with nothing inside it, had fallen over), Ben's backpack on the couch, Susie's roller suitcase, the coffee table pushed to one side, pickup sticks on the floor, a book on an armrest, kids everywhere, his mother's computer cord stretching across the parquet floor. When they were children, traveling, they used to sleep on sofas, they colonized many of his parents' friends' apartments, and all of this mess, people getting bored and restless, people resting, people arguing about where to eat, struck him as very familiar. Somehow the rest of them were all in it together, but not him. Something to be grateful for, maybe; or else to mind.

Julie was especially helpful with Cal. She loved babies. She was at that age where girls have identified what they get praised for, or what they think they get praised for. The kitchen was tiny for an apartment this size, just a staging area really, but it had a small side table, where Cal could sit, and Julie stood beside him, dipping a plastic spoon into the jar (whatever they gave him to eat, lamb, beef, chicken, looked like colored apple sauce) and poking it into his mouth. "He can do it himself," Paul said at first, but watching him make a mess wasn't Julie's idea of help, so he left her to it.

"How are you feeling, son?" Bill said. "I bought some fruit."

"I'm fine, all right. I feel all right." He pulled off a twig of grapes and picked at them.

"Don't worry about us," Bill said. "Do what you have to do."

"I'm not worried."

Some of the grapes looked faintly discolored, whitish instead of green, like the skin under a Band Aid, there were soft spots, and Paul put them down on a section of newspaper, feeling childish. As a kid, he couldn't bear any sign of ripeness in fruits, any rottenness, he was very particular about some things, and recently he had realized these feelings were related to the presence of his family, he needed to fence off certain areas.

Susie said, "What's Dana doing?"

"Spin class."

"On a Sunday night?"

Bill said, "She doesn't need to come out with us later."

"Even on Sunday nights in this city people spin."

Jean said, "She can come if she wants to."

"I don't want her waking up Paul when she gets in."

"How late are you guys thinking of going out?" Paul asked. "I mean, you're taking the kids, right?"

These conversations could go on and on. Maybe Dana was right—as soon as he saw his family he went into retreat mode. But it was always like this, before a tournament. Your levels of self-involvement go through the roof. Just to conceal the degree of self-obsession is a full-time job. There's something almost therapeutic about the process. Everything else burns away and what's left is a kind of hard, bright core. And the people around you feel it, too, they seem to respect it. There was something in his physical presence, a weird combination of nerves and calm. When he picked at his eyelashes, you could see the muscles in his forearm move under the skin. He didn't talk much; whatever he did, he did slowly, partly because he was wearing flip-flops. His feet ached, his pulse was somewhere in the forties.

Paul said to his father, "Don't worry about me, Dad. I had a run today, I hit a few balls, I feel good."

"Enjoy it, right? That's all you can do."

Jean said to her mother, "What's the password on your computer?"

Bill fingered Paul's grapes and asked, "Is something wrong with these?" and started eating them.

Susie said to Nathan, "How late are you willing to keep your kids up?"

"I'm not worried about it," he said. "It's not an issue."

Paul, listening to their cross talk, remembered something. Bill had a friend in London they used to stay with, an American guy who worked at the LSE. His apartment was in the penthouse of a student building, right in the middle of the city—you walked out of the lobby into a bus lane. Red double-deckers. There was a pub on the corner with etched-glass windows, the side street led to Covent Garden. The apartment itself felt like an island of Americana. Leather couches sat in front of an early large-screen TV, whose projector took up the middle of the room. One summer Jean and Paul got food poisoning or some kind of gastrointestinal thing on the flight from Austin. They spent the first five days of vacation horizontal, lying on

the couches, and watching Wimbledon. Bill kept offering to queue up for day tickets—he didn't mind leaving
the house at 5 a.m. or waiting in line for three hours. But
Paul felt too sick. Even now, he could hardly bear to sit on
leather furniture. Maybe he was thirteen years old, Jean
was ten. Sampras had just come on the scene; Paul was
an Agassi fan, Jean liked Lendl. The truth is, they had a
very happy week, drinking black tea with sugar and eating
McVitie's digestive biscuits. Arguing and annoying each
other.

Jean said, tapping at their mother's computer: "The
good places to eat are mostly downtown."

"That's fine with me."

"That may play a part in whether Dana decides to come
along," Paul told them.

"I'm not saying it's an issue. I'm just asking how late."

"So let's stay local."

"It doesn't have to be a consideration. I'm only men-
tioning it."

"Of course it's a consideration," Jean said. "Don't be
stupid."

And on and on. Ben had the right idea. He sat on the
sofa reading his book. Paul went in the kitchen to clean up
his son. Afterward, Susie offered to walk him home and
the three of them waited for the elevator and then got in.
Bill asked, "Will we see you before the match?"

"Probably not," Paul said, and they descended into the
lobby and walked out into the street. It felt much warmer
outside—uncomfortably warm, the apartment was well
shaded, it had windows only on one side.

As soon as they hit Central Park West, the sun beat down on them; it reflected off the pavement and the moving cars. The light was very white, you blinked against it. Whatever clouds there were just kept the heat in. More storms were predicted in the night. The air, like a dishcloth, needed to be wrung out again and again.

When Cal complained about walking, Paul lifted him onto his shoulders, still holding his hands. They crossed the street like this, and into the park, into its shade, and the traffic noise retreated, too, it was easy to talk.

"Let me take your bag at least," Susie said, but the strap was tangled up in Cal's legs and in the end she gave up. It bumped against Paul's hip at every step; his flip-flops slapped the sidewalk. They passed a playground, but it was partly hidden by trees, and Paul said, "If we keep walking, maybe he won't notice." Sometimes, even with his sister, he became aware of the awkwardness of being alone with another human being. There are formalities you have to go through. "Ben has grown," he added, but the formalities also make you feel a little sad, something genuine, which can open up the conversation. "Even since the last time I saw him. He seems very—self-possessed."

"I saw him cheating at pickup sticks just now. I don't know. He starts middle school next week. They don't always show it, but he feels like he's under pressure."

"Did you say something to him?"

"No. I didn't know what to do. I kept telling myself, it doesn't matter. But I was also a little upset. It's just a stupid game, but he's not one of those kids who wins at games, and part of me just wanted him to win, too."

With her hair pulled back in a bun, Paul could see the gray in it; but Susie didn't seem to care. Her face had grown narrower with age—she was one of these women who gets skinny with motherhood. Just from worry, she might have said, but the truth is, she also watched her weight. Her friends were health-conscious, competitive, and generally über-competent. Susie wore nice clothes but nothing fancy, most of them she bought from catalogs, she said she didn't have time to go shopping. When they were younger, Paul remembered, he used to tease her for being fat. The thought made him nostalgic.

"I know very few adults who cheat at pickup sticks," he said. "I don't think it's going to be a problem."

"But they cheat at other things."

Anyone seeing them, Susie thought, would think they were a family. And the park was full of people, walking dogs or pushing strollers, a sunny Sunday afternoon, kids throwing Frisbees on the Great Lawn, a softball game going, there was a boom box playing by the soda cart—"Batdance," from the movie, the vendor wore a bandanna and kept mouthing the words. His shoes, a pair of Hi-Tec high-tops, looked dirty and busted; his jeans were gray. From his expressions, you couldn't tell if he was angry or happy.

"Cal's falling asleep," she said.

"He goes to bed too late. Dana and I keep having stupid fights."

"About what?"

"About putting him to bed. Come on, buddy," he said, lifting him down and setting Cal on his feet. "You

snooze, you walk." But in the end, Paul carried him anyway, in his arms, against his hip, because Cal refused—he
kept flopping and falling over, as if his bones were made
of jelly.

"Did you tell anybody about me?" Susie asked. Her
tone was older-sisterly. None of the Essinger children had
a strong Southern accent, they mostly sounded like East
Coasters, but Paul also heard a class overlay in his sister's
voice (what you make yourself into, by fitting in), something sweet and tough, the tone of a woman with a role in
the PTA.

"No," he said. "I don't really see that as my job in
the family, to communicate. But I don't think they'll . . .
object."

Susie made a noise, like a "huh," through her nose.
"They'll think I'm giving up on my career."

"They think that anyway. But it's not you they're worried about right now."

"I heard. I'm sad. I like having a famous kid brother."

"I'm sorry I'm not more famous."

"Nobody cares."

"Bill cares, a little."

"Maybe he does, but not much."

They were coming up to the 86th Street Transverse:
somewhere below them, the footpath led over a bridge to
the reservoir, where Paul had run that morning. But you
could see the cars slipping by underneath, mostly taxis,
there was a pattern there, a lesson in fractions; and then,
at ground level, runners and cyclists passed them on the
road, you had to wait for a gap in the bodies to cross over,

toward the West Side, where there was another playground. This time Cal saw it and Paul gave him a turn on
the swing.

"I don't know if you're in a hurry," he said to his sister. As a young boy, Paul used to be obsessed with his
big brother—Nathan to him was all-in-all. But later, as he
grew older, he started to see things from Susie's point of
view. Nathan and Susie used to fight a lot; as first- and
second-born, they were caught in the middle of a deep
loving battle that Paul wasn't really a part of. Eventually he understood this and stopped taking sides. And Paul
and Susie formed another one of those alliances, the middle children, sensible and undemanding. They hosted tea
parties for their stuffed animals, he was very happy with
girls' games, and sometimes he felt guilty of a betrayal—of
Nathan. But you put the work into these relationships, at
eight or nine years old, and later, twenty or thirty years
later, there's a kind of muscle memory.

"If I want to go, I can just go," Susie said. They were
standing side by side behind the swing; every few seconds
Paul gave Cal a push.

"It's not really me or you they should worry about."

"What do you mean?"

Next to the swings was a picnic area, just a patch of
grass, where a woman sat sprinkling cheese into a Tupper-
ware container of pasta. She sat on her haunches, beside a
blanket. Another mother ate a carrot stick and continued
talking; a baby lay asleep on his back. The first woman
called out, "Riley, dinnertime," and Susie thought, you're
going to wake him up.

"Jean has gotten into a thing with her boss," Paul said. "He's married. I think she thinks she's serious about him."

"She told you?"

"She told Dana. I don't know who else."

"Does he have kids?"

"Yes."

"Oh," Susie said.

For a minute they stood there like that—Cal's swinging gave a rhythm to their silence. A girl came over and sat down on the blanket, Susie watched her eat. Eventually Paul said, "I have this idea, I don't know how crazy it is, of moving back to Texas. I'm in the process of buying a house outside Wimberley; there's land enough for me to build a whole . . . a series of cabins . . . room for everybody, that's my idea. Pretty near Canyon Lake. Well, I'm considering it. Money isn't a problem for me anymore, there's nothing I have to do. I just want to get out of this mess."

"What mess?" Susie said.

"I don't know. The whole thing. So when are you going to tell them?"

"Tonight, tomorrow maybe."

But Cal was getting bored on the swing, bored and tired, he needed to go to bed, and Paul lifted him up, first by the armpits, and then hoisting him, throwing and turning him a little, and shifting his hands to the boy's waist. Cal put his arms around his father's neck, he was very warm, and Paul said to his sister, with his face partly obscured, "They love you, they'll be happy."

"I guess we won't see you before you step on court."

"Probably not."

"I like watching you play," she said, before putting her arm around the two of them (she had to reach up) and walking back alone the way they had come.

It was almost seven o'clock, but the park was still full: people winding up a long day outside, lying in the grass surrounded by empty containers; joggers going for an early evening run, a bunch of them wearing some kind of uniform, green T-shirts with a company logo, colleagues training together; power walkers, too, a pair of women swinging their arms robustly; old guys, dog walkers, lovers. There really are lovers, she saw a couple of kids against a tree, the boy leaning in, with his arm raised above her and his hand on the trunk. So posed. The girl wore tiny shorts, almost painful, her legs looked pale, she was resting against the tree, as if in retreat. From time to time they each seemed to say something, one or two words, they kissed like that, too. Maybe they were sixteen or seventeen years old; he had white socks and skater shoes. Just the intensity of it is something you forget, thank God. Amazing how dense the life is here, and she stopped by the boom-box guy to buy a bottle of water.

The heat was getting to her, she didn't feel right. Some woman was ahead of her waiting for change, all she had was a twenty-dollar bill. Another song was playing now, "Don't Go Chasing Waterfalls," and the vendor peeled through the stash in his fanny pack, counting down—he had a lot of dirty singles. He lost count and had to start over; his hands were wet from the icebox. She had read somewhere that the license fee for operating these food carts was over two hundred thousand dollars a year. It didn't make sense. Who had that kind of money? Who would take such a risk? When Susie asked for an Evian, she almost couldn't hear herself. He said, "Here you go, lady" — she had the dollar and a quarter ready in her palm. Afterward, she sat on a bench for a minute to unscrew the cap and drink.

Something was bugging her, she didn't know what. Like a dream where you wake up and can't remember what put you in a bad mood. One of your stocks has fallen in the night. It wasn't just the cheating but the way Ben reacted to it. Maybe they pushed him too hard, it was partly her fault. Ben was very bored in first grade, he had learned to read early and was starting to misbehave, so they let him skip a grade. Who knows how much she was motivated by pride. I don't think much. But he was already young for his year, a September baby, and now he was hanging out with kids sometimes two years older than him and trying to fit in. There's a big difference between eleven and thirteen. You start pretending just to save face. David hated these kinds of conversations, he had a low tolerance for anxiety. Which only exacerbated her worries, as they both acknowledged. He also had a slightly English attitude toward childhood and thought it was bad for the kids to get too involved in their lives, that's not what childhood is for. But Bill and Liesel had always been very involved; they still were.

You can't just sit here all day, they're probably making dinner plans. And Ben will be wondering what happened to you, he's still your little boy. She started walking back to the apartment. The light had changed, the sun had dropped behind the buildings on Central Park West and what was left was a kind of uniform warm gray that cast no shadows even under the trees. The quality of sound had changed, too, it seemed farther away, you could hear parents calling for their children, everything echoed a little, like noises at a swimming pool, as though the surface of things had begun to ripple slightly. I need some sugar and she looked in her purse for the bag of dried apricots she usually carried around, in case the kids got hungry. Poor Paul. It's a weird career that you give up at thirty-three. Jean said that Liesel was worrying too much about Dana, and I said to Jean, just because she's your mother doesn't mean she's necessarily out of touch. But the apricots weren't there, she must have left them in the fridge. I don't feel right, and she explained to someone in her head, maybe Liesel, I need to eat little and often, every few hours. You know what it's like for me, being pregnant. You were the same. I guess I know why Jean was fighting with me, and she came out of the park at 81st Street, one of the four-way intersections, the trash cans were full, the trees leaning over the street were covered in dust, a bus rumbled past, and waited on the corner patiently until she could cross.

Dana said to Paul when they got in: "Where were you? I called the apartment, but they said you left half an hour ago. I've just been waiting around."

"What do you mean, waiting? You live here," he told

her. "Come on, buddy. Bedtime." But the boy started walking away and Paul made a game of catching him and picking him up.

"I can do this," Dana said. "You need to rest up."

Her hair was still wet from the shower, she was barefoot and wearing a dress. She had tough brown athletic legs and her face, after a workout, looked almost boyish — partly because she hadn't put her contact lenses in. When they first started dating, Paul used to take her to his club, they knocked a ball around, he wanted Dana to see something he was good at. But she moved very confidently, too, it was a real turn-on, she had played a little in high school before concentrating on crew, and even at thirty she moved like a woman who knew what her body could do. He felt her physical presence, a kind of equality in it, and said to her, with Cal in his arms, "I don't mind. You did it last night."

"I do it most nights."

"So tonight it's my turn. He calms me down."

"Just so long as it works out for you," Dana said.

"Give me a break, Dana." And then, with his face in Cal's neck, "It doesn't matter, it doesn't matter."

But his breath tickled the boy, who started wriggling. "Mommy do it," Cal said, and Paul let him go.

The phone rang while Cal was getting in the bath. Jean was on the other end of the line. "Okay, we're going to Carmine's, because there's room for everybody and the kids can have spaghetti and meatballs. Not my first choice, but it's also pretty near to you, in case Dana wants to come along. Or you."

"It won't be me, but I'll tell Dana." He had taken the cord-less phone to the sofa and was lying down. The water was still running; he could hear Cal's voice, at a different pitch, rising above it. "Hey, Jean," he said. "Is Susie back yet?"

"Not that I know of."

"You should be nice to her. She's got a lot on her plate."

"What does that mean? I'm always nice."

"You're mostly nice."

They were used to talking long-distance on the phone, they were used to silences, and eventually Jean said, "Don't feel like you have to lose tomorrow. I booked my flight back for next weekend, so you may as well make it to the third round."

"Okay."

Somewhere in the room with Jean, Bill was talking, part of the background noise. Liesel answered him and Bill called out, "I can't hear you when you're in the kitch-en." Jean said, in the same tone as before: "You know that everybody loves you."

"Except my son, apparently."

The water had stopped, but there was still a kind of banging going on, coming from the bathroom. Paul reached for the remote control, which was on the coffee table, and flipped on the TV. Dana stood in the doorway, there were splash marks on her dress, and she said: "Who are you talking to?"

"Jean. They're going to Carmine's."

"What'd he do?" Jean said.

"Picked his mommy to put him to bed." Dana heard this and stared at him for a moment, then turned back down the hallway. Paul switched off the television sound and started looking for a baseball game.

"Well, she's prettier than you."

"She's prettier than me."

Then Nathan, faintly but distinctly, said to Bill or Liesel or maybe to one of his kids: "I don't think this has to be decided now." They were all there together, in the middle of something, not necessarily happy or unhappy, but caught up in it, and Paul was on the outside listening in. Jean told him: "The table's booked for seven thirty, if Dana wants to come."

"She may be a little late."

"Not as late as we will," Jean said.

A few minutes later, Dana walked in with Cal in her arms; his face looked hot from the bath, he was in his pajamas, with a thumb in his mouth. "His hair got wet," she said, "so I washed it anyway." The boy had a sleek look, his eyes seemed hooded, darker than usual, full of feeling. Paul sat up. "They've booked a table for seven thirty. You should go if you want to go. I can take over."

"I don't want another fight. If I do it now, it will take five minutes. I can be five minutes late."

"You can be whatever you want to be," Paul said. "You don't have to go."

"Do you want me to go?"

"It's up to you."

"Is it rude if I don't go?"

"It's not rude either way. You should do what you want to do. I can't tell you what that is."

"I don't care, but if you want me to go, I'll go, if you

want me to see your family."

"Dana, I don't know how to say this any other way. It's up to you."

"I guess what I'm saying is do you want me to stay."

She shifted Cal onto her hip; he was getting to be pretty big.

"I'm happy for you to stay if you want to stay. In about five minutes I'm going to put a pot of water on for pasta. Then I'm going to eat in front of the TV. I'm gonna check my rackets, I'm gonna get the bags ready. Then I'm going to bed."

"Are they expecting me?"

"They're not expecting you or not expecting you."

"But they must have booked a table for a certain number of people."

"All right, go. You're making me crazy here. I can put Cal to bed and you go."

"No, I'll put him to bed."

"At least let me give him a kiss," Paul said, pushing himself up.

But Cal for some reason turned his face against his mother's armpit, so Paul kissed the boy on his wet head. The gesture was more intimate than he intended, he could feel their combined warmth, and put his hand on Dana's side, where Cal was holding her, too. "Sleep tight, buddy," he said, and left them to it, as Dana carried him away. She was gone for about twenty minutes, and when she came out again wore a different dress.

"I'm going to go," she said. "I think that's what you want me to do."

"Okay," he said, shaking his head humorously, but when she was gone it's true he felt relieved to be on his own. For too much of the day he had been looking forward to this moment, when he could lie down in front of the TV with a ballgame on. People just bugged him, even the people he loved. It's like everybody has this gravitational field — just being around them drags you somewhere against your will, unless you resist it, and that takes up energy, too. *You're in a dark corner, you have to fight your way out of it.* But even as a kid this is what he liked, hitting a tennis ball against a brick wall, there's a reason you become an athlete, solitude and repetition are not a problem for you. With crowd noises coming out of the television, like some kind of carbonation, rising up, he began working through his visualization exercises: backhand down the line, just inside it; backhand crosscourt, rolling his wrist over the shot; forehand crosscourt and down the line; moving your feet, keeping low, striking early. Even like that, with his head on one armrest and his feet on the other, he felt his heart rate quickening, and after a minute got up to put the water on.

—

The fountain in the courtyard was leaning slightly when Dana came out, and splashing over the brim of the pool; the wind had picked up and blew in through the arch on 86th Street. There was still that same gray light that Susie walked home in, after the sun went down. With her hair wet, Dana shivered a little but warmly — that feeling you get, coming in from a day at the beach. She had pushed herself hard at the gym and felt tired and cleaned out.

There's no use fighting with him the night before but you can't pretend either it's a temporary thing. All her life she thought of herself as a straightforward person, who took things head on. Even at thirteen, when she became aware of her looks and the effect they had on people, she thought, this is something you have to learn to deal with. But she also couldn't ignore the fact that she had basically drifted to this point. From one crowd to another. It was never a question of what she wanted to do, everybody wanted things from her. After a while you get out of the habit of asking what you actually think about anything. And then you have a kid and it doesn't matter. But Paul is right. You're making yourself ridiculous. If you want to go, go, if you don't, don't. Look, she felt like saying to him, I'm just as frustrated with myself as you are. You don't hear it but in my head, I'm shouting, Make up your mind! What do you want! Because *you* just sit there suiting yourself, I should, too. Screw your family. If you can't be bothered to see them, why should I? But the awful truth was, she wanted to see Liesel and Jean because she liked them and they were like Paul but still showed her some sympathy and interest.

This is stupid. You're doing it again. He goes into his shell for a week before the tournament and you act like it's a major crisis. Every time. And then after a while he gets sick of dealing with it, which I don't blame him for. When he loses, and gets over it, everything will be fine. But she didn't believe this either.

It was five blocks to Carmine's, walking along Broadway, with the traffic following and waiting and surging at the lights, but she took her time even though she was twenty minutes late. Something she learned from her mother, let people wait. It felt good to be out of the house, away from Cal. From Paul, too. People (men) looked at her, they scoped her out, even with a girlfriend on their arm. Not that it mattered, but it was like checking your bank account, she liked knowing that the money was still there. The wind felt rough against her face. Her dress hung loose, she could feel her body under it. The first person she saw was Julie sitting on one of the plastic chairs outside, under the restaurant awning, and reading a book.

"Hey, Julie," she said. "What are you doing out here?"

The girl looked calmly up at her. She had something of her mother's Middle Eastern complexion, but a kind of pallor, too, underneath it, especially under the eyes, so that she always seemed tired and patient.

"Waiting until the food comes. Everybody's fighting and behaving like children."

Then Jean came out. "Grub's up," she said and saw Dana. "Hey, you look nice." On their way in, she held the door for Julie, and then as Dana walked past, Jean said to her, "I'm not mad or anything, but I just want to know. Did you say something to anybody?"

"About what?" And then, when they were both inside: "I told Paul."

"It doesn't matter," Jean said. "I told Nathan myself but I just want to know who knows."

Even with Jean, Dana got little reminders of what it means *not* to be part of the family—stranger kindness or even distant cool familiarity. With her shortish hair, Jean was hard to place. She wore cowboy boots and her T-shirt said BRUKLIN HIGH ROAD in mismatched letters like a blackmail note; she dressed like a teenager. But she was also a twenty-nine-year-old woman who could make up her mind about people. If you crossed a line she could draw a new one that excluded you, and Dana, to make up for telling Paul about the affair, said, "Nice boots."

"They're totally phony. When I was a kid who actually lived in Texas, I would never have worn them."

The restaurant had the air-conditioning on, and Dana goose-pimpled lightly in her cotton dress. You could hear the noise of fans and vents blowing, the background noise of various televisions, low-level conversation sounds like pebbles dragging on a beach, under the waves, and they climbed a set of stairs by the bar to the mezzanine floor. Dana thought, if I didn't know them, what would I think of them? Bill had a friend along, a heavy-set old guy with finely drawn features; he looked ill, there was a cane resting by his chair. Liesel seemed unhappy about something, frazzled, which was one of her words, seventy-odd years old, the kind of person Dana would probably ignore at a party. Susie was talking to Ben in a slightly rising voice, explaining something, in the voice of a mother treating her child like a grown-up, but loud enough so that Margot could listen in, and some of the adults, too. Nathan, in a fresh suit, wearing a paisley shirt, looked like the big shot at the table, but still there was something slovenly in his appearance, he couldn't be contained by clothes. Margot sat on his lap and from time to time he kissed her hair—even he had his defensive gestures, his comforter. The girl seemed tired, she was five years old, and he cut up her meatball for her and fed her with a spoon. To a stranger's eye, it must have looked like what it was, a family reunion, though who could say if they were happy to see each other.

There was plenty of food on the table already, the portions were big, and everybody picked off other people's plates. Spaghetti with meatballs, fried calamari, pasta with clam sauce, a baked fish special, steaming in the foil, veal saltimbocca, garlic broccoli, shiny and oily, a big Caesar salad. Bill had held back one of the menus. "Order something else if you want to" was his greeting to Dana, as he passed it over, but when the waiter came all she asked for was a gin and tonic. A kind of statement of intent: I'm here to have a good time. Because she could sense already a sourness in the atmosphere, a tiredness or a kind of conversational tendinitis, that kept flaring up because the Essingers couldn't resist repeating certain arguments. Paul always said she had the wrong idea of what a family should sound like. Yes, she told him, I think they should sound like they're having a good time. But Paul said, it's not a *social* occasion, when we see each other.

Whatever the argument was, there was also something else going on, which she couldn't put her finger on. Nathan had taken over from Susie's explanation. "There are things you can do in a war," he said, "that you're not allowed to do at other times."

"Like kill people," Ben said. With his glasses on, he looked like an English schoolboy, pale and pink, pleasant and well brought-up.

"That's right. But it's not always easy to say what a war is."

Bill introduced Dana to his friend, an old law-school pal, now retired, named Fritz Kohl. A gentlemanly South African. Fritz used to work at Alston & Bird, but he regretted not taking the academic high road and clearly wanted to impress Nathan, he kept asking questions. There was a story in *The New York Times* that morning about the so-called Drone Memo, which *The Times* and various other parties, including the ACLU, had petitioned the government to release. It had been written to justify the murder or assassination "or execution or killing or whatever you want to call it" (Jean had joined in) of Anwar al-Awlaki, an American citizen fighting for al-Qaeda. His son died, too, both of them killed by a drone attack in Yemen. One of the authors of the memo, Daniel Ronstadt, used to be a professor at Harvard Law. Nathan knew him a little.

"He's a smart guy," Nathan said. "I don't know him well, but sometimes at the house we have a whiskey night. Everybody brings a bottle and we try different whiskeys. Daniel came once or twice."

"The people you know," Liesel said. The noise was getting to her, the restaurant clamor, but she sat straight in her chair, with her round brown face, white hair, and a red fat-beaded necklace on her neck—like some kind of Indian chief. In her German childhood she used to be known as *der schwarze Bomber*, the black bomber, because of her dark skin. One of her cousins once complained (they shared a flat at university), there are fat people and thin people, but she didn't mean looks, she meant that Liesel took up a lot of space. Somehow even her silence could be very expressive. Judgments were being made.

But Nathan was used to it and kept going. "His wife is an exceptionally smart woman. Clémence was on a panel with her or maybe they judged a prize together. She said she learned something useful from her. That when you're doing one of these public service things that people do in a half-assed way, if you come prepared, fully prepared, you get your way."

"As if all they think about is getting their way," Jean said.

"Of course that's what they think about."

Dana said to Julie, who was sitting next to her: "I don't understand what they're arguing about." And Julie said, "Nobody's arguing, they're just trying to get at Nathan."

There was a story Fritz heard that Ronstadt had cited one of Nathan's articles in the Memo. It was impossible to know because the government refused to publish it. And Nathan himself wouldn't say one way or another; he claimed he didn't know.

Jean said, "I'm sorry, but I find all this incredibly upsetting. You have no idea how—American all this sounds. Not just the drone strikes, which are bad enough. But the cover-up and the fact that the only reason any of this matters is that one of the people they killed was an American citizen."

"That's right," Nathan said. "Because that's the legal issue. That's where they thought they could pick a fight."

"Who do you mean, they?"

"*The Times*. The ACLU. It's a specific instance. That's what you look for in the law, a specific instance that tests the principle."

"Don't talk to me like that," Jean said.

"Like what?"

"Like I'm one of your students."

Liesel, smiling in a hot-and-bothered way, looked over at Dana. "You need to eat something, too," she said.

"I don't have a plate."

"Take mine, I'm finished. Too much food. Americans always give you too much food."

"It's an Italian thing," Bill said. His beard had crumbs in it, from the soft white bread lying half cut in wicker baskets on the table. But underneath his beard he looked like Paul, the same slightly earnest, slightly eager boy's face. "When I was a kid," he went on, "half the kids I knew were Italian. There were restaurants like this in Port Jervis. But we never ate there because they weren't kosher."

In the end Dana used one of the food dishes—Jean handed her the rest of the meatballs, on a platter, and Dana cleared some space in front of her. There was an old jam jar on the table with knives and forks, wrapped up in napkins. Susie said, "What can I get you?" and passed the broccoli toward her, and the Caesar salad. She wore a dress, with pixelated colors on it, reds and muted blues, and sat up straight in her chair, with her hair up. Looking proper and somehow touching, a still youngish mother dressing up for a night out. Even though it was only with her family.

It's true, Dana thought, taking the plates, I'm just hungry. And when you're hungry you can't make decisions, you know this about yourself. She had worked out hard that afternoon, and the first mouthful of meatballs and spaghetti tasted of calories to her, like a battery tang, energy coming back into the system.

"When I first met you, I was worried you didn't eat." Liesel looked on approvingly. "And then we took you for barbecue and I watched you eat. I was very relieved."

"The first time I had dinner with your family," Dana said, "I had to sneak off to the bathroom to cry."

"Are we so terrible?"

"I wasn't used to it. I'm an only child."

"Sometimes I think you ended up with the easy one."

"That's because you're his mother." It was Susie talking—she had a voice she sometimes used, sensible and sisterly, and certain expressions to go with it, when she was out with her girlfriends. "I'm sure Paul isn't easy to live with. He suits himself."

"That's what I mean," Liesel said. And then, with her round brown face, which always looked wide open somehow, totally exposed, she turned to Dana: "Which doesn't mean I don't worry about him."

"I know that."

"I'm worried about him now."

"He's doing all right. I don't know. He kicked me out tonight." Sometimes it surprised Dana, how much she wanted to confess things to Liesel. Even as a joke.

"Why? I don't understand." And she sighed, not quite honestly. "I feel I should apologize for my children."

"It just means he told me to come out for dinner, which is what I wanted to do anyway. It was my fault. I was being annoying."

"I don't believe that for a minute," Susie told her.

But this line of sympathy struck the wrong note. Dana didn't want to lump herself in with Susie, a woman married to a man with conventional ideas about marriage roles—she didn't want to complain about their "husbands" together. Partly because she knew Jean wouldn't like it. Jean always resisted this kind of easy gender identification. And Dana for some reason felt closer to her tonight, maybe because of what Jean had confessed to her about the affair. Paul sometimes complained, actually he wasn't really complaining, just describing the situation, that the family geography had all these ley lines of loyalty in it, which meant that whatever position you took, on any subject, you were also taking somebody's side against somebody else. That's just how it was. There was no point in fighting it. It was simpler not to have the argument at all or whatever the argument was pretending to be about. It was simpler for everybody just to admit, I like you today. And I don't like you.

Meanwhile, Jean was still arguing with Nathan, their voices were growing louder, and Dana heard her say, "That's not what this is about. This is about telling people in power what they want to hear, so that they can exercise that power without getting into trouble for it later."

"All right," Nathan said. "This conversation is over."

That kind of comment hurt him more than he let on. Margot was still on his lap, he kissed her again on the head.

As if to say, don't listen to these people. Dana sometimes thought the family gave him a hard time. But she could see it from their point of view as well. Nathan was bad at smoothing things over. He shouldn't talk to Jean like that, like the kid sister or secretary, somebody he had the authority to dismiss.

"I just worry about the people you're getting into bed with," she told him.

"I said it's over."

But Liesel chipped in now. "Excuse me, but Jean is right. It's not just a question of making an argument, but what the argument will be used for."

"That's because you don't believe in the rule of law," Bill said. It was sometimes hard to tell when he was paying attention. He had started cleaning up the leftovers from unfinished plates of food, reaching across the table and using the bread to mop up sauce.

"Excuse me, that's not true." Liesel raised her voice slightly; this was an old argument, they had had it before. "I believe very much in the law. In some ways, I believe in the law more than you do . . . But there is a purpose to the law, which the law serves. Lawyers should serve it, too."

"That's just what I said. You don't believe in the rule of law."

Dana's drink finally arrived. The waiter brought it over on a round tin tray, on which it looked unnecessarily precarious; the glass, as if sweating, was beaded with water. She took a sip and felt the little hit of liquor and excused herself. She said she needed the restroom, which meant that Julie had to squeeze in so that she could squeeze out and walk between tables to the back of the restaurant. *Essingers*, she thought, looking at herself in the mirror. It always took her a minute to get used to the atmosphere again, to acclimatize to the intensity of their relations. But what she felt was also more complicated than that, envy mixed strangely with a kind of pity, for Paul, who had been raised in this atmosphere and sometimes chose to opt out of it, like now. Her purse was in her hand; she touched the lipstick to her lips, very red, the rest of her face was unadorned, and looked at herself coolly enough. Okay, here we go.

"You didn't go out to cry?" Liesel said, joking unhappily.

"No."

Julie had to scooch in again, to let Dana through, and Ben, who was sitting opposite, said, "Okay, which is she?"

"I don't want to play this game."

"What game?" Dana said.

"Ben has a stupid, mean game they play at school."

"It's stupid," Ben said, "but it's not mean."

"It *is* mean. Either way it's mean."

Nathan said, mostly to Jean, "That's because you haven't thought seriously about the problem of evil."

"Have you seen any of the programs I work on? About immigration camps in Lampedusa? About for-profit nursing homes? I don't think you *can* have . . ."

"You think of evil as basically an American invention for describing the rest of the world. Which it often is. But you cannot understand geopolitics if you think of it as the reasonable disagreements of reasonable people with understandably different aims."

"Who says that's what I think. Mostly it's a question

of people with a lot of money making more out of people with less."

"That's what I mean: the disagreements of reasonable people with different aims."

"They don't seem very reasonable to me."

"Of course they do. Now you're just kidding yourself. Look at the way you live, look at *where* you live, and how much of your life, and your friends' lives, is defined by money and spent trying to get it."

"Okay, Nathan. First of all, I have a *room* in somebody's house, you don't know my friends, you don't know how they live, and I can't believe I'm having to say this to you of all people, given the house you live in and who your friends are . . ."

"I wouldn't deny it. I'm not trying to deny it."

"Please, Jean," Julie said. "Why are you shouting at Nathan?"

"I'm not shouting." But then she looked at her niece and said, "I don't mean to shout." And then, more calmly: "Okay, explain it to me."

"Explain what."

"The problem of evil."

"There is a kind of opposition that cannot be reasoned with or treated reasonably and one of the problems of power, of any government, is what to do with that kind of opposition without sacrificing the rule of law."

"So that's where you come in, right?" Jean said.

Susie said, "Stop picking fights. In front of the kids."

"Who are you talking to? You mean me?" Jean looked at her sister, wide-eyed, a little wild.

"I'm talking to both of you."

"It feels like you're talking to me."

"You feel that because . . . you think that everyone's getting at you."

"That's because everyone's getting at me. And I don't see what the kids have to do with it."

"Please," Susie said. "I find this upsetting."

"Well, I wouldn't want to upset *you*."

"Please." And in fact even Jean could see that Susie looked emotionally charged, bright-eyed with something, pity or worry, on the verge of tears.

"What have I done?"

"This isn't the conversation I wanted to have tonight."

"Well, maybe if I go you can have it." Jean stood up, pushing her chair out, but she had to wait for Ben to budge in before squeezing through.

Dana looked at her with a don't-leave-me look in her eyes. "Where are you going?" she said.

"To make a phone call. To get out of here."

"Vulpine or porcine," Ben said after Jean had gone. Dana could see her descending the mezzanine stairs, onto the main floor level. A waiter was carrying up a tray of food, and she stepped aside. She said something and he laughed, then she said something else and threaded her way between the tables to the entrance. But her neck, her shoulders, the way she carried herself, looked unhappy, as if unhappiness were a weight that affected her movement.

Eventually Dana said, "What?"

"Vulpine or porcine, that's the game. Everybody is one or another."

"It's mean," Julie said. "Either way it's mean."

"It can't be mean if it's mean to everybody. I don't mind. I'm porcine."

"Do you really play this game in school, with your friends?" Dana asked.

"I guess those are the kind of friends I have."

"It's not a nice game," Susie said, though she wasn't really paying attention. She blew her nose on a napkin. "I didn't mean to get into a stupid fight. We've basically been avoiding fighting all day."

"I'll talk to her," Nathan said. "I think I know what's going on."

"She told you?"

"Told you what?" Liesel wanted to know.

"Nothing," Susie said. "Nothing you need to worry about."

Ben was used to adults fighting at the dinner table; his parents often argued. For years, when he was younger, he could lighten the mood by being silly. "It's not a nice game, but it's not a *not* nice game either. It's funny. Which are you?" He looked at Dana.

"I guess I'm vulpine."

"You see, it's funny," Ben said, but he was trying too hard and could hear the effort in his own voice. His touch had gone, something had changed.

Bill said to Fritz, who was sitting at his elbow, "My father had Italian clients, he used to eat with them at these restaurants. I found that out when I was seventeen, and would you believe it, it came as a shock. You forget how young you used to be."

"I had my first cheeseburger at a Wimpy in Covent Garden." Fritz's accent still had a South African flavor, dry and sweet, a little clipped. "I was twenty-four years old. I had just passed my LLM and I thought, why not. The only people who would have cared were a long way away."

"Why is it por*seen*?" Ben said, still pushing. "Why is it vul*pine*?"

"Stop it." Susie finally snapped at him. "Stop it. I've said it's not funny. Stop it now."

Jean, in the rough warm evening air, on her own again, crossed Broadway with the traffic gunning for her but still half a block away and bought a copy of *Time Out* from the deli on the corner. She thought of buying a pack of cigarettes, too, but the truth is, she didn't like smoking much, it was more of a gesture. Henrik smoked sometimes, it was something she did with him, something else his wife didn't know about or pretended not to know about. There was an apartment building next door, with an entryway that had a light on, and she leaned against the wall and flipped through the movie listings, in case there was something she could see once the kids were in bed. But she found it hard to concentrate. All of the movies looked stupid to her. Once you get out of the habit of going to them it's hard to break back in.

Henrik was almost certainly asleep. It was three in the morning in Vranjic, though sometimes he stayed up late on holiday with some of the guys. They played rummy together; he would get drunk and sleep it off in the morning, go for a swim—letting their mother look after the kids. Just thinking about him made her realize how tired she was. The jet lag was almost like a fever, she felt vulnerable and unsure of herself, she needed to lie down. For a minute she watched the cars go by, surging and slowing at the lights, then she took out her cell phone and called Paul.

"Did I wake you up?" she said.

"No, but I'm about to go to bed. What's up?"

Paul was five blocks away—if a fire engine drove past, they could both hear the siren. But it was easier talking to him on the phone.

"I had a stupid fight with Nathan."

"What made it stupid?"

"Me, probably. I don't know. I get a kind of culture shock when I come back here."

But Paul wasn't paying attention or wanted to put her off. "Did you get the meatballs?" he asked.

"I don't want to talk about the meatballs. I don't understand what the big deal is. They're like totally ordinary meatballs in tomato sauce."

"Okay," he said, like she was taking a tone.

"I feel like, for the past twenty-four hours, or whatever it is, I've been engaged in this basically constant low-level warfare and I don't know why."

"Maybe because you're picking fights with everybody."

"Is that what I'm doing?"

"I don't know, Jean."

After a moment, she said: "It's like I get a kind of culture shock when I hang out with our family again."

"Well, you're not a kid anymore. You're used to being on your own."

"That's not what it is. It's because everyone else has kids, it's like the ground has shifted. You don't see it happening because you're part of the problem. I'm not really blaming anybody." Again, he didn't respond, and she eventually said: "Dana told me she told you."

"Yes, she told me about it."

"Am I a bad human being?"

"You're not a bad human being."

"You don't sound very convinced," Jean said. "You're not saying anything."

"I'm thinking. Whether people change because of what they do. Maybe they don't change."

"But what I'm doing is wrong . . ."

"I don't know, Jean. What do you think?"

She felt tired and teary, but all she said was, "Does Susie know?"

"Yes, she knows. I told her." But this time, he broke the silence. "What were you fighting with Nathan about?"

"The problem of evil." He laughed, too close to the mouthpiece, it sounded a little static, and she said, "Did you know about the Drone Memo? It's possible they cited one of Nathan's articles."

"No. I mean, I didn't know."

"Nathan wouldn't admit to anything. I feel like something is happening to all of us that I don't like."

"Yes," Paul said. "I can see that."

The cars kept coming, stopping and coming again, they left streaks of light across her eyes, the rhythm was the rhythm of falling asleep—she felt it in her legs, too, in the weight of her body against the brick wall.

"I need to get through to somebody," she said, in a different voice. "I need to have like a real conversation. Of course, I know what the consequences are. I know he has kids, I take all that very seriously. But at the same time I feel like, I like this guy, it doesn't happen often, I've been around enough to know that . . ."

"You haven't been around so much. You're twenty-nine years old. There's plenty of time to make your own life with someone."

"That's what I'm trying to do. What do you mean?" But she had lost the thread again, of whatever sleepy confession she had briefly felt like making. "I'm not trying to steal *her* life."

"I didn't say you were."

"Yes, you did. It doesn't matter. I don't want to pick a fight with you, too. I'm not an idiot, I know what's going on, people tell me what I already know, and I shout at them for it."

She could hear background noises on the phone, Paul was putting something down or picking something up, she could hear water running and said, "I'm sorry to dump my self-obsession on you like this. When you probably just want to go to bed."

For a few seconds, he didn't answer, and she tried to imagine what he was doing. Making himself something to eat or washing dishes or stocking his gym bag. Finally he said, "Don't worry about it. It makes a nice break from my own self-obsession. Is Dana still there?"

"I guess so, do you want to talk to her? They're still in the restaurant. I made a scene and walked out, I'm across the street."

"Just don't let Bill give her the doggie bag to take home. She can't say no to that kind of thing, but it gets on her nerves and then I have to hear about it later."

She could see Julie coming out of the restaurant and looking around, a kid in Doc Martens, dragging her feet a little. She looked cold, too, from the air-conditioning, she had bare legs. Ben was behind her, faintly self-conscious; he should have held the door and tried to push it open from outside. Then Nathan backed out, with Margot asleep in his arms. Somehow it didn't matter if you knew him, there was something charming about a man in a suit carrying a sleeping child. The girl's shoulder had rumpled up his collar, her hair was in his face. Bill held the door for Fritz, who hobbled past on his cane, elegant and elderly, slightly top-heavy. He used to be a rugby player but at a certain point in life the muscles just weigh you down. Susie and Dana followed, two pretty women in dresses, though Dana was taller and prettier. Even in the way she moved and stood waiting you could see her confidence in that fact; it was just a habit, she couldn't help herself. Everybody was waiting for Liesel. They were looking for Jean, too, but she, feeling wide awake now, had come out the other side of something and said into the phone, "How are *you* doing?"

"I don't know." The water was still running—maybe he was running a bath. "I don't want to play tomorrow. Part of me wants to walk out on the whole thing. You know, before they can kick me out."

"What whole thing?"

But Dana had seen her, and Jean waved back—she held up the magazine by way of explanation. Liesel came out, limping slightly; there were too many people on the sidewalk, anybody passing by had to walk around them. The kids kept getting in the way. Bill had a brown paper bag in his hands.

"Listen, Paul, I should go," Jean said, but she didn't go. The traffic intervened and she didn't want to get off the phone. "Should I worry about you, too?" she asked.

"I feel like I'm not being very nice to Dana," he said.

"So be nicer to her."

"I'm trying but maybe not hard enough."

"It shouldn't feel like trying," Jean said.

"Look, I don't want to start the whole business up again. But that's one of those things you say because you haven't been there before."

The lights changed and the cars pulled up at the other end of the block. "I have to go," Jean said. "I'm not mad, I just have to go. Don't worry about anything now. Listen, if I don't see you before the match, kick his ass. Kick his *ass*," she said again and ran across Broadway to join the others; her cowboy boots clicked and slipped a little on the asphalt.

Nathan was heading uptown. Margot still slept in his arms, he was going to take a cab and stood out in the street to flag one down, shifting the weight of his daughter to put out a hand. Jean stepped out into the street. "I don't want to fight with you," she said.

"Nobody's fighting."

Then a car pulled up and he waved Julie in. "Say good-night, Julie." Goodnight, she said—her voice had gone almost pale. After she was in, Nathan turned and, bending down, retreated awkwardly into his seat, so that Margot didn't hit her head on the door. Liesel watched them go, there were tears in her eyes; she was very tired, it had been a long day. All of these complicated arrangements wore her down, crosscurrents of sympathy. Nathan had such—he made himself so difficult to agree with, even when he was telling you . . . asking for help. But she always felt this way, even when he was a boy. And the more you disagreed with him, the harder he made himself to love. It was like a deliberate challenge. Susie was the other way around. If she didn't get her way, she burst into tears. Paul never wanted anything, he just watched. Jean always wanted everyone to be happy, according to her ideas. Like a dog with a bone, she wouldn't let it go until you were.

"He's a good father," Liesel said to Bill, whose knee felt stiff after sitting down for so long; he kept pacing around. She meant, I'm glad he has those girls to love him.

Fritz needed a taxi, too—he lived in Brooklyn. "I can drop you off *en route*," he offered, in his gentlemanly way.

But Bill wanted to walk. "It's not far."

"Liesel?"

She would have preferred a ride, but said to Fritz, "Thank you, I'll walk, too." Leaving him out, on his own, a single, childless man, returning home to his apartment. The taxi arrived and he put his cane in first then slid himself painfully along the bench seat.

"You and me both," Bill said. Fritz had to lift his knee with his hands to swing his leg in.

"In London, you can *step* into a taxi. You can *walk* in."

But he closed the door behind him and the cab pulled away.

Slowly they were diminishing—just the six of them now, a more manageable number. Liesel said to Ben, the last child left at the end of the day: "Do you know how I hurt my knee? Have I told you that story?"

"You can tell me again." His glasses both magnified his eyes and made them hard to read.

Dana and Bill walked a little in advance. Against the grain of the traffic on their side of the street, which was heading uptown, through Harlem and Washington Heights, some of the drivers making their way to the GW Bridge and the suburbs, going home on a Sunday night. They passed a bank, dark now but exposed, the arrangement of furniture, chairs around desks, a table somewhere, a long counter, strangely suggestive of a certain mood, a certain kind of friendliness . . . Then a pet store, with stuffed animals on display; another restaurant, half-empty, a couple sitting in the window over half-finished plates. She had her legs crossed, he was leaning back. Dana wondered what their relationship was.

"Is everything okay in the apartment?" she asked, in her good girl manner. "I'm sorry you can't stay at ours."

"It's an extremely comfortable apartment."

Susie and Jean brought up the rear—Susie had been lingering a little. "I should just tell you, because I already told the others," she said, and for a second Jean imagined the most terrible things, cancer or divorce, something to do with the boys.

"I'm pregnant," Susie said and Jean put her arms around her sister and held her so she had to stop walking.

Dana split off at 87th Street. Bill tried to give her the left-overs, but for some reason Jean stepped in. "She can give it to Cal tomorrow," Bill said, slightly hurt. "He probably likes meatballs."

"Dad, stop," Jean said. "She doesn't want it. I'll have it for lunch."

Dana, feeling uncomfortable, tried to avoid choosing sides. She made a funny gesture with her hands, as if to take it, and then not—yes, no, yes, no. A kind of dance with Bill. But Jean insisted. "I'll be up at four with jet lag. I'll be ready for lunch by nine o'clock. And if we throw it away, we throw it away. That's our business."

"Speaking of which," Bill said. Certain practical details gave him pleasure to think about. He had to hold himself back from discussing them, but then, when the opportunity arose, you could tell he had a kind of checked momentum. "How are you getting to the stadium? We could meet at Times Square and ride up together."

"I don't know. Paul's taking the car, but he'll drive in early to warm up. I haven't really started thinking about all that yet."

"We could share a taxi," Liesel said.

"Not everybody fits. We'd need two cars, and the 7 train goes right there."

"Dad," Jean said. "It's late. We can talk about it in the morning. Dana doesn't have to stand here listening to this."

"All right, all right."

In the end, Dana left empty-handed and walked along the half block to the back entrance suddenly alone—out of their presence. Some silly part of her thought, I could go anywhere, the night is young, but in fact, she said hello to one of the younger doormen (a kid, really, with a scratchy bit of stubble on his face; his cap looked too large for his head, he was pushing an empty brass-poled cart along) and passed through the little archway into the courtyard. The fountain sounded cool and quiet, it was the background noise of privilege, and reminded Dana that she had on nothing but a cotton dress. She felt chilly now and wanted to get inside.

Waiting for the elevator, she started thinking about Michael. For reasons she didn't totally understand, she found it incredibly embarrassing to have her "in-laws" staying at his apartment. Why? Because he was so rich? The Essingers were hardly poor, but she could imagine their reaction to the furniture, the gilt mirrors and Tiffany lamps and claw-footed sofas, the fake Roman frieze over the fireplace. Not Liesel's style; it wasn't really Dana's style either. Not anymore. Maybe what she felt wasn't so much embarrassment as resentment, at the way the Essingers colonize everything. There are so many of them, and they are all so sure about everything; it gets into your head. But she thought about Michael, too—about what he was actually like.

When they met, she was a junior at Amherst; he was

fifty years old and "semiretired" as he liked to put it. He had just given some money to the Isenberg School of Management, and so they "let me give a lecture," he said, "about leadership. You know how much this privilege cost me? A hundred thousand dollars. I plan to enjoy it." Dana was a history major, but she worked part-time for the Special Events Facility Staff and helped to serve drinks at the reception afterward. Michael chatted her up; she wore a little black apron, black shoes, she had her hair tied back. But her face looked serious—all that human contact stressed her out. Wandering around with a bottle of white in one hand and a bottle of red in the other. You have to think about when to approach a group of people and when to leave them alone. Around a third of the men try to start a conversation. Michael had a hard job persuading her to stop and talk. One of the things he said to her, in the course of the evening, something she never forgot, was this: you should get more pleasure out of being so handsome. It was a line, but that didn't make it less true. She felt he had noticed something important about her. Afterward, he asked her back to his suite at the Lord Jeffery Inn. ("This place is a four-star dump," he complained. "That's basically what four-star *means*.") One of them joked, it might have been Dana, that *she* was part of the hundred-thousand-dollar deal—a way of addressing the creepiness but also turning it into part of the game.

That was that, she thought, walking back after breakfast to her college dorm room. But the following weekend he invited her to New York, he sent a car to drive her, and three hours later she arrived at that apartment. Everything made a tremendous impression on her, the gilt mirrors, the Tiffany lamps, the Roman frieze, the little view of the Park from the Juliet balcony . . . Maybe this was part of her embarrassment. From her mother, Dana had inherited very conventional ideas of class and taste; Michael appealed to them. He was also smart, attentive, lively, healthy, and rich. And they had a good time. For a while, she thought of herself as the fun young thing, giving him new life, but later she realized, or maybe he realized, that in fact *he* was the one with the energy and the pleasure receptors, and she was holding him back—she was just an ordinary girl. The divorce was amicable and his idea, that's how far she had fallen. There was something wrong with her, she didn't have any drive, any initiative, she didn't know what she wanted from life, she just drifted along. Even Paul could sense this, or was starting to.

By this point, she was in the elevator, riding slowly up. The light kept ticking along the fantail of numbers over the door. Arriving like this at the place where you live makes the whole setup feel slightly imaginary—it's like coming through a portal or a wormhole, your apartment has no immediate connection to the rest of the world, it's floating somehow. She used to like this feeling, just the two of them, and then the three of them, alone together on their cloud-island in the city. But now she was thinking, as the elevator opened out on her floor and she reached into her purse for the key, I wonder if he's asleep. She also wondered if she wanted him to be or not, and if he *was*, whether she should sleep in the single in Cal's room or climb in next to Paul under the duvet at the risk of waking him up.

"Why wouldn't you let her take the food?" Bill said, when Dana was gone. "She's got a small boy. It's a lot of work, cooking from scratch every day."

"She doesn't want our leftovers," Jean said. Already she could feel a shift in alignment, she was taking sides again, on behalf of others, in this case Paul by way of defending Dana. She felt slightly happier.

"Then she can say so." Bill had reached the age when he was starting to lose these pointless battles. For the first ten years, that's all you do with kids—argue them into bed, or out of bed. Get dressed for school, get changed. You shout at them to finish their plates, to empty the dishwasher, to practice piano. And in the end, when you want to, you get your way. There's always some nuclear option on the table, you can raise your voice, you can pull rank. If you want to win, you win. Then they go away for a few years, to college, they make their own lives somewhere, and when they come back, slowly, you feel the tables turning. The power has gone, your rank is ceremonial, and something else is changing, too, more fundamental. You start to feel out of touch. Maybe you're wrong, maybe they know better. Doubt creeps in.

"She *can't* say so. Not to you. Think about it for a second. You paid for the meal. What's she going to say?"

"Then she can take it and throw it away at home. What's the big deal?"

"If she does that, Paul has to hear about it. He has to get involved."

"Why should he be involved? It has nothing to do with him."

"It's like you've never met a human being before."

"All right. I give up." And then, a minute later, to show he has a little fight left in him: "I still don't see what the big deal is." But it doesn't sound like fight.

Liesel, limping slightly, was telling a story—and Ben walked with her, touchingly slow, keeping pace. Susie followed a little behind, listening; her son could play the gentleman when he wanted to. One thing David always insisted on, in his English way, was manners. He could be very charming, especially with old ladies, which tended to annoy Liesel, who didn't want to be treated like one. Susie knew that David knew what he was doing, that it amused him to irritate his German mother-in-law by being extra-English and polite. You reach a certain stage in a marriage where the motives *all* seem ulterior. Not even that, but the whole point of an outer self is to suggest and withhold information about the inner; and once you've stepped through the curtain it's hard to keep believing in the magic show. In things like charm. But with Ben it was different. He was too young to appear condescending; he just seemed interested and well brought-up.

"Were you mad at your brother?" he asked. "Afterward."

"No, I felt sorry for him. He was very ashamed. He always took everything—*an sich*. On himself: too personally."

Liesel had told him how she first hurt her knee, years ago, when she was a twelve-year-old girl. It was the summer holidays, a few weeks after the end of school, and she kept following her brother around. Klaus was two years older and very handsome, with the sort of sensitive unhappy face you used to see in movie stars. Like Leslie Howard. ("Do you know who Leslie Howard is?") Not particularly masculine, though he was also very good with his hands, in the way boys were then. He could catch fish, he could build a fire, he could fix a bicycle. And Liesel kept tagging along, she wanted to be where he was. Mostly he was very patient with her, but in sly ways he also got his own back.

There was a hill near their house, in the middle of a park. Not a natural hill but man-made, piled up in layer after layer like a wedding cake, with a kind of crown on top—a platform for looking out. To celebrate some famous inventor or statesman, after whom the park was named. No, it was an astronomer, she couldn't remember his name. There were other things in the park, too, slides and seesaws, but Klaus decided the playground was for children. He used to push his bicycle to the top of the hill, climb on and let it roll down. There were ridges you could walk around, every ten or fifteen feet along the side of the hill; and when the bike hit a ridge, it flew. Klaus would skip into the air for a half second and come back to earth again, on the next slope, and keep going. Liesel wanted to try it, too. He told her she was too small. She said, in that case, why don't we play on the seesaw together. But he was too old for the playground. Children can spend hours like this, arguing back and forth. ("Maybe you know something about this.") Klaus had other friends around, too—all of the kids from his school ended up at the park. He couldn't back down.

So Liesel insisted on trying to ride down the hill. And finally he said, "*Meinetwegen.*" It means, if you must. Or, as far as I'm concerned. She pushed her bike to the top of the hill, over the ridges and up the slope, which was difficult enough—he refused to help her. If you're old enough to ride down it, he told her, you must be strong enough to push yourself up it. Which she did, at last. Everybody was watching, all of Klaus's friends; she couldn't back down either. And so she climbed onto her seat and pulled her feet off the ground. She didn't have to pedal; the hill took care of the rest. She remembers the first few seconds, gathering speed, feeling a jolt, her wheels left the ground, she was flying, really, and then she remembers lying in a heap at the bottom of the hill with a terrible pain in her knee.

At that time, which was just after the war, they didn't have all the complicated surgeries available for knee injuries that they have now. It swelled up and she couldn't walk on it for a week, they kept her in bed, but eventually it got better. Years later it started hurting again—like a kind of memory, returning.

"But I was never angry with him, I loved him too much. I wanted to be like him. And it was my fault. He was a child, too. Fourteen years old but in his own way still very young."

Jean, who was listening, said to Susie in an undertone: "Does Ben know? Did you tell him?"

"Yes, he knows."

So she said to Ben: "Are you excited to have a new baby in the family? When did you find out?"

It seemed to her strange, how little they were talking about the pregnancy; Jean wanted to redress the balance. Bill was walking five paces ahead, by himself—they had turned east on 82nd Street, which was darker and quieter than Broadway, and were passing the heavily wrought, slightly greenish iron doors of a church, with wide steps. Someone was having a beer on top of the steps, sitting down and drinking from a paper bag. He looked indulgently on; there was a backpack at his feet. He had the air of someone without access to a private bathroom. After the church, there was a dry cleaners; the shop front, with a panel over the window, hadn't been changed in thirty years. What surprised Jean was how old-fashioned it looked, the italics of the name and then the white all caps: *Fang* CLEANERS DRY CLEAN * LAUNDRY * ALTERATIONS FREE PICK-UP & DELIVERY. And then a telephone number. Already it had the faintly vintage feel of sawdust and striped awnings, part of the classy past. Next to it, the blank brick wall of an apartment building was stenciled with the shadow of the fire escape, a double zigzag like a slightly distorted reflection of the real red rusty thing, which stopped short ten feet from the ground. They reached the street lamp that was casting the shadow, and the lights and noise of Amsterdam on the corner.

"Mom told me this afternoon," Ben said.

"I wanted us to have a weekend together." Susie was using the voice she used around her children, that was partly addressed to them and partly to everyone else.

"Just you and me, before school starts, before everything starts."

"Just you and me and fifteen uncles aunts cousins grandparents . . ." Jean said, apologetically.

"He knows what I mean. Without David or William. When they're small like that, you spend all this time alone together, and then slowly . . . forces conspire." She put her arm around her son, who came up to her shoulder; she kissed him on the head and added, "To take them away." It worried her slightly that Jean might understand some personal reference to her situation, and so she went on: "We had a nice train ride into the city."

"I'm excited." Ben seemed to tolerate his mother's affections placidly. "I'm more worried about William. He'll have to get used to not being the baby anymore."

"Everything's hardest on the oldest." Liesel had a way of not quite responding to what had been said before. Also, she was still caught up in her story. Susie noticed that more and more of her mother's conversation took the form of recollection; it saddened her vaguely. Liesel had always told stories but now it seemed she couldn't help herself. "Klaus was really a wonderful big brother," she said to Ben. "Afterward, when he saw what had happened, he tried to carry me home. But I was too big. He had to put me down on one of the benches, and then leave me— he ran to tell our mother. One of the things he told her, which he admitted to me afterward, is that he always used the brakes on his bike when he came down the hill. He has a real honesty streak; he has to say the worst about himself. Whenever I'm angry with him these days, and Klaus can be a difficult and irritating man, I remember that for thirty or forty feet, when I was twelve years old, he tried to carry me home."

Bill was waiting for the lights to change. "What does this do to your teaching?" he asked Susie, when the others caught up.

"Nothing, really. I'm on an ad hoc basis anyway. This fall I've got a pretty full load and then nothing in the spring, and after that we'll work it out the way we always do."

Susie was used to the fact that her father expressed his love by worrying over practical details, and yet she couldn't help being disappointed by how little the atmosphere had changed. It was a Sunday evening; they were walking back from a restaurant. That's the problem with secrets, they never matter as much as you want them to. Her parents disapproved of the backseat role she had taken to David's professional career. That much was obvious — they resented him for it, too, which wasn't entirely fair. Because the baby was *her* idea, at least, it's what she wanted, more than he wanted it . . . It felt to Susie like a kind of renewed ambition, a way of taking interest in life again, and starting over. That's what she wanted to explain, but somehow the conversation never let her. It was like attempting to fit something bulky into the opening of a narrow plastic bag.

At least Jean was trying to make nice. She said to Susie, "Maybe at one point this weekend you can cut my hair. My fringe keeps getting in the way."

"You mean your bangs." A vague sort of tease, about becoming English; she didn't really mean anything by it, and Jean didn't notice.

"I refuse to pay forty pounds at a hairdresser. There are cheaper places in my neighborhood, but mostly for Afro-Caribbeans. There's a barbershop under the tracks by the train station, but I don't have the guts to go in. I've never seen a white person in there."

Susie suggested: "You could give me a five-minute backrub in return. David doesn't see the point of them anymore. He says it's what you do when you're courting."

A small admission, of something missing, to answer Jean's appeal. But as soon as she said it, Susie heard something else, too, in her own voice, a boast about the familiarity of marriage, which Jean was in danger of underestimating. As if what Susie really meant was this: there's a kind of superficial niceness in all these relationships that goes away. Oh who knows. When you're sensitive to something and still a little angry or upset (because your sister is sleeping with a married man who has kids), no matter how much love or good will you also feel, it's hard not to get hemmed in by subtext.

They were passing the Natural History Museum, walking beside the park where Jean and Susie and Ben had eaten their bagels earlier in the day. The building, lit up at night, strongly illuminated from below, looked like a court of law. There were still people on the sidewalk, a high percentage of dog owners, taking their dogs for a bathroom break before bedtime, but the park itself was closed and under the lights seemed vaguely threatening, deserted and under surveillance. All of these civic spaces have day selves and night selves. "Maybe tomorrow morning we should actually try to go in," Susie said. (Another little dig?) "What time do we need to leave for Flushing Meadows?"

"I'd like to get there no later than 12:30." Bill had thought about all of this more than anyone else.

"I wake up at six thirty anyway."

"You can eat the meatballs," Jean joked.

"So what does that mean? When do we have to leave the house?"

"It's about half an hour from Times Square."

"Longer than that," Jean said.

"Forty-five minutes."

"You have to get to Times Square first."

"What's the big deal? It's five stops on the 1 train."

"Unless we take a taxi," Liesel said. "In which case we can pick up Dana on the way."

"Then we need two taxis. And we get stuck in traffic."

"I don't know if Dana wants to be picked up. That's not the sense I got." And so on.

It was almost ten o'clock, the streetlights and storefronts and headlights mixed their glow. Clouds had come over the sky, rolling darkly over Central Park, which Susie could see at the end of the block—a row of trees on either side leading up to a green smudge, shapeless and shifting slightly in the wind. The temperature seemed to have skipped a step going down the stairs. End of summer feelings, rain coming, back to school. Susie had stopped entirely paying attention; she had the half-anxious, half-consoling sense that her real life was elsewhere. When she was fighting with David she sometimes thought, the people who really know me are Liesel and Bill, Jean and

Paul and Nathan; but then, in their presence, David somehow became a source of protection, something held in
reserve. She could talk to him about them afterward.

Eventually, as they waited in the lobby of Michael's
building for the elevator to take them up, Bill said: "Paul
should be asleep by now."

"I hate it, how public it is, what he has to go through."
Liesel was tired, she had walked too far, it was late, and
everything she felt had risen very near to the surface.

"What is he going through?" Bill for some reason had
a reservoir of indignation on this subject, which he could
dip into at will. "He's playing tennis."

Jean didn't want to take sides. "He's winning, he's losing."

"I'm glad it's almost over," Liesel said. "And he can live
the rest of his life."

"What is that life?" There are arguments you have with
your wife that acquire new energy when you have them in
front of your kids. "This is his life. What do you think that
life is supposed to be?"

But Liesel had an answer this time. "He said to me, he
wants to buy a house in Texas."

"What for?" It was Jean now who seemed indignant.
Who wanted to deny that her mother might have inside
information. "For a couple weeks in summer, so he can
take a break from New York."

"No, he wants to live there, he wants to move there."

"I can guarantee you," Jean said, "that's not what he
wants to do."

"He's already talking to architects, he's looking at land."

"Does Dana know? What's Dana's reaction to all this."

"I haven't talked to her."

"Because it's Dana here that you should really be worrying about in that case."

This is how they talked, Jean and Liesel, Bill sometimes chipping in. While Susie felt more and more removed from it all—and only slightly upset, though maybe the bruise would show up later. At the restaurant they had asked her about her due date, and Liesel said something about morning sickness, which she used to suffer from, too. More stories. But the focus of their attention was clearly on Paul, at least right now, which she didn't blame *him* for—even as a kid, he had the air of wanting it least. Probably the two go together. The elevator came and she stepped in. Even Ben looked tired now, though he wouldn't admit it; while the elevator rose, she took his hand but when the doors opened he let go of her again. Kids give you a few years of protection, from everything else, including your own family, your own childhood, but unless you keep making new ones the protection runs out.

MONDAY

When Paul woke up, too early, he could tell that the weather had shifted. It had rained overnight but the rain had stopped — now there was just a leftover glitter between the curtains. But he could hear the wind in the flaws of the contact between the window frame and sill, a kind of coming and going noise, which suggested to him for some reason a whistling circular motion, or somebody blowing out and in. He didn't mind the wind so long as it didn't rain. It sucked, waiting around for the courts to clear, everybody hanging around, Bill and Liesel, too, in the wet and cold (at least Paul could stay in the locker room), while you had to work out when to put food in your stomach. But a little wind would probably help his cause. Borisov was a heavy hitter, he had narrow margins of error. Dana wasn't in bed.

One of the things Marcello used to tell him on game days was . . . let everything go. Think of yourself as a stick in a current, don't fight it. That's what they said about airplane turbulence, too. The stress on the system is much higher if you try to keep still. Feel what you feel. As an athlete, you have to come to terms with this kind of mystic speak, which always made him think of Nathan, who despised it. Not despised it really but just thought it was dumb. Though Marcello in other respects, in other areas of life, was a fairly sensible hard-nosed guy, and Paul himself eventually had to admit that he believed some of this stuff. You don't know why a shot goes in sometimes and sometimes not. There are technical things you can correct but even that is just another way of deferring the uncertainty, pushing it back to another stage in the process, because who knows why you sometimes keep your elbow at a certain angle and sometimes don't when every time you practice a shot you try to practice it the same way.

His bedside clock, one of those radio cubes, said 5:53 . . . it was much too early to get up, the forepart of the day was going to seem long enough already. The cream curtains had lozenges of yellow and brown; Dana had picked them. Most of the apartment was a compromise between what she wanted and what he would put up with. Which was his fault not hers—she was always asking for more involvement from him. More and more his default state of mind seemed to be preoccupation, some kind of not paying attention. Because there was nothing he wanted to pay attention to. At least, nothing around him. Cal sometimes. The wardrobe on the far wall (from Ligne Roset in Gramercy Park) had a mirror running up the middle, and with his head on the pillow Paul could see himself. A youngish middle-aged man looking tired, wide-eyed and slightly blinky at the same time. Me. Even when they were fighting, he disliked sleeping alone. The bed without Dana in it seemed colder and lopsided. But there was also this . . . relationship to yourself that needed to be interrupted or interfered with for you to get a decent night's sleep. Otherwise you stayed up too late, reading, or woke up too early, or thrashed around under the covers, since nobody was there to mind or tell you to stop.

Paul was never good at lying in bed, even as a teenager. There was a steady moderately high-level current running through his body that kept pushing him around. But he tried to force himself for a minute to go back to sleep. That early morning, rainy light coming through the curtains is something he always liked, where you can't tell if it's just the dawn or the wet that darkens the day. He had heard Dana come in a little before ten o'clock last night, by which point he had already turned off the bedside lamp. But he was awake and waited for her. She seemed to be messing around in the kitchen, then he heard the noise of the TV, which annoyed him, because if he fell asleep now she'd wake him up coming to bed. It's terrible the stupid frustrations that mount up against your lover for being somebody else and not you. He could have called out to Dana, but in this mood he didn't want to shout or get up again, he was trying to wind down. And then he must have fallen asleep. She must have slept in the room with Cal.

Okay, feel what you feel but this is the kind of feeling you have to put out of your head. Unless it can serve as a useful distraction. Sometimes that works, too. Paul never much liked game days, he hated the fact that the only part that matters is a two-hour island in the middle, when you're on court. The rest of the day you may as well be dead. But the slow buildup of tension also has a purifying effect, like keeping the fast on Yom Kippur, which he used to do as a kid, to please Bill. You've got one thing to worry about, a game of tennis. At least this is the story you tell yourself. Because the truth is, what really happens, all these anxieties start rising up, you can't sleep right, you can't rest, you don't want to waste your energy either. You worry about the time, you worry about your bags. The Germans have a word for it, *Reisefieber*, the unrest you suffer from the night before a flight. It takes a certain kind of craziness to live like this. Every time he walks on court, he thinks, don't make me go out there.

Several years ago, before Cal was born, he rented a house in the Lake District after losing in the second round at Wimbledon. Just for a week to clear his head—Jean took the train up, too. They went hiking together, they ate pub lunches, he didn't play or watch tennis. One afternoon they rented a canoe and went out on Lake Windermere. A midsummer day, but the water was choppy, it had rained that morning, the lake looked swollen, the temperature was somewhere in the 50s. Like winter in Austin. Paul started goofing around. He wanted to see how fast he could push it and dug his oar in hard—the weight of his body pulled them over, and suddenly he felt a momentum that he couldn't reverse. The cold is what really knocks the air out of you. When he came up again, Jean was hanging onto the side of the boat, looking blue. "I don't want to be in the water, I don't want to be in the water," she kept saying, with rapid chattering teeth. The lifeguard had already seen them. He brought blankets, and they drank hot chocolate afterward in one of the lakeside hotels.

For some reason, the sight of his sister repeating in a slightly insane way this totally reasonable phrase stuck with him. *I don't want to be in the water, I don't want to be in the water.* For the rest of the week, he used it to make fun of her, even though (as she liked to point out) the whole thing was his fault. And sometimes when he walked on court, especially at a big tournament, when what you're walking out into is a lot of ambient noise, which turns into cheering briefly, and then back into ambient noise . . . at the moment you come through the tunnel, out of the shade, with your opponent walking beside you, whether you like him or not, Jean's line ran through his head. Just in that tone of voice she used, which wasn't whiny at all but extremely cold-sounding and matter-of-fact. Last night, when she called, he was shaving; he always shaved the night before a match. And he basically didn't want to be on the phone; he tried to work the razor over his cheek with the phone in his ear, switching sides as he went along. His attention span for other people was incredibly small at the moment—like one of those hardened arteries that can barely let through the oxygenated blood. But she got through anyway, and he felt like, if I tell you what I actually think about what you're doing, you'll have good reason to call me a hypocrite later on. Which doesn't mean that what I'm thinking isn't true.

One of the small mysteries of life is why you get up when you do. For several minutes you lie there, telling yourself, I need to get up, and nothing happens. Then suddenly you've swung your legs over the edge of the bed. The self makes decisions without informing you. More of that Inner Game of Tennis bullshit, which in spite of himself Paul basically believed . . . another way that he had let his family down. First you drop out of Stanford, and then these are the ideas you pick up. He pissed in the bathroom, holding his dick lightly in his hands and feeling his bare feet on the tiles. And for some reason some of the old hopefulness, which he couldn't help either, just the animal response to life, the current running through him, rose up. Everything ached less than usual. This is what happens when you ease up the day before. The muscles in the balls of his feet, his knees, the muscles in his thighs, his right shoulder, his elbow . . . It's easier to keep the body happy than the soul. Something else Marcello used to tell him. He washed his hands and face and picked at his eyes a little, staring in the mirror, with water dripping off his brows. Trying to get the blepharitis off, between the lashes. A nervous habit, which was basically satisfying, because there was an end in sight. Between his thumb and index finger he flicked the flakes of dandruff into the sink.

Cal's room was on the way to the kitchen, and for a second he stopped in the doorway to look in. He pushed the door gently open with the backs of his fingers. Dana was asleep in the single bed, her legs hung over the side and she had her face in the pillow. It's very hard to not like someone when they're asleep. She wore shorts and Paul could see, in one or two places, a tiny spidery explosion of veins on her thigh, which she felt self-conscious of and blamed on childbirth. A friend of hers had had them removed but they left a brown patch. Poor Dana. He felt distantly tender toward her, in the way you do toward someone you're about to hurt, before they find out. The crib stood against the wall, making an L-shape with the bed. Cal lay with his head back and his mouth open. Part of what was touching about the position, which didn't look very comfortable (his arms were thrown awkwardly outward, as if in surprise), is that no sound came out.

In the kitchen, where Paul fixed himself a bowl of cereal, the level early-morning light seemed strangely colorless. It reflected off the messy flashing of the apartment building roofs below and scattered against the raindrops on the wide sash window. Like a poked anthill, the city was beginning to stir. There was traffic coming down Broadway, you could hear the noise of trucks driving through wet, a few cab horns, and on the other side of the kitchen wall, the service elevator in operation. Another Monday morning, at the end of summer; people going to work.

—

Nathan had a meeting at nine o'clock; he was busy enough that whenever he had a reason to be somewhere, he tried to fit in other reasons on the side. But the kids would have to come along. There was a woman he knew in grad school, another Rhodes scholar, named Sandy Franks. She had just come back from a session of the International Law Commission in Geneva. Her day job, as she liked to call it, was teaching at Columbia, but there was also a Clinton connection. She had worked for Hillary in the State Department, and her husband, who was substantially older, sat on the Advisory Board of the Democratic National Committee. In term time, he moonlighted at the Business School. He was basically a hedge-fund guy, who had retired at fifty, divorced his first wife (their daughters were in college), and gotten involved in politics, which is how he met Sandy. They didn't have kids of their own.

Sandy suggested Community Food and Juice, near Columbia. It was basically around the corner from her office (she lived somewhere on Lexington, across the Park), and that way she could get some breakfast on her way in. Nathan resented the implication that she was making time for him, but what are you going to do. He generally had mixed feelings about this woman. At Oxford Nathan thought of her as a not-very-serious person. There were two basic categories of people and she belonged to the wrong one. But since grad school he had started to revise and expand his sense of the different kinds of intelligence. There were people who got things done, and Sandy had made the most of moderate intellectual ability—she did her homework, she followed through, she made connections. She made sacrifices, too, and spent her first six years after law school working with Senator Briscoe, the ranking Democrat on Ways and Means. You can't go from there to an academic job (she started at Georgetown before moving to Columbia) without putting in the hours. It's not a bad idea to keep in touch with people like that. He also thought it likely that Hillary was going to run in 2016, that she would probably win, and that Sandy by that point might offer real access to the president. So he gave her a call.

Community Food and Juice turned out to be the kind of place he tended to avoid: one of those organic coffee shops that overcharges for uninteresting food and bad coffee, where the barista is probably some college kid. (Nathan was sometimes tempted to go behind the bar and make it himself.) Most of the tables were communal, but they had a few plastic four-seaters under the awning outside, so he asked the waitress for a cloth and started drying the chairs. The weather was on the cool side for late summer, overcast but pleasant enough. Sandy was late and he set up Margot with paper and crayons—Julie could read her Laura Ingalls Wilder. And they could order what they liked. If you drag them along to this kind of thing, you have to let them win the small battles.

When Sandy showed up, he remembered why he disliked her. Her businesslike efficient friendliness, very American, which is how it seemed to him at Oxford—she used superlatives without enthusiasm or irony. It's wonderful to see you again. And these are your beautiful kids. Sandy's stepdaughters were both in their twenties. The younger one had just had a baby (the boyfriend, whom nobody approved of, was luckily out of the picture), and she was learning what it was like to help out. The laugh she laughed she must have laughed a dozen times before. It's amazing how quickly certain intimacies become public currency. But it's also true that for a childless married woman, who has just turned the corner of forty, you need some kind of protection against sympathy. You need stories to fill the gap made by what hasn't happened to you.

Mostly they talked about other things—the ILC, for example. Sandy had chaired a Working Group on the immunity of state officials, and Nathan was good at asking intelligent questions, even in subject areas of which he had no prior knowledge. In fact, she said, the trouble with these committees is that they rely too much on agreement; nothing gets done. It's one of the problems of internationalism, it produces bureaucracy. The minutes just . . . for some of these people you get the sense, the whole purpose is to add to the minutes. Nathan himself was working on an article about terrorism and the law: how the rule of law was applied to and affected by non-state actors, and how in turn the obligations of the state might adapt to the presence of new powers of surveillance. There were also privacy issues about the ways in which governments shared information. Margot while they talked was testing the slope of the table by letting one of her crayons roll down, but Julie had started listening to these conversations.

Sandy kept referring back to Oxford. "The way we lived. It was only two years of my life, but . . ."

The food arrived; she had ordered a bran muffin and a flat white. The coffee turned out to be not bad—Nathan had a double espresso. Julie stared, visibly shocked, at her eggs Benedict. She was experimenting, trying new things in restaurants, and usually ended up not finishing her plate, feeling annoyed at herself and slightly hungry.

"It was just so . . . civilized," Sandy went on. "I keep thinking, *that's* the kind of nation-state I'd like to be a part of."

Nathan couldn't figure out what she was trying to prove—making him jump through the hoop of reminiscence. "I don't know. The place was full of pettiness and narrow-mindedness. And also the lowest kind of intellectual snobbery. But I met some smart people."

"Just walking to the Bodleian every day. Sitting in the reading room."

"The New York Public Library isn't bad."

She smiled at him. "I suppose it's because in those days I could read what I wanted to. I didn't think of it as a business."

"It always seemed like a business to me. Maybe a different kind of business. Plato was in business. Rawls was in the same business as Plato." But he knew that this kind of arrogance was part of his appeal and felt slightly ashamed.

Julie, listening, could feel that her father didn't like this woman—she didn't like her either. Her face was covered in fine powder, practically the same color as her hair. In her matching lilac jacket and skirt, she was one of those people who looked like a cake in the window, not quite real. Clémence, Julie's mother, never wore makeup, except sometimes a little dark red lipstick that showed very brightly on her darkish skin. A few of the girls she knew in school had started to play around with eyeliner and foundation; some of them wore earrings, too. But Julie wasn't interested. There's a reason boys don't wear makeup, and it's not because they're missing out, she figured. She didn't understand why Nathan wanted this woman to like him.

But Nathan himself was changing his mind about Sandy. She had read, or read extracts and reviews of, Bobbitt's book, *The Shield of Achilles*, about the death of the nation-state—she knew his editor at Knopf. And last year at Davos, Tony Blair said to her . . . but it wasn't so much what he said as the fact that this is what he wanted to talk about. It's a mistake to think that ideas have no influence, that intellectuals don't matter. These people read books, she said. Or they listen to people who read books. The closer you get to real power the more you realize that it functions like other forms of power you've already known. In the faculty lounge, for example. She seemed very sure of herself, of the rules of her world. Part of the problem with talking to insiders is that you end up playing the whole conversation on their home court. And yet her face under the makeup also showed a kind of brittleness; someone more naturally confident wouldn't lay it on so thick.

In spite of himself (somehow he couldn't help it), Nathan mentioned his meeting with Michael Labro from the Justice Department. Sandy knew him, too; she said he had a difficult relationship with the Attorney General but wouldn't elaborate. In his private practice days, Holder used to be a partner at Covington & Burling—they did some work for the NFL, and her husband had a connection there that meant they sometimes ended up at the same events. "He likes to talk sports."

"That's not the sense I got," Nathan said. "I mean, about Labro and Holder. In any case, for me, it's just a means to an end." But you can't win these games; even in his own ears it sounded like posturing.

"The Justice Department's a mess," she told him. "It's too big, it's too political, and all the power lines are tangled up. Everybody's scrambling." Later, she added, "If we're talking about what I think we're talking about, you need to be careful what you put in print. But you know that; you don't need me to tell you."

Nathan, his eyes flicking back and forth, not nervously
but restlessly, felt chastened somehow. When you seek out
certain kinds of success you expose yourself to a lot of
good advice. And not just advice but you actually learn to
respect people you don't particularly want to respect. A
crumb of muffin, a flake of bran, had stuck in the powder
on Sandy's cheek, near the corner of her mouth. (Julie had
been watching it with fascination.) After Sandy finished
eating, she took a compact from her purse and in front of
them all examined herself briefly in the small round mirror. She adjusted her hair, she brushed the crumb off, and
looked up at Nathan, smiling—the meeting was over.

Margot had started to act up anyway. She was licking
her knife and sticking it in the jam jar, so Nathan called
for the bill, which Sandy insisted on paying. Julie, suddenly impressed, said thank you very sweetly, even though
she hadn't finished her eggs. She felt bad about leaving so
much on her plate. It made an impression on her, a woman in a suit who pays for your breakfast. They ended up
walking Sandy back to campus. Nathan felt vaguely that
he was giving in to something, her greater importance. It's
not clear how these fights get lost, but you know afterward, you can see the score. Margot kept putting her feet
on her father's good shoes. She felt tired after their late
night and wanted to walk like that, step by step. Eventually, Nathan lifted her onto his shoulders. He liked having a
kid on his head. As if to say, look, I've got other fish to fry.

They parted at the entrance to Columbia—a statue,
with stony flowing robes and a book in his hand, presided
between a hedge and a gate. A few students were already

walking out and in, though classes didn't start until the following week.

"Maybe," Sandy said to Julie, breaking the silence, "that's where you'll go to school one day." When she wasn't sitting down, you could see how short she was: Julie could look her in the eye.

"I'm going to Harvard," she said. "Because that's where Nathan teaches. We get a discount."

"That doesn't matter," her father cut in; but he was pleased, too, because on some level she was standing up for him. "You don't have to worry about any of this yet."

Sandy smiled again. "If you want I can talk to a friend of mine at the OLC. I take it that's what you're interested in?"

Nathan, awkwardly, ducked his head; he couldn't quite look at her. But he said thank you and kissed her powdery cheek, English-style. For a few seconds they watched her walking along the footpath between the lawns, slowly diminishing, just another short, brisk middle-aged woman in a suit.

As an adult, when Julie talked about her father, first at university, and later, to her own children, and finally after his death, she described him as the most rational human being she had ever known . . . It was a joke, because she knew this made her family seem crazy. But she also meant, the fairest, the most just. Even as a child, some feeling based on that thought was growing in her. The whole weekend stuck in her mind, for various reasons. Sandy became an occasional figure in their lives—in fact, she helped Julie after graduation get an internship on Capitol Hill. But she also thought, there are people in the world you have to be nice to, whether you want to or not. Realizing this, that Nathan was "being nice" for some personal reason of his own, upset her at the time; it colored the rest of her day. There were other undercurrents, too, like Paul's retirement. By glimpses and stages you become aware of adult life. Paul looked like her father, they sounded almost identical over the phone, and sometimes they talked the same. They said the same kind of things, probably because Paul was copying Nathan. And she remembered feeling jealous, on her father's behalf, because the whole point of everybody getting together was to watch Paul. That's why Jean had flown in from London, that's why Bill and Liesel had flown in from Austin, that's why Susie and Ben had taken the train from Hartford, and why Nathan had driven them down from Boston. To watch him play tennis.

They were supposed to meet the others at Times Square, at eleven thirty on the platform of the 7 train, which gave them half an hour to kill. So Nathan and the kids wandered around the Columbia campus. He showed them the Butler Library, and they spent a few minutes throwing pennies down the broad steps, trying to get them to land on a particular one. Nathan, when he wanted to, could draw on a large store of small inventions—games and tricks you pick up in the course of a long childhood, as the oldest of four kids. Then they walked back to the subway stop and caught the local down to 42nd Street.

Emerging from the first train, Nathan kept hold of Margot's hand. He had to pull her slightly, up the staircase toward the central concourse, and down a series of tunnels, and then more stairs. There were too many people, most of them moving in the same direction, but in a slightly zombielike way, taking short steps, shuffling, always straight ahead, until they ran into something and bounced off, and kept going at an adjusted angle. In addition to the usual craziness of the city, you could already see the US Open craziness, a lot of USTA merchandise on display, T-shirts and golf caps. Margot noticed a boy carrying an enormous tennis ball, as big as a basketball, and scribbled over in felt-tip. She poked Julie, and then Julie saw Bill, staring at her unseeing and then looking anxiously around the station and over her head.

"Bill," she said, and then, trusting her voice. "Bill! Bill!"

A train stood waiting with open doors, but they couldn't get everyone together in time, and so, much to Bill's annoyance, they watched it depart. "Maybe we should split up," he said, "and try to go in separate cars." Because their group was too large: Susie and Ben, Bill and Liesel, Jean, Nathan, Margot, Julie. Trying to squeeze eight people at a time, two with bad knees, three of them kids, through the same set of doors wasn't easy. At least Dana and Cal were making their own way. She was taking a cab: Paul had insisted. Bill also had a heavy tote bag over his shoulder, filled with sandwiches and fruit and other things, nuts and bagel chips, which he had picked up from Zabar's that morning. The food at the Open was overpriced and not very good. And this way, if anyone was hungry, and they found a seat, they could eat on the train.

"That's just not true," Jean said. "It's overpriced but perfectly acceptable—they've got a whole food truck thing going on. Most of the street food you get these days is better than what you eat in restaurants."

"Well, what we don't eat, I can take home."

Lines were already forming for the next train. Nathan, in his suit, with a briefcase in hand (he planned to do a little work, if he could, during the lulls) maneuvered his kids near one of the entry points, and when the double doors opened, he pushed them on. Jean, taking charge of Bill and Liesel, forced her way on, too, while Susie and Ben found the same car by another door. But there was nowhere to sit; the seats were quickly taken up, and you had to bump people along just to stand in the aisles. Ben said to his mother, in an undertone, "Maybe if you tell them . . ." but Susie shook her head: "I'm fine." At the other end, a handsome young man, a foreigner—he had a goatee and a slight accent, maybe he was Czech or Polish—offered his seat, smilingly, to Liesel. She ended up sitting down in front of Julie, who was tall enough to hold onto the overhead bar. Margot clung to Nathan's legs.

Jean said to Bill, "Let me take the bag," but he refused. "If it's this busy," she said, "you shouldn't carry it on your shoulder. That's not the etiquette. You keep banging people." So he stationed it dutifully between his feet.

Liesel offered, "Margot can sit on my lap if she wants to." But the girl was happy, she liked her father's legs. The train pulled out; Julie swayed a little, against a stranger, a fat man with his shirt tucked in, who didn't look at her or say anything but kept staring ahead out the window as if

there was something to see. Mostly his own reflection in
the dark tunnel, under the bright lights.

"When I was Margot's age," Liesel told Julie, "or a little
older, we caught the last train out of Gotenhafen before
the Russians came. Gdynia now, a part of Poland. It was
so full my father had to push us in through one of the
windows." She was sitting comfortably but the memory
was still strong, seventy years afterward. "He had to stay
behind, we didn't see him until much later. My mother had
to do everything, with five kids—four, I forget, because
Suze was a baby and they had already sent her ahead. Your
aunt Susie is named after her. It was twenty hours to Berlin
and Mutti stood the whole time. By the end, she couldn't
walk. Her legs had swelled up like sausages. My uncle had
to carry her from the station in a handcart."

"Why didn't your father come?" Julie said.

"He had to work, he had a job to do. He was an engineer, building ships. But he knew the war wasn't going
well and wanted to send his family as far from the front as
possible."

Julie's accent always sounded to her grandmother pecu-
liarly American—East Coast educated. The only thing
still childish about her voice was its clarity. "Did he want
Germany to win?"

"That's not an easy question. He was a German, but he
didn't like Hitler."

Bill thought: Right now, he's probably knocking a few
balls around, I don't know what the practice courts are
like. It's a little cool today, you don't want to get stiff. He
should take a shower before going out, to keep warm.

Nathan had promised to read something for Sandy in the next couple of weeks, and already regretted it. One of her students was going on the job market and needed help getting an article published—it was in his field, and she had sent it to him on her phone, over the coffee and muffins. Exchange of favors; you do these kinds of things out of a conscientiousness that has a flavor of complicity. But he was also listening to Liesel's story. When he was younger, a teenager with passionate political opinions, he used to argue with Liesel about what her father could have done differently. He built ships for the Nazis, *that* was his job. And for some reason it seemed very important for him to make his mother admit, there was culpability there. Part of an ongoing battle between them, about other things as well. The German side of the family always treated him like a kid. And Liesel herself took a pragmatic view of legal argument. There are principles at stake, but there are also ends in sight, sometimes conflicting ends, and you have to have sympathy for the fact that people are limited, there are things they can't do—maybe even things they don't want to do.

Most of the workers at the dockyard in Gotenhafen were prisoners of war; it was practically slave labor. And her father petitioned to get them better rations, successfully, as it happens. "Only so they could work harder," Nathan, fifteen years old, angry and not quite sure why he was angry, pointed out.

"Who knows why people do what they do. It isn't always possible to say. In his own way, your grandfather was an honorable man. He had a strong sense of duty."

"That was the problem, this is what I'm saying. His duty the way he saw it was to the state."

Liesel, unhappily, but also looking at her son with a certain admiration (this is the child I have made), said, "It is a very rare privilege not to feel any obligation, of any kind, to your country or the institutions that employ you."

"A privilege is exactly what it's *not*. It's your first duty, as a human being, to work these things out for yourself."

"Later, after the war, which you know perfectly well, he lost his job—basically for being a whistleblower, for pointing out financial irregularities at the engineering firm where he worked. And they fired him."

"Everything you say just convinces me more and more that he was at heart a company man. The only mistake he made was being surprised, that this is how a company treats its employees."

"You say that as if it's such a terrible thing to be." But now she said, to Nathan's daughter, "The carriage we were standing in had the toilet compartment. There was a soldier who sat on the pot the whole time, just for somewhere to sit. But my mother insisted . . ."

Hearing these stories reminded Nathan of the battles they used to fight. Somehow he still wanted to fight them. You don't outgrow that. But now that he was a father himself, he had a different insight into the position, as a child, his family had put him in. The argument with Jean at that lousy Italian restaurant was in his thoughts, too. A fight-picker, this is what they made him out to be— while Paul was the peacemaker. Because he didn't care about anything, much, beyond himself. Everybody gave him an easy ride, Bill especially. Because Paul was good at sports. Susie always cried to get her way. And Jean . . . Jean was like a kind of sheepdog, rounding everyone up. The youngest child has her peculiar burdens, too. She sees the family breaking apart, kids leaving for college, while she stays helplessly behind. As a father you have to be aware of these roles, you have to compensate, even if that means arbitrating sometimes against the interests of your own past self. Which isn't easy. Because nothing in his childhood had prepared him for the depth of his identification with Julie, his firstborn.

And nothing had changed much either, even in the old relations. Here they were again, twenty-odd years later, trooping off to watch Paul. There was a taste in his mouth, from that and other things. The meeting with Sandy Franks. The extent to which he was willing to involve himself with . . . what? Someone he considered beneath him. Asking her advice. Because what Jean had accused him of wasn't picking fights, it was chasing his own advantage. At the expense of his principles. Which is an argument you can make if you refuse to have anything to do with actual power and the decisions it requires of the people who exercise it. You can make your documentaries, about the migrants at Calais, about funding elderly care on the NHS, about all the avoidable tragedies that can only be avoided at the expense of some other tragedy. Which doesn't matter, because you never have to choose between them. But being serious at some point means being serious about power. If that's not the game you want to play, then you might as well stick to the junior circuit.

Yet sometimes it seemed to Nathan that the junior circuit is exactly what he was stuck in. In spite of the Harvard
chair and the offers to speak (which he received regularly)
at conferences in São Paulo and Tokyo and Oxford. Some
of his colleagues, not much older than himself, had been
invited to Downing Street to explain their views. Others
had given a keynote at Davos or sold a book for a million
bucks or appeared on the cover of the *New York Review*.
Paul's complaint, that you realize after a while that people see you in a certain light, as a certain kind of person,
a hanger-on, had made a deep impression on Nathan.
Because this was their inheritance, what they had learned
from Bill, another fight-picker, an eccentric, who had let
himself (and there's always some collusion) get elbowed
to the side professionally. Year after year. Nathan, thinking these thoughts, watched his father in his fraying sports
coat, with his uncut beard, hanging onto the subway bar
and clutching between his knees a Zabar's shopping bag.

Sometimes he thought that Jean was basically right:
there are conversations you can have inside the family at
a deeper depth or a truer height than any you can have
outside it. Because of the affinities and the stakes and the
shared history and private language. Nathan's friends
were extremely able, educated and ambitious people, who
were also capable of expressing unusually intelligent sympathy—but none of them could make possible the train
of self-reflection a weekend with his family in New York
had set in motion. First, the conversation with Paul, and
later that stupid fight with Jean. Just listening to Liesel
rehearse the old war stories for his daughter's sake, which

he had heard a hundred times before, brought home to him the fact that it isn't always easy to tell whether the views you hold now represent the natural evolution of the views you used to hold, as a kid, fighting these fights with your mother—or their opposite. Because it occurred to him that what Jean was saying last night, another way of putting whatever it was that she was accusing him of, is that he was in danger of turning like his grandfather into a company man.

After Hunters Point, the train ran elevated into Court Square. The ordinary light of day flooded the car. It was like drawing down a pale blind across the hot strip lighting. Until your eyes adjusted, people looked washed out, faded, but also dirty around the edges, like newspaper photographs. They swayed on the irregularities of the tracks. Residential streets, at odd angles, passed by—laid out like kids' blocks, and looking no bigger or better built. Then a shopping district, where the traffic stops and starts, appeared under the stanchions and continued on the far side before disappearing into a warehouse wall. Someone had spray-painted cartoon flames against the bricks. Gray skies and blue skies alternated overhead; a firm wind pushed the cloudscape along. While the train hurried the other way, retreating from the skylines of Manhattan, into the suburbs.

Jean, feeling the overhead bar warming up under her hand, went over her conversation with Henrik in her head. She had called him after the second time she woke up, around six a.m. in New York. The first time it was still pitch dark; she got up to pee and went back to bed. But at six a little light had started to come in, like something spilled and spreading slowly. "Can you talk?" she said, and then, after a half-second pause, a satellite delay, he answered: "Of course I can talk. It is nice to hear you"—a phrase he had picked up in England.

She wanted to say, *everyone's driving me crazy*, a little offering to him. But it wasn't quite true and would have felt like a betrayal anyway. So she said: "I can't get over the jet lag. I miss you." She had to speak quietly, cupping the phone against her neck, because of the time. Liesel and Bill were sleeping next-door. Ben and Susie were out cold, too. And she could almost hear, on the other end of the line, the lunchtime sunshine inflecting his voice—it was just another day at the seaside. He was in public mode.

"Not now," he said, to someone else. In the room, or outside, approaching him—she couldn't tell. "In a minute." And then, to Jean: "Our neighbors have gone away for a few days and left a dog behind. For the children to look after. A cause of great excitement." Tinker, their German shepherd, had died the year before and not been replaced.

"That *sounds* exciting." Jean, subtly, found herself entering into the spirit of his conversation. But also heard her bored kid voice.

"He is a *Weimaraner*." Henrik, like many Danes, spoke German almost fluently but always with a slightly mocking, very deliberate accent. "Or maybe it is a she. I don't look."

"Are you going for a walk?"

"The children can do what they like. I don't go anywhere."

"I miss you," she said again.

"Yes. I heard you the first time." She couldn't tell if the delay was technical or had some other cause. But then he said, "My sentiments exactly."

"Everybody here is picking fights with me." She shifted around in bed, because her legs were cold—she had sat up to reach her phone, which was on the bedside table, and the covers had partly fallen off. Now she pulled them back and lay down. As if, by making herself comfortable like this, something intimate had happened. "I told them about you and keep getting defensive."

"You told me this in an email." But maybe his own voice sounded harsh to himself, or too formal, because he went on: "It is not what I would want either. For my daughter."

"Not my parents. My brother. But everybody tells everybody everything, it doesn't matter. I keep on trying to work out how guilty I feel."

"And?"

Sometimes, even now, he spoke to her like one of his assistants. In the flesh, this mattered less—partly because it was easier to give in to him. He had a strong self-contained physical assurance. Making films was also a physical activity, shooting on location sometimes required courage, he was good with his hands, practical, and trusted his own sense of reasonable danger. All of this came across, in his presence: he was six feet tall and built like a rower or a sailor. You could see the muscles in his forearms. But over the phone, she had to make allowances.

"Where are you? What are you doing? I can't talk to you like this."

"Like what? I am sitting in the garden. What I am supposed to be doing is another question. Monica has gone
off to the shop, to buy bread. Something, I don't remember what, is supposed to have happened by the time she
comes back." After a moment, he added: "It is not your
problem."

So, just to keep talking, she said: "Paul is playing today."

"Who is he playing?"

"A Bulgarian named Borisov."

"Oh, a Bulgarian . . ."

"He's ten years younger."

"So he is inexperienced."

"And ranked around twenty points higher. Paul said,
this is it. If he loses today, he's retiring."

So she had made her little offering after all, of intimacy
or betrayal, laid at his feet. This is what it felt like to her.
And Henrik seemed to feel it, too, because he said, "That
is something . . . to be reckoned with."

In the distance, in the very far distance, she could hear
a dog bark—not loudly, and a child laugh, probably a girl,
and say (but it might have been a different kid) *no no no
no*—not unhappily, but as if she were pulling on a leash.
Jean realized that she was imagining the garden at her
mother's childhood home, in northern Germany, which
sloped down to a path running along the beach. But Henrik's house in Vranjic might look nothing like this. He
called it only "my wife's beach house." In most ways, Jean
didn't know him well.

There were more noises in the background, and Henrik
said, "Listen, I can see her coming with the shopping bags.

I should go. I will check his results on my phone." And
that was it, and she was lying alone again, in a strange bed
on the Upper West Side, waiting for her parents to wake
up. Her ear felt hot from the pressure of the phone against
it and her heart was racing. But she was annoyed at herself now, standing on the train next to Bill, that some part
of her reaction to her brother's match, whether he won
or lost, would be made up of the thought that Henrik,
an ocean and six hours away, might be checking the score
before he went to bed.

Julie asked, "Did you put that story in the book?" and
Liesel told her, "I put it in. I put them all in. None of them
feels true anymore. If you talk too much, it's like you
made everything up."

"Sometimes when I write a story I don't remember
what I made up and what I didn't."

"Your mother sends me your stories."

"I have your book in my bedroom. But I haven't read
it yet."

Over the windows, the subway map spelled out the
journey—dots of light appeared as you passed a station.
You forget how big the city is. None of these places meant
much to Bill: Bliss Street, Woodside, Elmhurst Avenue.
Their family roots were Lower East Side, that's where his
uncles opened their first Essinger Brothers store, on the
corner of Essex and Stanton. They sold Astor Coffee and
Comet Rice and Pillsbury Cake and Pancake Flour—Paul
once gave him a framed advertisement from the *Jewish*

Morning Journal in 1921, which he had picked up on eBay.
It was hanging now in the bathroom in Austin under the
stairs. Bill's father was a Dodgers fan; sometimes he drove
them down to Ebbets Field to watch a game—a little over
two hours by car. He never forgave them for moving to
LA, but Bill still followed the box scores in the morning.
Koufax was Jewish, this meant something to him as a kid.
And his career only really took off in LA, by which point
Bill was already at Stanford—in the same time zone. He
even played hooky on a Monday afternoon in October
(skipping his Macro lecture) and saw Koufax pitch against
Billy Pierce at Candlestick Park. Koufax lasted an inning,
gave up three runs and the Dodgers lost eight nothing.
Around this time the Mets also came along, but it was too
late by that point to switch allegiances. Queens was never
really his New York.

Who knows where the love of baseball comes from.
His kids didn't have it, not even Paul. But most days after
school Bill used to head over to the baseball diamond at
the corner of Ferry and Union. There were two diamonds,
facing each other, but sometimes if it was busy—a church
league used the grounds—you wandered over to City
Park across the street. There was no backstop there, and
the rule was, if you hit it into the river, you were out. They
lost a lot of balls and got wet looking for them: Eddie Kai-
ser, Bill Panofski (Big Bill), Steve Tauchman, Mike Schultz.
But the river rule never bothered Bill, he was a contact hitter. His high school coach once said to him, *Essinger, you
may be slow, but you sure are weak.* He had quick hands,
though, and played catcher for two years, when he was

still a fat kid and before he started concentrating on golf.

Sometimes, when the boys were young, he asked them if they wanted to watch a Longhorns game at Disch-Falk field—ten minutes by car, there were always tickets. For most of their childhood, the Longhorns were pretty good. It was a chance to spot a future major leaguer. Maybe he took the kids once or twice, but they sat there bored. Sometimes he played catch with Nathan in the backyard. Nathan had a decent arm. But the way childhood works, from one generation to the next, keeps changing. You try to re-create what you had but can't overcome the resistance. There was a park, Adam's Park, a short walk from the house, and he often spotted people playing basketball on the court by the fire station—there was a baseball backstop, too. But when you've got a hoop at home, a big yard, who needs to go out. His kids were rich man's kids, which shouldn't surprise him, because he was the rich man. They had no sense of community, of living in a neighborhood with other kids. And once Paul got hooked on tennis, he was happy enough banging a ball against the net Bill set up in the yard, or playing at Whitaker, by the law school.

It meant a lot to him to have a son to play ball with. Nathan had been aggressive, but not competitive. He didn't like losing and that's how you always start out, by losing. How you finish, too. Susie did her duty at YMCA soccer but quit when she was ten or eleven; she didn't want to spend her Saturday mornings out at Zilker Park when she could stay at home with a book instead. But Paul from an early age had a fixed expression on his face every time a game got played. If he didn't win, you could see him afterward, practicing by himself whatever you needed to practice, working things through. He was never especially communicative but if you paid attention like this he was easy to read, very single-minded. At four he was playing on Susie's co-ed soccer team, some of the kids were twice his age, but he held his own. Bill stood on the sidelines watching, trying not to boast but also feeling a strong affinity for the kid, sent out as it were into the world to do his business again, the business of childhood. Playing ball.

By the time Nathan left for Harvard, his little brother could challenge him at basketball, even though Paul was six years younger, still prepubescent and probably thirty pounds of muscle weight lighter. They played in the backyard, after school, or sometimes, under the lights, when dinner was over. The only way Nathan could win was by backing him down, using his butt and his elbows—Bill sometimes had to step in. The court was poured concrete, covered in abrasive paint. Sometimes Nathan said, I'm coming down the middle, knee-first; if you want to stand there and take the charge, feel free. Not while Bill was watching, but he heard about it afterward: Paul sometimes got hurt. Eventually they stopped playing together, which was a shame, because you never get back that intensity of relationship.

It transferred to Bill, who used to play tennis with his son on the university courts. Even when Paul was ten or eleven years old, Bill let himself go all-out. He used to be a decent player himself. Though his serve was soft, he had soft hands at the net, too, and liked to force Paul to pass him. "If you pass me, you beat me," he told his son.

Paul hated losing, especially to this old guy sweating into his sweatband, with a straggly beard, a lopey run, hanging shoulders—his dad. Sometimes, when the shots weren't falling for him, Paul would smash his feet against the hard court (jumping and then landing-kicking at the same time), to gee himself up. It was embarrassing to watch. These were semipublic courts, students used them, one of his colleagues might be playing alongside. But Bill had a thick competitive streak, too; it was like being a kid again, he loved going at it. As a father, you win for a certain number of years, and then, when the tide turns, it comes pouring in. You never win again.

Eventually the question started coming up, around Paul's fourteenth birthday: how much of our lives are we supposed to rearrange for this one kid? It's true (Bill remembered the conversations), Marcello thought he needed to enroll full-time at one of these academies. Most of the best were in Florida. They could have sent him away. But in other respects, Paul was a late developer, still a child, his mother's son. Liesel put her foot down about sending him to boarding school; and they weren't going to relocate either. Susie was finishing high school, Jean was just about to start junior high. Bill and Liesel had jobs and lives, they weren't the kind of family that moves to Hollywood or Florida—the truth is, it was never under consideration. Liesel also saw the danger of letting just one part of his personality colonize the rest. The tennis-playing part. He was a smart kid, with an interest in art, in painting, like Susie, and a good eye; he could draw like a Polaroid. He needed to go to college, he needed to figure out for himself, at a reasonable age, what he wanted to do with his life.

When Paul dropped out of Stanford, Liesel was almost too upset to speak to him. For several months beforehand, he had been calling to argue it out with her: they fought constantly. For some reason, he needed his mother to consent to his independence—the package couldn't be delivered without a signature. Which she refused to give; it clouded their relationship for several years. Then, when he made it to the quarters at the US Open, Paul felt vindicated and tried to explain this feeling to her, which started the whole thing up again. For Liesel it was an enduring disappointment that he should waste his life on a hobby. A bruise that doesn't heal because you keep bumping into it. It seemed to her one of those things America had done to her children. Whenever she watched Paul play, the tension between her mixed feelings was almost visible. Because she hated it when he lost, too, and couldn't bear that what he had turned out to be was a mid-ranking, top-100 professional. Who, at the age of thirty-three, needed to work out for a second time what he wanted to do with his life.

But for Bill, there was a special kind of national pride in having an athlete in the family. When your grandfather spoke no English, your uncles were in the grocery business, and your son, short-haired and handsome, appears on television as a tennis star, an ordinary American, some very deep itch is being scratched—a part of you that never expected acceptance has been recognized. Bill got phone calls from people who did not otherwise keep in touch, cousins and old fraternity buddies, after they saw Paul

playing on ESPN or in one of those commercials. Sometimes offering advice: *He's got a beautiful backhand, but
why doesn't he come to net? His second serve is just putting it in play.* And so on. For a while it wasn't clear how
good he would become, and then it was. He went up the
rankings, stopped, and started going down. It was like
watching the world conduct a highly refined and public
experiment upon your son, using the best researchers and
the most expensive equipment, according to which, at the
end of a ten-year trial, his talents (and its limits) have been
measured and graded to the decimal point. *This is who you
were*, they tell him, when it's over.

———

A t the sign for Mets–Willets Point, everybody started
pouring out of the train. The tournament still had a
Day One feel, people excited just to be showing up,
it didn't matter who they were seeing. A dad with teenage kids, his mother coming, too, clutching his arm, gangs
of guy friends, young men wearing college sweatshirts or
USTA-approved official gear, T-shirts and polos, fat-soled
sneakers, middle-aged women with tennis-preserved
bodies and exaggerated tans, every type and stereotype of
American (though most of them white), the straw-hat bri-
gade, Hasidim in dusty black coats, an old lady dressed for
a party, in pink feathers and an artificial boa, happy atten-
tion-seekers getting attention, and in spite of the crush,
everybody shuffling along, rubbing shoulders, according to some natural but also slightly formal American

principle of friendliness . . . *I flew in yesterday from Boca where it was 102 degrees, there are a number of food concessions of every variety, I saw Federer here last year in the second round, and my husband complained, that for the next two weeks* . . . out of the station, and across the echoing floorboards of the long pedestrian bridge, riding like a ship over a sea of parking lots, bus and train depots, sheds of corrugated metal, bulk containers, rusty tracks, while low-level construction activity continued with the small-scale urgency of bugs somewhere below (the intestinal operations of a great city, plainly on display)—everybody floating above it, until the wooden walkway opened onto a concrete concourse where the ticket lines were already forming.

There was an atmosphere of patient high spirits (everybody's got a long day ahead), but also of a kind of duty being done, people showing up to witness something of minor significance to the culture, playing their part by buying tickets, making their way to the suburbs of Queens, walking the distances they needed to walk, standing in lines, showing their bags to security, proceeding as directed to the courts in question, and carrying afterward the proof of a job done, as spectator and consumer, of tennis caps, signed balls, programs, and T-shirts that read, NOTHING BEATS BEING HERE, US OPEN CHAMPIONSHIPS NYC 2011. Along the way you pass a park, almost empty in tournament season, avenues of trees, bright blue public courts, dusty patches in the grass where the kids play soccer, a golf course, spreading greenly into the distance, but you turn your back on it, and on the far side of the ticket turnstiles, the tennis-industrial complex begins: trees dotted at regular intervals in the kind of open space Americans call a plaza, a convention center, a food village, with a series of landed spaceships growing in size, until you reach—at the end of another concourse, composed of alternating pink and white concrete bricks and lined with municipal shrubs and benches and street-lights—Arthur Ashe Stadium, looking as if it's about to take off.

At the security checkpoint, they refused to let Bill through with his Zabar's bag. The guidelines said *No Food, except in strictly limited quantities.* "How am I supposed to know this?" Bill asked.

"It's on the website." The guard was just some college-age kid, working a summer job. He wasn't stupid but he didn't really care. His cheeks were pink, his hair was sandy; he wore glasses. Any personal qualities he might have possessed were concealed beneath the official role— one of those people who play a functional part in your life and make no impression.

"What's a limited quantity. This is a limited quantity. I don't understand what strictly limited quantity means."

"I can let you through with the bagel chips or some-thing like that. Unless you have a medical reason."

"I need to eat, is that a medical condition." Bill wasn't really angry; he was enjoying himself. "If I don't eat, I starve. How about that?"

But the kid was already checking the next in line—he didn't have time for hermeneutics. Eventually Bill said, "You go ahead" to Liesel and the rest of them and stood by the side eating one of the sandwiches. "If anybody's hungry, I've got plenty." He offered food to some of the passers-by—this was his kind of scene. But there wasn't really room for standing aside, the lines were packed tight, everyone inching along.

"Come on, Dad," Jean said. As the youngest, she was traditionally best placed to reason with him. It was her job—no one gets mad at the baby of the family. "This happened a couple of years ago, too."

"It's a scam," Bill said, finally getting annoyed. The basic social conservatism of his children baffled him sometimes. Not just his children, it seems, but the whole generation. Their willingness to go along with the rules. Also, to spend money later on sub-mediocre food, at inflated prices. "There's no reason I can't bring in a few sandwiches. This is just some deal they strike with the food concessions."

"I thought you were supposed to be an economist. This is how the market operates."

Eventually the kid let him through, still eating, but Bill had to throw most of the rest away. "*You* eat it," Bill told the security guy. "Otherwise, it's just a waste." But the sandwiches ended up in the trash. There was a large container by every row, filled with soda cans and water bottles.

By this point it was twenty to one. Nathan said, "We probably want to eat before the match starts, which doesn't give us much time."

"Oh for Christ's sake." Bill shook his head. "I'm going in." But he didn't move, he just stood there.

"You do what you want to do. The kids need to eat."

"I need to pee," Liesel said.

She always felt uncomfortable in crowds, pushed around, she didn't like the mass conformity of them. There was a predictably long line in front of the women's restroom. (Another example of American mealymouthedness. She preferred the German *Klo*, simple and direct, short for closet, which children and adults could use without embarrassment.) Julie came with her; Nathan took Margot to the men's room. Jean and Susie and Ben started lining up for food—pizza was usually the safest bet with the kids. That or hot dogs. Jean had decided to suspend her culinary beliefs. For the past week, at work, she had been looking up food blogs about what to eat at the US Open. There was a food-truck grilled cheese sandwich with caramelized shallots that she wanted to try, but you get used to sacrificing your interests around people with kids.

Margot, walking among the legs, said to her father, "I know where they come out." She had been worried at the security check-in: everybody seemed to be coming in, no one was going. It was the practical problem that bothered her; the place was filling up. But then she noticed the flow of people toward Arthur Ashe Stadium—the tallest spaceship at the end of the walkway. It occurred to her that maybe it had access to an underground exit, like a subway station, like Times Square, which is why she couldn't see anybody leaving.

"Come out where?" Nathan said, and she tried to explain, but he wasn't listening or couldn't understand her. She didn't need the bathroom but he made her go anyway, after wiping the seat down carefully with wet toilet paper.

Everybody met up again outside Plazza Centro Pizza and Pasta. Jean practiced saying it in an Italian accent: *Plazza centro. Pizz' e pasta.* For some reason this amused her. It was now a few minutes to one—Bill kept pacing around. "We should have met at eleven," he said. "This is what I said." But when the pizza came, two large pies (a margherita and a pepperoni), he helped them by eating a slice. Just to keep things moving. "We can eat and walk," he said.

"Relax. He's on second." Nathan had decided to be in a good mood. "The schedule says, not before one o'clock."

"It's one now."

"The first match probably isn't over yet."

"It was a women's singles."

"Look," Jean told the kids. "If you fold it over like this, it's easier. That's it. Now you're New Yorkers."

Paul was playing on Court 12. It took them a while to find it, among the currents of people going in other directions: down a leafy alley (hedges on one side, zinnias on the other) that ran into an intersection of little pathways with a low bowl of a stadium at the end. Just a few tiers of bleachers, Nathan could look over the wall. Not much bigger than a pub theater, seats arranged around a small stage. Very much Off Broadway, there were a lot of empty rows. It was the first round, early in the day. You felt a kind of intimacy among the spectators, showing up for some second-rate match. Maybe because they knew somebody or had a hard-core interest in the sport. Several commentators had identified Borisov as a potential problem for Djokovic in the third round, if he made it that far. (His record against the Serb was two and three, though both of Borisov's victories had come on clay.) Though it's also possible that what people wanted was a place to sit down without standing in line—they didn't care who played.

In any case, the court was empty, apart from a few ground crew. Bill cheered up instantly; he slowed down. Jean saw Dana first, two rows up on the other side. She had spread out her baby paraphernalia along the bleacher to claim their seats: her bag, her coat, a change of clothes, a milk bottle and several containers of baby food. It looked like the aftermath of some buggy-on-buggy crash. Cal was standing up and trying to climb the rows. Dana held him around the waist, though whether in struggle or play was difficult to tell. A husband and wife rose to let Jean through, and then the rest filed past: Susie, Ben, Julie, Nathan, Margot, Bill, Liesel. "It's a convention," Bill said to the couple, retirees probably, late sixties. Bill liked talking to strangers.

"You got the whole family, I see." The man's acne-scarred face hung a little low in the cheeks, though he looked otherwise skinny enough. Maybe he had recently lost weight. His voice, though perfectly with-it, sounded like a marble rolling around a bowl, as if there had been some stroke damage in his medical history.

"My son is playing," Bill told him.

"Which one is he?"

"Paul Essinger." It was curious what happened to your name, when you said it like that.

"Go get 'em," the man said. Maybe there *was* some impediment there.

Dana started sweeping up the contents of her diaper

bag when she saw them coming. "I'm turning into one of you," she told Jean.

"What do you mean?"

But Liesel pushed her way through before Dana could explain. "I've got something for Cal," she said. "Something small." She looked through her purse and eventually brought out a little stitched-cloth finger puppet with a red hood. "*Rotkäppchen*," she called it and tried to take Cal by the hand. But he pulled away.

"Don't do that." Dana had been trying to keep him still for the past half-hour. She'd had enough. "Your grandmother wants to give you something."

Liesel said, "It doesn't matter," and put the puppet on her own finger. "*Weißt du wer das ist?*" she asked the boy. Do you know who that is.

But Cal never responded to German, even when his father spoke tenderly to him, just a handful of words, like *du* and *Kind*—for Paul it was still the language of endearment and childish comfort.

"Little Red Riding Hood," Liesel said, but they had both lost interest. "You can give it to him later, when he isn't distracted."

"I'm sorry."

"*Da nich für*," Liesel told her, using the German phrase, making a joke. *Not for that.* But Dana wasn't really paying attention; she had reached into her handbag to check her phone. After flicking the screen on, she put it away again quickly. Liesel said, to shrug off her annoyance, "It must be stressful for Cal, with so many people around. Stressful for both of you."

"I'm sorry," Dana repeated, but this time looking her in the eyes. "Inez's mother went into surgery this morning, but I haven't heard anything."

"What kind of surgery?"

"She's having a pacemaker replaced. I mean, the batteries. Apparently it's all very routine, but I told Inez to text me afterward that it was okay. But she's in Arizona. They're three hours behind."

Liesel made sympathetic noises, but somehow this wasn't the conversation she wanted to have. She wanted to talk about Paul; she wanted to watch Cal watching him. Probably he would never remember seeing his father play, but Liesel planned to remember for him. He was too young to know what was going on, but maybe he was old enough to get excited: look, there's Daddy. This is the kind of thing she hoped to talk about with Dana. But it didn't matter.

There was a noise, a few people clapping, and the players walked onto the court—one of them was her son. It upset her every time, how unprotected he seemed on the flat, brightly colored surface. Like a cell on a microscope slide. Just far enough away to look small, but not so far that she couldn't see his receding hairline and the one-night stubble on his cheeks: a slightly intense young man. Not so young anymore. Sometimes he checked the stands for friendly faces but usually not long enough to find them, and the rest of his expression was the expression of a private person in a public situation. There were chairs by the side of the court, folding chairs, and both players sat down. Paul undressed. He took off his windbreaker and warm-up pants and bent low to retie the laces of his shoes. One of his rituals. He still tied them the way Nathan had taught him, almost thirty years before: two loops, like a child; and then a double knot. Borisov was waiting for him, practicing his serve, and then they started to warm up together, hitting forehand to forehand crosscourt, and then backhand to backhand. One of those surprisingly gentlemanly conventions, from another age.

Susie had been trying to find something in her handbag, dried apricots or a piece of chocolate. Something sweet; she liked to eat something sweet after every meal. When she looked up, they were already playing, knocking the ball back and forth, moving their feet. For a moment she had forgotten who they were, it was just a couple of guys playing tennis. Then she felt the shock of recognition: her little brother. She took Ben's hand and squeezed it. She said, "Uncle Paul." Her eyes had suddenly filled with tears. Maybe she was conflating things, worrying about Ben, she was probably hormonal, too. When they go to school you can't go with them. Every day it's like sending them off to battle. How smart are you? How cool are you? Who likes you, who doesn't? Does anybody think you're funny? No wonder they come back . . . a little bit dirty. Maybe Paul is right. We should get out. When he was a kid, about Cal's age, she used to throw a Nerf baseball for him to hit with Bill's old squash racket. Sitting on the floor of the TV room. Already she could tell he was good at it—he kept wanting to do it again. Afterward, he ran and picked up the ball and passed it to her (often she had to chase it down again), and they started over. Back and forth. Nothing else mattered, and here he was, and it did matter and there was nothing she could do about it.

Bill thought, If he comes to net, he can beat him. But he has to come to net.

Nathan said, "Has anyone talked to Paul about what he plans to do next?"

"Please, can we not have this conversation now?"

But Jean ignored her father. "Apparently he told Liesel that he wants to build a house in Texas."

"That's what he told me," Nathan said. "But if he doesn't do some kind of job, he'll go crazy. Maybe he already is a little crazy."

"Give him a break," Bill said. "It's no joke, retiring at thirty-three."

"That's what I'm saying."

"This is why he needs to think twice. There's no hurry. When this is over, he should give himself some time."

Susie offered: "He talked to me about writing stories for kids. He wants me to do the illustrations."

Bill looked up. "That doesn't sound like a serious plan."

"He told me some of the titles he's come up with. *A Gap in the Fence. Last Light.*"

"Do *you* want to move to Texas?" Liesel asked Dana.

"All of this is news to me." She said it lightly but it wasn't easy to say. The way her life, the decisions they made together, had become Essinger family property as soon as she got together with Paul continued to upset her. But there was no point fighting it; she'd learned that much. "He doesn't really tell me anything. He kind of shuts down about a week before a tournament."

"I thought you were taking photography classes at the New School," Bill said.

"That's just something I do because I like it."

"I thought the plan was moving into TV."

"Maybe that was *his* plan. I don't know."

"My favorite," Susie said, "was, *Hey, What Was That For?*"

"I don't understand." Liesel for some reason looked indignant.

"It's one of those things kids say to each other."

The chair umpire called time, and the ball boys picked up the balls. There was a flurry of choreographed activity, then calm. Everyone took prearranged places, crouching, standing, sitting. Waiting. Borisov was serving first, the atmosphere had subtly changed. He lifted his hand in the air, to show the ball in it, and fired a serve a few inches long. *Out*—the call of the linesman (a woman, actually, leaning forward, with her hands on her knees) rang out. By this point the afternoon had started to clear, sunshine broke through occasionally, there were patches of clouds being blown around the sky. It was still fairly windy, and not exactly warm, but not cold either. A nice day, good kite weather. Some of the spectators had sunglasses on. The stands were about two-thirds full, and filling up. *Pluck*, and Borisov's second serve kicked off the blue hard court. Paul, raising his elbow, knocked it back and the match had started.

It wasn't only the atmosphere that had changed. Everything seemed to happen a little faster; you could hear them breathing, too, and grunting as they followed through.

Nathan couldn't believe how hard they hit the ball. Every
time he watched his brother he was stunned. Then he forgot, and a year passed and he watched him again. Not just
how hard, but how quickly he moved into position, his
air of efficiency. It wasn't just a question of concentration,
but of seriousness. This is what it means to be serious, to
be able to do this, whack whack whack whack. To hit a
ball at that speed, at that spin, so low over the net and
keep it in. Again and again. You can't do this and tolerate any bullshit in yourself, any laziness or delusion. It's
amazing, at this level, the human ability to eliminate error.
Paul once explained to him that the difference between the
Challenger Tour and the majors was that top ten players
could hit a shot nine ten eleven times in a row without
mistake; but lower down the ranks, after three or four
ground strokes, errors crept in.

Nathan remembered when they were kids, and Paul
beat him for the first time. They were knocking a ball
around on a Saturday morning, on one of the Whitaker
courts, while Bill finished some work in his office. Paul
had started chasing down everything. Maybe he was ten
years old, still red in the cheeks under a bowl haircut; who
knows where this kind of relentlessness comes from. But
Nathan couldn't hit it anywhere that Paul couldn't hit it
back. So he tried to force the action and made mistakes, he
got pissed off. It's hard to accept that your kid brother can
do things you can't. At the same time he also admired the
kid brother. In every other area of their lives, Paul deferred
to Nathan, he imitated him, but in this one area, he was
perfectly willing to kick Nathan's ass. Even though while

he was doing it he wouldn't look him in the eye. Out of guilt or sympathy or something else. And twenty years later this is where all that . . . relentlessness had ended up, on some side court where he'd probably finish his career. A first-round match against an unranked player, the US Open equivalent of the suburbs.

Even making arrangements for this kind of thing means making predictions. Nathan was supposed to inject himself with Avonex once a week. Clémence usually did it on a Monday morning; it varied according to his teaching schedule. But she wasn't there, and he often went through a twenty-four-hour period afterward of feeling mildly crappy (achy and shaky, he called it), so he'd put it off until tomorrow—they were driving back to Boston after the match; she was flying in to Logan, taking a cab. Hoping to get home before the kids went to bed. The drug had been linked to depression; twice a year he needed a liver test, and all of this was for what, maybe for nothing, but the guy he talked to at the Mellen Center said to him, if I were you I'd play the percentages. And this is what the percentages say . . . According to Paddy Power, Paul's chance of winning the US Open was less than a tenth of one percent. I shouldn't have started that conversation at the restaurant. Sometimes it's hard to know what you're trying to prove.

The sky felt large overhead, busy with weather. Borisov left a forehand short, and Paul, coming forward, followed his momentum to the net. But this is where the Bulgarian wanted him: he lofted a lob crosscourt that landed a foot inside the baseline and skittered away. Fifteen love. At this level, every weakness, every bad decision, gets punished. Just another point. Under the shadow of Arthur Ashe Stadium—you could see it rising over the bleachers on the far side of the court. They were on the outside, away from the action, the center, as the family always was. Borisov served again.

When Bill was younger there were courses the black kids couldn't play on. Not that he knew any black golfers. There were clubs Jews couldn't play at either—or even if they let you in, for some high school tournament, they found a way to make you uncomfortable. Bill was lucky; his name sounded German. But when he showed up, there was no disguising certain facts, and he didn't try to. At Stanford, he had to overcome the quota system. At Cornell Law School, too. You had to be the best Jew to get in. His mother was turned away from Columbia on this basis; she ended up at Syracuse, one of those things you just accept. When Arthur Ashe won Wimbledon in 1975, the same year Susie was born, part of what Bill thought was, That's right, stick it to that jerk Connors. As a kid he knew a lot of Jimmy Connors types. Ashe played the way Bill had been taught to play. Get to net when you can. Don't hit it any harder than you need to. And keep quiet out there.

But the game had changed. The way his son played was already old-fashioned. With those new racket heads, the topspin they could generate—everybody just pounded the ball. Even Federer. You watch your kid out there, made out of the stuff you're made of, shaped by you, and you can't help blaming yourself. For whatever it is that passed both of you by. Borisov won the first game to fifteen, and they took a short break before switching ends. Paul, sweating already, sat down and hid his face in his towel. A gesture meaning what, nerves? Relief? That the thing he was waiting for had finally started? Who knows. When the towel came off, when he stood up again, he looked expressionless. Some people play better when they've got something to lose. Hard to say what effect it might have on him, the fact that this could be his last match. Paul wouldn't know either. One of those things you find out about yourself, in the event.

Jean, on her way in, had overheard a woman saying, "He understood where I was coming from, but he didn't give me the response I wanted." Not a woman, a teenager. She had painted-on eyebrows and dyed black hair, but her voice sounded very reasonable. Paul had started serving and Jean thought, I wonder if Henrik will text me if he wins; or maybe only if he loses. What do I care if Henrik calls or doesn't. All day long she'd been having an argument in her head, first with her mother, then Nathan. With all of the Essingers. My friends say it's the best thing that's happened to me. It's like I'm finally leaving the nest. But then they point out, *You moved to England eight years ago*. And she says, Only because Nathan went there. *What friends are these?* He understood where I was coming from, but he didn't give me the response I wanted.

She was almost too nervous to watch him. For most of her childhood, all Paul ever did was win—at tennis, ping-pong, mini golf, tree climbing, running. At cards and chess, too, because he tried harder than anyone else. When he was a kid he told her, it doesn't matter how good you arc at anything. And she said, you only say that because you always win. It seemed like this was one of the facts about Paul, but later she realized it was only one of the facts about his childhood. As soon as he went out in the world, when he quit Stanford, it turned out that other people were also good at what they do. Borisov was known as a returner, he liked to stand in front of the baseline and take the ball early. Paul tried to jam him, serving at his body, but Borisov had quick feet. He could hit his forehand down the line while leaning away. Thirty fifteen. Thirty all. Forty thirty. Deuce. Paul, hoping to catch him by surprise, followed his serve into the net. So early in the match, it seemed a bad sign; hc wasn't normally a serve-and-volley player. His first serve wasn't strong enough, it hovered around a hundred and five, a hundred and ten. Borisov had plenty of time and opened up his forehand. Maybe too much time—the return went long. Advantage Essinger. Jean breathed.

The stupid thing is, she thought, Paul would like him. Henrik was good with his hands, he was intellectually practical. For someone who worked in TV, he seemed fairly immune to fads and trends. His emotional temperature was on the cool side. As a kid, in Denmark, he used to be serious about handball. Sometimes he still liked to sit with a beer and watch the Boxer Herreligaen, the Danish handball league. When they were stuck in her room, hanging out—he felt uncomfortable in the landlady's lounge, even though the TV area was perfectly in-bounds. So he sat on her bed with his computer. The internet had made all of these homesick appetites easier to satisfy. He was also unusually self-aware. You need a high cash-reserve of egoism to speculate in self-examination. He didn't mind if you pointed out his unattractive qualities; he was also willing to admit his guilt, which wasn't her guilt, he said, but entirely his own. "I'm going to be very selfish about this," he said. "The guilt is mine, not yours. You haven't done anything wrong."

"That's not what it feels like," she told him. "Anyway, what I feel bad about is probably just selfish. What I want is my own life with you."

Part of what upset her now, watching Paul play, was the thought that her brother might not be an easy man to be married to. When you're loyal to family life, as the youngest kid, you have this idea that you know these people (your brothers and sister) better than anyone else, because you love them more. So that if someone has a problem living with them, they're making a kind of mistake. After all, you lived with them for fifteen years, growing up. You know they can be lived with. But somehow, this weekend, she had started to feel sorry for Dana. Something was going on she didn't like. Paul had withdrawn his participation, or was withdrawing it, which he used to do even when they were kids, retreating into practice or into his room, but then there was always solid ground underfoot, there were relationships he couldn't withdraw from, that you can't opt out of, but the relationship he was in now you *can* opt out of, and maybe that's what he was doing.

When he lifted his arm to serve, his shirt rode up; you could see the hair on his belly, the muscles, too. Dana had met him for the first time at a black-tie fundraiser—he had one of those bodies whose shape and strength isn't immediately visible under formal clothes. She liked him because he asked a lot of questions. Later she realized this is just something he did, out of boredom or to deflect attention. But it seemed very flattering at the time. When he told her he was a tennis player, she laughed, it seemed like such a made-up job. But she was also excited by the idea, because . . . because it seemed like the kind of job you do when you haven't completely given up on your childhood, on the idea of yourself that you have when you're a kid. At that stage of her life she was in the market for somebody with this kind of faith or self-belief.

Also, Dana was a swimmer in high school; she knew what it meant to compete. Every morning, she woke at five to spend an hour in the water before school. Then a couple of hours after, too, before coming home to do her homework and go to bed. She quit senior year—she wanted to have a good time and told her parents she needed to concentrate on college applications. At Amherst, because she was tall, the rowing club recruited her as a freshman; by her junior year, she was rowing stroke in a coxless four. Then Michael came along and she started spending time in New York. Even before she dropped out of college, she had quit the team—something she still regretted, because it left other people in the lurch. Also, because it confirmed something she had started to suspect about herself, that she was a serial quitter.

One of the things that attracted her to Paul was his athletic discipline. She had had enough of good-time guys. She was always happiest when she was working too hard, at least that's what she told herself afterward; she liked teams, too. In the early days, when they were dating, she used to go running with Paul. Maybe he slowed down for her a little, but not much; she could tell he responded sexually to her competitiveness. They used to sprint the last few hundred yards. She started rowing again, on the erg machine, when he went to the gym. She lost weight, she felt good, she loved him. She liked going out on the town with him, feeling the muscle in his arm, under his shirt; they were almost the same height. They attracted looks. All of these feelings turn out to be short-lived.

She had already gone through one divorce. There's a period of identification, and then a period of separation. Even with Cal, maybe even because of Cal—she had what she needed from Paul. That's what she thought, listening to the Essingers discuss his future. It amazed her how they could talk like that when she was sitting right there. The way they treated everything connected to them as common property . . . For a while she was flattered to be included. As a kid she felt left out even of her parents' marriage. Her mother made it very clear who *her* priority was. And then the Essingers took her in. But it was also clear who *their* priority was: the guy on court, hitting a tennis ball. And yet she felt sorry for him, too. The way Liesel watched him, resentful with worry, not understanding what she saw. From time to time, she had to ask Bill what was going on, why something had happened. And

Bill, annoyed, answered as quickly as possible; he didn't
want to explain. To be the focus of such love, to have so
much of it concentrated on you. This is why he sometimes
couldn't look you in the eye, he shrugged away affection,
he wasn't good at it. Because he felt that his career was a
disappointment to them.

Sometimes he fought with Liesel about this—she refused
to admit it. What do I care about your ranking? she asked
him. Which put him in the position of explaining to her
why he had failed, the various ways . . . to instruct her
in his own sense of failure. Kids often have to keep their
parents up-to-date. Why do you fight with your mother
about this stuff, Dana asked him. She doesn't have to know
what it means to play qualifiers. You don't understand,
he said. They have this totally unreasonable perception
of me. They love you, she said, that's all. They're your
parents. But he insisted: it's very corrupting. You have to
make sure they know what's going on. Otherwise, you
start to believe it yourself, what they think of you. Would
that be so terrible, she said. But again, he wouldn't look
her in the eye.

Living with him was like watching him play tennis—
he was concentrating on something else. She watched him
now, against the bright blue surface of the hard court,
alone on his side of the net, moving and stroking the ball
and moving again, never looking up, entirely focused
on the task at hand, but also, in his own way, helpless,
exposed, when he sliced a volley wide into the tramlines.
Another deuce—the first service game is often the hardest, you just need to get over the hump. Because in spite

of everything, she wanted him to win, from a depth of love that was almost like anger. Come on, she thought, as he lined up his serve again, bouncing the ball to get a rhythm going. Her phone buzzed twice in her pocket but she ignored it. Come on! Come on! Come on!